THE GEISHA AND THE MONK

A NOVEL

BY

JULIAN BOUND

Novels by
Julian Bound

Subway of Light
Life's Heart Eternal
The Geisha and The Monk
The Soul Within
Of Futures Past
A Gardener's Tale
By Way of The Sea
Four Hearts
All Roads

Non-Fiction

In the Field
The Mindfulness of Wandering
Of Eden's Touch
The Seven Deadly Sins and The Seven Heavenly Virtues
Ten Minute Travels

Two souls born thousands of miles apart
each shall follow a similar path

Julian Bound

CHAPTER ONE

Morning breezes stroked the edges of newly formed petals, giving folds of pink and white a first taste of the short life Hanami would bring. This was how it was, how it had always been. The people of Kyoto saw the arrival of their beloved cherry blossoms as the start of a much welcomed spring, yet each were aware the fragile lifespan such beauty gave.

Many would come to see the cherry trees in full bloom and eat besides the ever flowing stream accompanying its display. Legend told how the trees knew of the crowds to arrive, taking pride their flowers gave such tranquillity and hope to those who appeared. Soon, laughter and chat would once more become part of the landscape, the way it had for generations before as families and friends joined together beneath rows of soft pink.

This would not be happening today. It was believed that even nature needed a period of adjustment, to simply just be before the world's prying eyes descended upon them. On the last day of March 1876, those fresh virgin buds were left their time alone, to delight in the serenity they in turn would produce in others.

As gentle winds continued towards hillsides blanketed in lush green, quiet rustling branches gave way to the sound of rushing water. These cool, clear waters winding through the countryside proved the life blood of cherry blossom season, and coupled with the fine rich soil Kyoto was so famed for gave its flowers such distinct subtle colours. It was often considered no other setting in Japan shared the same magnificence of a Kyoto Hanami, and the city had been preparing for weeks for the influx of tourists from far across the country to arrive.

A second breeze meandered across the silent row of cherry trees. Touching petal's fragile tips once more, this time the winds carried with them the first cries of a new born child.

"She's beautiful," Hiroko smiled, the deep creases around her eyes joining with grey temples.

"A girl?"

"Yes, Miyako, you have a daughter," the old midwife replied.

Wrapping her in the warm soft blanket awaiting her arrival, Hiroko handed the child for her mother to hold.

"She has her mother's beauty, you see, Miyako?"

As mother and child's eyes met for the first time Hiroko watched on. In all her years delivering new souls into the world she never tired of seeing the bonds form between the young and those who had carried them for so long.

Looking to the window beside her to sprawling countryside beyond, the old midwife's view rested on the cherry blossoms she had visited every year since a small child, warming to memories of paddling in the stream beside them.

She too had waited for these first signs of spring. A time of new beginnings when all that had gone before could be left where it belonged, in the past. With thoughts of returning blooms, Hiroko wondered how many times she had witnessed such a sight before returning to the young mother at her side.

"A cherry blossom child," she said. "Born on the first day of Hanami, a lucky girl."

Seeing rows of vivid pink and whites she thought would never come, Miyako gazed back down to her daughter. It was then she knew all that had gone before had been worth everything, all the heartache and upheaval in her life over the past five months accumulating to this one point in time, her child's warmth cradled in her arms only led to confirm these feelings.

"Sakurako," the old midwife said. "A cherry blossom child."

Brushing a finger across her new-born's cheek, Miyako shook her head.

"No, there are so many Sakurakos running around. This little one has far too much beauty for such a familiar name."

The baby soothed under her mother's touch as Miyako stroked her cheek once more.

"Her skin is so soft. It feels more like a peach."

"Momoko," Hiroko said. "A peach child."

"Yes, a peach child. That is just what she is," Miyako leant down and kissed her daughter's brow, her lips hovering on soft downy hairline.

"Momoko," she whispered. A faint murmur came from the small bundle in her arms.

"She knows her name," Hiroko joined the new mother. Both women peered down to tiny brown eyes and mop of black hair.

"She loves you very much, Miyako, do you see?"

The single tear rolling down Miyako's cheek, prompting Hiroko to place a gentle hand on her shoulder.

"It is time for you to rest now," she said.

Miyako's eyes did not leave her daughters as Hiroko took Momoko in her arms and settled her into the small cot beside them.

"There you are, Momoko, now you must let your mother sleep."

The old midwife turned to Miyako with a smile.

"She will still be here when you wake," she said.

Exhausted from a long labour another tear escaped Miyako.

"Momoko," she said before falling into much needed rest.

Pulling warm woollen covers across the sleeping mother and lifting a strand of hair from her cheek, Hiroko turned to the baby beside them.

"And your mother loves you very much also, Momoko," she said to the tiny face staring up at her. "Now, you must sleep also, then you both will not be tired when you begin to get to know one another," she added as Momoko's eyes closed beneath her calm tone and drifted off to sleep.

Happy and content her work was done, Hiroko stepped back and watched mother and child breath in rhythm together. She paused for a moment as Momoko stirred. The old midwife watched her return to her dreams then looked from the window once more.

Almost tasting the fragrance she knew lay beneath the blossoms far in the distance, she recalled a lifetime spent walking beneath them. A wave of sadness flowed over her and she glanced back to sleeping mother and child. Recalling how she too had once dreamt of having children of her own, that elusive wish had never appeared. Looking back to the cherry trees beyond her moment of sorrow lifted.

"You have brought many into this world, Hiroko," she whispered out to them.

She could still remember every small face of the children she had delivered, each one keeping her longing for her own child at bay for over forty years. A fragment of sadness remained on realising that soon her life's work would be coming to a close. Returning to the crib she looked to the sleeping baby within.

"Could you be the last?" She questioned to tiny breaths below. As Momoko wriggled to her words Hiroko tried to push away such thoughts, although she knew them to be true. It was time now.

Feeling the comfort in being besides Miyako and her new born, Hiroko remembered how she had somehow known from the start that these two would be with her for the last of her days. Brushing another lock of hair from Miyako's brow the old midwife sat down beside her bed. She recalled the late October day when she had first met the sleeping mother now at her side.

With the approaching winter upon them, the streets of suburban Kyoto had been alive with those preparing for the cold to come. Hiroko remembered how rays of early morning sun had cast across her cheeks, giving the boost needed after a long night delivering the twins so rare in her Kyoto district. Word had soon spread of the new arrivals and Hiroko enjoyed the smiles received from recipients of such news on her walk homewards.

Everybody knew the old midwife and she never tired of the respectful greetings that would come her way, knowing her own features were the first most along these streets had seen. As the years passed Hiroko would take pride in the knowledge she had witnessed all those children grow and have children of their own, which she too had delivered also.

Through all the nods and smiles entertained that morning Hiroko's thoughts lay elsewhere. That late autumnal day had carried with it the seeds of leaving the profession that had seen her through many lonely years.

"Hanami," she had told herself on nearing her small home. "When the first blossom's show. Then, Hiroko, then it will be time for you to retire."

Those plans had lightened her spirit. Although she knew her decision was wise, she wondered how she would cope with a life not bringing fresh souls into the world. Little had she known her answers were to appear that morning.

Walking towards her home, Hiroko had paused on catching sight of the lone figure stood outside her door. Dressed in a long winter's coat of finery rarely seen within the confines of Kyoto's southern regions, Hiroko tried to discern the features of its owners bowed head. Edging forwards the old midwife stopped once more as her unexpected visitor raised her chin on her advance. Taken aback by the sheer beauty greeting her that morning, her heart had filled with remorse to the sadness portrayed in such striking eyes.

"Are you, Hiroko?" The beautiful young woman had trembled.

Hiroko remembered nodding in reply, but had been unprepared for the torrent of tears her mysterious caller presented. Placing a reassuring arm around the young woman a sense of relief arrived within the stranger.

"Come with me, my child," Hiroko had instructed leading the way into her home, the young woman giving no reply and simply moving with her. With the front door closed to the world outside Hiroko had looked to the young woman. "What is it? What is wrong?"

The young woman undid her coat buttons. Her hand reached for the old midwife's and she placed it on the small bump across her midriff. Hiroko understood.

"Yes, I am here now. You are safe," she had told her, remembering how delicate features had formed into a charismatic smile as the young woman's hand pushed soft against hers.

"Tell me, what is your name?"

"Miyako," the young woman had replied as Hiroko's view fell from frightened eyes to the swollen torso beneath her palm.

"Hanami," she had said in such moments, knowing from experience the exact date this new soul would arrive.

Momoko's cries brought Hiroko back from her recollections. Lifting the baby from her crib, tiny wails transformed into a slight murmur.

"And here you are," the old midwife rocked the new born in her arms. Hiroko felt a new set of eyes fall upon her.

"Here we all are," Miyako said from her bed.

Hiroko nodded in silence to the new mother, each knowing no further words were needed between one another.

Momoko's birth proved to be the last of Hiroko's deliveries. The district in which she had worked throughout her life saddened to the news of the old midwife's retirement, yet her choice was greeted with the same respect she had always known. This respect also carried through to the other aspect of Hiroko's life, and no questions were ever asked to the reasons behind the arrival of the beautiful young woman with child on her doorstep. Aware of the gossip and tittle-tattle that ran through her home's small streets the old midwife's reverence within the community paved the way. Not once did she ever hear question of why she had taken in the stranger and now acted as guardian to her and her child.

Mother and daughter soon became accepted by those of southern Kyoto, and Hiroko fell into her role as doting grandmother with ease. It seemed only natural Miyako should remain within the old midwife's home and the small community beyond its doors warmed to the happiness Hiroko portrayed from her new household. As Momoko was introduced to the world the old midwife's neighbours received her and her mother's presence with welcoming smiles, and by the start of the next year's cherry blossom season the bonds between all concerned were complete.

On the eve of Momoko's first birthday Hiroko stood in the kitchen preparing her family's evening meal. Looking from the window onto her home's small garden, she watched Miyako play with her daughter beneath the winter's final setting sun. Her eyes fell to the cherry blossoms far in the distance.

Smiling to the last time she had seen such a sight, it was hard to believe a year had passed since Momoko had entered her life, a life she could not imagine without her now.

With her view returning to Miyako, the joy this beautiful young woman released as she laughed and played with her offspring gave Hiroko great delight. Ever thankful for the small family she had acquired, she admired the transformation in the frightened eyes that had confronted her two autumns earlier. She had never asked Miyako of her life before they met. Even Hiroko knew that everyone had a past. If the one who had brought such pleasure in her life's closing chapters choose to tell of those times, only then would she be there to listen. Although, Hiroko remained curious as to how such a dignified young woman should arrive at her door that cold October morning. This question only raised its head when Hiroko would at times notice a certain distance in Miyako's eyes. The old midwife felt the heartache and loss such a stare contained, but still she did not pry, knowing once more that when and if the young woman was ready to share her history, then she would with no prompt from herself.

Turning from the laughter outside Hiroko reached for the rice which would complete their evening meal. Taking care to weigh such precious grains, the container and its contents fell to the ground as the kitchen filled with Miyako's frantic calls.

"Hiroko," Miyako called again. "Come quickly."

The old midwife rushed from the kitchen and out into the garden.

"What is it?" she said as Momoko filled her view.

"Do it again, Momoko," her mother smiled, unaware of the panic she had unwittingly caused. "Show Hiroko how clever you are."

Turning Momoko to face her surrogate grandmother, Miyako released her hold on her daughter. Momoko took three unaided steps towards her. The fright that something had happened to her precious child soon left the old midwife and she walked towards the owner of tentative steps.

"Look at you," she leant down to the toddler.

Reaching out with both hands, Momoko stumbled and wrapped her tiny fingers around Hiroko's.

"Such a happy child, Miyako."

"Yes, she has her father's smile," Miyako replied.

Falling silent to her admission, her eyes did not leave her child's. Hiroko saddened as the beautiful young woman's lonely gaze returned. Momoko sensed her mother's change in emotion.

"Come now, Momoko," Hiroko swooped the child up into her arms before the flow of inevitable tears. "You must be hungry after such hard work."

A smile formed in reply to the old midwife's words. With Momoko held tight to her, Hiroko walked back to the kitchen, where setting the child down at her feet, Hiroko looked to the garden's lonely figure.

The old midwife had yearned for Miyako to break her silence on what had gone before. Now that moment had arrived she saw it was only shrouded in sadness.

"She won't be long," Hiroko reassured the child playing at her feet, her view not leaving Miyako.

As late evening winds rose Miyako turned to meet with wisps of cool air. Closing her eyes, the young woman's silk like blue black hair swept away to reveal a high cheek boned profile of porcelain skin.

The old midwife's thoughts towards Miyako's past grew in the natural beauty displayed before her. Having often supposed the past of one of such exquisiteness she had never voiced her assumptions. Now, as Miyako exposed the unique beauty she had passed onto her daughter, Hiroko's view only confirmed her thoughts on the matter. Sensing Hiroko's gaze, Miyako turned from the prevailing winds. She nodded once and raised a slight smile before leaving her solitude and joining her family for dinner.

Miyako said little that evening as the trio ate together and soon retired to bed after settling Momoko down for the evening. On saying goodnight she paused at her bedroom door.

"Thank you," she said to her friend and guardian. Hiroko smiled in reply, her silence validating the understanding each held of that day's events.

Two years passed and as Momoko grew Miyako embraced her new life within southern Kyoto. In return, her community gladdened to their much needed replacement midwife. With Hiroko's teaching, Miyako soon became as adept at her work as had her teacher, the joy encountered from delivering those young souls bringing her a strength and compassion never experienced before.

Hiroko was proud her life's work had found a suitable successor in the beautiful young woman who had arrived so unexpected to her home. It seemed the old midwife's career had come full circle and she treasured every moment spent with her new found family, her life at last complete after so many years spent alone.

As the spring of 1880 began, Hiroko and her small family walked beneath the pink and white flowers that always marked Momoko's birthday. With a small hand in each of her guardian's, Momoko laughed to the delight of having Hanami to herself.

"Tomorrow, Momoko," Hiroko said. "It will be so hard to walk this path."

"Is it because today is my birthday that no one else is here?" Momoko asked.

Her mother looked to Hiroko.

"Not even we should be here today, Momoko," she said.

"Hiroko?" The child frowned. "Is it not because I am so special that I have the whole of Hanami to myself?"

Hiroko laughed to the child's pride.

"In a way that could be true, Momoko."

Looking ahead she released the small hand in hers.

"Run on, Momoko, find me some flowers for the kitchen."

Breaking free, both women watched her race from them.

"And stay away from the stream," Miyako called.

Turning to Hiroko as they walked together she considered if she should speak her fears. The old midwife's smile encouraged her to tell what bothered her so.

"You see it in her also, Hiroko?"

"Yes, she knows she is special, that is true. But…"

"But she has a lot to learn," Miyako interrupted.

"Yes, Miyako, she has, but remember, she is still a child. In time, her modesty will come." Hiroko paused. "Her lessons will be learnt, as I suppose, Miyako, yours were once also."

Coming to a stop, Miyako looked to Hiroko's mischievous grin. Glancing back to Momoko playing ahead she gave the old midwife a coy smile.

"You are a wise one, Hiroko. Have you known all along?"

"And what is it that I know, Miyako?" Hiroko said before walking on alone.

Watching Hiroko stroll from her, Miyako's attention fell to the waters beside her. Becoming lost in its constant flow she too recognised how her life had moved forwards, much like the twisting currents she looked to now. Was it now time for her to share the past she had tried so hard to forget? Watching her daughter present Hiroko with a small posy of pinks and whites she walked to them.

"Hiroko," she said on her approach. "You have been so kind to Momoko and I."

The old midwife smiled down to Momoko and raised her chin to the tall grass lining the edges of the path they now stood.

"Momoko, do you think that some of those would go well with my flowers?"

As Momoko ran onwards towards her new quest Miyako turned to the young woman's tears.

"Hiroko, tell me, what is wrong?"

Reaching out, her actions evoked memories in them both to their first meeting five years earlier.

"I owe you so much, Hiroko. I feel I owe you everything."

"You owe me nothing, my child," Hiroko shook her head. "It is more that I am in debt to you," she nodded over to Momoko.

"Not once have you asked of my past. Not once," the young woman cried. "It is only now that I am ready to tell you what has gone before." Wiping away the last of her tears her daughter raced towards them.

"Here, Hiroko," the child handed over several fine strands of grass.

"Thank you, they are beautiful, Momoko. We shall put them with the flowers when we return home. Are you ready to go?"

Momoko nodded and then raced homewards leaving Hiroko and Miyako alone.

As the two women looked to each other Miyako knew it was time to release her history. She wondered if telling of the moments that had gone before would bring the peace she sought.

"All in good time," Hiroko told her as they walked towards their home.

CHAPTER TWO

Nourished by thawing winter snows, the Nyangchu River broke free of its swollen banks. Cutting through the Tibetan midlands, these building waters signalled the beginning of a much anticipated spring on its race to merge with Yarlang Tsangpo, a waterway famed for leading onwards to Lhasa, home of all that was.

The inhabitants of Gyantse welcomed the sounds of these rising torrents, its eternal rush echoing through their small village to confirm the commencement of a new season after harsh cold months. All knew that soon the surrounding fields would once again begin to fill with sweet scents of barley, peas and mustard, a rich harvest granted from the melting plains of snow and ice beneath clear blue skies.

On the last day of March 1876, a young shepherd glanced back to his small herd of goat and sheep before edging towards the lip of Nyangchu's new waters. He sighed to raging white rapids now barring his usual passage homewards. Looking further upstream for the ford that would ease his path, he dreaded the laughter he knew he would receive on his arrival back home. Now it seemed it was his turn to become the one cut off from his village by spring's sudden flow of water, an initiation all those of Gyantse had experienced at one time in their youth. Tired and hungry he called his livestock to him and began his journey towards their unknown crossing, thinking once more of the amusement his elders would reveal at his expense.

Trudging through the remnants of winter, he neared Gyantse's small collection of mud brick houses, longing to feel the warmth of the fires he knew lay within and eat the tsampa his body craved. In the ice cold water separating him from his home he began to count his family's treasured animals. His heart sank in finding one was missing. Looking around, he watched in horror as a stray goat began to wade across the river. Running to the beast a smile spread across the young shepherd's wind chapped cheeks. The animal had found the small inlet for which he searched. Gathering up the remainder of his herd he made for the opening in haste, fearful it would soon bar their way once again.

As the last of his herd reached the safety of the banks opposite, he began to follow their path homewards. Considering if his elder's teasing was still to come, he paused as the sound of weeping carried across Nyangchu's calming waters. Looking in the direction of that sorrow, he saddened on recognising the home which held such grief. Aware of the new arrival his neighbours awaited the young shepherd stepped forward through the shallows, preparing for the sad news that was to greet him and the rest of Gyantse's small community.

From his home's window the old man watched the young shepherd guide his flock across the river, remembering how he too had faced the same trials when a boy. So many years had passed since those days. Memories of such times faded on returning to the cries beside him.

"Gyaltso," he placed an arm around his son's shoulder. "She has left us now."

"I know," Gyaltso reached out for the one gone from them now. Holding his wife's lifeless hand tight in his, he turned to his father.

"Why?" He asked.

"That I cannot answer, Gyaltso, it is not for us to ask why." Seeing his words offered little consolation the old man looked to the far corner of the room. "You must be strong now, my son. For there is another who needs the love you once showed."

Gyaltso followed his father's gaze to the small crib he had spent the winter months labouring over in expectation of their new arrival.

"Come now, it is time," the old man led his grieving son to meet with their new addition.

As both men peered down to the young soul the old man saw recognition in his son's eyes.

"Yes, Gyaltso," he said. "Now you see how she will always be with you?"

A tear escaped him on seeing his wife's smile play across his son's tiny lips. Leaning forwards he brushed his fingers down the side of their child's cheek.

"Such wise eyes for someone so young," he said.

"Of that he has, Gyaltso," the old man warmed. "He has been here many times before, of that I am sure."

Looking to the one with whom his love had spent so little time, Gyaltso reached down and took the new born in his arms.

"Tenzin," he said to the small brown eyes staring up at him.

A small wriggle accompanied the child's flawless smile on hearing his name for the first time.

"You see, Gyaltso? He knows his name. Tenzin, a true keeper of knowledge," his heart lightened once more on seeing the bonds between father and son begin. That joy faltered as Gyaltso carried Tenzin to where his mother lay.

"It is time for us both to say goodbye now, Tenzin," Gyaltso whispered and placed a final kiss on his wife's brow before lowering their child down to do likewise.

"She loved you very much," Gyaltso fought his tears and returned to his father's side. The old man smiled as Gyaltso settled his son back down into the crib.

"Tenzin's farewell shall always be with him now," he said, placing an arm around his son again. "Come, you must rest, we have much ahead of us now."

Gyaltso sank into his father's embrace and glanced from the love he had lost to the one who he hoped would now replace such emotions.

Covering his daughter-in-law with the blanket once shared with his grieving son, the old man wiped his eyes and smiled down to her.

"Goodbye," he whispered, keeping check his emotions did not disturb those who slept around him.

Aware the strength his household now needed, he pushed away his pain in the loss of such a kind and gentle heart. Turning from his sorrow he walked towards the crib where his grandson lay.

The old man paused as he passed Gyaltso. He leant down and pulled the warm woollen blanket up around his son's chin, the way he had always done for him since a child. Gyaltso murmured before returning to the sleep his body craved, causing the old man to wonder if his actions were to be emulated now his son had himself become a father.

"We will see," he said, stepping forwards to meet with the new soul once again.

"Tenzin," the old man looked to his grandson. "Are you not tired?"

Small almond shaped eyes stared back up at him and he too saw the mother's smile that had brought such comfort to Gyaltso, yet he also recognised something else lay within Tenzin's features. Shaking his head, he dismissed such notions and stroked the soft crown below him.

"Your Grandfather is just tired," he said. "Come now, Tenzin, you too must sleep, there will be many people for you to meet with soon."

Tenzin smiled back up to his words, only adding to the assumptions the old man held towards their home's new arrival.

The bonds between Gyaltso and Tenzin grew as the residue of winter passed and spring advanced into rich summer months. With great joy the old man watched their union flourish. Aware of the sorrow still containing his son, he was thankful for the solace found in the child whose smile mirrored one missed so much. The old man understood the loss of another. Gyaltso's mother had also passed away at such a tender age leaving him to rear their child alone. This enhanced the connection between their small family and the old man's selfless support, which was returned in the pleasure of seeing his son and grandson's love strengthen.

The small community of Gyantse also grieved for the loss of Tenzin's mother. Their unyielding compassion welcomed the village's new member. They too recognised the child's special qualities the old man had witnessed in the first few hours of his arrival, doting over the soul whose smiles never ceased. Gyaltso was also aware of his son's unique composure, although he dismissed his own ideas from where such traits had come. All that mattered now was that Tenzin was here, safe and warm within their small home.

With his day light hours spent tending village crops, Gyaltso's thoughts would remain with the one who gave such comfort to painful memories of another's affection. Tenzin's world soon became his as he buried his sorrow in the wellbeing of the one they had waited so long for. Those hidden emotions would only surface late at night when watching over their son, with Gyaltso suppressing the wish his love stood beside him, and trying to understand the reasons behind their parting.

As always, those answers evaded the young father and he would turn from Tenzin's crib for his own lonely bunk, longing for dawn's rise so may see that familiar smile once more.

Without a word the old man would watch Gyaltso's anguish each evening. From experience he knew only time could heal such hurt and that there were no words which could release his son's heartache. Gyaltso knew the support his father summoned. His silence revealed the answers to his grief lay deep within the core of his own being, causing his love for the man who had guided his upbringing throughout the years to grow, a love he hoped he would one day share with his own son.

As the last of Gyantse's crops were harvested for impending winter months, the old man caught glimpse of the lifting sorrow that had lain within the walls of their small home. The approaching snows seemed to ease Gyaltso's pain, as did the emergence of Tenzin's own unique personality on reaching his seventh month. Those characteristics developed as he and his family saw through the coldest of Tibet's seasons, and by the eve of Tenzin's first birthday the old man felt confident his son's period of grieving was at last coming to a close.

That evening the old man watched his son and grandson play in the small dirt track outside their home. Leaning in the doorway his hand rested on the mud clay brick walls which had protected them from the harsh winter months, he smiled on feeling the warmth those walls now held having been touched by rays of early spring sun.

Turning to Tenzin's giggles the old man recalled how Gyaltso had also laughed to his father's antics years ago in the same place they now played. These memories brought with them appreciation of times passed since those carefree days. The old man joined with the laughter of the grandchild he could not imagine a life without. Looking from the cherished child, he glanced up to the mountains standing tall beneath a dimming evening sky of pink and blue, their sheer granite face revealed by spring's welcomed thaw. He knew the tips of those snow-capped peaks would remain throughout the year, much the way they had since he himself had first arrived into this world. He was also aware they would continue to do so long after he had gone. Leaving their home's doorway he walked towards father and son.

"Tenzin," he called to never ending smiles always received. "You are pleased to see your grandfather?" The old man watched tiny arms raised towards him in expectance.

"Show him, Tenzin," Gyaltso said. "Show your grandfather what you can do."

"And what is it you have learnt?" The old man asked his grandchild.

Looking deep into Tenzin's dark eyes, he felt the same recognition of another that always accompanied such a stare. Gyaltso broke the old man from his thoughts.

"Go on, Tenzin," he encouraged. "Show us all what you can do."

With another glance back Gyaltso, Tenzin looked up to his grandfather with arms outstretched. The old man knew what was to come and reached forward. Allowing small fingers to curl around his, Tenzin rose to his feet and took his first teetering steps towards him.

"Well, well, look at you," the old man laughed.

Sweeping Tenzin up into his arms he turned to Gyaltso and winked. Holding Tenzin close to his chest the old man's eyes moistened on seeing his son's joy return, knowing of the sad anniversary both would share the next day. Gyaltso's peace faded on sensing the thoughts his father held. He nodded to him, knowing of the difficulty each was to face and reached for Tenzin's hand.

"Tomorrow, Tenzin, you will have been with us for one year," he said. "Your grandfather and I will make a promise to you now. No tears shall be shed on your special day, Tenzin. Not one."

"Not one," the old man echoed as his grandson reached out and caught the tear rolling down his wrinkled cheek. Looking to Gyaltso, he saw his son's emotions matched his own and collected his feelings as best he could.

"Tenzin," the old man smiled. "Come with me now, for I suppose you are ready to eat after showing us your talent. Gyaltso, will you join us?"

Gyaltso walked from them towards the edge of Nyangchu's building waters.

Throughout the winter months he had dreaded the return of these raging torrents, aware its resonance would carry the grief encountered on its last arrival. Turning back to his home he watched his father and Tenzin enter its door. Comforted the trials now faced were not to be spent alone, his gaze returned to the swirling white waters before him.

From their home, the old man saddened to his son's pensive manner. Although neither had spoken of the coming day, father and son respected the private sorrow each contained. Pride came to the old man on recalling Gyaltso's vow made to his son.

"No tears," he said to the child perched on the worktop beside him.

Looking back to Gyaltso stood alone on the river banks both men had known since a child, he found some comfort Gyaltso had at last come to accept the suffering within him. Knowing that acceptance would lead to the key to unlock such torment, the old man lowered his chin on sensing a second surge of grief enter him. He raised his head in surprise to the soft touch across his hand.

"Tenzin?" The old man stared down to the tiny hand now placed on his and then to the compassionate stare accompanying such an action. "Thank you," he whispered to his grandson, once again witnessing the acts of another from his own past.

In the following two years Gyaltso's longing waned as the seasons passed and he came to acknowledge his wife had gone, channelling his life towards the child who brought both him and his father a joy never expected from such harrowing times.

Tenzin's smiles continued much to the delight of Gyantse's residents, yet the child who gave such happiness to others never played on the empowering emotions recognised deep within him. Watching these modest traits his grandfather said no word of his assumptions.

Although Gyaltso continued to leave his heartache behind the old man saw a fragment of that pain remained and gave no mention to the causes for Tenzin's self-effacing position.

This did not stop his growing ideas as to the origins of the compassion this soul revealed to all he encountered. He knew his neighbours were also aware of Tenzin's unique gift in bringing hope to those who had mislaid the trust once held in others, and themselves.

For these reasons the old man kept his silence, somehow

discerning the destiny which would one day call out to his treasured grandson.

Tenzin laughed as he swung through the air, his small hands clutched tight in his father and grandfather's. As they lowered him back down between them his laughter ceased and he looked to the rising waters beside them.

"Another birthday, Tenzin," his grandfather said.

"My fourth, Grandpa," Tenzin smiled up to the old man.

"Of that it is, Tenzin. Are you happy to feel the sun on your cheeks once more?"

Tenzin looked to his father's question. The child nodded and returned his view to the river's edge.

"What is it Tenzin? What can you see?"

Tenzin's lips broke free of his elder's grasp.

"Let him go," the old man told his son. Seeing apprehension in Gyaltso's eyes he understood the anxiety held in the thought of losing another close to him.

"Stay away from the banks, Tenzin," Gyaltso called. Turning to the old man, a smile formed in recalling when he too had been a boy.

"Yes, Gyaltso. I too remember how I would call to you. Like your son, you also did as you pleased."

"And you, old man? Were you told the same by your father?"

The old man looked to his grandson, his admissions answered with a slight grin.

Walking onwards alongside Nyangchu's growing surge both men watched Tenzin enjoy his new found freedom in exploring his village's life blood.

"A special child," the old man suppressed his want to speak his thoughts towards Tenzin's true calling. Although the repercussions of such admissions at times worried him, he saw his son was ready to cope with these ideas, yet something still held him back from voicing his notions. Gyaltso sensed his father's trepidation.

"I know Tenzin is special," he said, "and that others see this in him also."

"That they do, Gyaltso."

The old man stared at the one he had raised alone, wondering if now was the time to tell of his ideas on Tenzin's fate. Those needs left him as Gyaltso called out to his son.

"Tenzin."

"He's fine, Gyaltso," his father reassured. "What have you found, Tenzin?" He asked the child peering down to the ground on all fours.

Tenzin raised his head to his grandfather with a familiar gaze before looking back to the stone and dirt beneath him. Nearing his grandson, the old man calmed his son again.

"Wait, Gyaltso."

Both hovered over Tenzin in awe of the child's actions.

"Here you are," Tenzin said down to the insect struggling on its back before him.

Gyaltso hesitated in reaching for his son, he too having experienced the painful nip of a stag beetle's jaws. He stopped his want to protect Tenzin from a Tibetan child's rite of passage.

Tenzin found a short twig in the dirt beside him and gently wedged it beneath the beetle's hard shell.

"Patience," Tenzin whispered down to its flailing legs before flipping the stranded insect over.

"See," Tenzin clapped his small hands together as the righted stag beetle disappeared into riverside shrubs.

"Tenzin," his grandfather held out his arms. "Come to me."

The child stood and with a final look to where the beetle had lain he ran into the old man's embrace. Lifting him up, his grandfather frowned.

"What is it Grandpa?" Tenzin's smile faded.

"Tell me, why did you help that creature?"

"Because it was the right thing to do."

"Yes, Tenzin," Gyaltso nodded. "It was."

"Your father is right," the old man lowered his grandson to the floor. "Now why don't you run ahead of us home and see if there are any others in need of your aid."

Staring up to Gyaltso, Tenzin giggled once more on receiving his father's permission.

"Go," the old man clapped his hands then turned to Gyaltso as the sound of tiny feet raced from them.

"A special child," he said once again that afternoon as they too began to walk homewards.

In silence, each man thought of the compassionate actions they had just witnessed in someone so young. Summoning the courage to ask what he had always denied himself, the old man knew of his son's words to come. His soul lightened in the knowledge that at last his son was ready to hear his ideas as to Tenzin's true identity.

"You have something say, my son?"

Gyaltso's looked away from his father and nodded.

"You two have met before," he said, his view not leaving the child now running ahead before them, a glimpse of awareness arriving as to where his son's destiny may lead.

CHAPTER THREE

Hiroko looked to Miyako as they stood together in Momoko's bedroom doorway. The old midwife's eyes sparkled in amber candle light watching unconditional love flow from mother to child. Aware of Hiroko's gaze Miyako turned to her.

"Thank you," she said.

Hiroko's view fell to the sleeping child and the small doll clutched tight in her arms, its red dress coated in warm rich light against a backdrop of silk black hair. Sure her daughter slept, Miyako crept forward and blew out the lone candle. She paused as Momoko stirred and pulled Hiroko's birthday present close to her before returning to young dreams.

"She loves her doll," Miyako said walking from Momoko's bed.

"So peaceful," the old midwife nodded and left the doorway to clear the remnants of Momoko's birthday meal.

"And you, Miyako? Do you share the same emotions as your daughter?"

Knowing of what Hiroko now spoke, she glanced back to Momoko.

Pulling the bedroom's slat door closed, Miyako stepped forward and reached out to Hiroko. Her delicate fingers curled around the old midwife's hands. She smiled in feeling a gentle pressure in return.

"I am close," she said with tear filled eyes, afraid to speak the words she knew would provide a peace yearned for. Calming to Hiroko's soft touch, her eyes closed as aged finger tips placed a strand of hair behind her ear. Looking back into kind eyes, Miyako gave a faint smile.

"You are closer than you think, Miyako," Hiroko reassured before

21

leaving the young woman alone with her thoughts.

Watching the old midwife walk to the kitchen, Miyako's heart filled with the same hope felt on their first meeting. She had known from that cold autumn day she could confide in the old midwife and that her story would be received with no judgement. The guilt at not sharing her past with the one who had shown such compassion to her and her daughter only added to the torment her soul contained. Wondering again if the history she wanted so much to reveal would banish the heartbreak burning within her, Miyako stepped towards the kitchen. She stopped. Turning back to Momoko's bedroom she edged forwards and slid its paper door open, careful as to not wake her sleeping daughter.

From the bedroom's single window, moonlight filtered through wooden blinds, casting a silver sheen across Momoko's blanket rising and falling above tiny breaths held within. Mesmerised by the tranquillity such a scene contained, the question which had hounded Miyako for so long came forth. Can I really attain the same peace? Miyako knew this to be true. As her heart filled with hope once more, she tiptoed into the room, leant over and placed a soft kiss on her daughter's crown.

"New beginnings, Momoko," she whispered before leaving to join Hiroko's side.

In the entrance to the kitchen Miyako looked to the small vase's collection of subtle pinks and whites Momoko had picked earlier that day.

"They are beautiful," Hiroko felt Miyako's presence behind her.

Nothing escaped the old midwife and for a moment Miyako considered if she already knew the tale she was to unfold that evening.

"Yes, Hiroko, they are," Miyako stood beside her friend. "Here, let me help you," she plunged her hands into the washing bowl's hot steaming suds.

Miyako knew Hiroko waited for answers. She hesitated. Was it time now? Could the answers to the search of breaking from the past result from her recalling it? All these notions swam through Miyako.

She knew Hiroko would never force her to tell of what had gone before. Only she could break that silence. Staring down to the remaining plates and pots she raised her head to the moonlit landscape before them.

"You know, Hiroko, I once vowed to never wash another plate in my lifetime again."

Hiroko turned to her and nodded towards the living room and its small fireplace.

"These will still be here tomorrow," she reached for the cloth beside her. "I'm sure we have much to talk of tonight."

"Yes, I'm sure we have," Hiroko replied. Easing within Hiroko's simple manner she followed the old midwife to sit on the mat besides their home's fireplace.

Settling down Hiroko pulled her shawl around her shoulders and glanced back to Momoko's room.

"She has enjoyed another birthday, Miyako."

"Yes, thank you for her present. You can see how much she adores it."

"Oh yes, very much so. Momoko seems to like the finer things in life. A trait she gets from her mother I suspect."

"It shows that much," Miyako giggled, aware these words hinted to the origins of her past. Confirming her story was ready to be shared, Miyako's laughter faded and her view fell to the fire.

"I was no older than, Momoko," she began. "When Auntie first found me."

Hiroko kept her silence as Miyako unravelled her tale. Telling of the woman who had visited her parent's home in the poorer districts of Tokyo one cold winter's morning, it seemed talk of Miyako's beauty had spread as she explained how her parents had somehow expected the arrival of one of Tokyo's geisha house owners.

"And she took you from your home? There and then?"

"No, Hiroko," Miyako said. "At least, not straight away."

Hiroko glimpsed the hurt such deep rooted memories held for the beautiful young woman sat before her.

"I am sorry," she said, annoyed her interruption should deter Miyako from her story. "Please, continue."

Understanding the oldwife's concern, Miyako knew that now her story had begun there would be no cause for her to stop, no matter how painful such recollections proved to be.

"I can still remember seeing Auntie for the first time," Miyako continued. "Even now after so many years I remember the rich material of the blue kimono and its intricate gold braiding she wore. And you know what her reaction was on seeing me for the first time?

She gasped, Hiroko." Miyako's stare drifted to her daughter's bedroom door. "That was when I knew all that was to come. That one day I would be the same as the beautiful woman who visited my parent's home."

Hiroko listened as Miyako told how she would join her father's side to visit Auntie within her Okiya home. Always sitting quiet as the two discussed matters her young mind could not understand, Miyako explained that although it seemed she was left alone during that time, she always longed to return to Auntie's home, so in awe was she of the comings and goings around her. Never before had she seen such a collection of attractive women, each of which would greet her with a respect unknown to a child of Miyako's age. With their fine silk clothing, elaborate hairstyles and pale white makeup, Miyako longed to be like the willowy figures surrounding her, paying little attention to the endless dialogue between her father and the one she had come to know as Auntie.

Those brief visits soon developed into a week, and then another, until Miyako's home became the small Okiya in the heart of Tokyo's Hanamachi district.

"Did you not miss your parents?"

Miyako looked to Hiroko with a sadness the old midwife had witnessed many times before.

"At first, of course. But." Miyako paused. "It must sound strange to others, Hiroko, a child taken from their parents at such an age, but it was not like that. My parents would visit me, yes, yet as I grew older those visits became less frequent until after my first two years with Auntie, my mother and father never came to see me again."

Seeing the shock on Hiroko's features, Miyako leant forwards and took the old midwifes hand in hers.

"Do not be sad for me, Hiroko," she smiled. "You have to understand that Auntie became both my parents to me. And I had many older sisters who cared for me also. That was how it was. Soon my life with the geisha was all I knew, all I had ever known."

Hiroko looked to the young woman's hand still held tight in hers. She squeezed it once, willing Miyako to release her history. Miyako reached forward and with a gentle touch, tucked Hiroko's shawl around the old midwife's shoulders.

"As the beauty Auntie had discovered in me developed, my name soon became known throughout Tokyo. Although this did not stop my duties within the Okiya," Miyako glanced to the kitchen and its remaining pile of unwashed bowls. "I had my chores to keep me busy, long before I could even touch one of my sister's kimonos, let alone dream of owning my own one day."

Hiroko also glanced back to the kitchen, understanding her dislike of house hold chores.

"But you became…"

"A geisha? Oh yes, eventually, Hiroko," Miyako laughed. "Auntie was always so kind to me. She gave me such encouragement, such support in my early years. As my time came to learn the art of becoming a true geisha, the love she showed to me surpassed all I had known before." Miyako's excited words drifted from her and she looked down into her lap.

"What is wrong, Miyako?"

Their silence was broken by the fireplace beside them. Miyako looked to the offending log, its cracking spit replaced by a melodic hiss.

"I owed Auntie everything," she continued. "But not even I could have foreseen what was to happen."

Aware the sorrow that had contained Miyako since their first encounter was at last beginning to surface, the old midwife stood.

"Miyako," she said. "Choose your words. Tell me of what has gone before. For we both know it is time now."

Miyako nodded as the old midwife made for the kitchen, leaving her alone with her thoughts. Hiroko soon returned with a pot of green tea she knew would always calm Miyako, their silence remaining as the old midwife poured the hot amber liquid into two small worn wooden bowls. Savouring her first sip Miyako felt its bitter flavour invigorate her body.

"I was chosen, Hiroko," she said, her bowl warming her palms.

"A suitor?"

"Not as such. More a benefactor, someone who would not so much own me, yet I would belong to them."

"A slave?"

Miyako giggled and her eyes softened to Hiroko's question.

The old midwife's naivety had been part of the reason Miyako loved her so. Throughout their time together she saw how her own life differed greatly to the kind woman who had always lived within Kyoto's southern district. These traits in no way mirrored the harsh reality of a geisha's false love Miyako had grown accustomed too.

"No, Hiroko. I was never a slave," she smiled. "My benefactor was to be the only one I would dance for, talk with, and share my time in his company."

"Then what happened? Was he cruel to you? Did he hurt you in some way, this, this benefactor?"

"No, Hiroko. He was a kind man, a gentle soul." The young woman's gaze returned to the fire side. "In a way that was what made things worse."

"But how could that make it worse? Did Auntie's love for you change because of him?" Hiroko put down her bowl and reached for Miyako's to refill its contents.

"Auntie's feelings for me never changed, and neither did my patrons. You see, it was my own heart which became my undoing."

"There was another?"

Miyako smiled to the oldwife's startled expression. The young woman understood then the sheltered life Hiroko had led. Her smile grew as she saw the hidden intrigue Hiroko held towards affairs of the heart, her love for the old woman growing more in the process.

"Oh, yes, there was another," Miyako's eyes sparkled. Their light soon dimmed. Hiroko sensed aloofness from such a familiar gaze.

"Tell me of him," she said. "No matter how much pain your memories hold."

She too knowing the need for her tale to be told Miyako continued.

"He always made me laugh," Miyako smiled. "But any liaison between us was strictly prohibited. Auntie suspected at first, of that I am sure. Although she said nothing, and I in turn kept my benefactor happy. You see, Hiroko, his dowry to Auntie kept the Okiya going. Such was my patron's position and wealth within Tokyo, the price he paid to keep me to himself and from other men made Auntie the most powerful Okaa-san in the district. I held the keys to such respect. For news to spread of my forbidden love would have brought ruin and great shame upon my home and those with whom I had grown."

Hiroko held her silence. She knew the ways of such places having delivered the occasional child within those confines. Each time the affair had been treated with much secrecy, a concealment Hiroko had always found distasteful.

"I was chosen to be Auntie's Atotori, the one destined to succeed her position when time came for her to retire." Miyako's voice softened and Hiroko sensed the guilt such tones produced. "All that was lost as my love for another grew."

"Was he handsome, Miyako?"

Seeing the wonder in the old midwife's question, her innocence touched Miyako once again.

"Very," Miyako smiled. "We met by chance one morning as I walked beneath the cherry blossoms on the first day of Hanami." Miyako glanced to Momoko's room. "Always a special day," she added.

"Was he not wealthy also, Miyako? Could he not have taken care of you as your patron did?"

"No, his life matched my parents. He lived from day to day on what little he had, finding his only funds by selling the occasional fish caught on Tokyo's harbour front. But that mattered little to me. His soul was what my heart craved, for in the moments we spent together I was alive in no other way I had felt before."

"Then why did you not leave your life as a geisha behind so you could be together?"

"That is not the way, Hiroko. My whole existence was in debt to Auntie and the man who paid for all surrounding me. In no way could I leave that behind." Miyako's head shook from side to side to confirm her words. "Not at first that is," tears formed in her eyes.

"Our love for each other happened so quickly. I knew as did he, what we had found in each other was precious, something magical. A blessing words cannot describe."

"Then what happened, did he come to you or you to him? And your patron, did his objections reach Auntie?"

A part of Miyako shamed to the way her story had enlightened hidden desires within the old midwife she loved and respected so dearly.

"Hiroko, those first months we spent together as spring faded into summer flew by so fast. It was so hard to find time for one another, but we made it work, our secrecy only adding to the passion encircling us both."

Miyako watched Hiroko's cheeks turn crimson to her statement. "I am sorry to embarrass you, Hiroko."

"Not at all," Hiroko giggled, her features flushing once again. "I am not as innocent as you may believe," she winked. Both women shared a moment of laughter together before Miyako spoke again with a more solemn tone.

"It was the third week of July when I told my love of the little one we expected. To my relief he was as thrilled as I to the news, yet as we held each other close that summer's evening we both knew our child would bring a new set of problems."

"How to tell, Auntie."

"My benefactor's feelings did not matter to me, I knew his heart was pure and he would understand my position as best he could. I was also sure that Auntie would forgive me in her own way. It was I who bore the guilt of such consequences. As I have said before, I owed all I had ever known to Auntie and her kindness."

Hiroko understood. She knew of the ways of geisha life, its benefactors, patrons, business deals and acumen. Miyako's loyalty for the one who had raised her from a child shone through, which in turn verified the honesty and allegiance she had always known this beautiful young woman to hold.

"Then how did you end up here in Kyoto that late autumn morning?"

Hiroko reached for Miyako on seeing the pain her question induced. Her hand warmed to Miyako's touch as she received the gesture. Wiping her tears Miyako began to unfold the ensuing drama that led to her arrival to the old midwife's door.

"We had a plan, my love and I. We both knew it would not be long until proof of our child began to show as a geisha prided herself on holding a trim figure. We were both aware that soon, not even the most heavy of sashes and bows would conceal the telltale bump growing larger by the day." A deeper pain seared in Miyako's eyes and her grip tightened around Hiroko's fingers. "As the cooler winds came and our child became more prominent, we knew time had come to escape Tokyo's restrictions. New beginnings, my love would say on talking our plans through, his hand soft upon my torso."

"And so you decided on Kyoto to be your new home? The new beginning you both dreamed of?"

"Yes, Hiroko. Here would be where we could start a fresh, with no one knowing of all that had gone before. A full moon was due and we decided such an auspicious moment would prove us right for our passage to a new life together."

"Then how did you come to arrive here alone in Kyoto?" Hiroko asked.

Her words brought grief to Miyako once again and she clasped another hand around hers, summoning the words telling of the betrayal she still felt after so long.

"I waited in our secret place that night. I waited and waited for him to come."

"He never did?"

"No, Hiroko, he never came to me. I could not understand why. I wondered if it was I who had made a mistake. The wrong night, the wrong place."

"But you left without him?"

"I panicked. I knew I could return to the Okiya and to the love and safety Auntie had always shown me, but my guilt was such that I knew my heart would break on seeing those I loved shocked by the admission of my situation." Miyako's cheeks glistened in the flicks of orange and yellow flames beside her. She glanced into the heart of the fire and then back to Hiroko.

"He never came," Miyako repeated, her voice distant once more. "Without him I felt I had nothing. And so I left in the night, alone, cold and scared of what my unknown future held."

"You came to me, here in Kyoto," Hiroko nodded. "Tell me, when I found you that morning in front of this very house we now sit, you asked for me by name." The old midwife paused. "How did you know I was here?"

"Hiroko, you are famous in geisha circles," a smile returned to Miyako's lips as she saw surprise in the old midwife's eyes. "Yes, we all know of the work you have done for others in a similar position as I found myself in. The respect others hold for you extends further than these small streets of southern Kyoto. Many have talked of the discretion your kind heart reveals, never judging those with child that come your way. I knew then as I travelled to your home that you would keep me safe with no questions asked towards my arrival."

A tear fell from aged eyes as Miyako reached forwards and held Hiroko in her arms.

"And I was right, Hiroko, I can never thank you enough for your kindness."

The old midwife warmed to her embrace, recalling how long had she waited for a family of her own.

"Mamma? Hiroko?" a young voice carried through the room.

Both women broke apart as Momoko's bedroom door slid open.

"Come, Momoko. Come sit with your family," Hiroko tapped her hand on the mat beside her.

The child looked to her mother and smiled as Miyako nodded the permission she awaited. To the tiny patter of feet across her small home, Hiroko watched Momoko race to join them, her birthday present clutched tight in her hand, its red dress flowing at her side.

"Happy birthday, Momoko," Miyako whispered as her daughter snuggled into Hiroko's lap. Momoko smiled to each of the woman and after a final wriggle her eyes closed. Miyako looked to the sleeping child held tight in Hiroko's arms.

"Your love for Momoko has always been unconditional, Hiroko. Of this also I can only give thanks."

"Momoko has brought such pleasure to my closing years, and so, my child, have you." Hiroko wondered if after all she had learnt that evening she should ask the question burning within her.

This time it was Miyako who read the old midwife's thoughts.

"Yes, Hiroko, I am sure Auntie would have shown the same love also." Miyako's eyes returned to the fireplace. "That is what I am afraid of," she said into its flames. "That one day she may find us both."

CHAPTER FOUR

"Are you not full yet, Tenzin?"

Tenzin looked up from his wooden bowl to his grandfather's words.

"You have you father's appetite," the old man winked to Gyaltso.

"Of that he has," his son said as Tenzin returned to his birthday meal of hot momo dumplings.

Even after the onset of spring their small home still held its winter chill and Gyaltso made for the fireplace to feed its dying flames

Watching his father reach for one of the logs he enjoyed helping gather beneath his village's steep mountain back drop, Tenzin saw the nod given to his grandfather as he ate the last of his dumplings.

"Have you finished now?"

"Yes, Grandpa."

Wiping his mouth, he tried to understand the smirks between his elders.

"Good. Now are you ready for your surprise?"

"A surprise?"

"Yes, Tenzin, now close your eyes and hold your hands out."

As his son did as told Gyaltso waved his hand in front of him. Happy he could no longer see, he looked to his father and nodded once more. Reaching into his jacket pocket for what he had laboured over in secret since the snows had first appeared, the old man placed the gift into Tenzin's small expectant hands.

"You can open your eyes now," Gyaltso said, eager to see surprise spread across his son's features.

Slowly opening one eye and then the next, Tenzin gazed down to the gift rested in his palms. With no hesitation he raised the small red

31

flute to his lips and blew as hard as he could.

"Tenzin," his father called out, his fingers planted deep in his ears. The piercing wine stopped and Tenzin laughed to the response his playing gave.

"You just need some practice," the old man told him. "Here, let me show you."

Placing his gift into lined hands the boy watched on as his grandfather's fingers found the positions he too had learnt when reaching his grandson's age. Glancing first to Gyaltso and then back at Tenzin, he took a deep breath and began to blow soft into the flute's delicate reed.

Fascinated by the sweet tones before him, Tenzin saw his father also succumbed to the old man's melody. The child leant forwards with chin rested on clasped hands. Seeing his grandson's posture the flute's soft tones came to an end.

"Why have you stopped, Grandpa?" Tenzin asked.

The old man placed the flute back onto the table. Collecting his emotions he smiled to his grandson.

"I will play for you tomorrow, Tenzin," he said. "And I shall also teach you how to play." Gyaltso recognised his father's unsettled tone and looked to Tenzin.

"Tenzin, have you had a good birthday?" He asked.

"Yes, thank you for my present."

Long forgotten memories resurfaced within the old man and he looked away from the table. Tenzin reached out for his hand.

"What is wrong, Grandpa?"

"I am just happy to be here with you," he said, his eyes revealing their true feelings as a tear escaped before his treasured grandson. Gyaltso wrapped his fingers around Tenzin's other hand.

"Your grandfather is tired, Tenzin," he reassured. "As I am sure you are also."

Tenzin's yawn prompted Gyaltso to stand and take him into his arms.

"Good night, Tenzin," the old man said to his grandson's heavy eyelids. Watching Gyaltso carry the child to his bunk, his view returned to the red flute lying between empty plates and bowls. Memories of another returned as he waited for Gyaltso to sit with him once more.

Returning back down beside his father he picked up the red flute and looked back to the sleeping bundle at the far end of their home.

"Tenzin loves his gift," he said.

The old man gave no reply, his pensive stare revisiting the myriad of lines running across aged features.

"You will teach him to play?" Gyaltso pressed for a response. The old man's view returned to the flute. He nodded once to his son then rose from the table.

Watching the old man walk to their small kitchen, Gyaltso grinned to his return and reached for the bottle of amber liquid his father carried with him. Taking out its stopper, he poured them each a draft of the last of the winter's supply of beer and handed one to his father now sat opposite. Both men raised their cups and took a large sip.

"Now that spring is here we can look forward to some fresh chang," the old man broke his silence and took another drink. His son saw the fermented hops had brought his father back to him, yet something still preoccupied the old man. Raising their cups father and son drank together for a second time, each aware of the words to come.

With the bottle reaching its half way mark Gyaltso leant back in his chair. "Why did you stop playing?" He asked.

The old man looked to the flute. Was it now his son ready to hear his thoughts?

"We all have a past, Gyaltso."

"I know," Gyaltso looked down to the table. He soon raised his chin. "Tell me of yours," he said.

"Is it only now you have a child of your own that you realise your father had a life before you came?"

Gyaltso flushed in the old man's laughter.

"It is ok, Gyaltso. This is the way of things. I too never thought of the life your own grandfather held before you arrived."

Refilling their cups, Gyaltso's insight encouraged his suspicions.

"Father, is it true? Have you and Tenzin met before?"

The old man gave no reply and took another draft of beer.

"I see the way you are together," his son continued. "The understanding you hold with one another. I have seen this since Tenzin first came to us. Tell me of the past when you were together."

The old man looked to his son's need for answers.

"Where to begin?" He said, preparing to tell the thoughts which had hounded him since recognising his grandson once more.

"Yes, Gyaltso, it is true. I am sure Tenzin and I have talked before. With each day that confirmation comes to me. His ways, his mannerisms, all these things point towards the one who once taught me so much. The one I knew I would sit with once more."

The old man smiled to his sleeping grandson and then to Gyaltso, his thoughts resting with the teacher who had shown him great kindness as a child.

"My years have not always been spent besides Gyantse's flowing waters," he nursed the last of his chang. "I was Tenzin's age when they came for me."

"Who came for you?"

"Patience, Gyaltso. I think you know the ones of whom I talk." His son reddened again much to the old man's delight. "All will become clear," he added on beginning to recount his childhood.

"I can still see the heavy burgundy robes my parent's visitors wore. I remember the fascination I held towards their arrival peering up from behind my mother, and the broad smiles I received from each of those four holy men as they entered our home."

"These were the ones who took you away?"

"Yes, Gyaltso," the old man nodded. "Although it was not that I was so much taken. I choose to continue with them on their journey to Shigatse."

"You choose to leave your family behind?"

"My leaving brought such happiness to my family. You have to understand that I had been recognised by our guests. I was deemed to be the one who now housed the soul of their one time fellow teacher. This brought great respect to the parents who had conceived such an honour. The pleasure received in seeing their child led away to serve that honour replaced any heartache they may of otherwise held."

"So you went with them to Shigatse of your own free will?"

"Yes, but remember I was a child. My young mind could not recall the life I was told I had lived before. Of course my heart yearned to stay with my family, but there was something within me, something calming my soul, telling me my actions were true. That the life I embarked on was the one I was destined to lead."

Gyaltso sensed sadness in his father's voice. Reaching forwards he took his empty cup from him and refilled its contents, anticipating his act would encourage the old man to continue.

"Thank you," his father smiled. He too knowing the words now spoken were at last ready to be aired.

"For three days and nights we travelled northwards, following Nyangchu's racing waters towards my new home. Wrapped in warm blankets, my bonds strengthened with those who took turns to carry me on their back. It was on arriving at Shigatse's city walls, the memories of my own family began to fade as my young soul merged with those I felt I had known forever."

"You forgot all you had left behind?" Gyaltso glanced to Tenzin's bunk. Seeing his son slept on he looked back to his father. "I mean, how could you forget the life you had always known?"

The old man shook his head.

"Gyaltso, my heart stayed with those who had raised me, and always continued to do so. Yet even at such a young age, I knew the life ahead of me and felt comfort in the knowledge that the parents I had left in Gyantse felt little remorse for my leaving, they too respecting the path I had taken."

Reaching for Tenzin's gift he held it gently between his fingers and became lost in its red sheen.

"My young decisions were soon confirmed the morning of my arrival, when I first met with the one who would guide me through my formative years."

Both happiness and regret swam within the old man's eyes and he looked to the fireplace. Gyaltso also saw its dying embers had returned and reached for another log to fuel its welcomed heat. He hoped his actions would prove enough respite for his father to continue. Settling back down they sat together beside new found warmth.

"Father," he said. "Tell me of your guide."

A smile formed across the old man's lips as he met with Gyaltso's anticipation.

"Lama Jampo," his eyes recovered the sparkle his son had always known. "I knew from the moment he crouched down before me and took my small hands in his that I was destined to be at his side."

"Lama Jampo?"

"Jampo, the gentle one. His name portraying the kind nature he held."

Warmed to his father's memories he saw the old man's features soften in the telling of his past.

"From that first day onwards I would remain at his side, listening and learning from the one who became both parents to me then." The old man paused. Pushing away his apparent regret he trusted his story would ease the words he must now tell his son.

"As I grew, my life within the walls of Shigatse's Tashilhunpo monastery became all I had ever known. With Lama Jampo's wisdom and tender guidance my understanding of the world expanded. I took on the role revealed to me just weeks after my fourth birthday with a reverence I could not have imagined."

"You became a Lama?"

"No, I did not become a Lama, nor was I destined to do so. My fate it seemed lay in another direction."

"Where? In which direction did you go?" Gyaltso tried to keep his voice from carrying to Tenzin's bunk. "What happened, father?"

"It was so long ago, yet still I remember those days so clearly."

Taking another sip from his cup he motioned to Gyaltso and poured the last of the chang. "Lama Jampo and I would sit like this," he continued. "Beside the fires of his home, we too would talk as we do now." The old man reached for Tenzin's flute. He once again became lost in its fragile stem. "And as I have played briefly to you both this evening, so would he for me."

"Did Lama Jampo teach you those notes also?"

"Yes," the old man sighed. "Of that he did."

Joining his father's gaze into the flames beside them, he considered if he should continue to press for the old man's tale. Those thoughts were answered in a smile tinged within a glow of rich orange light.

"The days I spent with Lama Jampo were as treasured then as they are to me now. It would be another who would take me from my guide, teacher and, friend."

"Tell me," Gyaltso's heart broke to the tears flowing before him.

"I am sorry," his father wiped at his cheeks. "Like I have said, so many years have passed, but still they remain fresh in my old mind."

"Who took you from Lama Jampo?"

"She did not take me. It was I who chose to leave what I considered all that was."

"She?"

"For so long I believed my happiness could come only from the monastic life I had known since a child. That was until my eighteenth year when I encountered the one I knew I could not live without."

"My mother." Gyaltso understood who his father now talked of.

"Yes, my son. It is your mother who we now remember."

Gyaltso waited for his father's words, battling grief as to the anniversary of his own loved one's passing.

"I know of your pain also, Gyaltso," the old man spoke softly. "It seems our fate reflects each other's. We must not dwell on such painful events. We must be happy for the short time we spent with those now gone from us. This leads only to enhance their memory, defining the soul we once loved to remain with us always."

Gyaltso became lost in recollections of the one he would still dream of often.

"So you left your life in Shigatse for the love of another?" He asked. "Was Lama Jampo angry with your choices?"

"No, Gyaltso. It was quite the opposite. He saw the love your mother and I held. If any resentment came from the situation it was only from my disquieted soul"

"Then did you remain friends with Lama Jampo?"

"No," the old man saddened. "I would never be in his company again." He glanced back to his sleeping grandson then returned to Gyaltso with a wry smile.

"That is until now."

"You mean?" Gyaltso's view rested on the woollen blanket covering Tenzin.

"Yes, I believe with all my heart that Tenzin is indeed my former teacher, Lama Jampo."

Shocked in at last hearing what he suspected his father always knew, Gyaltso denied his own ideas as to the young soul's true identity and turned to the old man.

"No, that cannot be. Tenzin is unique, special."

"And so was my guide," his father replied. "Have you never wondered how such a young mind can hold the compassion you, I and the rest of Gyantse witness every passing day? Have you not considered that his concern for others comes not from his own family's lineage, but from somewhere else?"

"His mother," Gyaltso said. "She held the same traits as the son she never got to know. It is her reverence for life Tenzin has inherited."

"That may be so, but other reasons lay behind my thoughts. Ones that have made themselves apparent to me as Tenzin's characteristics have flourished over the years."

"The flute," Gyaltso whispered.

Both men gazed down to Tenzin's gift between them and then to each other. "Was that why you stopped playing, because it reminded you of your teacher?"

"In a way, but that was not the true reason why I stopped."

"Then what else did you see?"

The old man's eyes recovered their sparkle as he recalled his past once more.

"When Lama Jampo and I would sit together, he would often ask me to play for him. I would do so on every occasion. I knew when my melodies were enjoyed by my teacher's posture as he became lost in my notes, leaning forwards, his chin rested on clasped hands."

"The way you saw Tenzin do tonight also?"

"His appreciation to my music could not have been mirrored in any other way. It was not until tonight that I truly knew I sat with my guide and friend once more."

Gyaltso's view returned to his son. He understood his father's notions. Part of him believed Tenzin could not be anything else but the incarnation of another's kind soul, although his anxiety remained in thoughts of one day losing the one who made life real to him.

"But how can you be sure? You never saw your teacher again. How do you know he does not still live within Shigatse's walls?"

"It was four years ago today that I received the news I awaited. The morning of Tenzin's birth, I carried with me the knowledge my friend had gone, brought to me by our neighbours as you wept over your loved one's passing."

"Then why did you not tell me, father? So I too could share in your grief?"

"Your own sorrow required all the strength you had without my adding to it."

As blurred recollections of that day retuned to him, Gyaltso considered if it were true Tenzin was indeed the favoured Lama his father now spoke of.

"Was that the moment you knew of Tenzin's destiny?" He said. "On that very same day he first took his first breaths?"

The old man watched his son begin to warm to his assumptions.

"It was not until that evening when I turned from your sleeping and to Tenzin's own slumber that I saw the one who had shown me such wisdom in my youth, revealed in the gaze my grandson's eyes gave to me."

Sensing Gyaltso's growing apprehension and aware he too understood the fate which may lay ahead of his treasured son, he rose from the table placed a hand on his Gyaltso's shoulder.

"Come now, it is late," he embraced his son as he too stood before him.

"Do not worry so, Gyaltso. It takes many years for those who seek to find such a soul. Maybe I am wrong in my ideas. Maybe this old mind of mine has failed me at last. Who knows? And just maybe, the love I hold for my cherished grandson has biased my opinions as to the unique character he shows to all concerned."

"Maybe, that is so," Gyaltso replied before bidding him goodnight and walking to his own bunk.

Gyaltso slept little that night. Lost in the words spoken to him, his view stayed on the gentle breaths lifting the blankets of the child sleeping across the room.

Allowing himself a moment to imagine he once more shared his bed with the wife he had lost, he wondered what she would have made of her father-in-law's ideas towards their son. Would she too have believed Tenzin's destiny lay elsewhere?

Feeling the pain from evoking tender memories, Gyaltso pulled his blanket up around him. He looked to Tenzin's moonlit bundle.

"Could it be true, Tenzin?" he whispered and rolled over to face where his love had once lain, his heart heavy with the possibility he and his son may one day be parted.

CHAPTER FIVE

Miyako continued her work within the suburbs of southern Kyoto. Guided by Hiroko, her skills progressed until she needed no further teaching and soon began to receive the same respect as her predecessor. Knowing those lessons were no longer required, Hiroko would smile as Miyako left their home for another's expected arrival, remembering how she too had once held the same passion and excitement as the beautiful young woman rushing from her door, the former geisha who had brought such richness to the old midwife's life.

As Momoko grew so did her mother in spirit. Hiroko knew the cause of Miyako's new found happiness, yet not another word was spoken of the history she had revealed one Hanami evening. The release of that past had brought a deeper bond between the two, the pain buried deep within Miyako laid to rest amongst the diminishing embers of her home's fireplace.

Miyako's joy for life developed as the seasons came and went, her smiles confirming the words revealed that night the key to her new existence. It would be on the eve of Momoko's sixth birthday that Hiroko would notice a distance in Miyako's eyes she had not seen for many years. The old midwife did not question the reasons behind such pensive stares and instead waited for Miyako to approach her first, the way it had always been between them. Her wait would not be long as Miyako soon joined her side one evening after seeing Momoko to bed. Knowing the expectations her daughter's soul always held before her birthday, Hiroko smiled as Miyako sat with her on the living room floor.

"She is excited for tomorrow?" The old midwife asked. Miyako nodded in silent reply.

"Momoko told me how she enjoys having Hanami to herself, Hiroko. That she is glad only the three of us walk together beneath her cherry blossoms."

"She knows she is special," Hiroko laughed.

"She knows that she is different," Miyako said. The young woman's head bowed in apology for her sharp retort "I am sorry," she said. "It is just that I worry for Momoko."

"Worry, in what way? Your daughter is healthy, she is strong. She has the face of an angel."

"That is the problem," Miyako looked from the old midwife. "Even at this young age, she knows the power her looks wield over others."

"Yes, Miyako, but you know as well as I that Momoko has always been aware of her beauty."

"But she wears her beauty as a prize, a way of gaining what she wants from others. Not as the gift it truly is."

Seeing the truth behind Miyako's words, the old midwife also recognised the worry that hounded the young mother.

"She is young, with many things to learn." she reassured. "I am sure you too as a child encountered the same as Momoko does now."

"That is true. I too was aware from a young age the command I held, and the manipulation of others came easy to me also. But I seldom used such ways. This is what worries me." Miyako paused. She glanced to the room where her daughter slept. "Momoko understands the influence her appearance carries."

Hiroko understood. She too had seen a slight arrogance develop within Momoko. At times she worried it would one day override the child's true soul, yet her love for her surrogate grandchild took precedence over all thoughts.

"She will learn in time, Miyako, do not worry so. Momoko's lessons will arrive as did yours many years ago. Then together we will see her take on the modesty she has yet to encounter." Hiroko reached out and took both Miyako's hands in hers. "All in good time, wait and see."

The remnants of Hanami lay beneath Miyako's feet as she walked homewards after a long night delivering another soul into Kyoto's community. As dawn light caught the edges of scattered petals she looked down to brown tinges replacing the pinks and whites she so adored, confirming her belief that nothing lasts forever.

It had been three weeks since Miyako had aired her worries for Momoko's lack of humility. Although not another word had been mentioned on the subject the matter still lay heavy in her thoughts.

Emotions had surfaced within her that contradicted her love for Hiroko, adding to the weight she now carried. She knew the old midwife recognised her daughter's unpleasant traits, but her love for Momoko had dismissed such feelings. This angered Miyako. Confused, she battled to understand how her contempt towards the one who had saved her grew each day from such denial. As Miyako neared home, her mind raced with the decision to confront her daughter's unpleasant problem once more, wondering how the old midwife would react to the words she was to speak.

On reaching her home, Miyako paused before the front door that had been her salvation several years earlier. Looking to the laundry hanging from the porch beside her, Miyako's eyes fell to the doll and its red dress drying amongst her family's clothing. The present Hiroko had given Momoko two years before wavered in the morning's cool breeze and a smile came to Miyako's lips, aware this was the only time of year her daughter could be parted from her treasured gift. Having become an unspoken tradition for Hiroko to wash the doll once a year as Hanami came to a close, Miyako recalled how the old midwife had explained to a distressed Momoko on each occasion that her actions were to mark the beginnings of a new cycle of seasons. These recollections calmed Miyako's frustrations and for a moment she considered if she should continue with her intended confrontation.

Her view drifted to Momoko's own prized dresses. The pride her daughter assumed when parading through the streets in her finery haunted Miyako. Her concerns pushed to the fore again. Miyako knew from experience that Momoko would not listen to her mother's advice. Only Hiroko held that power within their household. With a deep breath, she entered her home, determined to convince Hiroko to broach the subject of Momoko's growing vanity.

Closing the front door behind her, Miyako's confidence grew in that she and Hiroko would not be disturbed in their talk. It was still early and Momoko would not be from her bed for another half-hour before readying herself for school. This would give them time to speak, remembering how on early mornings like these she and Hiroko would often sit together in their small garden to watch the sunrise cascade across the surrounding landscape.

Hiroko looked to the fireplace. She could not understand why its hearth did not contain the golden flames which always welcomed her mornings. For all the years she had lived with Hiroko, she had never known the old midwife to sleep through daybreak's rising sun. Continuing to the kitchen expecting to be greeted by smells of Momoko's breakfast, she looked from its window and rushed out into the garden.

"Hiroko," Miyako crouched down besides the old midwife's frail body. Pulling her close to her, the old mid wife's eyes opened to Miyako's touch.

"Miyako," she smiled, her voice weak. "You are here."

"Yes, Hiroko, I am here. What happened? Let me get you inside."

Beginning to lift the old midwife she stopped as Hiroko shook her head.

"No, my child. It is time," she glanced to the orange sun emerging from the hillsides beyond. Her eyes returned to Miyako's. "Stay with me," she said.

Miyako nodded to her friend's request. Cradling Hiroko in her arms, tears ran freely down her cheeks.

"Do not be sad," Hiroko smiled once more. "My life has been long and full. You and Momoko have brought such happiness to me in my closing years. I could not have asked for anything more."

"But, Hiroko, you cannot leave us now."

"Miyako, I will always be with you, with you both. You know this don't you?"

Hiroko's expectant gaze broke Miyako's heart. With no reply, she wiped at her tears, leant down and kissed the old midwife's brow.

Guilt towards her thoughts that morning filled Miyako and she turned her view to a distant sunrise.

"She will be fine, you will see, Miyako," Hiroko said, aware of what troubled the beautiful young woman. "Wait and see, my child," Hiroko's hand found Miyako's. "Now let us enjoy the morning sun together for one last time."

The lines around Hiroko's eyes softened and for a brief moment and Miyako caught glimpse of the beauty the old midwife had once held many years ago.

"Yes," the old midwife saw the young woman's recognition. "I was once the same as you, Miyako."

Hiroko gave her hand a gentle squeeze and no further words were said as they enjoyed their last moments together, bathed in the first rich rays of morning sunlight.

Holding Hiroko close, Miyako willed the old midwife to stay with her. Yet she knew in her heart it was time to say goodbye. On feeling Hiroko's final breath leave her, she placed a kiss upon her temple.

"Thank you, Hiroko," she wept. "Thank you for everything."

Looking back to the morning sun they had watched so many times before, Miyako saddened she would never share such a sight with her friend and confidant again. A shuffle of feet broke Miyako from her grief. She turned to see Momoko standing in the kitchen doorway behind her.

"What's wrong with, Hiroko?" she asked her mother. "Is she sleeping?"

Miyako shook her head, summoning her emotions to tell her daughter of Hiroko's passing. She stopped as Momoko turned away and stared at her own reflection in the kitchen window. Paying no attention to the situation played out before her, Momoko tucked a stray strand of hair behind her ear. Miyako's tear filled eyes widened in disbelief as she watched her child become absorbed in her own appearance.

In time, Miyako came to accept Momoko's ways. In no way did this detract from the love she held for her daughter and would sometimes consider if the characteristics she so disliked in her child somehow increased her unconditional emotions towards her. In Miyako's quieter moments, she wondered if she in turn would pay less attention to Momoko had she not the failings of pride and vanity surrounding her. In memory of Hiroko, Miyako had tried to gently guide Momoko towards the modesty her daughter needed. To no avail did her child recognise such a quality. Taking comfort in the old midwife's final words, Miyako waited for Momoko to reveal her hidden humility, hoping the manipulative ways she witnessed blossom in her child would one day cease to be.

By the morning of Momoko's eighth birthday her mother's wishes had still to be granted, and as the two walked beneath the cherry trees on their second Hanami without Hiroko at their side, Miyako hoped this year would present the sentiments so lost from her child.

"I miss, Hiroko," Momoko said, her fingers wrapping round her mother's hand.

"I know you do," Miyako looked to the stream beside them. "But she is always with us. Can you feel her presence now?"

Momoko looked up to her mother. "Yes, Mamma," she nodded. "Always."

Miyako wiped a single tear from her eye and crouched down to her daughter. Cherry blossom season brought mixed emotions to her now. Once she had been so enamoured by thoughts of new beginnings, the child before her was testament to that, yet the brief lifetime such beauty carried held with it memories of the friend she had lost as the last chapters of pinks and whites came to an end.

"Never forget, Momoko, Hiroko is always by your side, where ever you are."

Raising a small finger, she wiped a fresh tear from her mother's eye.

"Don't be sad, Mamma, Hiroko is with you too you know."

Miyako looked deep into her daughter's eyes. Could this be the beginnings of the selflessness she had longed to see in her child? Was it only now as they remembered the one who had shown such kindness to them both, that the empathy concealed in someone so young began to flower? Taking Momoko in her arms, Miyako held her close to her.

"I know," she said.

Breaking apart, mother and daughter's hands slipped into one another's as they continued to walk the empty pathway of their own private Hanami. Miyako looked to Momoko. Delighting in the young eyes accepting the world afresh each time, she remembered her own days as a child in Tokyo's poorer suburbs when all had been new to her also. All those years seemed so far from Miyako now and she gave Hiroko a silent thank you for the chance given to her.

"Look," Momoko pulled Miyako from her memories.

Following her daughter's finger to the lone figure walking towards them Miyako peered closer. It was unusual to see someone walk the same path as they on Momoko's birthday. Something familiar about the stranger's gait reached deep within Miyako. Many years had passed since she had seen such elegance.

As each dignified footfall neared Miyako froze on recognising who now approached them.

"Hiroko," her daughter cried out.

Miyako said nothing as Momoko drew her hand away. Watching her daughter run towards the old woman, Miyako bent down and picked Momoko's doll from the ground, its red dress more than ready for its annual wash. Raising her eyes to the figure ahead, Miyako rose to her feet and prepared herself for the encounter she knew would one day come. A faint smile came to her lips as her daughter and their visitor's laughter evoked lost memories, recollections she knew could not remain hidden forever. As the two came to a stop before her, Miyako looked to the one who had once provided her with long passed opportunities.

"Mamma," Momoko giggled, her hand held tight in the old woman's. "Doesn't she remind you of Hiroko?"

The old woman looked down to the child and then smiled as her eyes met with Miyako's. Momoko fell silent. Staring up, her young mind tried to understand the intense gaze held between the two adults.

"Hello, Miyako," the old woman said. "It has been a long time."

Miyako returned the visitors smile and bowed once in respect for her elder.

"Yes, Auntie," she replied. "It has."

Although their meeting had been brief, Miyako knew Auntie would uphold her promise made that day.

"Now that I have found you both, I shall return in one week's time," she had told Miyako beneath Kyoto's famed cherry trees before leaving for her own home.

Momoko's joy to Auntie's words confirmed the fears Miyako held to the old woman's unexpected arrival. As the following days advanced towards Auntie's return, Miyako considered the events she was sure were to unfold, her daughter's eager expectance only adding to her worries.

That day soon arrived and as the three dined together that evening within Miyako's home, she studied the fascination her daughter and Auntie held for one another. Miyako's heart sank in seeing the same bonds she herself had experienced as a child were present between them both.

"She has your eyes, Miyako," Auntie said on returning from Momoko's bedroom.

"You are honoured, Auntie," Miyako avoided the old woman's complement, knowing in which direction her former guardian directed their conversation. "Momoko rarely takes to those she does not know so soon."

Auntie glanced back to the closed bedroom door.

"Momoko understands the great beauty she holds."

"She does, Auntie, more than I ever did at her age."

Auntie reached for the steaming pot of green tea between them and raised an eyebrow to Miyako. Miyako bowed her head in return.

Watching Auntie pour their drinks, Miyako marvelled to how at ease she felt in the old woman's company once more. It had been so long since the two had talked together. Those years seemed as days now as Miyako observed the love each still held for the other. Auntie recognised those feelings rise in her former protégé.

"Here, Miyako," she held out one of the wooden bowls Hiroko had once cherished. "Drink, my child."

Taking the bowl Miyako's memories filled with those of the old midwife. Auntie watched as Miyako's eyes closed on tasting the bitter liquid.

"You know why I am here, Miyako?"

Miyako's eyes opened to reveal tears within. "I am in your debt, Auntie," she said.

"Of that you are." Auntie paused. "But this is not the only reason why I am here."

Miyako stared at her visitor. Was the forgiveness she had yearned for to be granted? Those hopes were shattered as Auntie spoke the words Miyako feared would arrive.

"You know of the life of a geisha, Miyako. Tell me, can you still remember those days?"

Miyako knew the connotations behind those words. Nevertheless, Miyako saw no malice lay in the old woman's enquiry and once again eased to the calm felt in her company, a peace gained from the long history they had once shared together.

"How did you find us, Auntie?"

"Miyako," Auntie laughed. "We all knew of the kind old midwife from Kyoto." Her joy faded and Miyako noticed a distance enter the old woman's eyes. "I was once a geisha also."

"You knew I was here all along?"

Auntie took a long sip from her tea before continuing.

"I too watched your stomach rise in those last summer months, as aware as you of the forbidden child you carried. When you did not return to the Okiya that moonlit evening I knew the place to which you ran. With all my heart I fought my want to find you, but I was determined to let the one I had raised as my own live the life she wanted."

"Then why? Why now after all these years have you decided to come to me?"

"Miyako, I am old. When you left I thought I would find another Atotori to take my place. In my search I found no one worthy of your grace and beauty."

"Then you have come here to ask me to return? To be the successor I was groomed to be?"

"That was my plan, Miyako. Until…" Auntie looked back to Momoko's bedroom door.

"Until what?"

"Until I saw the one whose eyes matched yours, Miyako, then I knew I had at last found my true heir."

Miyako's fears resurfaced. Glancing to her daughter's room, she knew of the life Auntie could provide Momoko, opportunities once given so freely to her. She saddened on realising how that existence suited the vanity so natural in her own child.

"It is late, Miyako," the old woman rose to her feet. "Remember, what I ask is not for your consideration. We both know only the child can make that decision."

Miyako nodded, she understood the ways of her former profession and watched her guest walk to her room. Auntie paused beneath its doorway.

"I shall return to Tokyo in the morning," she said. "In one weeks' time I shall revisit your home and the one who shares her mother's beauty. Good night, Miyako."

Miyako's years of training pushed forwards. With no objections, she bowed in respect to the one who had always shown her kindness and compassion.

"Good night, Auntie," she said, her eyes fixed on where her daughter slept.

*

A week soon passed, each day fuelled by the same sleepless nights Miyako had experienced from her first encounter with Auntie.

Momoko once again anticipated Auntie's arrival and in answer to her many questions Miyako did her best to explain the complexities of geisha life to her. Listening to her mother's words, Miyako's heart sank to the awe her daughter portrayed from her tales. She understood the fascination the young child held, she too had once felt the same way, but Miyako knew she had eventually chosen a different path. A route she hoped Momoko would take one day also.

Arriving late one evening to Miyako's home seven days later as promised, Auntie had retired to bed with only a few words spoken to her host. Miyako understood the reasons behind their brief welcome. For the first time, she saw the true age of the one who had discovered her in Tokyo's poverty stricken back streets decades earlier. Miyako's insight only increased her awareness of the need for the Atotori the old woman craved.

The next morning as dawn light broke Auntie was woken by Miyako.

"Auntie," she said. "I must go, my work calls me."

The old woman looked from her bed. "I understand, Miyako," she said. "Do not worry for Momoko, I am sure I can prepare her for the day. As I did you so many times before."

"Thank you, Auntie," Miyako replied, recalling her own moments as a child when Auntie became the parents she had left behind. "I will not be long," she raced to join the soon to be father waiting nervously outside her door.

Miyako walked homewards, pleased the delivery of another young soul had been swift and without complication. Anxiety returned to the young woman as she neared her home, wondering if in her time away Auntie had enchanted her daughter with stories of the geisha house that had once been her world. Miyako remembered how Momoko's eyes had shone on first hearing of the bright silks, elaborate hairstyles and makeup which were part of that life. Hesitating outside her door, Miyako tried to shake her feelings of impending loss. She was aware her daughter was already slipping from her grasp.

'Hiroko, what would you do?' She thought on walking into her home.

"Miyako," Auntie smiled beside a roaring fire. "You are here at last."

Miyako bowed once. "Where is she, Auntie?" She asked. "Where is Momoko?"

"Momoko," the old woman called out. "Are you ready?"

The bedroom door slid open and Miyako gasped to the sight of the small child shuffling from within.

"Do you like it, Mamma? Am I as beautiful as Auntie told me you once were?"

Her eyes not leaving the elaborate red silk Kimono wrapped around her daughter, fresh tears formed in Miyako's eyes.

"What is it, Mamma? Am I not beautiful?"

Miyako walked to Momoko. She wiped her cheeks on kneeling down before her daughter.

"You are more beautiful than I could have ever been, Momoko." Another tear escaped as she watched Momoko stand upright and parade around the room.

"Look," she squealed. "I look the same as my doll."

Momoko held up Hiroko's gift to her, its red dress as new from its yearly wash.

"You see?" Momoko jumped up and down.

"Momoko," Auntie called out.

Momoko froze, her chin falling to her chest.

"Now that is not the way for a young geisha to behave? Is it?" the old woman said.

Miyako saw then the command Auntie held over her daughter. It seemed Momoko too had fallen under Auntie's spell.

"Come, Momoko," Auntie spoke softly. "Come sit with me and your mother."

The kindness in the old woman's voice brought a smile to Momoko's lips and she did as instructed. Joining her mother and Auntie's side she slumped to the floor.

"No, Momoko, you must now always sit how I showed you," Auntie said. "I see you have not forgotten such ways, Miyako," she added, glancing over to Miyako's perfect posture.

Miyako reddened, realising how the old woman's teaching had stayed with her from a child. Reaching for her daughter, she helped her attain the position she herself had mastered a lifetime before.

"Very good, Momoko," Auntie commended.

Her heart breaking to the delight Momoko showed from such praise, Miyako knew in that moment the life she had once lived was to become her daughter's.

Miyako's assumptions proved true as the summer months advanced. Momoko's short trips to Tokyo became more frequent until soon it was customary for her to spend a week at a time with the one she too now called Auntie.

Miyako knew the procedure well. The drawing of a child from her family was a delicate business, and Auntie saw to it that neither party were harmed by such actions. Alone in Kyoto, Miyako would reassure her actions for letting her daughter become inaugurated into the life of a geisha, remembering the debt owed to her former guardian for her sudden departure. This eased some of the loss Miyako suffered, always allowing herself the thought of Momoko deciding the new life offered was not for her. Those indulgent hopes were dashed each time when an excited Momoko returned home from her trips away, her young eyes wide and bright on telling of her moments there.

It would not be until the first week of October that Momoko announced her desire to stay with Auntie on a full time basis. Her mother took the news as best she could in front of her child, her sadness amplified with the guilt of how her own parents must have also felt from such news.

Momoko's gradual absence over the previous months had helped Miyako to confront the inevitable and for that she had only Auntie to thank. Knowing the life that lay ahead for her daughter, Miyako took comfort in the knowledge she would remain safe from harm in the old woman's familiar hands.

As the morning came for mother and child to say goodbye, Miyako looked deep into her daughter's eyes.

"We will be with each other again," she held back her tears.

"We will, Mamma," Momoko nodded, even though neither knew when that would be.

Momoko reached out for her mother and both embraced each other tight for a final time before Miyako watched her tearful child join the one chosen to escort her to her new life. Walking from her, Miyako battled her want to race after the two and take Momoko back, yet in some way she knew this was the life her daughter was destined to live.

Momoko stopped as she neared the corner of the street on which she had grown. She turned and raised a small hand. Her mother smiled as she waved back to her child, fighting her instincts once more as her tears fell on watching Momoko disappear from sight.

That night Miyako sat alone besides her small home's fireplace.

"Thank you, Hiroko," she said into its flames, understanding how the old midwife's life work would now be her redeemer. Miyako smiled as she saw how her role in life had taken on the one that had shown such kindness to her, and as she did every day, she wished her friend was by her side now.

"Yes, Hiroko," Miyako smiled once more. "I can feel you now," she recalled her words spoken to Momoko six months earlier. A fresh wave of grief entered Miyako to such thoughts and she walked to Momoko's bedroom.

Kneeling down beside her bed she reached out for the blanket that had once kept her daughter warm and held it to her.

Breathing in the scent of her child salty tears met with woollen fabric. As Miyako placed the blanket back she noticed the red material peeking out from beneath the bed. Crouching down, she reached out and pulled Momoko's cherished doll to her.

"She forgot you?" Miyako said to its round face and bright red dress. "Then you will have to come with me."

Feeling the child emerge within her, the young midwife rose to her feet and walked to her own bed, Momoko's doll swinging at her side.

CHAPTER SIX

True to his word, the old man opened Tenzin's world to the notes and tones hidden within the red flute. Each night after supper the child would play to his household, delighting in the pleasure he gained by their smiles. Watching his son perform as the sun fell behind their small home, Gyaltso would nod in approval to his father's tuition as Tenzin's skills grew, concealing his thoughts as from where such talents came. He had not forgotten his father's tale that birthday night Tenzin had received his gift and felt some relief that no word had been mentioned on the subject since.

As these evening recitals came to a close, Tenzin would redden to the praise received from his elders and pass the flute on to his grandfather. Taking the instrument, the old man would give his own rendition whilst watching his grandson assume the position of his former teacher. Sitting with them, Gyaltso dismissed his true feelings towards the origins of such traits, his fear of losing his treasured son resurfacing in his mannerisms. Aware of his son's trepidation, the old man played on. He knew one day Gyaltso would come to understand the inimitable destiny he was sure Tenzin was to take.

Life within Gyantse continued as Tenzin's birthday marked the commencement of another hailed spring. As the seasons rolled by, he would join his father in the surrounding fields of Nyangchu's flowing waters, his young mind learning the farming skills handed down by generations before him.

Soon, Tenzin's presence became common place amongst those reaping the harvest that would see them through the foreboding harsh winter, his endless smiles welcomed by the village's farmers and their own children who too helped reap tall grasses of barley and wheat. As Gyaltso watched his son laugh and play with all those he encountered, he would return to his toil, his thoughts staying with the one who had once shared that same smile, the doubts to Tenzin's true soul fading in the joy such a playful nature gave others.

With the dawning of another spring upon them, Tenzin walked between his father and grandfather besides the river's increasing torrents, enjoying his time with those he loved as they celebrated his sixth birthday.

"Grandpa, what lies behind the mountains?" Tenzin pointed up to snowcapped peaks. The old man glanced to Gyaltso. Sensing the apprehension his son held to Tenzin's growing curiosity he gave a reassuring smile before answering his grandson.

"Why do you ask, Tenzin?"

"No reason," the boy shrugged. "It is just that I wonder."

"What do you wonder?" Gyaltso questioned.

Tenzin recognised his father's concern.

"I wonder if there are others."

"What others, Tenzin?" his grandfather smiled.

"Oh I don't know," Tenzin looked from both men. "Others like me I suppose," he said out to the surrounding landscape.

"Tenzin," Gyaltso turned from his father and crouched down to the young boy. "Now you are six, I think you are old enough to run ahead and explore your home," he hid his disquiet to his son's interest in the world beyond all he knew.

"Really?" Tenzin's eyes widened. Gazing up at his grandfather, he laughed to the old man's grin and reached out to Gyaltso. "Do not worry, father, I will keep from the river," he said before running from them.

Seeing his son kept his vow, Gyaltso and the old man walked behind Tenzin's trail besides Nyangchu's winding path, each caught up in their own thoughts. Nearing their home, the old man looked once more to Gyaltso.

"Tenzin has a curious mind," he said.

"Too curious, father. Why does the outside world concern him so when all he could ever ask for is here in Gyantse?"

The old man nodded to Gyaltso. Watching the joy his grandson held in being free to explore his surroundings, he said nothing of the same want of independence he knew had contained another from his past.

"Gyaltso, Tenzin's want of knowledge to the world beyond his homelands will only grow with each coming year. Both you and I know this. It seems it is his soul's destiny to explore and seek new horizons. Something we must allow him to do so if that is his wish."

Gyaltso saddened. He understood his father's advice, yet his heart could still not admit the unknown fate he felt Tenzin headed towards with every passing season. Looking back to the mountain tops that had triggered his son's inquisitive young mind, he smiled to his father.

"Did Lama Jampo hold the same curiosity to the world?"

The old man saw his son's first signs of awareness towards Tenzin's future.

"Yes, Gyaltso. He often talked of the faraway lands he had visited before settling in Shigatse. Nonetheless, there are many other similarities Tenzin holds with my former teacher."

Gyaltso knew his father wished to carry on with their taboo subject, admiring his patience in waiting for him to make the first move. Considering if it was now time to hear more on Tenzin's supposed life before arriving to Gyantse, he decided to listen to the old man's words.

"Gyaltso," he began. "Do you remember two springs ago when we watched Tenzin's actions that day?"

"When he set that beetle free?"

"We both knew then something unique lay within Tenzin's behaviour. The reverence he showed to that creature's life led to confirm by beliefs."

"Lama Jampo showed the same respect towards the life of others?"

"Since leaving my friend's side, I had never encountered such compassion until that day, shown in the hands of someone so new to this world."

Looking to his home Gyaltso waved to Tenzin stood outside its doors.

"If what you say is true, what will happen if Tenzin is discovered by those who once knew him?"

"That will be Tenzin's decision," the old man replied. "Not yours, not mine, nor the ones who seek the return of their former teacher also. Only the child can choose the life offered to him." He too waved to his grandson as Gyaltso mulled over his words, a peace coming to him as his son began to understand the great undertaking that may lie ahead of them all.

"Then only time shall tell," Gyaltso said and walked towards Tenzin's beckoning call.

In the months that followed, no words were spoken concerning the old man's belief that he sat once more in the presence of his teacher. Gyaltso saw to that silence. Of this his father was aware and paid his respect in waiting as accustomed for his son to question that which he knew to be true.

The turmoil coursing through Gyaltso in denial of his son's fate played heavy on the young man's conscience. A part of him had begun to believe his father's assumptions. The wise look in Tenzin's eyes as he watched his grandfather play his cherished melodies each night confirmed what he tried so hard to refuse. Yet the fear of Tenzin leaving his side fuelled his dread that those who sought their favoured Lama would one day visit his homelands.

One evening as their household slept, Gyaltso rose from his own bed to watch over Tenzin's bunk. With each of his son's tiny breaths, he became aware that his thoughts on the matter must be told. Hovering over Tenzin that night, Gyaltso view fell to his sleeping father. His heart aching for some relief from his suffering, he knew it was time to confront his pain. Walking towards the old man he stopped. Staring to the one who had raised him alone, he recognised the peace his father held and turned from him.

"Soon," Gyaltso whispered and let him sleep on as he made back to his own fitful slumber.

Returning from the fields one summer's afternoon, Gyaltso knew it was time to speak of what had troubled him for so long. Leaving Tenzin playing happily in the grass lands with his friends, Gyaltso's confidence grew in the knowledge this would give him time to talk alone with his father to discuss Tenzin's possible future. As he reached the door to their small home, Gyaltso hesitated. Searching for the courage to continue onwards, he looked up to the surrounding mountains and shielded his eyes from the sky's bright glare.

"You must do this," he whispered out into the vivid blues he had always known and then marched forwards, determined to know the truth of Tenzin's soul.

Pushing the door open, Gyaltso stopped once again. Glancing around its only room he frowned in seeing his father was not there. Gyaltso could not understand why the old man was not besides the fire to greet him as he always would.

Turning to leave, any relief Gyaltso felt in putting off their confrontation was soon lost in the slight groan from his father's bunk. Racing towards the bundle of blankets, he fell to his knees besides the old man hidden beneath them.

"Father, what is wrong? Are you sick?"

Caught in a shaft of sunlight flowing through his bedside window, his father opened his eyes and smiled.

"No, Gyaltso, I am not sick."

"Then what is it? I have never known you to sleep in the day."

Warm sunbeams playing over his lined features.

"I am not tired either, Gyaltso," he said. His smile faltered as a tear rolled across his cheek. "It is my time now."

Gyaltso's emotions brought through the same tears in understanding his father's words.

"But you can't leave us," he reached out for the hand he had known since a boy. Feeling its grip around his, Gyaltso wiped his eyes and drew closer to his dying father.

"Gyaltso, do not grieve, for my life had been long and contained such happiness. There comes a time when a soul must leave behind all it has known."

"But there is so much more for you to teach me."

"Gyaltso," the old man hushed, his hand squeezing the one in his. "You have your own child to guide now." He looked to the doorway. "Tenzin? Where is he?"

"He will be here soon, father."

Smiling to the comfort the old man gained in his words they said no more, a lifetime of experience entwining their silence.

As the sun's rays moved across to meet with Gyaltso's tears, both men looked back to the figure stood within the doorway of their home.

"Tenzin," Gyaltso called. "Come talk with your grandfather."

Watching his son's cautious gait towards them, he greeted the boy with a silent nod.

"Grandpa," Tenzin smiled. Taking the old man's free hand he too knelt down besides his bunk.

"Is it time now?" He asked.

Gyaltso settled back on seeing the bonds between Tenzin and his grandfather. Thinking of his reasons for returning early from work, he saw within their stares his questions in some way had been answered, that this lifetime truly had not been the only one these wise souls had experienced together. Seeing this recognition in Gyaltso, the old man's eyes told of the gratitude he felt.

"I understand now, father," Gyaltso said and reached his arm around Tenzin. Holding him close, father and son's view returned to their elder.

"Until we meet again," the old man whispered up to each of them.

"That we will, Grandpa," Tenzin replied before falling back into his father's embrace as the old man closed his eyes and was gone from them.

Consoling each other's grief it was Tenzin who spoke first.

"Do not cry, father," he smiled. "We shall be with him again."

Looking into his son's eyes, for the first time he saw the old soul his father had talked of housed within Tenzin's young body. Nodding to him, he leant forwards to the old man's calm features and placed a kiss on his lined forehead.

"Yes, father, until we meet again," Gyaltso whispered his father's parting words, humbled by the lesson revealed by his young son.

Tenzin remained at his father's side through the hot summer months, their companionship growing as carefree days led into autumn and then settled once more into another harsh winter. In the year that passed since his father's death, Gyaltso came to understand the beliefs the old man had held towards Tenzin's true identity. His eyes opened by their last moments together, Gyaltso came to accept the unique compassion his son held to all those around him.

Tenzin's kindness shone through as the advancing winter approached. Proving both friend and confidant to his sole parent, the bonds Gyaltso had watched form between Tenzin and his grandfather now became his, bringing them a union he had not imagined possible before.

Watching his son sleep at night, Gyaltso would glance to where his father had once slept and smile. "So you were right old man," he would whisper, understanding the kind- hearted qualities Tenzin displayed may have once belonged to another. Even so, Gyaltso's growing awareness did not mask his fear that those who sought the same soul might one day knock upon their door. Gyaltso hid this anxiety from Tenzin, yet he knew his son saw through such concealment and never mentioned his observations. This pleased Gyaltso, although at times he would find himself longing for him to do so. At least then they could talk of the trials which may lay ahead.

On the morning of Tenzin's eighth birthday, Gyaltso watched his son edge closer to Nyangchu's river banks, its waters replenished by the mountains they lived beneath.

"Tenzin. Do you want to make it to another birthday?"

Tenzin saw through his father's stern words.

"Yes, father," he laughed.

"Do not worry so," he returned to his father's side and placed an arm around his waist. Continuing onwards, Gyaltso gave no reply as they neared the trail which would lead them home. Having noticed his father's distance that morning, Tenzin looked to him.

"Where are you today?" He asked.

Recognising the suffering in his father's eyes, the boy pressed no further, aware of the sorrow his own anniversary held of the mother he never got to know. Gyaltso saw his son's understanding.

"Will I be with her again also, Tenzin? One day, in my next lifetime?"

"Of course, father," his son replied. "As will I also."

Glancing back to his homelands, Gyaltso warmed to his son's counsel.

"Thank you, Tenzin," he said.

Any relief Gyaltso gained from his son's insights wavered on looking to the figures approaching them. He paled to the delight the young boy showed as he too watched the four burgundy robed men draw closer.

"Say nothing," Gyaltso whispered down to Tenzin.

"But why, father?"

"You must do as I say," Gyaltso snapped. The young boy silenced. Trying to understand his father's sudden change of mood, he glanced back to their nearing visitors and suppressed his excitement.

Gyaltso readied himself for what was to come. He had spent too many sleepless nights worrying about the arrival of those who now walked the same trail as he and his treasured son. Taking a deep breath Gyaltso summoned a smile.

"Hello," he said to the smiling faces before him.

His welcome received, Gyaltso's heart raced as each figure's view fell to his son.

"Hello," the elder of the four monks smiled down to Tenzin. "And who are you?"

Tenzin could not help but smile back to the stranger.

"Tenzin," he replied with a slight bow. Looking back to the three monks behind his questioner, the boy saw the awe each held to his actions. Looking back to what had triggered the young boy's wonder, the old monk nodded to the others before returning to him.

"And what brings you here today?" Gyaltso asked.

Tenzin knew his father's instructions to remain silent, yet something within the old monk's tone brought his words forwards.

"It is my birthday," Tenzin said. "My father and I always walk besides the river on this day."

Ignoring the excited whispers behind him, the old monk nodded to the boy.

"Then happy birthday, Tenzin," he said and gazed to the rooftops of Gyantse. "And this is your village?" he continued. "Tell me, which one is your home?"

Watching Tenzin's hesitation, the old monk smiled to Gyaltso in hope of releasing the boy's answer. Gyaltso nodded to Tenzin, as aware of the serendipity surrounding their encounter that morning as the four holy men before them.

"Show them, Tenzin," the old monk said.

Masking his fear, Gyaltso watched his son raise his arm and point towards their home.

"Good, now we know where it is you live, I hope we can become friends."

Within Tenzin's laughter the old monk returned his attention to Gyaltso

"You have a happy child," he said and motioned his entourage to continue their walk.

"I am sure we shall meet again," He too walked from Gyaltso and

Tenzin.

Each monk stopped and turned in unison to father and son. Gyaltso's anxiety returned as his son repaid the farewell to the four with his small hands held together before his chin, the way he had watched his own father teach his grandson to do.

"Will we meet them again, father," Tenzin asked as the monks continued along the river banks, puzzled by the suffering in his father's eyes.

"Yes, Tenzin," Gyaltso said. "I am sure that day will come."

As the summer months came, Tenzin learnt not to ask his father of the monk's inevitable arrival. Trying to understand the pain his questions produced, he in turn kept his wishes to himself, each day hopeful for their return. Gyaltso sensed his son's restraint.

This only added to his sorrow as he watched Tenzin's expectant look out onto the river banks with every given moment as they worked together in the fields of Gyantse.

Longing to be at his father's side once more, Gyaltso knew the old man would have given some comfort to Tenzin's fleeting glimpses, an answer to the reasons behind their spring time encounter. He resided to the fact that he was gone from them now and it was he who must be strong for their remaining household.

Working through those hot summer months, Gyaltso's anxiety eased as they approached the beginning of a new season. With no sign of the monk's return, Gyaltso began to forget their meeting besides Nyangchu's rising waters and eased once more into village life. Tenzin saw this change in his father. The joy in seeing that happiness return to his guardian was only tainted by his own yearning to talk with the old monk again. Once more Tenzin kept his silence for their return. Not wanting to cause his father any more suffering, he would hide his eager gaze to the river side path, confident that one day he would be in their presence once more.

On the first day of winter, Gyaltso looked to his son as they ate breakfast together besides their home's rekindled fireplace.

"Tenzin," he smiled. "Are you happy now our work has finished for the year?"

"Yes, father," Tenzin looked to the flames at their side, thinking of the rich harvest that would see them and his neighbours through the cold months to come. Those thoughts were interrupted as three sharp knocks filled the room.

"Who could this be?"

Once more concealing his hopes as to who stood outside their small home Tenzin watched his father rise from the table and walk to greet their callers.

"So early," Gyaltso mumbled as he reached for the door. Pulling it wide open his heart sank in seeing who now faced him. He glanced back to Tenzin, his sorrow increasing in his son's elation.

"Hello again," the old monk smiled to them both. "May we come in?"

Tenzin raced to his father's side. "Can they, father," he said, his eyes not leaving the four smiling figures.

Gyaltso nodded. Standing aside to allow their guests to enter their home he reached for Tenzin's hand.

"Don't worry, father, they are my friends."

From the fire place the old monk looked to his companions, they too smiled on hearing Tenzin's words.

"Tenzin," he leant down to the young boy. "We have still yet to be properly introduced.

I am Lama Norbu, and these are my students."

Tenzin clasped his hands together and bowed to each one. The monks echoed his welcome and then looked up to his father.

"And I am, Gyaltso," he told their guests. "Tenzin's father."

"Then you know why we are here," Lama Norbu replied.

The room fell silent as Gyaltso looked to each of their unexpected arrivals. He glanced down to his son and then back to the old monk.

"Yes," he whispered. "I know."

Tenzin's shuffling feet broke the stillness as he gazed up between his elders.

"Tenzin," Lama Norbu smiled to him. "Your father and I must talk now, would you permit us to be left alone?"

"Is that what you wish, Tenzin?" Gyaltso asked.

Watching the old monk wait for his answer, Tenzin nodded. "Yes, father. Like I said, they are my friends," he told his father again and grabbed his winter's coat before running from his home and pulling its door closed behind him.

Gyaltso's view remained on where his son had stood, dreading the events to unfold. Lama Norbu saw his apprehension and raised an eyebrow to his students.

"We are only here to see if Tenzin is indeed the one we once knew," he reassured Gyaltso.

"I understand," he looked to the bunk that had been his father's. The pleasure the old man would have had in seeing his grandson receive such an honour gave him the confidence to continue as he watched Lama Norbu take his students bag and walk to him.

"Gyaltso, I am sure your father told you of the bonds he held with our friend Lama Jampo."

"You knew my father?"

"Yes, Gyaltso. Although it was many years ago since we last talked, I was saddened to hear of his passing."

"You were aware of our family?"

The old monk nodded. "Gyaltso, we have always known of Tenzin. Although it is not until now that we believe our old friend Lama Jampo has come back to us once more."

Gyaltso eased in knowing he now stood with one who once knew his father and he looked to the bag in Lama Norbu's hands.

"Yes, Gyaltso," the old monk said. "Here may lay our answers," he began to empty its contents out onto the fireside table.

As his father summoned his son back into their home, Tenzin's eyes sparkled on seeing the blue cloth spread across the table. He edged closer to see its display.

"Tenzin," Lama Norbu said. "Do you see what once belonged to you?" He pointed to the nine items set out before them.

"Yes, Lama Norbu," Tenzin's heart racing as he leant forwards and picked up one of the three golden bells before him. Striking it once, its familiar tone echoed around his home and he handed it to the old monk.

"Good, Tenzin," Lama Norbu smiled. "Now, is there anything else?"

Tenzin looked to the two rows arranged neat along the table. His view fell first to the three sets of red coloured wooden beads and then to the orange scarves parallel to them. Glancing to Lama Norbu once more he reached for the beads he knew were once his.

"These," he passed them to the old monk.

As with the other monks present, Lama Norbu took delight towards Tenzin's choices.

"Now, Tenzin. Do you recognise any of the scarves before you?"

His small hand hovering over the three remaining items, he made for the one closest to him. Picking the scarf up, Tenzin felt its silk sheen lay soft across his fingers and then set it back down. He tried once again to find what had belonged to him and then took the orange scarf furthest from him.

"Here," Tenzin said. He saddened to the disappointment evident in his guest's features.

"Was this the wrong one?" He asked.

"Tenzin, your choices were yours and yours alone. How could that ever be wrong?"

Handing the orange scarf back to the old monk Tenzin looked up to his father.

"It's ok, Tenzin," Gyaltso said, his heart saddened by his son's confused expression. "You did very well."

"Very well indeed, Tenzin," Lama Norbu tried to calm the boy's regret. "Will you allow your father and I to talk again?"

Tenzin nodded and made for the door again. He paused before leaving and smiled back to the old monk.

"May I try once again?"

Receiving only a smile, the boy knew his answer and with no further word closed the door behind him.

Gyaltso turned from Tenzin's upset and looked to the old monk.

"Well?" He asked. "Is my son the one you seek?"

Lama Norbu watched his students gather the table's contents and place them back in the bag with care before replying.

"Tenzin decided wisely. Lama Jampo's bell, and his treasured beads, were all reached for with no hesitation by the child. Yet we must be certain that our friend's soul has chosen to return in your son's body."

"Then will he be coming with you now?" Gyaltso's eyes filled, his worst fears at last arisen. Guilt came in his relief as the old monk shook his head.

Lama Norbu reached back into the bag and produced the orange scarf which had evaded Tenzin's touch. "Here is the reason why," he too hid his own disappointment. "As I have said, we must be sure as to whom Lama Jampo has chosen to house such a compassionate soul."

"Then it is not to be Tenzin?"

"Who is it to say the true identity of Tenzin's soul?" Lama Norbu replied. Taking a breath he began to continue with his explanation.

He stopped as music flowed from outside and into the room.

"Lama Jampo," one of the student monks whispered from the fireplace.

Lama Norbu smiled back to his apprentice and then to Gyaltso.

"You recognise my son's playing?"

Looking to the expressions before him Gyaltso's heart sank once more that morning, aware Tenzin's destiny had as last begun to take shape in the guise of his beloved red flute.

"Yes, Gyaltso," Lama Norbu said to him. "I too recognise my old friend's musical talents."

In the weeks following Lama Norbu's rediscovery of his old friend in Tenzin's sweet notes, Gyaltso helped his son prepare for his new life as an apprentice within Shigatse's Tashilhunpo Monastery. Watching his son play, Gyaltso found it hard to conceive that Tenzin had once been his own grandfather's teacher. Yet it seemed even those in Lhasa talked of Lama Jampo's new incarnation, found within Gyantse on the banks of the Nyangchu River. Deep inside Gyaltso, he knew his son's soul once belonged to another. The compassionate nature and reverence for life Tenzin had showed from an early age led to his understanding, although these insights gave little to comfort to the prospect of losing his only child.

On the eve of Tenzin's departure, he and his father walked for one last time besides the waters they had always known. Gazing up to their mountain landscape, Tenzin pointed to the snow now blanketing the summer month's granite they had become accustomed to.

"Father," Tenzin smiled. "The snow that now covers the mountains, what will happen to them when the spring comes?"

"You know as I, Tenzin. They shall melt."

"Yes, but what will happen as winter comes?"

Gyaltso frowned. "The snows shall return."

Looking back to snow-capped peaks his understanding came in the lesson his son now gave.

"The snows shall return," he said once more out to them before picking his son up and carrying him towards their home so they may share their final meal together.

The next evening, Gyaltso looked to the two empty seats beside him and rose from the table. Walking to the fireplace, he stoked its dying embers and then reached for another log. Placing it snug onto the fire a tear splashed onto his hand.

Returning to his seat and wiping his cheek, he looked once again to the place his son would always take and then to the chair where his father had once laughed and talked. Resting his hands beneath his chin, Gyaltso considered the life of that which Tenzin now embarked. Certain his decisions on allowing his son to travel such a path were right, his sorrow still remained.

Glancing from the fireplace's new found flames, Gyaltso looked to Tenzin's empty bunk as his tears fell down wind chapped cheeks in an unbroken stream.

CHAPTER SEVEN

As a rich Tokyo sunset betrayed the surrounding cool winds of early winter, Momoko snuggled into her escort's warm woollen coat and looked up with tired eyes.

"We are nearly there, Momoko," her companion pulled the child's blanket across her. "Better?" she smiled.

Momoko's eyes closed, unaware the life she had known in Kyoto was already beginning to fade from her. She awoke as their carriage came to a halt.

"Momoko, you are here at last," Auntie smiled down to her. She laughed as Momoko reached up and wrapped her small arms around the old woman's waist.

"You are pleased to see me, that is good, my child."

Lifting her to the ground, with a simple nod to the three women waiting to greet Momoko also, their new arrival watched as one of the young Geisha she had come to know as one of her elder sisters bowed to Auntie and ran to pay the driver and Momoko's kind escort. Momoko's young mind saw and understood the respect her new guardian commanded, her pride growing as Auntie took her hand as they walked through the doorway of her new home.

"Now, you are home." Auntie stopped and crouched down to Momoko's eye level. "Are you happy?"

Although this was where she had spent most of the previous six months, it felt strange to know it was now to be her home all the time. Glancing back to her three sisters, Aiko, Hanako and Tamiko, Momoko eyes fell to their bright coloured kimono's and svelte figures. She looked to Auntie and smiled.

"Yes, Auntie," she reached out to hold the old woman once again.

"I am glad," Auntie whispered into Momoko's neck and held her close before gently prising the child from her.

"Momoko," she said rising to her feet. "Now you are to be with us always, you must understand this is your home now and we all want you to be happy. But, there is one thing we must ask of you, Momoko, if you are to stay within these walls."

Momoko smiles left her as she stared up to the old woman.

"Do not worry, sweet Momoko," Auntie smiled also to the child's reaction. "All I ask is that now you are here, you act as the young lady I know you are to become. Can you do that for me?"

Momoko's reply came in her returning happiness.

"Good," the old woman nodded. "Now run along to your room and I will come for you when supper is ready."

Momoko picked up the small bag her mother had helped pack that morning and raced to her room. She stopped half way along the short hallway and turned to her new family.

"Thank you Auntie." Momoko hesitated and then bowed once before waving to her sisters' smiles and continuing onwards.

Auntie watched her new protégé race from her. Her eyebrows rose to the three Geisha at her side, knowing they too saw she had chosen wisely.

Looking around her bedroom, Momoko opened her small suitcase. Rummaging through her clothes, tiredness pushed her on for what she sought and delved into her belongings again.

Repeating her search several times, tears welled in her eyes and she sat down on her bed and began to cry. Her door slid open to the sounds of her sobs. Momoko peered up to Auntie's concerned features.

"What's all this?" Auntie walked to her and sat down.

She looked from the floor's small pile of clothes and then to the weeping child. "Tell me," she whispered.

"She's gone," she sniffed.

"Who's gone?"

"Hiroko's doll. She's not here," Momoko's tears increased and she fell into the old woman's chest. "She's not here."

Auntie reached down and kissed Momoko's crown. "I am sure she will be ok, my sweet," she raised Momoko's chin with her finger. "You are tired after such a long journey. That is the reason why everything seems so sad."

"But, but what will she do now I am not with her?"

"Shh," Auntie hushed, rocking Momoko gently as she did so. She knew who the child in her arms now truly talked of.

"I am quite sure Hiroko's doll likes her home in Kyoto." Auntie waited for Momoko's gaze to fall to her own. "As much as someone else we both know."

"Mamma?" Momoko brightened as Auntie nodded to her.

"Yes, Momoko. Your mother loves her home, and the work she does there delivering all those beautiful new souls into the world. You must be proud of her choices to stay behind and continue to do that."

Momoko's tears stopped and she wiped her eyes. "I am, Auntie," she said. "But."

"But what, Momoko?"

"But I bet those new souls won't be as beautiful as me."

Auntie looked away from the child. She had noticed Momoko's vanity from their first encounter. Putting such an unpleasant trait down to age, her fears for the lack of humility in one so young never hampered Auntie's desire to mould the child into the Geisha she knew she truly was. One as exquisite as her mother had once been, Auntie considered looking to the clothes strewn floor.

"Momoko, you must hang your clothes up yourself now you are living here," she said. "Come, my sweet," Auntie knelt to the floor. "I will help you to do so on this one occasion."

Momoko's sight never left her guardian as together they folded her belongings and placed them in the small wardrobe at the foot of her bed. Aware of the young eyes upon her, Auntie looked to Momoko.

"Your mother became so famous within these streets of Tokyo, Momoko."

"And will I become the same, Auntie?"

The old woman raised her head to the child. Taken back by the drive in someone of such tender years, she recognised the same determination Miyako had once shown at a similar age.

"Of that I am sure. But tell me, is that what you truly want?"

"Of course it is, Auntie," Momoko laughed. "Why else would I be here?"

Auntie remained silent. Stunned by Momoko's reply, she

wondered if the decision for her successor had been as wise as she once thought. Looking to Momoko, she dismissed such ideas. She knew from experience that the training on which the young child was to embark would rein in her self-importance and took some comfort in that knowledge.

"Tomorrow you shall begin your life as a novice. From that first step, Momoko, we can only wait and see if you prove to match your mother's standing. Are you excited?"

"Yes," Momoko's eyes widened. She turned to her bedroom door as it slid open.

"Auntie, supper is ready," Hanako, peered into the room. Momoko giggled again as the face winked at her.

"Good, we are both hungry," Auntie took Momoko's hand and they left the room to enjoy their first family meal together.

The next morning, Momoko began her first steps towards the life of a Geisha, although that training proved far from what she had expected.

"But why must I cook and clean, Auntie?" She scowled down to the rags and tub of polish placed before her.

Giving no reply, Auntie questioned her decisions for a moment, recalling her own training when she too had demanded such answers. Looking back to the frowning child, she knew then her choices were correct. As Momoko was deemed successor to one of Tokyo's most successful Okiya's, it was quite unknown for said heir to take on the menial duties of a Shikomi. Auntie saw in Momoko's glare that to skip the first rites of passage to becoming a Geisha would have been a mistake in one so self-assured.

"Momoko, we were all Shikomis once," she smiled. "Myself, your older sisters. Even your mother. We all had to start somewhere."

"But, Auntie."

"No, Momoko," the old woman replied not losing her warm smile. "You have so much to learn, my child, before becoming that which you desire. Answer me this, are you not excited for your lessons to come?"

"But I want to be a Geisha now, Auntie," Momoko snapped.

Within moments she realised her harsh manner would not get her what she wanted. Momoko tilted her chin to the floor and looked upwards. "I am sorry, Auntie," she said in fake innocence.

The old woman hid her grins to Momoko's attempts of manipulation. Once more, she saw she had chosen well. Never before in all her years had she seen such empathy for another's feelings. The knowledge Momoko also held of how to play on those emotions only confirmed the old woman's belief that one day, the child may even surpass even her mother who had been famed for such skills. Yes, she thought, this child has all the makings of a true Geisha.

"These chores I set you will only be temporary," Auntie reassured. "You must take pride in your work. This will only enhance the schooling you are to receive on the skills to become what you want."

"When do my lessons start?" Momoko brightened. Her mentor paused before replying.

"Soon, Momoko. But there is a condition to your starting there."

"What is it, Auntie? Tell me."

The old woman said nothing and glanced from the cleaning materials between them and the hallway Momoko had resisted polishing.

Once again Momoko understood the wants and needs of another. Without further word, she lifted the bucket of rags and wax and left Auntie's side to begin her chores.

As the months passed, the old woman watched Momoko take to the toils she had been given. With all her experience of those Geisha she had raised and guided herself, Momoko attested to be the one who showed most verve in her tasks. Ever aware of Aunties watchful eye, Momoko would increase her work load in hope of meeting her prize sooner, seeing her chores as merely a means to end until when one day she too could sleep until mid-afternoon like the older sisters she now pandered for.

Momoko despised her role as the Okiya's Shikomi, yet not once did her guard slip. It soon became a game to appear happy and content to the rest of the household as she scrubbed and polished, raising a practised coy smile to the praise of how hard she worked. Although, her duties were not without compensation, with the enticement of becoming a student in her district's Geisha school there was another reason for Momoko to hide her contempt.

Sat alone in the early morning hours, Momoko would wait for the arrival of her elder sisters. It had become her duty to aid the often inebriated Geisha as they laughed and giggled on their return from an evening with their chosen patrons.

Exhausted from a day of cleaning and laundry, Momoko still relished such times. Caught up in tales of wealth and splendour, she would listen to her superiors talk of what Momoko knew would one day become her world, laughing to Geisha blushes whilst helping unravel yards of expensive silk kimono as they talked of the men who paid their way.

Those moments drove Momoko to continue her chores with extra vitality. Determined to prove to Auntie she had what it takes to become the regarded Geisha she so promised. Momoko's ambition flourished under such circumstances, her heart set on the spoils of wealth and status she lay witness to on those candle lit mornings.

Mistaking Momoko's hard labour as a sign of new found humility, the old woman showered the child with affections unknown to those around her. As a new summer began, she looked to the one whose eyes mirrored her mother's with each passing day, and true to her word, Momoko was enrolled into Tokyo's most revered Geisha school.

Momoko lived for those three days when at last her soul could lay the foundations for the life she demanded hers. Accompanied by Auntie and introduced to her tutors on that first morning, Momoko revelled in the surprised glances her new teachers delivered. Listening in silence to comments of the advancing beauty she knew she held, their expressions reminded Momoko of her and Auntie's initial meeting beneath Hanami's pink and white blossoms, causing a rush of pride to flow through her young veins. Playing on such admiration, Momoko repeated the timid smile she had honed in her time spent with Auntie and her older sisters, delighted her counterfeit emotions misled those who held the knowledge she required.

Within weeks of her enrolment, Momoko eased into the Geisha lessons she had longed to receive and as the months advanced it was clear this was where the child belonged.

Her drive and ambition soon surfaced and Momoko would compete with her fellow class mates at any given moment. Yet the tenacity Momoko demonstrated in her want of coming first only widened the gap between those she sat amongst. The other students recognised the skills within Momoko, but instead of adhering to her aptitude, Momoko was regarded in awe and treated with the quiet respect only regarded for someone of higher advancement. This suited Momoko. She had no time for those who took her teacher's valuable time away from her. Those same teachers noticed this divide also, but there was no mention of such matters as Momoko worked her instinctive charm and ability to sway her elders from broaching the subject.

As was expected, she excelled in the gentle nuances of dance, calligraphy and elaborate tea ceremonies, her subconscious memories serving her well of the one she had once called Mamma.

Momoko's thoughts seldom reached for the mother she had known in her younger years. Auntie was the one who saw to her needs now. She was the one who would kiss Momoko goodnight and nurse her when ill, and any recollection of Kyoto's beautiful young midwife lay hidden in Momoko's young mind, pushed far away where her pain remained concealed.

Taking on her role of guardian and confident, Auntie would often visit Momoko's school unbeknown to the child within. From the building's far recesses, she would watch Momoko undergo the trials she had once herself taken, her love for her growing on seeing the proficiency in learned movement of dance and walk.

Auntie knew these fundamentals would produce the valued Atotori she yearned for, yet a sadness remained as the old woman compared her prodigy with another.

"Why, Miyako?" she would whisper on returning to the Okiya, trying to understand how such mastery had been forsaken by a simple act of love.

Momoko's tenth birthday soon approached, marking the second year of her arrival to Tokyo's Hanamachi district. Continuing her chores as her Okiya's only Shikomi, Momoko's schooling advanced, as did her talent to perform the sophisticated dance arrangements once considered far beyond the ability of a student so young. With all her training there was one discipline that still escaped Momoko's grasp.

"I can't do it," Momoko mumbled, placing down her Shamisen. She paused and looked to her fellow students, hoping they had not heard her words. Momoko smiled. Her frustration remained unseen and she returned to the four stringed instrument that still baffled her after almost two years of study.

"Momoko," her tutor called out, causing his other students to peer over to their star pupil.

Momoko gave a hidden glare to her audience and then smiled sweetly to her teacher.

"Yes, Master?"

"I see you have still to understand the notes I have shown you so many times before," he replied. The corners of Momoko's lips fell. How dare he talk to me this way, her mind raced as her eyes darted to the satisfied smiles of those she had so little time for. Ignoring her classmates delight, Momoko collected herself and then looked up coyly to her teacher.

"I understand the notes. It is just that."

"It is just what, Momoko?"

"It is just that they never seem to come out in the right order."

The teacher's eyebrows rose to the laughter erupting throughout the classroom.

Momoko gave a steely glare to all present. "But I do understand," she protested over her tutor's calls for the others to settle down.

"I do," Momoko called out again, but her declarations remained unheard over the din.

Seeing the disruption Momoko's misdirected words had produced, the teacher smiled to her once and then turned to his other student's giggles.

"I think that is enough for today," he told them. "I am sure your Okiya has plenty of chores waiting for you all," he added, waving his students away with a flick of his wrist.

Momoko glared at her fellow Shikomi's smirks as they filed past her, presenting each one with the curt stare she was so famed for.

"Momoko," her teacher called as she began to pack away the Shamisen that caused her so much trouble. "It is vital that you master that which is so far from your reach."

Momoko gave no reply. Her instincts begged her to throw the instrument across the room at the one who had caused her such dishonour that day. She withheld her wants. Momoko knew the repercussions that would entail from such an act and hiding her anger, bowed once to her teacher before running home to the safety of her Okiya.

Beneath the cherry trees she would walk most days, Momoko's rage subsided on nearing her home. Glancing up to small buds yet to flower, she smiled on seeing the signs of her coming birthday and relaxed her pace. So what if she could not play that silly instrument, Momoko thought, I have other skills, she looked up once more to bare branches waiting to blossom.

Walking onwards, Momoko soon spied her Okiya. She stopped on seeing Auntie and her three sisters stood outside its doors. Panic gripped Momoko as her household's eyes fell to her, considering if they knew the shame she had experienced that day at school. Momoko tried to reason how they could know so quickly of the difficulties she faced. She knew Auntie often visited to watch her progress behind hidden walls, but if she had seen her efforts in trying to master the Shamisen that afternoon, then how had she made it back to the Okiya before her? Auntie raised a hand and beckoned to her, her customary smile broadening as she did so. This eased Momoko's mind somewhat, although she continued her walk with a slight frown to welcoming faces.

"Momoko," Auntie welcomed her. "A good day at school?"

Momoko nodded. Receiving her sisters smiles also it became aware that they held no understanding of the day's events.

"Come, Momoko," Auntie said leading her ensemble into the Okiya. "I have a surprise for you."

They dually followed and Momoko looked back to her sisters. Her frowns returned. Each one smiled down to the child and hurried her forwards until all sat before Auntie in the grand room normally reserved for guests and clients.

"Hanami will soon be upon us, Momoko," the old woman began. "And we all know what day that will bring."

"My birthday," Momoko replied with the pride that often worried Auntie. The old woman pushed away her concerns and nodded to the Geisha sat beside her.

"I think she is ready now, don't you?"

Momoko watched Hanako leave the room.

"What am I ready for, Auntie?" she asked.

The old woman glanced to her charges before staring over to Momoko.

"I have had many reports from you tutors, Momoko. Each one tells me how well you have done in your lessons. This is why today, I and your older sisters wish to give you an early birthday reward for all your hard work."

Momoko looked to all those in the room and then to her older sister's return.

"For me?" Momoko said, staring down to the present placed down before her.

"Yes, Momoko," Auntie said. "Now open it quickly, we want to see if we have chosen well."

On those instructions, Momoko reached for the plain white paper wrapped around her gift. Pulling it apart with a gentle tear, her surprise was evident to what lay within. Momoko gasped and stood up, holding the blue silk kimono to her.

"Thank you," Momoko bowed to Auntie and then repeated the courtesy to each of her sisters. "May I wear it now?"

"Yes, my child," Auntie replied. "But first we have another surprise for you."

"Another present?"

"Yes, Momoko." The old woman nodded and looked to the doorway.

"Keiko," she called and then turned back to Momoko. "A new sister for you," she whispered on following Momoko's gaze to the small figure that entered the room.

"Come, my sweet, do not be shy," Auntie coaxed the young girl to step forward.

With her hands held behind her back, Keiko did as asked and stopped before Momoko.

"You are nearly the same age," Auntie smiled. "Keiko shares her birthday with the end of Hanami. Momoko, you have at last become an older sister by only a few weeks."

Momoko raised a slight smile to Aunties' words and continued to stare at the timid young soul before her.

"Can you dance?" Momoko asked.

"Keiko has received the same training as yourself," Auntie cut in. "She comes to us from Kyoto also, the same as you."

Momoko watched Auntie smile to her new Shikomi. The same smile the old woman only ever reserved for her.

Auntie saw Momoko's noticed exchange between them. Stepping up to Keiko, the old woman placed an arm around her.

"Keiko has come to stay with us, Momoko. She too has many gifts, as do you."

"And what gifts are they?" Momoko gave her new equal a demure smile.

"Tell her, Keiko," Auntie persuaded. "Tell your new sister what you have learnt already."

"I can dance," Keiko began after some hesitation, her kind-hearted temperament revealed in soft tones. "I enjoy calligraphy, and tea ceremonies. But most of all." Keiko paused. She looked to Auntie's gentle nod and then back to Momoko. "Most of all," she continued. "I like to play the Shamisen."

Momoko stepped back from Keiko's announcement. Catching her emotions, she summoned a smile to mask the feelings raging within her.

"Then you will miss playing when seeing to all the chores of the Okiya," she replied. Keiko's eyes shot to Auntie's, a tear escaping her from Momoko's words.

"Momoko, you are mistaken," the old woman kept her composure. "Keiko will be joining you with your lessons." Wiping a lone tear from her new protégé's cheek, Auntie looked to the young Shikomi and smiled. "One day, Keiko, you too shall become a Geisha."

Once again, Momoko raised a smile to hide her true feelings. Her expression faltered as Keiko's hands fell to her sides. Staring down, Momoko's sight fixed onto the doll clutched in Keiko's small hand, its bright red dress evoking long lost memories within her.

CHAPTER EIGHT

Flanked by his three student monks, Lama Norbu glanced back to his new apprentice. With their two day trek following the Nyangchu River northwards to the city of Shigatse coming to a close, he wondered how Tenzin would accept his new life within Tashilhunpo monastery.

Tenzin caught his teacher's stare and nodded to him. Aware of the thoughts containing the old monk, he smiled once then reached down and patted the strong neck of the horse beneath him.

"Nearly there," Tenzin whispered down to the beast, encouraging its short stubby legs which had carried him safely over the winter's rising snow and ice.

Lama Norbu noted the compassionate action. Coupled with the child's knowledge that they now neared where he had never ventured before, the old monk concerns left him, sure was he that he once more rode in the presence of his old friend.

As dusk drew in around them, Lama Norbu pulled Tenzin's mount aside and pointed ahead.

"Tenzin, your new home," he laughed on hearing his apprentice gasp.

Cast high on a hill in the centre of the city, the monastery's red washed walls struck Tenzin with an awe never before encountered in his years spent in Gyantse. Looking to Tashilhunpo's tiered levels, he could not believe buildings so tall existed and stared back to Lama Norbu's.

"Tashilhunpo," Tenzin said. "I am here at last."

Within one hour of seeing his new home, Tenzin rode through

Shigatse's winding streets. He reddened to the attention received from those who stopped and bowed their heads as he and his small group passed them by. The young boy understood the city's people knew of their new addition, and was in no doubt that most had known him before in the body of another, yet these insights gave little comfort to Tenzin, his modesty to such matters brought forth in his blushes. Lama Norbu and his students recognised these humble traits. Glancing to one another, they knew the joy each held that the eight year search for their former teacher was now over.

Reaching Tashilhunpo's entrance, Tenzin stared up at its tall walls and then to the lines of burgundy robed men who awaited his arrival. He looked to Lama Norbu, his cheeks continuing to flush from the interest his presence gave.

"Your brothers are pleased to see your return, Tenzin," the old monk said as he and his students dismounted. Helping Tenzin down from his horse, the old monk watched as the child placed a small hand on his rides matted neck and thanked the animal. Also seen by Tashilhunpo's dwellers, Lama Norbu smiled up to the gasps of recognition in Tenzin's actions, confirming his own beliefs towards their new novice.

"You must be tired, Tenzin," he said. "Come, I will show you where you shall sleep from now on."

Pulling the warm woollen blanket to his chin, Tenzin looked to the old monk at the foot of his bed and then to the candle beside him, finding comfort in the shadows flickering across deep red walls.

"Lama Norbu?"

"Yes, Tenzin?" the old monk watched his apprentice gaze over his new surroundings.

"This will be my room now?"

Lama Norbu nodded, confused by the hint of sadness in Tenzin's eyes.

"Tell me, Tenzin. What troubles you so?"

Tenzin view fell back to the candle. "This is the first time," he whispered into its flame.

"First time?" Lama Norbu's frown deepened. He smiled as Tenzin's stare returned to his.

"That there has only been one in the room, alone."

Lama Norbu nodded again. He understood the child's concern.

Recalling his own first nights as a boy beneath the rooftops of Tashilhunpo, the old monk knew the fear in not hearing the customary sounds of his sleeping family nearby.

"Mine and my brother's rooms are only across the hallway from you. There is no reason to be scared."

"I am not frightened," Tenzin giggled. His laughter faded as he looked into the candlelight once more. "It is my father I worry for, Lama Norbu. It is he who is now alone in his room."

Taken back by the child's reply, Lama Norbu warmed to Tenzin's compassion. Never before witnessing such empathy in one so young, he looked to the shadows playing all around them, his thoughts remaining with the Lama who had taught him such lessons many years ago.

"Tenzin, your father understood the path you yourself have chosen to walk, it is now time for Gyaltso himself to walk his own."

Understanding Lama Norbu's words, Tenzin gave his reply with a silent tilt of his chin. The old monk hid his surprise in the gesture he had received many times before. Peering closer to the child's expression, he glimpsed his old friend's features in the room's dim orange glow.

"I see you are aware of such things already, young Lama," he whispered.

The old monk studied the child's profile in hope of seeing Lama Jampo reappear to him again that night. In his heart he knew such things were seldom revealed. Those insights now lay within the soul of his new apprentice.

"Come now, Tenzin," Lama Norbu broke their silence. "Tomorrow you shall begin the life you are destined to lead."

Tenzin reached for the small bag he had carried from Gyantse and took his treasured Grandfather's gift from there.

"It is too late for music now, Tenzin. You must sleep, so you may be fresh to meet with the one you once knew so well."

"Who, Lama Norbu? Who am I to meet?"

"You will know, my child. Sleep well, Tenzin," the old monk closed the door behind him and made for his own quarters.

The next morning, Tenzin stretched out across his bed, confused by his new surroundings. In those few waking moments his memories of the journey from Gyantse came to him and he fell back onto his pillow.

"Tashilhunpo," he smiled.

Staring up to the ceiling above him, he studied its painted sheen. So different to the wooden criss-crossed thatch he had always known, Tenzin's thoughts returned to his childhood home, and of the one who now shared it alone. Recalling Lama Norbu's kind words the evening before, he somehow knew the one who had raised him would soon take to solitary life with ease. Finding some comfort in this he raised up onto his elbows. He saw the deep red robes folded neat on the end of his bed. Wondering who had left them there as he slept, Tenzin reached forwards and picked up the string of worn wooden beads placed atop his new clothing. Recognising them as the ones he had chosen before, he held them in his hand and flicked each bead over his finger with his thumb. Tenzin grinned to the peace his actions produced and then pulled the robes to him. Feeling its course warmth he wrapped it around him and threw the remainder of material over his shoulder before jumping onto his bed to look through the small window above. Tenzin caught his breath to the number of monks that walked the courtyard below all dressed the same as he. Tenzin watched hypnotized by each smiling face milling around beneath. He turned his head to the footsteps behind him.

"I see you are ready to start your day," Lama Norbu laughed from the doorway.

"Yes, Lama Norbu," Tenzin replied climbing down from his bunk. The old monk glanced down to the beads clasped tight in Tenzin's hand and then to his robes.

"I see someone has already been to show you how to wear your robes."

"No, Lama Norbu," Tenzin frowned. "I dressed myself."

The old monk gave a faint smile. With a heart full with the recognition such an act provided his eyes met with his old friend's again.

"Then you are truly ready to begin," he beckoned his young novice to him.

"Where are we going?" Tenzin stared up at his guardian as they walked the cool narrow corridors leading from his room. Lama Norbu continued forwards without a word. The old monk's silence only enhanced Tenzin's adventure and he looked to the walls they now walked between.

Shielded from daylight for more than half a century, murals of deities stared back down at Tashilhunpo's new apprentice, their eyes lit only by the numerous candles lining his path. Tenzin grinned back up to his observers, finding little fear in their mythical glares as he marched onwards at Lama Norbu's side towards beams of light at the far end of the corridor.

"Here, Tenzin," Lama Norbu said as they at last walked outside and into warm, rich sunlight. Reaching into his robe the old monk handed his novice three orange scarves.

"Do you recognise these now?"

"This was the scarf you showed me before, Lama Norbu," Tenzin looked to the silk material in his hand. "But what are the others for?"

"They are presents, Tenzin."

"Presents? For who?"

"For the one your soul has always known. The one we are to meet with now, Tenzin."

"But what shall I say?" the young novice asked, his anxiety mounting in the thought of his unknown encounter. "Does he know me too?"

"Of that he does, young Lama. Do not worry so," he laughed. "I shall tell what is needed of you. Now come, he is waiting."

Tenzin listened to his guardian's instructions as they walked through the large courtyard he had spied from his bedroom window. His young mind calmed in hearing the simplicity of the actions to be rendered. Returning the smiles he encountered on his path, Tenzin warmed to the reception received from his new brothers and looked forward to talking with those he felt sure he had known before also.

Reaching a large set of open wooden doors, Lama Norbu stopped and looked to Tenzin.

"We are here, Tenzin," he said. "Can you remember what it is you must do?"

"Yes, Lama Norbu," Tenzin bowed his head as instructed as they entered the great hall before them.

"Stay by my side at all times," the old monk tutored, acknowledging the welcomes given to him by those the same age as he.

Tenzin gazed to his feet as they came to a stop in the vast chamber. Daring not to look up, his curiosity grew and with all his will he could not help but peer up ahead of him. Lama Norbu watched his apprentice give in to his temptation, recalling his old friend and teacher's similar disposition he allowed Tenzin to study the golden throne on the other side of the hall.

"Are you ready to greet your master Panchen Lama, Tenzin?" He asked.

Tenzin nodded and assumed the position he had been told. With his small hands held together in prayer before him he felt the three scarves lay soft between his fingertips as he walked across the hall, his body stooped low beneath the throne, yet keeping his eyes on his master's seat at all times.

"Panchen Lama," Tenzin smiled on reaching the small crib. "These are for you," he laid the three scarves down on the red mat between them.

Tenzin's smiles broadened to the tiny giggles coming from the child who received his gift. His sparkling eyes held Tenzin in his place until the novice monk backed away with hands still clasped together, as was his gaze on the child's continued laughter.

"Good, Tenzin," Lama Norbu smiled as the young monk returned to his side. His novice grinned up to him. He followed his lead as they left the chamber and headed back to the courtyard outside.

"Lama Norbu?" Tenzin said as they walked together beneath a cloudless blue sky. "I thought the Panchen Lama would be." The young monk paused. Not wanting to offend his guardian, he considered if he should continue.

"You thought he would be older, Tenzin?" Lama Norbu spoke for him. "Old like me?" He laughed.

"Well yes," Tenzin agreed. "But he was only a child." The old monk's laughter ceased.

"Well of course he is, Tenzin," he smiled. "It was only one year ago that the eighth Panchen Lama left our side and found refuge for his ninth incarnation in the body of young Nyima, the one you have just met."

"So he was the Panchen Lama?"

"Yes, Tenzin," Lama Norbu nodded. "Our search took less time than it did to find you besides the banks of Gyantse. Our astrologers told us Lama Jampo would return to us when the Panchen Lama reached his first year, and," the old monk raised his eyebrows, "here you are."

"Yes, here I am," Tenzin replied, knowing then with all his heart that this was where he belonged.

As the months flew by, Tenzin would often visit young Nyima, Tibet's revered ninth Panchen Lama. Watched over by Lama Norbu and his peers, they saw the bonds between each child grow as they rekindled their friendship from lifetimes past. This pleased all concerned and throughout Tashilhunpo word soon spread of Tenzin's compassionate nature, the young novice's traits once more bringing joy to all those he encountered.

Memories of his early years spent besides Nyangchu's waters began to fade from Tenzin as he took to his new role. Although at times he would pause and think of his father, those recollections were surpassed by his emersion into the monastic life he now led, his young mind adjuring to the customs and lessons he seemed to know so well.

Given free reign of Tashilhunpo's maze of corridors and chambers, Tenzin explored his home and would often stop to talk with those who held him in the same regard as he to Lama Norbu. The respect Tenzin received never tainted his kind nature and he treated each encounter with equal reverence, his time within the monastery enhancing his views that everyone shared the same desire and want for knowledge as he. With all Tenzin's regard and admiration there was one simple deed which brought him as much pleasure as the lessons he would take every day with his fellow apprentices.

Each evening as the sun began to set above Tashilhunpo, Tenzin would race from his schooling to the kitchens that fed him and his brothers. Giving a fleeting wave to the greetings he received there, the young monk would run past the smiling cooks and to the large brass urns at the end of the kitchen.

It had taken Tenzin many months to decipher how to carry these urns without spilling a drop of the hot, sweet yak butter tea contained within. Destined for his peers, the young monk would lug the container across the courtyard and to the Great Hall where he knew Lama Norbu and the other Tulkas awaited his arrival. Kicking his sandals off outside its grand entrance, Tenzin would watch the old monk's grin on his arrival, their wise eyes all watching for the telltale drops which often trailed behind the brass container. As the seasons passed, Tenzin reddened to the courteous nods he would receive from each respected Lama on seeing not a drop of tea had been wasted.

This simple chore gave Tenzin an insight into the life he would one day live, his humble beginnings never forgotten in the surroundings of gilded golden statues and splendour. The friendships formed in his formative year at the hill top monastery also fared the young monk well, his modesty and soft manner accepted by even the most austere Lamas within Tashilhunpo's walls.

As Tenzin celebrated his first year of life amongst Lama Norbu and his brothers, his childhood recollections of Gyantse and the ones who had raised him became lost from him and were replaced by the providence in which he now revelled. With his schooling, his chores and the company of so many the same as he, Tenzin spent every waking hour within the moment. With no thoughts of his past or future, only the present mattered to him now, and those who enhanced the life he was sure fate had provided for him.

Lama Norbu kept his own thoughts towards his young novice's advancement to himself. Aware of the attention Tenzin brought to those around him, he knew the young monk's progress may in some way be hindered if it were known the esteem his modest acts produced. Holding that silence, Lama Norbu continued to act as guardian and confidant to Tenzin whilst allowing the child to find the keys to his own path and the wise soul his predecessor had once held.

He knew Tenzin was aware the majesty such a soul contained, yet as with all young minds, that finery was often lost in the physical world around them. Too much emphasis was played on the laughter and gossip which fuelled life within his surroundings.

The old monk understood this rite of passage, he himself succumbing to the same going-ons when he too had been a boy. Lama Norbu's faith in Tenzin's abilities to see past such illusions never faltered in those primary years. With gentle guidance he began to etch his subtle direction onto the child until with no further prompt from himself, Tenzin's spirit cast aside his want to play and hear talk of another's actions, and settled into the destiny his own pure heart desired.

With Tenzin approached his tenth birthday, he reflected over the time spent in his new life as he sat amongst his fellow students. Watching the young monk's mind wander, his teacher called across the small chamber which acted as classroom to his many apprentices.

"Tenzin, where are you?"

Tenzin opened his eyes to his classmates shuffle as they too looked at him. Seeing their smiles, the young monk's back straightened and he met with his teacher's gaze.

"I am sorry, master," Tenzin said, his head bowing once to the one who shared his knowledge with Tashilhunpo's young apprentices.

The old master smiled to Tenzin's words.

"Do not be sorry, young novice. Be here now, in the present. You know as I that there is no other moment to be in."

Understanding the methods of the meditation he now tried so hard to attain having at times glimpsed the benefits such peace gave, his frowns pressed his master to continue.

"Are your thoughts hounding you once again?" He asked the boy, aware of the trials a calming mind battled.

"Yes," Tenzin replied. His cheeks flushed with discomfit to his admission. "Sometimes my mind is still, the way you have taught us all. But…"

"But what, young Tenzin?"

"But my thoughts break free and I drift with them." Tenzin glanced around the classroom. The young monk found some relief in seeing his young brothers also encountered the same problems as he. Looking back to his old teacher, Tenzin straightened once more and waited for his answer.

"We all meet with this, you are not the only one to be swept along by your own thoughts." Turning to the large window on the far side of the classroom, the teacher pointed out to the view beyond. "Look above us. Tell me, what do you see?"

"Blue skies."

"Are there any clouds across these blue spring skies?"

"No, Master," Tenzin shook his head. "There are none."

"Will there be ever again?"

"Of course, master."

"And where shall they go when they appear?"

"They will drift by,"

"Only to be replaced by?"

A smile formed on the young monk's lips as he began to understand his lesson.

"They will be replaced by another, Master."

His teacher held Tenzin's stare and then with a nod turned to the rest of his students.

"The trick is not to let your mind notice these clouds, or wait for the inevitable others to follow. If they come, simply let them drift by. We must stay focused on the blue sky's empty form and pay no attention to the clouds which pass over its consciousness." His view fell back to Tenzin. "This will unlock the peace our heart seeks, young novice. So we may be one with the moment we now sit."

His spirits lifting in the insights shared, Tenzin stared back to the clear blue void above, closing his eyes once more, determined to empty his mind and ignore its own passing clouds. His goal was interrupted by a rap on the classroom door.

"I am sorry, Master," their young visitor said. "It is Lama Norbu, he has asked for Tenzin."

All eyes fell to Tenzin.

"It seems your presence is wanted elsewhere today, young novice," the teacher nodded his permission and then with the rest of his class watched Tenzin run from the room and into the courtyard outside.

As Tenzin ran he looked to the vast blue skies overhead. Its vivid gleam brought an extra understanding to the lessons revealed to him that afternoon and he hurried forwards to Lama Norbu's outline opposite him.

"Thank you for joining us, Tenzin," the old monk greeted.

"Us?"

"We have a new novice amongst us, Tenzin," Lama Norbu grinned. "And it has been decided that you are to be the one who shall aid in his arrival." Turning from Tenzin he raised his hand and called the lone figure from the shadows behind him.

A small boy walked towards him.

"Your younger brother shares the same age as you Tenzin within a few months," the old monk continued as the boy took a place beside him.

Looking to him, Tenzin could not believe the new apprentice's tiny stature matched the same age as his own. A full head in height above him, Tenzin smiled down to the boy.

"Hello, my name is Tenzin," he welcomed with hands clasped before him.

The child gave no reply.

"Tell your older brother your name," the old monk encouraged.

"Yes," Tenzin echoed his guardian. "What is your name?"

The boy glanced up to Lama Norbu. Seeing the old monk looked from them and out towards the surrounding mountains he turned back to Tenzin.

"My name is Ketu," he sneered and edged closer to Lama Norbu.

Tenzin frowned as Ketu's scorn towards him vanished and he smiled up sweetly to Lama Norbu.

"Good," the old monk returned to the boys. "Now you have been introduced, I am sure you shall become great friends. Tell me, Ketu, are you hungry?"

"Yes, Lama Norbu," the new apprentice smiled. He then turned and glared at Tenzin.

Once again the old monk missed Ketu's scowls.

"Then we must visit the kitchens," Lama Norbu laughed. "Until later, Tenzin," he bid farewell and made for the Tashilhunpo's kitchens with Ketu close to his side.

Standing alone in the courtyard, Tenzin's frown deepened as he glanced between the two figures walking from him. Trying to understand the distaste towards him held in Ketu's tone, Tenzin looked back to the skies above and soon became lost in the new clouds forming across its blue sheen.

CHAPTER NINE

Momoko watched Auntie in silence as she introduced Keiko to her teachers and the rest of the class. Raising a smile when only in her elders view, she scowled to the warm welcome her new sister received from all in the room, the one whose presence took such attention from the blue silk kimono she now wore. Looking to those seated around her, Momoko smirked to her fellow student's innocent acceptance of the new arrival, her determination to surpass them all fuelled by their delighted smiles.

"Momoko," Auntie called.

Momoko stood and bowed once to the old woman. "Yes, Auntie?" she said, her scowl lost in the false virtue she now portrayed.

"I must leave now," the old woman said. She put her arm around Keiko and smiled. "Momoko, it is up to you look after your younger sister today. Can you do that for me?"

Taking care to hide her true emotions she looked first at Keiko and then to their guardian.

"It will be my pleasure, Auntie," she said, adding another short bow to confirm her words.

Auntie replied with a nod, her eyes closing to conceal her suspicions from the one she knew held such a perceptive grasp of another's thoughts. Saying her farewells to those that had taught so many of her own Shikomi through the years, Auntie smiled to both Momoko and Keiko before leaving them to start their day ahead.

"Keiko, come sit with me," Momoko called, patting the floor beside her.

Giving Keiko a warm smile, she reached for her own satchel and with a slight tilt of head looked to see if Auntie watched from her usual hiding place.

Glimpsing the old woman smile on seeing her Shikomi sat together, Momoko grinned, happy she remained unaware of the young eyes upon her.

"You must pay attention at all times, Keiko," Momoko whispered. Keiko nodded and Momoko saw the relief her new sister held in being by her side. She looked back to see if Auntie still watched them.

"And there is one other thing you must do," Momoko's smile faded on seeing they were no longer spied upon.

"What must I do?" Keiko replied, her eyes revealing their timid nature.

Glancing to the others in the room, Momoko leant forwards and a cupped a hand between her lips and Keiko's ear.

"You must never forget," she whispered. "That I am your older sister."

That evening, after the Okiya's dishes and pots had been cleared away, Momoko and Keiko said goodbye to their three elder sisters as they left the Okiya to meet with their patrons. Leaving Keiko's side, Momoko sat down besides the fireplace and looked into its flames, anticipating the return of those she would help undress whilst listening to tales of the men who showered them with gifts and praise.

"Momoko?" Auntie frowned on walking back into the room. "Why are you not in bed?"

Momoko looked to her guardian with an equal confused expression.

"I am waiting for Aiko, Hanako and Tamiko, Auntie," she replied. "The way I always do." The old woman closed her eyes and called Keiko to her.

"Keiko," she smiled. "You must be so tired after your first day at school."

"Yes, Auntie," the young Shikomi replied. "But it is my duty to…"

"Not tonight, my child," Auntie told her. "From tomorrow that responsibility shall be yours. Now run along, I am sure Momoko can manage for this evening."

Keiko bowed to the old woman and then looked to Momoko with tired eyes.

"Thank you, older sister," she bowed once more before running to her bedroom.

Momoko watched her leave and then stared up to Auntie.

"What will be Keiko's duty?" She asked.

"Momoko," Auntie sat down beside her. "You are no longer the youngest member of the Okiya. It is now Keiko's chore to greet and see to your sister's needs in the early hours of the morning."

"But, Auntie," Momoko pleaded. "It was never a chore to me to help my sisters."

"And that you did so well, my child. But now it will be Keiko's duty to do so."

Momoko stared over at Keiko's bedroom door. "But, Auntie," she whined, her sight not leaving the paper slats masking the one who had taken away her pleasure.

"Momoko, look at me." Auntie waited until she had her full attention. "You have to understand that this is the way of things. This is how it is, how it is has always been. Tonight you can welcome your sisters to the Okiya for one last time, and then it will be only Keiko who shall do so."

Momoko lowered her head from Auntie's gaze. "Yes, Auntie," she mumbled. "I understand." Her chin rose as Keiko's bedroom door slid open to reveal the cries of her younger sister.

"Keiko," Auntie rose to her feet and rushed to the child. "What is wrong?"

"She's gone," Keiko sobbed to the old woman crouched down before her.

Auntie understood the cause of her new Shikomi's distress and glanced back to Momoko.

"Keiko, will you do something for me?"

"Yes, Auntie?"

"Go and wash your face, my child. A Geisha can never be seen to have shiny cheeks," she gave a warm smile. A smile came to Keiko's lips also from her guardian's kind words.

"I will find her, do not worry," Auntie reassured "Now go, quick before anyone sees," she giggled.

Auntie watched Keiko race from her to the bathroom. She paused and then walked to Momoko's room.

Momoko followed the old woman and stood in her bedroom doorway. Preparing herself for what was to come, she watched Auntie pull back the woollen blanket that kept Momoko warm each night and then lift up her pillow. The old woman reached down, looked back to Momoko and then sat down on the bed.

"Momoko, come sit with me," she beckoned. "Can you tell me how this got here?" She asked as Momoko lowered herself down beside her.

"No, Auntie," Momoko stared down at Keiko's doll held tight in the old woman's hands. Her young features betrayed the untruth and Auntie remained silent as she raised her eyebrows to the child beside her. Momoko knew she could not deceive the old woman. She knew also that to continue to do so could jeopardise her future in the Okiya.

"I took her, Auntie," she said, lowering her head in shame of her actions. "I am sorry."

The old woman shook her head and leant close to Momoko.

"But why, Momoko? Why do such a thing?" Auntie waited for a reply yet none came from the child. Setting the doll down beside her, she reached over and lifted Momoko's chin with her finger to continue her questioning. She stopped, surprised by the tears rolling free down Momoko's cheeks.

"Come, my child," the old woman embraced her protégé, allowing her to release her sorrow.

"I'm sorry, Auntie," Momoko repeated into her guardian's chest. "Keiko's doll reminded me so much of Hiroko."

"I know," Auntie whispered down to Momoko's crown. "I understand," she let the child set free the grief so well hidden from all around.

With Momoko's heaving body in her arms, Auntie peered down to the doll and its red dress. Recalling Momoko's anguish on the first night of her arrival, she appreciated the reasons behind her stealing Keiko's only comfort. She also realised that the one she now consoled was still a child. With compassion, Auntie raised Momoko's chin once more and witnessed the innocence she had encountered on their first meeting.

"Momoko, we shall not tell Keiko of this," the old woman smiled.

Momoko stared up to her guardian. "Then you are not angry with me?"

Auntie paused and reached for the doll.

"Momoko, what you did was wrong. But we must all learn in our own way. Your punishment shall be to remain here in your room tonight."

"But, what about my sisters? This will be my last night with them, Auntie."

The old woman nodded. "Yes," she agreed. "I am afraid you have forsaken that privilege, Momoko." She looked to the loss in the child's eyes and raised her eyebrows for the second time that evening. "You must always remember, my child. That there are always consequences for your actions."

Momoko nodded and looked to the doll's red dress. "Auntie," she smiled, wiping her eyes. "Shall we wash Keiko's doll for her? In time for her birthday?"

Once again, Auntie glimpsed the untainted soul within the child beside her, devoid of the vanity and egotistic traits she was so accustomed too. Rising to her feet, the old woman leant down and kissed the top of Momoko's head.

"That is a lovely idea," she smiled. Walking from Momoko, the old woman paused in the doorway. "Now, I will see to your elder sisters this evening while you sleep. Goodnight Momoko."

"Goodnight Auntie," Momoko bowed as Auntie left to return the doll to its rightful owner.

No further words were mentioned of Momoko's actions that night and under Auntie's watchful eye, she kept track of the forming relationship between her Shikomi. However, the old woman's wants never came to fruition.

Watching Momoko's development for the first two years within the Okiya, Auntie had considered that taking Keiko into her household would impede her talented Shikomi's aloof manner. The old woman could not dismiss the approach Momoko had towards others of her own age and had spent many sleepless nights wondering why those Momoko encountered were deemed a threat to her progress. Momoko's obsession to come first among others would serve her well in the years to come, of this the old woman understood within the world of the Geisha. She knew too well the battlefield a tea room could be, full with beautiful women vying for the attention of men.

Recalling her own time within such a setting, Auntie had no

concerns that Momoko would not prove the champion of those around her. Even her elder sisters saw the skills Momoko held now as a child would one day mature into a powerful weapon against her adversaries, yet their admiration did not account for the vanity which surrounded the child.

As the years progressed and Momoko reached her fourteenth year, Auntie watched those eyes that promised so much develop into the ones she had known to belong to another. Yet, with all the resemblance of Miyako's fabled beauty, Auntie could still not understand the escalating self-interested Momoko held in her own appearance. Each morning, the old woman would watch her Shikomi preen and pout in the mirror reserved for her sisters at the entrance of the Okiya, its complacent reflection smirking with every glance.

By the nature of her chosen profession, Auntie knew these traits were to be admired, but never before had she seen the vanity of another take on such ferocity.

Auntie saw that Keiko's beauty had also begun to blossom, and where her fellow Shikomi advanced in appearance, Keiko's qualities grew in the friendships she formed with ease of all she met, a closeness Momoko seemed so determined to avoid. At times Auntie considered if her own actions contributed to Momoko's remote want for companionship, taking into account the gentle prising of mother and child she had administrated years earlier. Remembering such events, the old woman put paid to her doubts. Her experience in those matters of choosing a new Shikomi had been the key to her Okiya's success. Many times before she had taken the young from their families. On each occasion this had been done with the pure consent of those involved and if the child had wanted to return to her family then this had been allowed in every instance with no animosity standing between parents and Okiya. These facts once more confirmed her uncertainties towards Momoko's conduct and with time, Auntie came to accept such a detached characteristic laid embedded deep within the child.

Auntie's confidence in both Momoko and Keiko's abilities grew also in this time. Aware of the skills each held, she knew her choices had been wise. Keiko's affinity for all she encountered balanced the sheer presence Momoko commanded from all concerned, making them both a formidable asset to the Okiya.

As the summer of 1890 began, Auntie knew it was time for her

Shikomi to take the next step towards their chosen destiny. It would be a quick turn of events within the Okiya that pushed Momoko and Keiko closer to their goal.

"Where is Aiko?" Momoko pointed to the empty space opposite her. Her two remaining sisters bowed their heads to the dining table to avert their eyes from Auntie's glare. Keiko echoed her senior's actions. She peeked up to Momoko willing her to do the same.

"I only asked," Momoko scowled at Keiko. "I just wanted to know where she is." Glancing to those seated around her, the old woman sighed and turned to Momoko.

"Aiko is gone," she said. Holding the child in her stare, the old woman raised a subdued smile. "Now all of you continue with your meal."

Following her elder sister's lead, Keiko summoned the nerve to encourage Momoko to do likewise once more. As Momoko returned to her meal with no further questions, Auntie watched her fight her want to speak out as the Okiya ate in silence.

Looking to the child's eyes, memories of Miyako flooded to her, realising how another of her Geisha now followed a similar path.

Auntie knew Aiko's actions were a hazard in the career of a Geisha, recalling how she too had once been tempted to leave all she had known for the love of another.

Lost in recollections of young love when all that had mattered were the embraces of a forbidden suitor, Auntie allowed herself a moment of longing for such times to seep through. Her feelings were quickly censored as she remembered how her childish romance had succumbed to the trials of honour and duty to her Okiya.

Feeling Momoko's sight upon her, Auntie titled her head and raised an eyebrow to the child. The juvenile beam greeting her mannerism evoked further memories of the reasons behind Miyako's desertion and Auntie nodded to the smile so like her protégé's unknown father.

With their meal finished, Momoko and Keiko began to clear the table. They stopped as Auntie signalled them to cease their nightly chore.

"Please, remain seated," the old woman said and glanced to Hanako and Tamiko.

The experienced Geisha sat upright, eager for their assumptions to be true. Auntie nodded to each in turn to confirm their thoughts before setting her sights on the two confused Shikomi beside them.

"Momoko, Keiko," she began. "Now our Okiya has only two Geisha, would you agree that we are in need of someone to replace Aiko's position?"

Momoko gasped, she knew of what her guardian spoke. Glaring at Keiko, Momoko's eyes narrowed.

"Keiko," Auntie said, aware of Momoko's thoughts. "How long have you been with us now?" she smiled.

"Four years, Auntie," Keiko replied, her voice wavering under Momoko's unwanted attention. Auntie ignored her other Shikomi's agitation and smiled at Keiko once more.

"And tell me child, after all this time, is the life of a Geisha still what you desire?"

"Yes, Auntie, more than anything." Keiko's heart raced to the old woman's question and she too disregarded Momoko's continued scowls. "My teachers tell me I have come far in my lessons and…"

"Yes, my child," Auntie said. "I have already talked to those at your school. They tell me you are more than ready to advance to your next stage of training. If," Auntie paused, her smiles fading. "That is what you really wish for."

Looking to those she sat amongst, Keiko's confidence dipped under Momoko's glare.

"Well?" Auntie continued. "Do you want to leave your life as a Shikomi behind you? Are you ready to become the Minarai I know you are?"

Keiko straightened and her eyes fell to Tamiko. Her favourite elder sister smiled and nodded, encouraging the answer she knew Keiko held within her.

"Yes, Auntie," Keiko gave her guardian a slight bow and then grinned back to Tamiko. Auntie recognised the bond held between the two and had done so from Keiko's first arrival to the Okiya. She knew Tamiko would prove a worthy onee-san for Keiko and could be relied upon to teach the techniques of conversation and feminine virtues unspoken of in her present schooling.

"Then, Keiko, if Tamiko is willing to take her younger sister under her wing, you may at last forget your chores within the Okiya," Auntie raised her chin to the Geisha in wait of a reply. Tamiko rose to her feet and glanced over to the young expectant face.

"It would be my pleasure for Keiko to become my imouto-san, Auntie," she said with an accompanying bow to her guardian.

From the edge of the dining table, Momoko watched Keiko race to Tamiko and fling her arms around her new onee-san's petite frame.

Looking to Momoko's flushed cheeks, Auntie recognised the rage twisting within her remaining Shikomi, and she considered her choice for Keiko to enter the second stage of her training. Feeling the old woman's stare, Momoko righted her tormented expression and gave her guardian the demure smile she had perfected over the years.

"And you, Momoko," Auntie hid the admiration for her protégé's skills. "Are you happy for your younger sister?"

"Of course, Auntie," Momoko replied. "How could I not be?"

Remembering the talent glimpsed in their first meeting, she saw how Momoko had honed her ability to hide her true emotions from others, a flair she knew would serve her well in the coming years. The Shikomi's composure confirmed her actions and with a fleeting glance to Hanako, Auntie frowned at Momoko.

"And do you think you are also ready to hold the title of Minarai?"

"Yes, Auntie," Momoko replied, her eyes darted to Keiko and then softened on looking back to her guardian. "My teachers tell me I have come far in my lessons also."

"This is so, Momoko," Auntie nodded. "They tell me in all their experience, no other student has excelled in dancing such as yourself." Glimpsing Momoko's smirk to Keiko on hearing her tutor's praise, her voice took on a different tone. "But, my child. They also tell me of one matter in which your talents do not lie."

"What is that?" Momoko already knew her answer.

"Your teachers have spoken of your difficulty with music and the problems you meet playing the Shamisen." Auntie raised a finger to silent protests and waited for Momoko to settle before continuing. "Momoko, the playing of that instrument is as valuable to the Geisha as dancing and good conversation. Is this not true, Hanako?" Momoko's elder sister smiled to Auntie and then nodded.

"Auntie is correct, Momoko," Hanako began. "Our work is to entertain and delight, and without the Shamisen our talents are not complete. It will only take the shine from our other skills if we are presented to the world lacking the basics of our profession."

"This is why, my child," Auntie leant closer to Momoko. "I am uncertain of your ability to become a Minarai with your younger sister."

With all her strength and will, Momoko could not conceal her emotions on hearing Auntie's words, nor could she disguise the contempt held towards Keiko. Witnessing Momoko's scorn, her guardian waited to see if fate would take the course she had envisioned.

"And, Keiko," she asked. "Now that you are no longer a maid within the Okiya, what are you views on Momoko's position?"

Lowering her head and glanced over to her onee-san, with a slight tilt of her chin, Tamiko once again encouraged Kieko to speak out. Looking up to Momoko, Keiko saw the beauty her adversary held, an appearance she was aware she could never match. Her talents lay elsewhere. Keiko knew this. Yet her admiration for Momoko remained, as did the kindness embedded within her soul. Glancing back to her onee-san she turned to Auntie.

"I can help Momoko," she said.

"In what way, Keiko?" the old woman replied, hiding her joy on seeing her plans come to light.

"I can teach, Momoko how to play the Shamisen."

Momoko's pride revealed itself across young flushed cheeks. Auntie watched the conceit swirl throughout her intended Atotori.

"Momoko, will you accept Keiko's help?"

Momoko glared at Keiko's offer of assistance.

"Will I then become a Minarai?" she said, her eyes not leaving her younger sister's. Auntie hesitated. Momoko's powerful gaze enthralled the old woman. She recognised the fearful command such stares held on those in her presence. Considering if her plans for Momoko's intended humility would be justified, Auntie looked to the child. She knew without doubt Momoko would one day become a formidable ally to the Okiya, but still the child's lack of modesty worried her.

"Well, Auntie? Will I?" Momoko whispered.

She turned to her guardian, her expression melting into the charming smile reserved for those who held what she needed.

Taken by such an adept transformation, Auntie nodded.

"Yes, Momoko. You may become a Minarai. If that is, you chose to accept Keiko's kind offer."

Retaining her amiable expression, Momoko bowed her head.

"I accept, Keiko," she said, her smile not faltering to Keiko's broad grin. Turning to Hanako, Momoko lowered her eyes. "And Hanako, will you be my onee-san?"

"Of that I will, Momoko," came her reply.

As a grinning Momoko sidled up beside her older sister, Auntie registered the trepidation in Hanako's manner. Dismissing these insights, the old woman addressed both her Minarai.

"Keiko, Momoko. Tonight your duties shall remain," she said glancing down to the table between them. "However, tomorrow you may both forget your chores, for your new life shall begin under the guidance of your onee-san. Now, these empty plates will not clean themselves," the old woman prompted with a smile.

With delicate hands, Hanako and Tamiko covered their giggles and soon Keiko joined them in their laughter.

Momoko did not retain her household's joy and began to clear the table of discarded plates before her.

"Come, Keiko," she said rising to her feet. "We have work to do. Younger sister."

CHAPTER TEN

Tashilhunpo's residents welcomed the dawning of another spring, their joy in seeing the surrounding thawing snows evident in the smiles each held. After another harsh Tibetan winter, life within the monastery walls soon regained its easy manner and tranquil ambience, aided by the sun's warm rays coating its courtyard and tiers.

Tenzin soon took to his duty of becoming guide and confidant to Tashilhunpo's new arrival, yet the pleasure he witnessed in those around him escaped his own soul. Never before had the young monk encountered the abrasive manner handed to him by the small boy Lama Norbu had instructed him to look over.

Confused by the animosity he received on trying to help Ketu settle into his new life, Tenzin turned within, looking deep inside his heart to try and understand the hostility he met with on each occasion. With all his searching, to no avail did he find the answers he sought and considered sharing his crisis with his own guardian, Lama Norbu. Something within Tenzin stopped his desire for council. He wanted to show his cherished teacher that he could himself manage the trials he now faced and draw on the well of compassion he knew his soul contained.

All but brief, that empathy surfaced as Tenzin recalled his own formative days beneath the rooftops of Tashilhunpo. He too had experienced the fear so apparent in Ketu's tiny frame.

These fleeting insights gave the young monk the courage to continue with what was asked of him. He was also aware of the damage such an energy put upon his own being. The torment of being pulled from sympathy to aversion to Ketu's callous nature weighed heavy on Tenzin's heart, but still he continued to show the young boy a kindness inherent to the lineage his soul was destined to portray.

There was another dilemma Tenzin encountered as he pushed forwards in his aim of guiding Ketu in the direction expected of him. Lama Norbu saw nothing of the novice's spiteful demeanour. Once more, Tenzin's young mind became torn by the actions so visible to him and could not comprehend how Ketu's insensitive acts went unseen. Was it his own perspective that was wrong? Was it he who in some way lay at fault in not being able to reach out to the boy? These thoughts hounded the young monk. His longing for the life he adored before Ketu's arrival surfaced with each advancing day, but still he persisted in trying to reach out to the one chosen to put at test all he had learnt; all his soul had always known.

By the end of the first month of Ketu's arrival to Tashilhunpo, the compassion Tenzin yearned to find towards the boy waned. It would be a simple chore within the monastery which would revive the empathy hidden deep within the young monk.

"Tenzin, Ketu," Lama Norbu looked to each young monk stood before him. "Thank you for coming to my calls."

"It is my pleasure, Master," Ketu bowed, giving Tenzin a sideways scowl as the old monk sat down and motioned for his apprentices to do likewise.

"What is it, Lama Norbu?" Tenzin asked, wondering why they had each been called to their guardian's chambers. Had the old monk at last seen through Ketu's façade?

Waiting for his answers, he felt Ketu's glare upon him once more. Tenzin ignored his charge's glare as he had done already on numerous occasions that morning.

"Tenzin," Lama Norbu turned to him. "How long have you been with us now?"

"Two years, Lama Norbu."

"Two years," the old monk whispered. He turned to Ketu. "And you, my child?"

"A whole month, Lama Norbu."

Tenzin's spirit sank in seeing the elation his guardian held from Ketu's sweet tone. His heart raced as he waited for the judgment he knew would one day come.

"Ketu," Lama Norbu continued. "Now you have been here so

long, do you not think it is time for you to become a part of your elder's daily life?"

Tenzin glanced between them.

"But, Lama Norbu," he said. "I have shown Ketu all the happenings within Tashilhunpo. What else is there for him to learn?" He quietened as the old monk's smile faded.

"Tenzin, I am surprised to hear such words from you. There is much to learn, I myself have not begun to understand all that occurs within these walls."

Feeling his cheeks burn, Tenzin lowered his head. "I am sorry," he said into his lap.

He sensed Ketu's pleasure beside him.

"Never forget this, Tenzin," Lama Norbu said and looked to Ketu.

"Now, myself and my peers have decided that we would like to see much more of you, Ketu."

"Of me?"

"We have decided that, as from tomorrow, it shall be you will bring us the sweet yak butter tea Tenzin here has provided us with for the last two years."

"But."

"But what, Tenzin?"

The young monk lowered his head again. He knew to continue would only enhance Ketu's growing confidence. "Nothing, Lama Norbu," he said and then turned to Ketu. "Ketu, I am sure your skills shall exceed my own, for the great honour given to you here today." Looking to the boy, Tenzin could not understand the revulsion in his eyes from being given such a treasured chore.

That loathing vanished as Ketu smiled sweetly to his elder.

"Thank you, Lama Norbu," Ketu bowed. "I promise to uphold my respect to your wishes."

The old monk delighted in his apprentice's declaration and continued to do so as he watched the young monks leave his chambers.

Tenzin looked to Ketu's sullen expression as they walked together across the courtyard.

"What's wrong, Ketu?" He asked. "You have been given a great honour today. It is not everyone who is chosen to enter the Grand Hall when our elders talk of great things."

"That's your opinion," Ketu grunted. He stopped and stared over to Grand Hall.

"Now it is I who has to carry that big urn I see you struggle with each day," he flicked his head to the ornate entrance. "Tell me, where's the pleasure in that?"

Looking into Ketu's malevolent glare, Tenzin searched within him to find a way in which to release the repugnance he now felt towards the boy. Studying his small frame, he glanced back to the kitchens and then across the courtyard to the Grand Hall.

Tenzin saw the path that would lead him to the compassion he sought.

"Ketu, you are right," he said. "The tea I once carried for my elders was heavy, and indeed it did take me many months to do so correctly."

"Yes, but it is ok for you now. Now it is me who must fetch and carry for these old men."

Tenzin concealed his shock in hearing Ketu's disrespect. Delving deep into his heart, Tenzin looked to him.

"Ketu, I can help you," he said.

"How, Tenzin? It is me who has to be seen delivering the tea. How can you help?" Tenzin took a deep breathe to calm his mind.

"Ketu, you cannot see the courtyard from within the Grand Hall."

"So?"

"So what if I carry the urn for you from the kitchens to the entrance of the hall where our elders sit. Then you can take the tea the rest of the way without their knowing your journey has been so short."

Ketu's solemn features left him.

"You would do that for me?"

Tenzin hoped his offer would ignite the hidden bonds between them. Staring back at him, Ketu shrugged. His eyes flowed across the courtyard and then returned to Tenzin.

"I shall think about it," he sneered and then marched away from his young guardian.

In the days to come, Tenzin watched Ketu struggle with the large tea urn. Recalling his own first days undertaking such a task, his heart went out to the small boy who looked hopelessly back at the trail of hot sticky liquid behind him.

By the end of the week, it would be Tenzin who carried that pot across a heat scorched courtyard, his conscience eased in Ketu's unabashed cries for help.

Every day, Tenzin carried the urn from kitchen to Grand Hall entrance. Waiting there in the shadows, Ketu would appear each time and take the container from him with a stifled grunt, preparing himself to walk the few steps expected of him. Ignoring the boy's lack of thanks, Tenzin would leave him to the task which had once been his, battling the envy he knew his heart must dispel.

Their deception continued unnoticed and soon it became customary for Tenzin to aid Ketu in this way. Always hopeful his actions would bring awareness to the small boy's soul, it would not be until one month had passed when Tenzin believed Ketu's wakening essence had at last begun to flourish.

Walking from the Grand Hall, the young monk glanced back to Ketu's small frame carrying the urn almost the same height as he. Tenzin smiled as he turned from him and made for his room, his steps lightened by the long awaited thank you he had received that day.

Racing to his quarters, Tenzin considered if his compassion had in some way made an effect on Ketu's character. Knowing such things took time, the young monk thought once more of the thank you Ketu had mumbled at him moments earlier and wondered if more were to come his way. Lost within these thoughts, Tenzin walked the long corridor to his room. He stopped on noticing his door had been left wide open. Tenzin could not understand why as it was not like him to forget to close his bedroom door and it would be several more months until the autumn winds arrived and did likewise. Shrugging, Tenzin entered his room. He paled on seeing the shards of red lying across his bed.

"No," the young monk crouched beside his bunk. Reaching out, he picked at the remains of his flute. "How?" he whispered. Flinching, Tenzin dropped his treasured instrument. Holding his finger up to the window, the young monk pulled out the tiny splinter imbedded in its tip.

"How?" He questioned once more on watching a droplet of blood form below his finger nail and placed it to his mouth. Tasting the warm salty liquid play across his tongue, Tenzin looked back to what had once been his delight. He could not understand how his red flute had come to lay across his bed shattered beyond repair. Gazing to up to the window again, the young monk wondered if a bird had entered his room and caused havoc with his belongings.

Peering around his small room, he saw none of his other items had been touched and his gaze fell to his open door. Tenzin shook his head to the thoughts now entering him. Those notions multiplied on staring down beside him to the gift his grandfather had spent so long to make. His recollections of the old man's kindness triggered hidden memories within Tenzin and he slumped down on his bed as his father's smiling features revisited his young mind.

"Father," he whispered and reached for red wooden splinters again. He looked in the direction to the shuffling feet outside his room.

"Father," a voice called from the corridor. "Why, father?" it continued.

Tenzin rose to his feet to meet with the sniggers that accompanied his taunts.

"Ketu," Tenzin called out. "Where are you?" he demanded.

Squinting through the dark hallway, Tenzin watched the small figure stride towards him, readying himself for what was to come.

"Yes, Tenzin?" Ketu smirked on reaching the young monk's doorway. Tenzin remained silent. Holding his glare on Ketu, he moved aside so the boy could gain full view of his bed and the broken flute.

"What happened?" Ketu grinned. "Had an accident?"

Tenzin glanced back to his prized possession and then to whom he knew had destroyed his gift.

"Why, Ketu?" he asked, his gaze boring deep within the boy's heart.

Losing their conceited expression, Ketu's eyes showed the fear brought forward from Tenzin's glare.

Sensing the panic his stare created Tenzin kept his eyes trained on Ketu. Edging towards him, the young monk stopped in seeing the tremble his actions produced.

"I am sorry, Tenzin," Ketu's mumbled. Backing up to the corridor wall he held his hands up in defence. "Don't hit me."

"I won't strike you, Ketu," he said edging closer to him.

"Please don't," Ketu raised his hands up once more.

Tenzin glanced back at the broken flute.

"Why do such a thing?" He turned back to the boy. "I thought we were friends. I helped you in your chores." Tenzin waited for a reply yet none came. "Why, Ketu?"

Realising the slight shrug of shoulders before him would be his only answer, Tenzin walked back into his room to the sound of running feet.

Listening to Ketu's footfalls fade from him, Tenzin sat on his bed. Reaching for the flute's torn reed, the young monk curled his fingers round its delicate edges and began to cry.

Tenzin remained sat perched on the end of his bunk for the remainder of the afternoon. Deep within his own remorse, he paid little attention to the dimming light outside his window. Neither did he notice a second set of footsteps approach his room, such was his grief for what was now lost.

"Tenzin, why do you sit here alone in the dark?" Lama Norbu asked from the doorway. Tenzin wiped his eyes on seeing the distress his features gave the old monk.

"Tell me, my child," Lama Norbu sat beside him.

Tenzin watched his guardian reach forward and light the room's lone candle. The old monk sighed as its flickering flame lit the wooden shards which had once given such delight.

"What happened, Tenzin?" he said, taking a large red wooden splinter into his hand.

Tenzin hesitated in his reply.

Aware that Lama Norbu saw no bad could ever come from his other young novice, Tenzin considered what implications would arise should he tell of Ketu's spiteful actions. Wiping his cheeks once more, he turned to the old monk and summoned a faint smile.

"I do not know," he whispered and looked up to the window. "I think a bird may have entered my room." Tenzin gazed at his feet, the guilt of his untruth causing him to divert his eyes from the one who cared so much for him.

"I see," Lama Norbu replied and placed the splinter back with the others. He sighed once again as he looked to Tenzin.

"My child, I see your suffering. Tell me, young Lama, can you see the reasons behind such emotions?"

Tenzin lifted his head and stared back at the old monk. He glanced to the broken flute and then back to him with a frown.

"I cry because my flute is broken, Lama Norbu. That is why."

"Of this I understand," the old monk nodded. "But you must look beyond such things. Take your mind away from what once gave you your delight. There, Tenzin," he smiled, "you shall find your answer."

Tenzin watched Lama Norbu gather the flute's broken pieces together and scoop them up into his hands.

"Here, Tenzin. These pieces once brought you such pleasure, did they not?" The old monk waited as Tenzin nodded to him. "And now, my child," he leant forwards and dropped them to the floor. "Now they are gone."

Watching the scattered flute and its shadows play long across his small mat, the young monk drew on his teachings. Lama Norbu saw his apprentice's understanding dawn.

"Yes, Tenzin, we must learn that all which comes to us will at one point leave us also. By holding onto these attachments our fears grow in that we may one day be without them. When that moment of loss happens and we cling on to the memory of what was once ours, the pain released comes in the form of the suffering you yourself now hold."

Tenzin understood the old monk's words, although his heartache to what was lost still remained.

"But, Lama Norbu," he said. "My grandfather made the flute. It was all I had to remember him by."

"Are there no other things that you recall of him, Tenzin?"

"Yes," Tenzin stared into the flame beside them. "His kindness towards me."

"And is this kindness now lost to you also?"

"No, that love will always be with me, of that I know."

Lama Norbu rose to his feet.

"Tenzin, these are the things to remember, these memories can never leave us. As will other's memories of yourself. This is what keeps our spirit eternal, everlasting. It is our acts that will be remembered, be they treasured or despised, this is only up to us to decide."

Once again, the young monk stared up to his guardian. His thoughts racing with the new lessons he sensed he had always known.

Lama Norbu saw this recognition within the child before him. His heart warmed in the fleeting memory of the one who had once taught him the same lessons he now bestowed to another. Standing beneath the doorframe he smiled to Tenzin.

"All we do, all we say, how we act. This is what counts most. You must always show reverence to all those you encounter, young Lama, no matter how callous their deeds may be to you or others. Only compassion may reign in such moments, a forgiveness with understanding that overcomes all adversity. This is the only way, Tenzin. Never forget this," the old monk smiled once more as he closed Tenzin's door behind him.

"That I will," Tenzin gazed at its wooden panels and then back to the floor.

Becoming lost in the flutes shadows once more, he replayed Lama Norbu's words, trying to find his compassion towards the one whose cruelty had revealed so much to him that evening.

With Tenzin's true nature shining through, the young monk continued to help Ketu carry the large brass tea urn his tiny stature struggled to lift. Soon two years had passed since Ketu's malicious actions towards his young guardian and Tenzin had hoped that in those passing seasons his compassion and forgiveness would restore the tinge of modesty he once glimpsed in the boy.

Watching Ketu battle his own splintered emotions, Tenzin's soul persisted in reaching out to him and saw the want in Ketu's eyes to attain the knowledge others held, the peace which eluded him so often. With all the kindness Tenzin's heart could muster, Ketu remained as distant and bitter as he had on his first arrival to Tashilhunpo.

Taking his task at hand, the young monk's benevolence never ceased. As the years continued, Tenzin would often feel Ketu's gaze upon him. His charge's stares often brought some pain to the young monk on recalling the shower of red wooden shards that had greeted him that afternoon. Remembering Lama Norbu's wise counsel, Tenzin would consider if Ketu's heart held any redemption in his wicked acts.

On the eve of Tenzin's fourteenth birthday, the young monk began to understand the reasons for the trials he now undertook.

Aware of the extent his soul battled against the one who pushed his compassion to the hilt, it came of some relief when he caught sight of the destiny his own soul thought forgotten, his reprieve coming in the guise of his summons to the Grand Hall one spring afternoon.

"Thank you for coming to us, young Tenzin," Lama Norbu said.

Tenzin nodded to the old monk and then repeated his actions to the several Tulkas before him. His view fell to the Panchen Lama, sat high on his golden throne between them, his habitual warm smile beaming down on all present.

Tenzin looked to the boy who now approached his sixth year.

"Nyima, are we to play today?" He bowed to his young Panchen Lama. His smiles stopped on seeing Lama Norbu's serious expression.

"No, Tenzin. You have not been asked here so you may play."

Tenzin tried to discern his guardian's tone.

"I am sorry, Panchen Lama." Tenzin's heart beat thumped with the anxiety now surrounding him. Looking back to Lama Norbu, he eased under the smile he received from the old monk.

"Tenzin," Lama Norbu began. "Once more I must instruct you that these are not the reasons for you presence here today."

The young monk's view flowed over the faces ahead of him, his soul foreseeing the words to come.

"Is it time now?" He asked.

Watching each revered monk nod to him in turn, Tenzin could not contain his joy and his attention returned to Nyima, the young Panchen Lama he had come to regard a brother.

"Yes, Tenzin," the child said. "At last you are ready to join us."

"Yes," Lama Norbu spoke up. "Your years amongst us have proved that you indeed hold the soul of the one we would once laugh and talk with."

The old monk glanced to his peer's respectful consent. Warmed by their approval, Lama Norbu turned back to Tenzin.

"My child, all here are certain that Lama Jampo lives amongst us once more within you, and so it has come to pass that you are to be ordained as the Lama your heart portrays."

Knowing this day would come, Tenzin raised his hands together and bowed to all before him.

Enjoying the silence amongst those he would sit with from now on, Tenzin began to settle into the life expected of him. The Grand Hall's tranquillity was soon shattered by a deafening clatter behind him.

Swinging round on his heels, Tenzin looked to the warm milky puddle spreading out towards him and then up to its assailant hovering above the upturned brass urn.

"Ketu," Tenzin mumbled, his moment of bliss fading in the envy of his charge's scowls.

CHAPTER ELEVEN

The life of a Minarai is a silent one. Momoko understood this and held her tongue as she accompanied her onee-san to the various banquets and tea houses she had longed to be part of. Although always arriving as an uninvited guest to such parties, the tradition of welcoming a respected Geisha's imouto-san never wavered and Momoko revelled in the warm smiles she would receive on each occasion.

In Momoko's role to observe the gentle nuances of Geisha customs, she would sit quiet besides Hanako and watch all played out before her.

Adorned in the elaborate Minarai Kimono designed to do all the talking needed, Momoko's delicate painted features masked the frustration dwelling within. She knew this life already. Looking to those who had completed their period of silence, the young Minarai studied the surrounding Maiko so undeserving of the position she knew belonged to her. At times, Hanako sensed her charge's irritation to those so close to reaching the status of Geisha, yet she never spoke of such emotions, her admiration for the child's talent in hiding her true thoughts opposing any want of reprimand. Although, there were other reasons Hanako remained quiet. She knew of Auntie's plans for Momoko to inherit the Okiya that too had been her home since a child.

Aware of Momoko's want for the title of Atotori, Hanako saw the ruthless traits her younger sister held towards others in her path and feared the repercussions crossing such a soul would carry, knowing she and Tamiko may one day answer to the child.

In her experience within the closed feminine world of the Geisha,

Hanako had witnessed such acts of revenge administrated with shocking results, where a simple word spoken to a prospective patron was often all it took to demolish an opponent's reputation, made all the more potent if coming from the lips of a regarded Okiya owner.

It was not that Hanako disliked her chosen imouto-san. Her love for Momoko was and always had been unconditional from the first day she had arrived to the Okiya. Hanako also knew Auntie's feelings for the child matched her own. Coupled with the respect gained over the years towards the confident presence someone so young demanded, Hanako recognised attributes of her own personality in Momoko, causing their bond to strengthen as her own vanity surfaced in the future esteem rewarded from having been older sister to such a formidable Geisha. With these considerations, Hanako kept her silence towards Momoko's inner superiority and continued to teach the subtle crafts her own onee-san had once shown her also.

With Hanako's gentle guidance, Momoko embraced her new world, learning with ease the rituals she knew to be her birth right. Yet the difficulties of remaining still whilst Hanako laughed and talked with Tokyo's wealthy business men infuriated the young Minarai.

Listening to their banter, Momoko devised her own way in which to soften her frustrations by composing her own sassy retorts for those in her company. 'One day I will use these remarks to capture you all,' she would calculate, her reserved expression never changing under such thoughts.

Keiko and her own onee-san would often accompany Momoko and Hanako to these banquets within the heart of Tokyo's Hanamachi district. Sitting apart from Tamiko and her imouto-san, Momoko would watch Keiko's awe in the surrounding celebrations, taking note of the tiny slips the young apprentice would make from time to time. Hiding her dismay, Momoko would allow herself an occasional smile on seeing her younger sister's mistakes, knowing these moments would empower her standing when under the tuition of her rival.

Auntie's conditions for Keiko to teach Momoko the skills of playing the Shamisen pained the young Minarai, her pride bruised in having to pay attention to someone younger than herself. Each morning Momoko would summon the patience to sit opposite her younger sister. Trying to decipher the notes and scales of the instrument so alien to her, she would listen to Keiko's kind tones as she explained the subtle sounds she produced with little effort, and once more, Momoko concealed her scowls from her adversary, the one who held the knowledge needed for her advancement.

Watching her young Minarai work together each morning, Auntie would listen for Momoko's Shamisen to reach its desired pitch, thus signalling the preparations needed for the penultimate stage of a Geisha's training.

The old woman knew both Momoko and Keiko were more than ready to obtain the title of Maiko. Having proved their confidence within the company of potential clients there was still one elusive factor her protégé had yet to attain.

As Momoko began to master her playing technique, Auntie continued to wait for the child's hidden modesty, even going to the unknown action of lengthening her and Keiko's time as Minarai. To no avail did that wanted humility surface during their extended period, and on the eve of their second year of leaving the chores of a Shikomi behind them, Auntie resigned to the truth that such a quality existed far from her intended Atotori's grasp.

Auntie listened to her Minarai play together from the doorway of Keiko's room. She glanced back to Hanako and Tamiko awaiting her instructions and nodded to each in turn.

"Hurry," the old woman watched them scurry away to prepare her plans before looking back to her two Minarai.

"Momoko. Keiko," she called to young surprised features. "You must leave your playing for now. We have other matters to attend to." As Auntie walked from them a wide eyed Keiko stared at Momoko.

"What can it be?"

"How do I know?" Momoko shrugged and placed her Shamisen down on the floor. Ignoring Momoko's mumbled reply, Keiko jumped to her feet.

"Well, I'm going to find out," she said, resting her beloved instrument onto her bed and racing past Momoko to the Okiya's dining room.

Joining Auntie and Keiko's side, Momoko bowed to her two elder sisters sat facing her at the opposite end of the dining room table.

"Sansun-kudo," she noted the large bottle of Sake between them.

Auntie remained silent, proud her protégé had deduced the ritual to come.

"Yes, Momoko," she looked to both her Minarai. "Momoko, Keiko. Now you have both reached your sixteenth year, do you not think it is time you became a Maiko?"

In Keiko's joy she looked to her onee-san. Realising the importance of the occasion, she lowered her chin as Tamiko retained her blank expression. Watching her younger sister's crimson cheeks glow from her actions, Momoko bowed once more to Auntie.

"Yes, Auntie, I know I am ready," Momoko gave a sideways glance to her fellow Minarai.

"And so too is your sister," the old woman replied, putting a comforting arm around Keiko's shoulder. "Now both of you sit opposite your onee-san," she instructed and walked from them to the Okiya kitchen.

She soon returned with a collection of small and large ceramic cups.

"Do not worry so," she saw Keiko's concern, placing a small cup in front of both her and Momoko.

Momoko stared down at her container. She knew of the ceremony to follow and grinned to her elder sisters and their identical drinking vessels.

Taking the large bottle of sake from the centre of the table, Auntie poured the clear liquid to the brim of all four cups. She motioned to Hanako and Tamiko and then stepped back to watch the proceedings that would mark her Minarai's initiation into becoming a Maiko. Reaching for the full cups, together they raised them to their lips. Closing their eyes, the two Geisha finished the sake with three delicate sips, sat the cups down and then looked to their young apprentices, encouraging them to do likewise.

Momoko was first to reach for her drink. Knowing the protocol needed for such a ritual she waited for Keiko to follow her lead. With a quick glance to Auntie, Keiko's hesitant hands curled around her cup. With Momoko, she too raised the sake to her lips and took the desired three sips.

"Good," Auntie walked to them and replaced the empty cups with four larger ones which she also filled to the top with alcohol.

"Now, we must continue," the old woman bowed and then edged

back from the table. She studied her young novices as they stared down at their drinks. As expected, the alcohol had already taken its effect on Keiko, yet Momoko showed no sign of succumbing to the intoxicating spirit. 'That will all change,' Auntie gave herself an inward smile, recalling the same rite of passage she too had performed many years ago.

Once again, Hanako and Tamiko raised their cup, drained its contents with three large sips and invited their imouto-san to copy their actions. Both Minarai complied and as Auntie returned to the table and refilled their cups, Momoko scowled at the giggle escaping her younger sister.

"Keiko," she hissed, staring at their third measure of sake. "There is only one more after this," she said. Keiko glared at Momoko with glassy eyes.

"You're not the guardian of me," she slurred and raised her cup to Tamiko. "Kampai," she laughed aloud and began to take her three sips.

Auntie and her two Geisha suppressed their smiles to Keiko's performance, paying little attention to the rage seething within Momoko.

"What?" Keiko frowned at Momoko and then grinned up at Auntie, eager for her final drink. Momoko gave no reply. She looked to her onee-san and waited for the final cup of sake that would seal their bonds between them. There will be plenty of time to see too Keiko's misgivings later she considered as the four completed their final three sips.

Clearing the empty cups, Auntie looked down to each of her new Maiko, expressing the elation she held.

"Welcome," she said.

Momoko looked up to her and then turned to her onee-san who nodded once to show her equal delight. Hanako's sight then fell to the apprentice beside her.

"Keiko?" Auntie bent down to the young Maiko. "Are you still with us?"

"I think so," Keiko mumbled under heavy eyelids.

Seeing her tiny figure waver, Auntie raised her eyebrows to Tamiko and called her to her. Keiko's onee-san did as prompted and put her arms around her novice.

"Keiko, come. You need to sleep," she helped her imouto-san to her feet.

Momoko watched her adversary being lead to her room and began to plot the reprisal for the disrespect Keiko had given that morning, her wrath still burning inside from such an act.

"And you, Momoko?" Auntie broke her scheming. "How are you feeling, young Maiko?"

Dismissing the light headed swirl encountered on her measures of ritual sake, Momoko looked up to her guardian. "I feel fine, Auntie," she summoned a drunken smile. Seeing through Momoko's sober veil, Auntie and Hanako stifled their smiles once more.

"That is good, my child," Auntie continued. "You will need all your wits about you this coming evening." The old woman paused as Tamiko returned to the table. "Your elder sisters and I have arranged a small party, here in the Okiya, to introduce my new Maiko to the world."

"Tonight?"

"Yes, Momoko. Tonight." Auntie took note of the pleasure on Momoko's features. "Now, Momoko, you too must sleep off the effects of our little ceremony. So you may be fresh to greet your future clients." The old woman's eyes flicked to Momoko's onee-san and Hanako rose to her feet to guide her apprentice to her room.

"I can do it, onee-san," Momoko declined her offer of help.

With a knowing smile, Auntie, Hanako and Tamiko watched the young Maiko stumble from the table. Reaching the doorway, Momoko turned to each of the women.

"Thank you," she said with a long bow.

Catching herself before toppling forwards, Momoko waited for their silent replies. When sure her superior's gaze had left her, she made for Keiko's room.

Sliding the slat door open, Momoko peered inside to the sleeping child. Seeing Keiko curled up on her bed deep in slumber she crept forwards and hovered over the young Maiko. Momoko smirked down to the gentle purrs below her and then looked for the prize she sought. Her eyes fell to Keiko's beloved Shamisen. Careful not to wake her rival, she edged closer to the instrument, reached out and held it in her grasp.

"Now we will see who your superior is, imouto-san," she whispered.

As dusk fell, Momoko shook the residue of sleep from her and raised her head to Keiko.

"You look beautiful," she said.

"Thank you Momoko, so do you," Keiko tried to ignore the uneasy feelings such praise gave her from Momoko's rare compliment

Watching from the dressing room doorway, Auntie held back a tear on seeing the beauty within, remembering each of her charges as the young frightened child she had taken into the Okiya eight years previous. Gazing to her Maiko's bright coloured kimono and its distinctive long sleeves, the old woman then looked to the pale white faces framed by freshly coiffured blue black hair.

"Are you both ready?" She asked them both.

The two apprentice Geisha nodded up to their guardian.

"Good," the old woman raised a customary eyebrow. "Momoko, Keiko, you look wonderful, I am sure tonight you shall both shine. Come now, we have many people to meet." As Auntie walked from them, the Maiko turned to one another and gave a slight bow.

"Good luck, Keiko."

"And to you too," Keiko replied, her trepidation to Momoko's kind manner increasing as she followed her sister and Auntie to be introduced to their guests.

Both Momoko and Keiko settled into their role of Maiko that evening. Taking the unprecedented step of allowing her young apprentices' free reign to talk at will, Auntie looked on as both devoured the opportunity to at last speak with those they sat.

Under her watchful gaze, she studied her Maiko's performance amongst the invited company of Tokyo's wealthiest men. True to her word, Momoko utilised the sassy retorts stored within during her silent time as a Minarai, and although her skills employing such impertinent remarks were far from polished, Momoko's striking beauty made up for her strident manner and she soon captivated her audience.

Keiko also displayed the talents bestowed to her. Where Momoko's raucous methods attracted the smiles and laughter of those beside her, Keiko's demure nature soon drew as many suitors to her as her sister. Auntie gained pride in the way Keiko portrayed her true Kyoto background, bringing to the table a grace and serene temperament such Geisha there were renowned for.

Looking to her two Maiko, Auntie perceived how different each character was. Yet with all their diverse traits, she still regarded both her charges with the same unconditional love she had known from their first encounter.

Returning her gaze to Momoko, Auntie smiled to the command held over those in her wake. She found it strange how the one who shared Keiko's Kyoto upbringing did not portray the same innocent characteristics. The old woman recalled Momoko's mother, the one who had also shown such confident playfulness amongst men. This was where Momoko gained her qualities, Auntie confirmed, her heart filling with recollections of how she had witnessed Miyako's first outing as a Maiko also. She saddened on realising how she too had shown the same virtues as her daughter did now. So much promise lost, the old woman remembered, listening to Momoko's laughter. Daring to wonder if she too would one day share a similar fate as her mother, her thoughts were interrupted by calls for music.

"Thank you, gentlemen," she smiled.

The men seated before her fell silent as Auntie raised a hand to their pleas, displaying to all in the Okiya her years of experience in such a command.

"That's better," she said with an added wink. "Now, tonight we have a treat for you all."

Her eyes trailed across her guest's drunken features, producing a new found respect from her two Maiko as their guardian enchanted all concerned.

"Keiko," she said. "Will you play for us this evening?"

"It would be my pleasure Auntie," Keiko replied.

Ignoring the surrounding cheers of those she was to entertain, Keiko reached for her Shamisen and prepared for her first official recital.

"Please, settle down, gentlemen," the old woman told them.

As silence fell throughout the room once more, Keiko struck her first string.

Momoko waited as her rival began the first part of the melody she in turn had learnt so well from the young Maiko sat opposite.

Looking to the rapture portrayed across faces of wealth and status, Momoko anticipated the second movement of Keiko's performance when the Shamisen's top string would come into play. Her eager want soon came. As Keiko plucked her fourth string her perfect presentation faltered with a dull twang. The young Maiko stared down at her instrument. She calmly reached for the peg of the offending twine and gave a sharp twist. Keiko frowned. Instead of tightening, it span loose in its designated hole. Peering up to her onee-san, Tamiko reassured her imouto-san to continue. Keiko nodded to her and turned the peg once more only for it to spin loose again.

Momoko concealed her pleasure as she watched Keiko's confidence melt from her.

"That will teach you," she whispered into her chest. Her pleasure was short lived as the room filled with applause.

"Thank you, Keiko," Auntie gave a respectful bow to her guest's generosity.

As a smile formed on Keiko's embarrassed features to her unexpected praise, Momoko's joy faded on submitting her plans for the Maiko's demise had failed.

"Now, let the celebrations continue," Auntie called out and opened a large bottle of rich, clear sake to more thunderous applause.

As the evening wore on, Momoko's fury grew to Keiko's regained composure. Using skills learnt as a child she masked her true feelings, empowered by the wealth of attention she received. Momoko realised how these men who now showered her with admiration for the beauty she held would prove the key to her new existence. A life she had always dreamt of. A kept woman granted with all the money and status her heart desired. Laughing to her potential benefactor's inane chatter, Momoko's grins expanded. This shall be my goal, she vowed on her first night as a Tokyo Maiko.

Auntie looked to Keiko's tired eyes.

"It has been a pleasurable evening," she announced across the table, aware of her young Maiko's want for sleep.

To drunken appeals the old woman bowed her head once to her guests, signifying the end of celebrations.

"I hope, gentlemen," she said. "That you have enjoyed our company as much as we have yours."

In silence, each visitor stood. They bowed first to their host, and then to both her Geisha before paying the same respect to the young Maiko's who had kept them entertained that night. Momoko and Keiko returned the gestures and looked to Auntie for their prompt.

"Hanaoko, Tamiko, myself and Keiko shall see you to the door." Auntie nodded to her youngest Maiko. She glanced to Momoko for any sign of animosity in choosing Keiko over her. Momoko smiled back showing no remorse.

"Thank you again, gentlemen," the old woman called. "Now you all know where you may find such pleasing company." She turned to Momoko once more, confused by the lack of hostility for not being given the honour of seeing their guests from the Okiya. Glimpsing the young Maiko walk from the room, she considered if Momoko had at last found her hidden modesty and returned to her Geisha and Keiko's side to prepare their farewells.

Looking over her shoulder, Momoko grinned on seeing the room empty. Knowing of the extended goodbyes to follow outside the Okiya's doors, she retraced her footsteps and grabbed a knife from the deserted table. Checking once more she was alone, Momoko picked up Keiko's Shamisen and twisted a second peg from its long slender neck.

"Next time it will be worse, imouto-san," she began to file down the peg's fragile wooden grooves. Lost in her intended sabotage, Momoko did not hear the tiny footsteps behind her.

"Momoko," Keiko called out. "What are you doing?"

Momoko turned to the pale startled face and shrugged. "I am helping, Keiko," she replied, her knife still wedged into splintered wood.

"Helping?" Keiko reached out for her instrument and yanked it from Momoko's grasp. Peering to the small cuts in her beloved Shamisen, her tilted head caused fresh tears to run down her cheeks. "How are you helping, Momoko?"

"I am helping myself," Momoko replied to the salty tracks running through Keiko's white make-up.

Holding her there in her stare, Momoko frowned to the soft twinge in her stomach. Glancing back to the damage she had inflicted, she acknowledged her feelings of regret. For once she revealed her real emotions.

"I am sorry, Keiko," she whispered. "Please forgive me."

Keiko considered the remorse in Momoko's words, yet her sister's unknown quality baffled her.

"But, Momoko, I thought you were my friend," she cried.

"I am your friend, Keiko," Momoko reassured.

Keiko stared down to her broken Shamisen and then back at its assailant.

"But friends don't do things like this to each other," she said, a new set of tears escaping her. Watching the sorrow before her, Momoko's regret returned.

"We can mend it. Together," she added with an expectant smile.

With eyes closed, Keiko shook her head to the offer of help.

"No, it is ok, onee-san. I can do it," she replied with a slight bow and ran back to the sanctuary of her own room, the damaged Shamisen clutched tight to her chest.

Finding herself alone once more, Momoko placed the knife down. She paused besides the table that had produced such laughter that evening. Looking at discard plates and half full cups of sake, she saddened how those hours of jollity were now tainted by her actions. Momoko rubbed her eyes trying to dismiss her feelings of regret.

"I'm just tired, that's all," the young Maiko whispered.

Still not understanding the emotions coursing through her, she pushed the unfamiliar sentiments from her, the way she had learnt to do so many years ago.

Staring at where she had sat for that night's celebrations, Momoko recalled her backchat amongst men more than twice her age. A broad grin spread across her soft features to such moments and forgetting Keiko's heartbreak, she smiled all the way to her own bed.

From the dining room doorway, Auntie watched her prized Maiko leave. The old woman shook her head to what she had witnessed.

"Why, Momoko?" She mumbled, having watched Momoko's treachery played out before her.

Auntie had wanted to intervene from the moment she saw her pick up the knife and head for Keiko's Shamisen. Something had stopped her from doing so. She knew of the child's spiteful tendencies, yet had overlooked such traits, putting them down to a phase of the young, but now Momoko advanced towards adulthood she wondered if this despicable behaviour would indeed cease in her coming years.

Another reason came to Auntie for her lack of intervention. Throughout the night she had watched Momoko shine amongst Tokyo's wealthiest classes. Not only had her startling beauty bewitched those men, but Momoko's lightening wit had also been brought into play. Auntie knew from experience these attributes would lead to her becoming a great Geisha. Much the same as her mother had once promised, the old woman remembered.

Her thoughts fell to Keiko, recalling the pain across her pretty face. She too had shone in her first outing as a Maiko and Auntie was sure she would entice as many clients as Momoko.

It was true that Momoko's brash sensibilities had won her several admirers that evening, yet it seemed Keiko's demure manner had acquired a near equal amount.

Looking to the remnants of the Okiya's small banquet, the old woman warmed to her charges' performance and found herself considering for the first time which of her Maiko deserved the title of her Atotori.

CHAPTER TWELVE

Within weeks of their audience, Lama Norbu and his respected peers saw to the preparations of Tenzin's ordination into Lama hood. With spring in their midst it seemed only fitting the young monk should fill the place of his past soul's line, now that the neighbouring mountains snows and ice had melted to reveal buds of mustard seed and barley. These new seedlings were seen as a great portent and it was deemed Tenzin's new role would ignite within the surrounding landscape's new found fertility.

Tenzin felt little apprehension towards the position he was now to partake. It seemed his destiny had always lain in such matters, his gentle heart taking the responsibilities to come with an ease which even amazed his soon to be fellow Lama's. The young monk was aware of such an undertaking. His confidence strengthened in knowing his path would meet little hindrance with Lama Norbu's guidance and friendship, Tenzin no longer considered Ketu's presence a threat to his own standing within the walls of Tashilhunpo monastery.

On the morning of his ordination, Tenzin pulled at his robe and contemplated the celebrations ahead. Running through the steps he was about to make, the young monk adjusted his ceremonial robes once more and turned to greet the footsteps approaching his bedroom door. He knew by heart to whom those footfalls belonged. With a hint of trepidation he awaited their soul's arrival.

"Good morning, Ketu," he said. "And what brings you to me this hour? Should you not be with our brothers in the courtyard?"

Ketu returned Tenzin's welcome, his eyes wide on seeing the

finery of Tenzin's formal attire.

"I, I," he stuttered. "I have just come to wish you luck today, Tenzin."

Looking to his young charge, Tenzin fought the mistrust encircling his words. Could it be now, after so long, that Ketu had at last seen past his own wants and put another's heart before his own? Tenzin hid his suspicions and beckoned his visitor forwards.

"Thank you, Ketu. Please, come join me in my wait."

Nodding to Tenzin's invite, Ketu stepped into the room and sat on its single bed. Looking around him, his view fell to where Tenzin's flute had once rested on the small table opposite. Tenzin noticed his guest's gaze and walked between his view, his heart recalling the hurt caused many years previous.

"I was only looking," Ketu muttered, aware of Tenzin's actions.

The young monk gave no reply and instead lowered himself down beside Ketu.

"Ketu. You understand the reasons behind my ordination today, don't you?"

"Yes, Tenzin. In a way."

"In a way?"

"I know that if I had worked as hard as you in my schooling, then it would be you watching me become a Lama today." Ketu paused. Glancing to the room's small window and the sounds of their brothers below, he stared back at Tenzin. "Then it would not be me having to look on from the crowds as you are given such a right."

Tenzin concealed his thoughts once more. He tried to fathom how Ketu could misunderstand the most basic of fundamental beliefs within the life each led. Was it due to the selfish heart Tenzin had tried so hard to breach throughout their time together? With these considerations the young monk.

"Ketu, the reasons for my becoming a Lama are not down to hard work or favouritism, nor have I been chosen so I may fill a gap within the Lama council. It has been my birth right since my return to these Tibetan lands to become what I shall today." Tenzin raised another smile to Ketu's intent concentration on listening to every word spoken. "My path is linked with those before who once walked the corridors and courtyards of Tashilhunpo, long before you and I were ever dreamt of."

"Then if I had worked harder, and shown more compassion to

others," Ketu frowned. "I still would not have become a Lama today?"

"I am afraid not, Ketu."

Empathising with Ketu's misinterpretation of such important matters, Tenzin wondered if this had been the cause of the boy's frustrations. Standing, he lit the lone candle before them and leaning forwards watched its wick take before returning to Ketu's side.

"I know you have found great difficulty in adjusting to life within these walls, Ketu," he said in a warm soft tone. "This life is not for all, yet those who are fated to follow such a way must indeed pursue that which their soul requires."

"I understand. It is true that I have at times found great difficulty being here. Especially when..."

"When what, Ketu."

Ketu stared back at Tenzin, his features bearing no expression.

"When it is you I have always had to look up to. You take to this life with an ease I can never imagine. You, you make it seem so easy, Tenzin."

Tenzin's view remained on Ketu. The young monk began to understand the years of bitterness portrayed in the boy and felt some shame that he himself had been cause of such a callous nature.

Seeing Tenzin's remorse Ketu leant to him.

"Tenzin," he said. "Do not feel any guilt for your actions. I too am aware that my behaviour towards you may have at times proved better than it has. I am sorry for my ways. As you have told me this day, we must all pursue the life our heart calls us to lead."

Startled by Ketu's confession, Tenzin's guilt amplified in hearing his admissions. Gazing back to the flame before them, he became lost in its early morning glow, his doubts towards Ketu's uncharacteristic sympathy returning.

With all his being he wanted to believe that here in the room which had once contained such hurt from Ketu's malevolent actions, his adversary had at last begun to discover the ways inherent to Tenzin's own soul.

Looking to Ketu, Tenzin joined his smiles, his heart yearning to at last trust the new found goodness hidden within the boy for so long.

Holding each other's stare, Ketu's veiled envy remained hidden from the soon to be Lama. Smiling to the deception he had mastered that morning, Ketu joined Tenzin's gaze to the figure stood in the doorway beside them.

"I see you have a well wisher already, young Tenzin," laughed Lama Norbu and acknowledged Ketu's presence with a playful wink.

"I, I only came to say good luck, Lama Norbu," Ketu rose to his feet.

"That is fine, Ketu, I have always found such pleasure in seeing the friendship you hold for one another."

Catching glimpse of Tenzin's brief frown, the old monk raised an eyebrow. "I see you are ready for your ceremony, Tenzin."

"Yes, Lama Norbu," Tenzin looked down to his robes and deep orange sash. "Have you come to take me there now?"

The old monk confirmed Tenzin's expectant stares and turned to his other young novice.

"Ketu," he said. "It is time for you to join your brothers in the courtyard. Now, run along."

Ketu turned to Tenzin, the joy he had portrayed earlier lost from him.

"Good luck, Tenzin," he mumbled and then squeezed past Lama Norbu to watch the ceremony he still considered belonged to him.

Lama Norbu watched Ketu race down the corridor. Seeing his small frame vanish into the shadows, the old monk turned to Tenzin.

"Now we are ready, Tenzin," he swept his hand to the open doorway. "Lead the way, my friend," he smiled, once more seeing his former teacher in Tenzin's dark almond shaped eyes.

At Lama Norbu's side, Tenzin looked to the corridor walls he had walked between for more than half a decade. Their Deities and Gods continued to stare down at all passersby and Tenzin wondered how many lifetimes before he had strolled beneath their timeless gaze. Glancing up to the old monk he saw his guardian also acknowledged those his life adjured to and wondered of the times they had walked the same passages together lifetimes earlier, long before his arrival to Tashilhunpo.

"You are in their favour, young Tenzin."

He recognised the fascination the young monk held, he too having experienced a likened awe in the same painted faces since a boy.

Recalling how he and Lama Jampo had talked endlessly of the meanings and devotion behind those frescos, he was sure that in years to come he would share the same dialogue with the boy beside him.

Tenzin understood the old monk's wishes but held his silence. His thoughts remained with another who had once looked over him as a child and dared not imagine if he too awaited his appearance that morning.

"Are you ready, Tenzin?" Lama Norbu whispered as they neared the end of the candle lit passageway.

Tenzin nodded up to him and with a faint smile walked into the shaft of rich sunlight marking the courtyard entrance. Trying to keep his composure, the young monk could not help showing his surprise to the sight greeting his arrival.

"You will be fine," the old monk reassured and encouraged Tenzin with a slight nod to take his first steps towards the life deemed to be his.

Stepping forwards into the courtyard, Tenzin raised his head above Tashilhunpo's devotees sat either side of the small path he now walked, his entrance signalling the deep droning hum of long wooden horns which resonated from the edges of his course. Accompanied by the melodic chants he knew so well, Tenzin's confidence faltered in sensing Lama Norbu's absence and he glanced back to him. From the doorway the old monk's smile restored Tenzin's poise. Encouraged once more, Tenzin turned to face his audience and continued his march between his brothers.

Viewing the sea of deep red from the corner of his eye, Tenzin's heart warmed that he knew the souls contained within those surrounding robes. With new found composure, he edged ever closer to the empty seat amongst the row of Lama's before him.

Watching Lama Norbu take his place on the raised platform ahead, Tenzin looked to the young Panchen Lama sat high above his peers. The delight the child held on his approach gave the young monk an insight into the life he was destined to lead and Tenzin suppressed a smile to Nyima's familiar giggles.

Reaching the end of his path, the sound of chanting and horn came to an abrupt halt as the young monk climbed the small steps leading to his seat.

Sitting down on its red satin cushion, the young monk trembled in the silence shrouding the ceremony and stared ahead. Feeling Tashilhunpo's gaze rest upon him, Tenzin's heart beat calmed as Lama Norbu looked to him, persuading the young monk to commence the vows he had learnt to recite to all those before him.

Tenzin's voice shook as he recounted the first few lines of refuge he promised to uphold, yet those nervous beginnings vanished as he recounted the declarations so close to his heart, his homes silent mood fuelling his want to prove his devotion.

Glancing across to his fellow Lama's, Tenzin continued, his words finding new meaning within him as he sensed the unconditional love ebb from wise eyes. It would be the youngest of his these who gave Tenzin the assurance to maintain his blessings. Catching the young Panchen Lama's smiles, Tenzin's mind escaped and he fell into their kindness. For the briefest of moments, Tenzin felt his soul rise and join his young brother's side to listen to the words flowing from him. The pleasure emitted by such verses touched his heart as he watched himself recount his vows before returning to himself.

As his recital came to close, Tenzin willed his soul to be beside Nyima once more, yet as his last words left him he knew these wishes would not be granted. He smiled to the young Panchen Lama. Aware his superior knew of their experience, Tenzin's wants eased and he watched Lama Norbu rise from his seat and stand before him.

The old monk's gesture produced a single drum rap from the crowd and Tenzin soon became lost in its endless beat echoing across monastery walls. Looking down to Tenzin, Lama Norbu understood the apprehension the soul before him experienced, yet his faith in whose presence he now stood before dispelled such concerns and he glanced down to the yellow curved hat in his hands. He raised it high above them both before lowering the ceremonial head piece gently onto Tenzin's shaved scalp.

"Young Lama," he bowed once to his old friend before returning to his seat.

Tenzin looked to his guardian and then the remaining Lamas he now sat amongst. The young monk realised his fate lay amid these wise souls, his epiphany causing him to look out to the courtyard's thousand smiles below.

Refreshing their pulsating hum, the rows of horns that had accompanied Tenzin's walk filled the air once more as Tibet's juvenile Panchen Lama jumped from his seat and walked towards him.

"Lama Tenzin," the child smiled.

His hands held before him, he bowed to Tenzin and then took the orange sash from between his fingers and placed it around Tenzin's neck.

Feeling its silk sheen fall across his shoulders he once more became lost in the Panchen Lama's enduring gaze, his soul comforted by the ease in which his company bestowed. Giving his reply with a look far beyond his six years, the young Panchen Lama revealed his many lifetimes in a sparkle of deep brown eyes.

With another respectful bow, Tenzin watched as he returned to his place only for Tashilhunpo's other Lamas to rise to their feet, each making their way to him with their own ceremonial orange scarves destined to be draped across the new Lama's neck.

Each wise soul paid their respects and Tenzin's modesty brought with it blushes to his new title, an emotion which enhanced the already present smiles before him, evident in the resurgence of chants across the courtyard.

Looking to his musical blessings, Tenzin prepared himself for the rows of monks forming so they may to pay their good wishes to the newly ordained Lama.

With the last Lama seated, his brothers took to the platform and one by one bowed down to Tenzin before allowing his successor to do likewise.

Aware of the honour such actions held, Tenzin focused his thankful nod to each individual, hoping his attention gave them the foresight that only their soul was present for that moment within the Tashilhunpo.

Although remaining in that present moment, Tenzin's mind returned to his earlier thoughts. A sorrow entered his spirit as he considered if the one who had raised him on the banks of Nyangchu's icy waters watched his ordination that day.

Lama Norbu recognised his novice's wandering mind. He knew the secret wants Tenzin contained. Allowing the young monk to let his thoughts come, he remained optimistic such notions would soon pass on remembering the traits his old friend had once held also.

Looking to Tashilhunpo's never-ending flow, Lama Norbu spotted the small frame of the one that would jolt Tenzin from his past, somehow knowing Ketu's approach was sure to pull his friend back into the now.

"Lama Tenzin," Ketu grinned.

True to Lama Norbu's hopes, Tenzin's perception returned.

"Ketu," he said. "Thank you," he added as Ketu bowed to him.

Watching his young charge raise his head, Tenzin's smiles faded to Ketu's scowls.

In the months following his ordination as Tashilhunpo's new respected Lama, Tenzin settled into the life he felt certain belonged to him.

Sitting each afternoon with his peers within the Grand Hall, he would listen to their discussions, held safe in the good humour that always accompanied their lively talk.

As Tenzin's experience grew, he too was encouraged to speak up and tell of the knowledge his own soul contained. Lama Norbu gladdened in the way his apprentice took to these requests. The old monk's spirits lifted as he watched Tenzin's trepidation leave him and join with his fellow Lamas heated debates on the divine mysticism shrouding the lands they had always known. At times the words spoken from the young Lama's lips touched Lama Norbu's soul in ways long forgotten, and once more he warmed to the foresight he had held in recognising his old master, Lama Jampo, on the banks of Gyantse' mighty flowing river eight years previous.

Tenzin was aware of the power his words held amongst his fellow Lamas, as was he of his new standing within the monastery walls it felt had always been his home.

With all the prestige his soul now encountered, Tenzin's pure heart remained untainted by such adulation. Knowing his birth right placed him above those with which he had grown, Tenzin retained the compassion imbedded deep inside him, his reverence for life revealed by his want to help those learning souls so they may advance to the new found peace he himself sometimes glimpsed. The young Lama's fortitude was acknowledged by those he would sit with each afternoon, bringing his wise contemporaries a new outlook towards the path they too now travelled.

With all the duties Tenzin's position created, he still found time to help his young charge's struggle with the large tea urn he himself had once carried to Grand Hall. It seemed strange that it was now he who received such a gift each afternoon and drank the favoured yak butter tea at his Panchen Lama's side.

At first it had proved difficult to aid Ketu's chore and remain unseen in his actions. Tenzin's tenacious spirit found a way. Carrying the urn across the courtyard, Tenzin would rush back to his place amongst his fellow Lamas, silent in the knowledge that Ketu waited outside the hall's ornate opening until sure their ploy remained hidden before entering.

As the autumn winds descended onto the Tibetan midlands, their strategy continued, yet it would be one such blustery afternoon which would put an end to their deception.

"Ketu," Tenzin called from the kitchen entrance.

Ketu turned to his aid. "What?" He stared down at the brass container freshly filled to the brim with steaming hot tea and then back at Tenzin and scowled.

"I cannot help you today, Ketu," Tenzin edged closer to the boy. "I have been asked to teach Tashilhunpo's new novices."

Ketu nodded. He understood the tribute given in such a request.

"That's ok, Tenzin," he said. "You have been given a great honour today. I am sure I can manage this once."

"No Ketu, I cannot help you any longer."

"Why not?"

"My teaching duties have begun. You must continue alone from now on."

Any guilt in no longer being able to help Ketu eased as he looked to the sly smirk before him.

"I understand, Tenzin. It is time that I took responsibility for myself."

"Thank you, Ketu," Tenzin replied, unsettled by his reply. "I am truly sorry."

"Think nothing of it," Ketu reassured. "You have been gracious enough to me over the years. It is now me who must try to prove the kindness you have shown. I will be fine, Tenzin."

Although the boy's words aimed to soften his conscience, Tenzin could not explain the foreboding racing through him.

"I must go now, Ketu," he said. "Good luck."

"And to you too with your teaching," Ketu hoisted the large urn to him.

Watching the boy battle to keep from spilling the urn's contents. Tenzin hesitated in helping Ketu for one last time. Ketu's words to him that afternoon had touched Tenzin. Was it now that the one who had challenged him throughout the years understood the responsibilities each soul must be held accountable for? As Ketu left the kitchen Tenzin dismissed his suspicions and prepared himself for the students he was to guide, trying to dispel the uneasiness Ketu had forced upon him.

Tenzin followed Ketu's footsteps and walked out into the courtyard. His heart sank in seeing the trail of milky liquid behind Ketu's awkward gate. Once more he knew his help would hinder the boy's awareness and with some sorrow he made for the apprentices who awaited his arrival.

On reaching the Grand Hall's entrance, Ketu looked back to the puddles behind him. He grinned on seeing Tenzin disappear into the classrooms opposite him.

"Now we will see who belongs here," Ketu reached into his robes.

He had waited for his chance since Tenzin's luxurious ceremony and smirked down to the small bag in his hand.

Lifting the urn's brass lid he took the red and white toadstools he had collected over the months and sprinkled them into the Lama's drink.

"Now we will see," he giggled on watching the fungus dissolve below him.

He paused before replacing the lid and looked back to where Tenzin had stood. Ketu's smile broadened and he reached into the tea. Cupping his hands, he raised the noxious liquid to his lips, his soul delighting in the repercussions to come as he lapped at the tainted brew.

CHAPTER THIRTEEN

In the years that followed, Auntie continued to consider which young Maiko would one day become her chosen successor. The events witnessed on the evening of Momoko and Keiko's initiation had stayed with the old woman and as each young woman flourished in their role of pleasing others, her observations of them both only added to the quandary.

As predicted, Momoko's abilities grew in strength. Accompanied by the exceptional beauty promised in someone so young, she soon developed an invaluable asset to the Okiya, her name becoming synonymous throughout Tokyo's elite circles for the wit and charm escorting such exquisite features. Momoko's burgeoning popularity only enhanced the traits Auntie held such misgivings towards.

The old woman would watch her protégé enjoy the trappings of adulation and praise, holding great anxiety towards Momoko's false belief in others.

Auntie knew the customers her household entertained. It had been her life's work to cajole and flatter these men, who in turn yearned for the same admiration they gave the young woman of Tokyo's Hanamachi district. Those needs for respect and acknowledgement always astounded the old woman. Through decades past since her own time as a lowly Shikomi, Auntie's experience of such matters brought with it the foresight of how every soul longs for some form of appreciation, her thoughts made evident by the charade played out between Geisha and client in their eternal circle of recognition.

Given the famed reputation Momoko received, Auntie's other young Maiko also made an impression within Tokyo's world of affluence and power.

Keiko's own talents had blossomed alongside her fellow Maiko's progress, and although not holding her predecessor's beauty, Keiko's submissive confidence reigned within the confines of the parties and banquets she would frequent at her onee-san's side.

With her reserved charm and high musical skills, requests for Keiko's talents inundated the Okiya and Auntie noted how the desire for her sweet Maiko's time often came from the more sophisticated of clients. Those who understood the art of Geisha life from generations of dignified breeding would often call for Keiko's presence, a clientele so different from the uncouth young men shrouded in newfound wealth demanding Momoko's company.

Auntie overlooked these divides. The praise she encountered for her skills in producing such adored young women amplified her unconditional feelings towards them. Their differences never hindered the love she held for both her charges and the old woman saw Momoko and Keiko in the same light as she had always done, understanding the diversity in their abilities, yet also seeing the strength each cherished Maiko possessed.

With these insights, Auntie continued to watch over those she had taken in as mere children and in time came to acknowledge the marked opposite persona each held.

Even though accepting the characteristics setting them apart, the old woman's decision as to who should inherit the position as head of her thriving Okiya remained unmade.

As Momoko and Keiko reached the summer of their twentieth year, Auntie saw both Maiko were ready to leave their life as a novice behind them. Their training in all fields had proved them well and with the years spent at their onee-san's side each had come to excel in the art of conversation and hidden influence of others.

In this knowledge, the old woman made the necessary arrangements and welcomed the cream of Tokyo's male society into her Okiya to celebrate the emergence of her treasured apprentices into the enduring world of the Geisha.

Looking around her visitors, Auntie's thoughts on Momoko and Keiko's progress were confirmed in seeing those guests were already aware of her former Maiko's attributes. Nevertheless, she knew such formalities were needed. The contacts made that night would see her

The Geisha and The Monk

new Geisha through the years and the old woman considered if maybe a Danna would appear to them that evening.

Auntie recognised the importance such a patron held. To be offered the financial rewards only said benefactor could provide proved the goal of every Geisha. Auntie suppressed her wishes. She knew the relationship between a Geisha and her benefactor was carefully chosen and could take years to cultivate. These hopes carried her through the evening's festivities.

A forthcoming Danna never appeared that night of Momoko and Keiko's initiation. Auntie submitted to her relief in this. With all her wanting, she understood her young charges were far from ready for such an undertaking, her experience verified by the loss of her favoured Geisha two decades earlier.

Overlooking the benefits such a relationship produced she knew the restrictions a Geisha's patron enforced.

Momoko's need for the recognition and company from more than one client at a time added to the reasons for Auntie's relief, determined this beautiful young Geisha would not befall the same fate as her mother.

Free from their constraints as apprentice, each young woman took to their position with ease. The life they had longed for had at last arrived and both Geisha prospered on foundations laid years before. Auntie took great pleasure in watching Momoko and Keiko leave the Okiya each evening to meet with their prospective clients, only to be greeted by her new young Shikomi Auntie hoped would one day also live up to her household's expectations.

The characters of the men each Geisha would entertain in their endless rounds of banquets and private functions remained the same. Calls for Momoko's attendance continued to come from those with an easy virtue born of Tokyo's growing economy. Auntie hid her distain for such clients from her protégé. Their disposable capital aided the old woman's concealed distaste and she instead focused on the charming clientele who requested the sedate presence of Keiko's placid manner. Auntie was happy for the demand her cherished Geisha drew, yet she saw how this differing clientele within the Okiya brought with it a strain on the already tenuous bonds between Momoko and Keiko.

Under Auntie's gaze, Momoko always treated Keiko with respect

135

within the Okiya's communal rooms and had never re-enacted the malice once shown her younger sister. Although Keiko shared Momoko's civil manner, Auntie saw through their pleasantries, knowing from her other prized Geisha the silent conflict Momoko would present to Keiko when their engagements clashed.

The old woman was grateful these occasions were rare and thanked their client's diversity for this as both Hanako and Tamiko relayed their concerns to Momoko's disregard for her fellow Geisha and never understood Momoko's want for dominance over a soul as kind as Keiko's. Learning that Keiko showed no such behaviour in return to her sister's hushed glares across the tables of Tokyo's most prestigious banquets, the old woman's dilemma returned as to which young woman deserved the title of Atotori.

Momoko had always been the old woman's protégé, the one chosen to be her successor on merit of her mother's wasted abilities. As a child she had known this from her first days within the Okiya and had acted in accordance to such knowledge. Auntie understood the plans to rid Momoko of her advancing superiority by introducing Keiko into her household had failed, made apparent by Momoko's continued egotistical approach to those she supposed a threat to her own interests.

With all the young Geisha's faults, her status within Tokyo's affluent districts had grown since her first outing as Hanako's imouto-san. Aware how this held Momoko in good stead for the coveted position of heir to her Okiya, an Atotori that would shine amongst others, the old woman knew of no other Geisha in the whole of Japan who could lay claim to nearing Momoko's unbridled beauty.

Remembering Keiko's arrival to the Okiya, Auntie recalled the young frightened eyes which had greeted her that early spring morning. Experience serving the old woman well, she had seen past the child's timid nature and into the core of her true being.

The serene soul witnessed that day had indeed thrived under her onee-san's guidance, producing the composed good natured Geisha Auntie always knew she would one day become. It was true that Momoko's growing list of clients surpassed that of Keiko's, yet Auntie saw within her sweet Geisha, the strength and compassion often needed to rule a household solely composed of women.

As the years advanced, the answer to Auntie's selection remained hidden from her. Watching each season fall into the next, the old woman knew her time to retire crept ever closer, but still she could not determine who should succeed her life's work.

She knew each of her charges wanted the coveted position, which eased her anxiety somewhat, still there was another predicament that troubled her. In their three years of reaching the status of Geisha, her young contenders had yet to find their elusive Danna. This only added to Auntie's worry for the future of those she had raised. Lost in her dilemma, the old woman was aware a decision had to be reached.

In the opening weeks of 1900, a few months before her candidate's twenty-fourth birthdays, her answers would arrive in the proposition of another.

"Momoko, Keiko," Auntie called out to her charges and waited for them to join her in the Okiya's dining room. As each young woman entered they bowed and took a seat at the table.

Looking to both her Geisha, Auntie saw the unchanging beauty Momoko held even in her premature waking. She noted that Keiko also retained the qualities she was renowned for, sitting upright and attentive with quiet dignity, a sentiment so different to the slouch of her sister's lithe frame. The old woman raised an eyebrow to Momoko's posture.

"Sorry, Auntie," the young Geisha righted herself. She gave Keiko a sharp glance before smiling back to their guardian.

"I have news for you both," Auntie began after a brief pause.

She stopped again on seeing Momoko guessed the words to be spoken.

"Late last night, I received a visitor. Sitting here at this very table, my guest offered me a proposal that concerns you both."

A broad grin spread across Keiko's features as her thoughts reached Momoko's.

"Was it a Danna, Auntie?" She asked, ignoring her sister's second glare that morning.

"Yes, in a way, my sweet Keiko. Of that it was."

Momoko straightened, her assumptions proving truc.

"Who did he ask for? Was it me or Keiko?"

With another raised eyebrow, Momoko settled down, her chin

tilted to the floor in apology for her outburst.

"Momoko, you must control your actions," Auntie scolded.

Taking a deep breath, the old woman regained her composure.

"Now, I must explain the reasons behind my calling you to me this morning. Yes it is true, my guest and I talked of a possible benefactor. However, he was not the one who desired one of my cherished young Geisha. He was merely a representative."

"A representative?" Keiko's eyes widened causing a faint grin from her guardian.

"Yes, Keiko. You see, this potential Danna lives far from our Okiya, yet he has been charmed by tales of each of your abilities."

"How far away?" Momoko asked.

Hearing the want in her young Geisha's voice, Auntie considered if she should tell of the distance Momoko's fame had reached.

"Yes, Auntie," Keiko shared her sister's excitement. "Where do they know of us?"

Aware she must disclose the location of their probable Danna, Auntie paused and leant towards each expectant face.

"America," she said.

Keiko gasped. "America? Where in America?"

"San Francisco, Keiko."

"San Francisco," the young Geisha repeated.

"Keiko, you don't even know where that is," Momoko smirked beside her.

"Momoko." Auntie patted Keiko's arm. "I will show you on a map, sweetheart," she smiled to red cheeks.

Watching Keiko smile back to their guardian, Momoko grew restless. She had no time for her timid imouto-san. Not now there were more pressing matters at stake.

"So which one of us has been chosen, Auntie?" She asked.

The old woman looked to Momoko's want. "That, my child, has yet to be decided."

Auntie sat back to each confused face opposite her.

"There is to be a banquet held in honour of your prospective Danna's name. He of course will not be there, but his representative shall be," she studied each Geisha in turn.

"My visitor last night has invited you both to this occasion, so he may choose which one of you shall become his superior's own private Geisha. There was one condition he made in your acceptance of his offer." Auntie glanced to Momoko, aware of the competitive fire deep within the young woman.

Enthralled by her wants, the old woman smiled to both sisters. "Momoko, Keiko. My visitor stipulated that it was of the utmost importance his identity remains a secret."

"But how will we know who it is we must please?"

"Yes, Auntie. How?" Keiko joined Momoko's puzzled features.

"This is the reason for such secrecy," the old woman laughed. "So you won't know who it is you are meant to impress. This will bring the talents I know you both hold to the fore, with no biased performance to the one who holds the key to your future."

Momoko and Keiko stared to one another and then back at the old woman.

"Do you understand? Both of you?"

Each young woman nodded to her words.

"When is the banquet to be held?" Momoko asked.

"Tonight," Auntie replied. "Now both of you. Hurry along," she instructed with a clap of hands. "This evening you must appear finer than you have ever done before. Can you do this for me?"

"Yes, Auntie," her Geisha answered in unison.

"Good, then off you go," she shooed them away.

Auntie watched each young woman race to their rooms to prepare for the festivities ahead.

The answer to her problems had come at last. Considering which of her Geisha would be departing for America that coming spring, Momoko's striking eyes came to mind. Aware of the ease in which she would charm her unknown client, thoughts of Keiko's reserved allure mixed with her sister's unabashed methods of seduction. Could Keiko be the one? The old woman looked to the slat doors where Momoko and Keiko readied themselves, knowing that whoever's appeal reckoned unsuccessful that night, would in turn achieve the position of Atotori and heir to her Okiya.

Reaching the entrance to the hall accommodating their banquet that evening, both Geisha came to a stop before tall red lacquered doors.

"Are you nervous, Momoko?" Keiko whispered.

"Not really," Momoko lied. She looked to her sister and smiled. "You appear so pretty tonight, Keiko," she added, pleased in seeing the untruth gave her rival such false security. Keiko gave a short bow in thanks.

"And you look so beautiful in your new kimono, Momoko," she replied, in awe of the tailored white silk material enfolding Momoko's elegant frame.

Momoko gazed down at the garment she had saved so long for, happy her wait for its first appearance had been saved for an occasion such as tonight.

Stroking its soft fabric, Momoko smiled up to Keiko.

"You know, Keiko. I hear San Francisco is a magnificent place to be."

"It is?" Keiko's eyes widened.

"Yes, Keiko, they say it is all you have ever dreamed of," Momoko continued, sensing her sister's growing want for the same prize as she. "And more, much more," she added placing both her hands on the doors before them.

"You make it sound so wonderful, Momoko."

"Yes, I suppose I do," Momoko smirked and gave the doors a gentle push. She paused before entering and smiled back to Keiko.

"It is a pity you shall never see such a place, imouto-san," she laughed and walked onwards to their awaiting clients.

Striding through the long hallway, Momoko ignored the shuffle of Keiko's feet behind her and collected her emotions. Edging closer to the evening that would provide the Danna she had longed for, Momoko turned and smirked at her younger sister once more as a second set of doors opened before them.

Paying little attention to Momoko's malice having become accustomed to her spiteful ways over the years, she instead focused her thoughts on what was to come, her desire to see that wonderful American city for herself growing with every footfall.

Joining Momoko's side, both young women looked to the vast table ahead and the several other Geisha present. Their attendance only enhanced Momoko's ambition to be the one to leave Tokyo behind her. She gave a curt nod to each rival and then suppressed her scowls as each Geisha raised a smile and beckoned Keiko to them.

Watching Keiko leave her side, Momoko frowned.

She had never understood this camaraderie so important to her sister. As they had grown together, Momoko could not remember a time when Keiko had not been without friends, most of whom were here tonight waiting for Tokyo's wealth to join them also.

Those men of means soon arrived and Momoko dismissed her lonely opinions to concentrate on the allure she was so famed for, determined to be the one to succeed over all others.

Momoko soon found the representative she was destined to charm and took her place beside him. Keeping her emotions hidden, she had allowed a faint smile on how easy it had been, her understanding for the wants of another surfacing from years of experience.

Looking to the remaining men present, Momoko realised how she despised the others of her chosen profession as they fawned over those who could offer them so little. She knew she now sat with the one who would give her so much more. The way he dressed, his dignified composure, all these signs confirmed he was the one who would tell his superior of her wit and beauty and award Momoko the life she knew she deserved.

As the hours advanced, Momoko saw Keiko had too gained the affections of those around her. She gave no notice to her younger sister's admiration, aware her demure charisma could not compete with the beauty she herself held.

Tilting her chin downwards and staring up to the representative, Momoko knew her perfected look enchanted the man she entertained, her years of training coming into play as she pretended to hang on every word said, making sure she retained their gaze when pouring the expensive imported red wine the banquet's overseers had provided for him.

Glancing across the table to her adversaries, Momoko noted the fatigue each held. It had been a long night and with the party still showing no sign of coming to an end, Momoko wondered if her own exterior had faltered in some way.

"Please, excuse me," she said and waited for permission to leave the table. Her wishes granted, Momoko gave Keiko a short sharp glare and then hurried to examine her appearance.

Entering the small bathroom provided, the young Geisha's reflection grinned back at her.

"You are as beautiful as they tell you," Momoko whispered on seeing her doubts were in no way justified. Listening to the laughter and chat from the walls beyond she considered her rival's false hopes once more.

"You are the only one they want, Momoko," she smiled.

Becoming lost in her own gaze, Momoko's self-interest faded on hearing the banquet's constant drone come to a stop, this time her reflection frowned, an expression that soon turned to horror as the sounds of a Shamisen pierced the silence.

Momoko knew no other who could produce such sweet notes.

"Keiko," she snarled, and with a final glance to her appearance rushed back to her client's side.

Momoko paused in the bathroom doorway. Watching Keiko delight her audience with her revered musical talents, her view fell to the man she had charmed throughout the evening.

Observing his pleasure gained from her sister's dulcet tones, Momoko raced back to her place beside him and waited for her return to be recognised. When that acknowledgment did not arrive Momoko looked to her surrounding Geisha. Seeing they too were enamoured by Keiko's skills, she reached a hand out under the table and brushed her fingertips across the representative's knee. The man frowned to Momoko's brazen call for attention.

"I am sorry," Momoko whispered.

She lowered her head and resumed her faultless gaze. Caught by the young Geisha's innocent stare once more, the representative glanced to Keiko then back to the unique eyes his superior had instructed him to witness. Granting Momoko's forgiveness with a slight nod, he smiled as the corners of her lips rose also.

Momoko's anxiety eased as Keiko's recital came to an end. By the praise the man beside her continued to give, she knew her rival had not damaged the chances of securing her deserved passage to America. With the Shamisen's diminishing notes, Momoko broke into a soft applause.

"Thank you, Momoko," Keiko bowed to her sister and then all others present. Her gaze retuned to Momoko. "Would you care to continue?" She smiled, lifting her Shamisen up in offering.

Momoko concealed her anger, yet she felt a twinge of admiration towards her young sister. Keiko knew Momoko rarely practiced the instrument so detrimental to her profession, relying only on her quick wit and good looks to gain the affection of others.

"Well, Momoko? Are you willing to play for our guests this evening?" Keiko asked once more. Momoko hid her wrath from the representative's expectant stare.

"Of course, Keiko. It would be an honour," she smiled. "Please, may I borrow your Shamisen? I mean, it plays so well."

Keiko dismissed the slur on her abilities and rose to her feet.

"My pleasure," she smirked. "Here, let me bring it to you."

Momoko glanced to the other guests. Each Geisha knew of her struggle with music. Momoko retained her calm exterior, battling her fears as Keiko edged nearer with the dreaded instrument.

"Here you are, Momoko," Keiko hovered above her, waiting for the Shamisen to be taken. Momoko remained still. Not wanting to lose face in reaching over to her younger sister, she waited for it to be presented to her.

Aware of her duty, Keiko enjoyed her moment of power. That slight feeling of authority faltered as she became trapped in Momoko's glare, past experience telling her the implications behind such a look.

"Here, Momoko," Keiko whispered and passed the instrument down to her. She cringed as the Shamisen rang a hollow chord on connecting with the neck of the tall foreign bottle between them.

Feeling the warm red liquid seep onto her thighs and midriff, Momoko glared first to the offending bottle and then up to Keiko.

"I'm sorry," Keiko mumbled.

Her apology broke the rooms silence and Momoko stared back down to the burgundy stain spreading across her lap.

"It was an accident, Momoko," Keiko spoke again.

She looked to her sister's once pristine kimono and a tear fell from her. "It will come out," she added, although she knew this to be untrue. Momoko's finger jabbed at the deep red patch and then rose to Keiko.

"Look what you've done," she pointed at her younger sister. "Look."

Momoko sensed Keiko's remorse. She knew it had been an accident, but that mattered little to her now. The kimono she had worked so hard for was ruined.

"Look," she grabbed at Keiko's Shamisen. Pulling it from her sister's grasp, Momoko held the instrument to her. She paused and looked to the shocked faces surrounding her.

"What?" She growled across the table, not caring for the thoughts of the other Geisha, or for the rich boring men they had grovelled to all evening. As Momoko's anger grew she also forgot the promise of a new life in America.

"Keiko, this is for you," Momoko whispered.

Climbing to her feet with Keiko's treasured Shamisen, she looped her fingers under its four strings and with a smile, prized them from their long slender neck.

"There," Momoko handed it back to the tearful young Geisha before marching homewards through the banquet's astonished silence.

The next morning as dawn light shone through the Okiya's dining room window, Auntie looked to the two young Geisha sat before her. Leaning forwards, she poured the hot green tea prepared before summoning them from their beds and encouraged each to drink. Taking a sip from their small ceramic bowls, neither Momoko nor Keiko's eyes left their guardians.

"You should both know by now," Auntie said. "That nothing misses my attention."

Each young woman bowed their heads and peered up to the old woman.

"Yes, Auntie," they whispered together.

"I have been informed of your conduct, and hope for your own sakes that word of such exploits does not harm the Okiya in which you now sit."

"No, Auntie," both answered in unity again.

"Now," Auntie's tone softened. "Even with the closing events of last night, it seems that earlier in the evening each of you shone in your abilities. Your later dishonourable performances have somehow been overlooked."

Momoko and Keiko lowered their tea and stared back at the old woman.

"Yes, my young Geisha," she said. "I have already talked with your prospective Danna's representative. It is my duty now to tell you a decision has been reached."

CHAPTER FOURTEEN

Running towards Tashilhunpo's small infirmary, Tenzin's thoughts raced as to the reasons behind the calls for his presence.

Leaving his novice students alone, his concerns for those closest to him increased with each hurried footfall across the courtyard. On reaching the monastery's makeshift hospital Tenzin burst through its doors. He shook to the scene greeting his boisterous arrival.

"Lama Norbu," he called to the old monk lying drained and exhausted on one of the infirmary's full beds.

Rushing to his side, Tenzin became aware of the others who joined in his guardian's sickness.

"Nyima," he mumbled out to the young Panchen Lama's prostrate body.

Tenzin's heart sank on seeing the Lamas he would sit with each afternoon lay covered in the same beads of feverish sweat.

"What happened?" He said down to Lama Norbu's closed eyes. Edging closer Tenzin took the old monk's hand in his. "Tell me, my friend," he appealed. "Tell me."

Watching his guardian's chest rise and fall under shallow breaths, a tear ran down his cheek and he looked to the infirmary overseer's kind smile.

"Lama Norbu will be fine," the carer reassured. "As will the others." Dabbing at the old monk's moist brow he turned back to Tenzin. "They have been very lucky," he continued. "Another cupful of that poison would have seen an end to them all."

"Poison?" Tenzin gasped.

His eyes shot around the room across his peers silent souls and then fell back to the carer.

"Yes, Tenzin. Were you not told?"

Shaking his head he gazed back down to Lama Norbu's pained expression.

"Where? How?"

"It was the tea, Tenzin," the carer replied. "Something within that brew caused the illness you see around you."

Realising how his fellow Lamas had fallen sick, he felt a temper within him never experienced before.

"Ketu," he muttered, the young monk's eyes retaining their glassy sheen from his rage. The carer stepped back on sensing Tenzin's wrath.

"Yes, Ketu is here also," he pointed into the shadows at the far end of the room. "It seems he too has enemies within his home."

His anger was soon replaced by a confused anxiety new to his soul. Knowing only Ketu had access to the tainted liquid which had caused the sickness surrounding him, Tenzin was also aware that the boy's malicious streak suited the offence. Yet he could not understand how Ketu came to lay with those he had harmed.

Walking to his bedside, he hesitated in seeing his adversary's eyes open on his approach. Fighting his fears, the young monk stepped forward.

"Ketu," he whispered down to him. "Why do such a thing?"

Ketu's eyes narrowed, accompanied by the sickly smirk Tenzin had witnessed since first meeting with the boy.

In the weeks that followed, Tenzin stayed at Lama Norbu's bedside, his hopes for the old monk's recovery, fulfilled in the re-emergence of the soul who had always played guardian and friend to his own.

With Nyima and his elderly peers also making the swift return to the health predicted by their carers, Tenzin was credited for the tenacious compassion he demonstrate to all concerned. With all his empathy and vigour, the young monk remained unaware of his tests soon to come.

During his time within those infirmary walls, Tenzin would consider the causes for his fellow Lama's illness. In his heart he knew Ketu lay behind such matters. Although the boy's actions held the malicious traits Tenzin had grown accustomed to, the young monk could find no motive behind Ketu's wrong doing and considered if it were he who had pushed Ketu to destroy all which was sacred to

Tashilhunpo.

Tenzin dismissed his guilt once more. He was aware of the tool Ketu would often use against him and continued to search for the reasons behind the boy's wicked intent, optimistic he would soon find his answer.

Determined to know the truth, Tenzin would question his wants to aid Ketu's recovery. Each day he battled his intentions on seeing the boy regain his strength, unsure as to whether his need for Ketu's wellbeing came from the compassion he had always held towards his charge, or from his burning to desire to find out why he had carried out such a callous deed. These internal battles hounded Tenzin's being as there was another situation raised within the monastic community Tenzin adored.

The young monk came to realise not one of Tashilhunpo's residents looked to Ketu with the same suspicions he contained.

As each Lama's recuperation came to an end, Tenzin would watch them leave the infirmary beds for their own bunks. On every occasion his peers would smile to Tenzin and commend his vigilance in staying at his master's side, although their true praise always fell on Ketu as he helped the Lama's back to their rooms, each elderly seer oblivious to the boy's scowls directed at Tenzin on their leaving.

Delving deep within his heart, Tenzin searched for the empathy he knew would rid him of the injustice surrounding his soul.

At times Tenzin found what he sought, an understanding in his forgiveness towards the one who persecuted all which proved revered within him. Those compassionate glimpses gave Tenzin the strength to continue his bedside vigil and to his joy Lama Norbu too was soon ushered back to his own bed.

Within a few days of his guardian's full return to health, Tenzin anticipated the afternoon discussions he had missed during his fellow Lama's illness. With so many questions left unanswered, the young monk longed to be amongst those who could provide such answers. It came as some surprise when the young monk was asked to arrive an hour earlier for their first meeting.

"Ah, you are here at last, young Tenzin," Lama Norbu said as the young monk entered the Grand Hall. "Please, step forward."

Bowing to each Lama in turn, Tenzin frowned to the response he received. Accustomed to the smiles his arrival always created, he could not understand the lack of acknowledgement now present as the Lamas turned to one another. Straining to hear the whispers his entrance produced, Tenzin walked to his seat beside them. He stopped as the room fell silent in his actions.

"No, Tenzin," his guardian called out. "Today you must stand before us. There are some questions we would like you to answer."

"Yes, Tenzin," the Panchen Lama's young voice commanded. "Speak fair and true, for we shall know in your voice that which is not."

Tenzin's stomach turned as he stared at all sat before him.

In his years spent within Tashilhunpo's walls he had never experienced the tense atmosphere which encircled him and his contemporaries now. Looking to Lama Norbu, he tried to ignore his torso's sickening churn.

"I do not understand," he said. "What is it that I am being asked here today?"

"Do not tell us that you do not know," one of the Lamas called out.

Sensing the acrimony within his words, Tenzin felt some relief as Lama Norbu raised a hand to silence his fellow Rinpoche.

"As our Panchen Lama stressed," the old monk said. "It is I who shall hold court here this afternoon."

Paying little attention to the frustrated huffs beside him, Lama Norbu's view returned to Tenzin.

"Now, young Lama," he continued. "As Nyima has instructed, your answers must remain true, for we shall know the untruths you may choose to speak."

Tenzin's eyes glistened in the flickering candle light surrounding him. His body began to tremble on guessing the reasons behind his inquisition.

"Yes, Lama Norbu," he replied. "I understand."

"Good, my child," he whispered, his eyes too gaining a similar sheen. Looking to the others, he reached into his robes and paused. Glancing back to his apprentice, a sorrow entered his soul as to what he was to ask.

The other Lama's saw his trepidation.

"This must be done," the Lama beside him spoke up once again. He silenced to his Panchen Lama's glare and nodded to Lama Norbu, encouraging him to continue.

"What must be done?"

Confused by the intrigue played out before him, Tenzin also held his tongue as Nyima caught his eye.

"Please, Lama Norbu, continue," the Panchen Lama instructed, and Tenzin noticed his soul matched the sadness containing his guardian.

The old monk pulled his hand from his robes.

"Tell me, Tenzin," he held up a small bag. "Have you ever seen this before?"

Tenzin edged forward and took the bag from the old monk. Peering inside he frowned to the deadly selection of toadstools he had known from a child never to touch.

"No," Tenzin's head shook from side to side.

"Then you must tell us, Tenzin," the Panchen Lama leant towards him. "Why were they found beneath your pillow?"

Tenzin stumbled on hearing Nyima's words. The Panchen Lama reached out for Lama Norbu's arm as the old monk motioned forward to steady his charge.

"No, Lama Norbu," Nyima whispered. "Tenzin must stand alone this day."

Leaning back, the old monk's hands returned to his lap and he nodded once to his startled apprentice.

"Tell us, Tenzin," he said. "Tell us how we came to find this poison within your bunk."

"I don't know," Tenzin mumbled to his feet. Looking up to solemn faces a tear fell from him. "You have to believe me," the young monk implored. "I do not know."

"He doesn't know?" Piped up another Lama.

Ignoring Nyima's calls for silence, the Lama continued.

"Then how were they discovered in your room? Don't tell me, somebody put them there."

Tenzin's view fell to Lama Norbu. Trying to find comfort within his guardian's gaze, he considered telling of his suspicions towards Ketu's behaviour. The young monk hesitated in his want to speak of the spiteful streak which seemed to go unseen to all those before him. Recognising his trepidation Lama Norbu leant forwards.

"Tenzin, is there something you want to tell us?"

"I." The young monk stopped, aware that if he were to continue with his words the accusations against him could multiply if it were seen he tried to blame another. Torn between saving his own reputation and destroying another's, the young monk held his silence, unsure of what actions to take next.

"You guilt seems evident in your lack of reply," the Lama sat beside Nyima said. Turning to his young superior, his eyebrows raised. "Panchen Lama, is it not obvious that it was Tenzin here who tried to see to our demise?"

Tenzin's heart thumped. How could these wise men before him think that it was he who poisoned them that day? Was it not clear to them that Ketu was to blame?

"I have never seen these before," Tenzin lifted the toxic bag to all present. "You must believe that I do not know how they came to be in my room."

"Then how else did they end up beneath where you lay your head each night, Tenzin?" Nyima asked.

Witnessing the compassion the young Panchen Lama contained towards him, Tenzin's anxiety lifted.

"I don't know," he insisted. His sight flowed across sombre glares as he searched for the words to bring an end to the torment his soul now experienced. His heart was in no doubt that Ketu was to blame. Besides himself, he knew only Ketu had access to the tea that had nearly caused such tragedy.

"Tenzin," Lama Norbu pulled him from his thoughts. "What has happened here has brought great uncertainty to your future within Tashilhunpo. Someone must answer for the wickedness portrayed within these very walls." The old monk leant to Tenzin. "You understand this, my child?" He asked. "Do you not?"

Tenzin wiped his cheeks and nodded up to his guardian, his memories recalling the kindness the old monk had always shown towards him.

Wondering once more if he should speak his thoughts of their true betrayer, Tenzin looked over his shoulder on hearing the Grand Hall's doors open behind him.

"Ketu," Lama Norbu called to the boy lugging the large tea urn towards them. "Were you not told that we would not need your services this afternoon?"

"No, Lama Norbu," he said and glanced to Tenzin.

The young monk saw the pleasure in his charge's eyes. He knew Ketu had been told not to come here today, and that the only reasons for his arrival was to watch the investigation he himself should be a part of.

"I am sorry," he said.

Tenzin sickened as each Lama raised their first smiles that afternoon, and revelling in the praise received, Ketu looked back to Tenzin.

"Are you ok, Tenzin?" He smirked.

Tenzin nodded, his heart submitting all was lost to him now.

"I am fine, Ketu," he whispered and gazed up to his guardian.

A shard of hope came to the young monk as he saw Lama Norbu had witnessed the exchange between him and Ketu. Was it now that the boy's treachery would be unmasked? Tenzin's optimism faltered as the old monk beamed to Ketu's false innocence.

"Ketu, for so long you have struggled to carry our afternoon tea and my brothers and I have grown accustomed to your presence. Tell me, do you enjoy your duties?"

Tenzin's frowns returned. How could his guardian miss the malicious traits housed inside Ketu's small frame? Wanting to speak out, the young monk bit into his lower lip, intrigued by what his adversary had to say.

Ketu saw Tenzin's actions and shuffled on his feet as he tried to find an answer.

"I, um," he muttered.

"Yes, Ketu?" Nyima asked.

Looking from Tenzin to the Panchen Lama, Ketu straightened.

"I am aware of the honour you have given me," he said. "It has been my pleasure to carry your afternoon drink across the courtyard each day."

"Yes, Ketu," Lama Norbu smiled. "That may be so. But has it not been a misery. I mean, you are no taller than the large tea urn before you. Has it not been a struggle for you to carry such a thing through the rains, snows and hot sun our seasons bring?"

Ketu glanced to Tenzin. Each knew it had not been Ketu who had traipsed through such harsh elements year after year. For a brief moment, Tenzin considered if the boy would reveal the truth to his elders.

"Well, Ketu?" Nyima pressed. "Has it?"

Waiting for Ketu's reply, Tenzin tasted salty drops of blood brought from his clamped lip and glared over to the boy. His heart sank to the grin he received.

"As I have said," Ketu turned to his audience. "It has been an honour."

Tenzin shook his head and gazed down to his feet. He cringed to the newfound praise given to Ketu on his reply.

"Tenzin," Lama Norbu caused a hush to fall over the room. "Thank you for speaking to us today. I must now ask you to leave us, so my Rinpoches and I may discuss your future."

Glancing to Ketu, the old monk smiled once more and bowed to him. "And many thanks to you also, my child," he said. "Please, will you excuse us also for we have much to talk of."

Returning his respect to the row of Lamas, Ketu grinned to Tenzin again as he accompanied the young monk from the Grand Hall. Sure his elders watched their departure he motioned for Tenzin to leave its doors first with a gracious bow.

Stepping out from the Grand Hall, Tenzin adjusted his robes to ward off the late afternoon chill and looked out onto his home's surrounding mountains. Seeing the beginnings of winter's ice and snow form upon them, he wondered if he would be here to watch these change of seasons again.

Despondent and worried for his future, the young monk sat down on the Grand Hall's steps, his heart heavy with the prospects of having to leave the one place he knew he belonged. Lost within that unknown future, Tenzin stared ahead, paying little attention as Ketu lowered himself down beside him.

Tenzin's sight flowed across the courtyard and to the path he would walk each day with Ketu at his side, free from the struggles of carrying the large tea urn which had caused such grief. Feeling his charge's gaze, Tenzin turned to him.

"Why, Ketu?"

"Why what?" The boy sniggered.

His laughter faded in Tenzin's glare.

"How many times have I helped you across this courtyard?" The young monk pointed before them. "Tell me, Ketu, have I ever asked you for anything in return?"

"No," the boy beside him mumbled. Lowering his head he shrugged as Tenzin continued.

"Then why do such a thing? Why try and harm those who have shown you a kindness seldom found in others?"

Annoyed with Ketu's lack of response, Tenzin turned his body to face his adversary.

"Ketu, what is it that I have done so wrong to you?" he demanded. "Tell me."

The change in the young monk's voice caused Ketu to raise his head and display the pent up emotions swirling within him.

"You have it all," he sneered.

"What? What is it that I have, Ketu?"

"Well look at you. Everyone admires the way you are, the way your compassion touches all those you meet. It makes me sick to see the smiles that trail behind you each day."

"But, Ketu, you are also liked within Tashilhunpo. Can you not see this?"

"No," Ketu snapped. "Why should they? I don't need anyone and no-one needs me. That's the way it's always been, all I've ever known. Don't you understand this, Tenzin?" He added with a snarl.

Listening to the resentment within those words, Tenzin's unyielding empathy surfaced.

"I understand, Ketu," he recognised the deep embedded hurt enveloping the boy. Throughout their time together, the young monk had known his own actions were not to blame for Ketu's unfortunate traits. Now as they sat together, Ketu's declaration only confirmed the pain Tenzin knew lay within this bitter soul.

"To let others into your heart will bring you a happiness never before imagined, Ketu," he smiled. "This will only lead to the peace your soul seeks. Bringing the same joy to you as those you hold such envy towards." Tenzin leant back, his smile growing as he watched Ketu mull over his words.

The young monk's delight faltered as Ketu lost that glimpse of peace he had waited so long to touch.

"And what do you know, Lama Tenzin?" He growled. "Your life here is at an end now. Can't you see that? Everyone thinks it was you who poisoned our elders."

Ketu grinned ahead of him and then turned sharply to the young monk.

"At least I did one thing right," he laughed.

"Then it was you," Tenzin said.

He shuddered as Ketu replied with an exaggerated nod.

"Of course it was me, Tenzin. Do you know how long it took to collect those toadstools? For weeks I hunted in hope of seeing to your demise."

"But why, Ketu?"

"I've told you before," the boy snapped once more. "It was not our elders that I wanted to harm, they were just a gateway towards your downfall. No, Tenzin, it was you I wanted to hurt. To put an end to the love you receive from so many and see your departure from the home I know you adore."

"So you planned all this? So it would appear that it was me who poisoned everyone?" Anxiety gripped Tenzin in the sound of Ketu's malicious laughter.

"Yes, Tenzin," Ketu giggled. "At last you get it. Yes it was me who tried to end the lives of those who tell us what to do and how to live. Yes it was me who poisoned those old fools." Tenzin trembled to the inane grins before him as Ketu continued. "You talk of praise and love from others, young Lama. But I have found such admiration in my own actions, a respect given to myself, from me, towards my own cunning."

"When you drank the poisoned tea yourself?"

"Yes. No one would suspect me then, would they? Not when I lay sick and you remained healthy." Raising his head high, Ketu stared out to the distant horizon. "The only Lama to not be effected," he smiled. "And it seems my plan has worked, Tenzin. For I do not suppose your soul shall spend another night beneath Tashilhunpo's sacred rooftops."

Ketu rose to his feet and stared down at Tenzin. The young monk hesitated in reaching for the one who had caused so much harm and instead returned his view to the mountainous skyline that had always accompanied his thoughts. Finding the solace those familiar peeks gave, Tenzin became lost in their tip's evening glow of orange and yellow, unaware of the two figures behind him.

"Lama Norbu," Ketu whispered.

The boy's hushed words broke Tenzin from his contemplation and he looked up to Ketu's pale features. Turning to his guardian, Tenzin's eyes fell to the small hand clutched tight in the old monk's.

"Tenzin," the young Panchen Lama smiled to him. "We are sorry."

"Yes, Tenzin," Lama Norbu echoed. His smile faded as he turned to Ketu.

"Lama Norbu, how long have you been stood there?" Ketu asked.

"Long enough, Ketu," the old monk sighed. "Long enough."

Ketu shuffled on his feet and tried to raise a sickly smile.

"But all I have said was just to make Tenzin feel better in his anguish. I was only joking."

"Silence," Lama Norbu shouted, startling both Tenzin and Nyima alike. Never before had they heard the old monk raise his voice, their hidden admiration concealed from Ketu's stunned gaze.

Collecting himself, Lama Norbu beckoned Tenzin to his side.

"You too, Ketu," he demanded. "It is time for your elders to hear of your deception. Come now, child. Your fate awaits us all."

With a tentative step, Ketu did as asked and followed the three Lamas into the Grand Hall. His heart sank on witnessing the old monk look down to Tenzin and whisper his apologues to his young apprentice again.

To the other Lama's gasps, Lama Norbu and the young Panchen Lama recounted Ketu's overheard words, the compassion each wise elder held portrayed in the softening glances they at times gave the boy.

As the room settled down from such news, Tenzin accepted his peer's requests for forgiveness with a courteous bow to each. Looking to Ketu's quaking frame he stepped forward and addressed his contemporaries.

"Now you know that it was not I who was to blame, may I ask what actions you are to take against Ketu now the truth has been spoken."

Watching his peers shuffle uncomfortably in their seats, Tenzin knew then of the ominous outcome.

"Tenzin," Lama Norbu spoke. "Your compassion and reverence for all life's creatures serves you well, a characteristic most seated here within these chambers can only dream of achieving in this, their present incarnation." The old monk paused and regained his familiar smile. "However, your own deceptive ways have not gone unnoticed either, young Lama."

"Mine?" Tenzin frowned.

"Yes, my child. We are all aware of how you yourself have carried that large tea urn for the one who has tried so hard to destroy your tender spirit. A commendable endeavour indeed, for your charitable actions have given us all such pleasure, confirming to us that Lama

Jampo has truly returned to his home amongst us."

"I am sorry for my trickery," Tenzin lowered his head. He raised his eyes as his guardian continued.

"Tenzin, we are aware your deception carried with it only good will towards Ketu here. But, my child, there are other matters at hand. Tell me young, Ketu," Lama Norbu looked to the boy. "Is your repentance greater than we imagine it to be?"

Ketu's gaze ran across the room to each present and stopped at Tenzin.

"Tell them, Ketu," he encouraged his adversary. "Tell them your regrets."

The boy scowled at the young monk's request and then turned to Lama Norbu and the seated Lamas before him.

"My only regret is." Ketu's malicious grin returned. "My only regret is that Tenzin has not been cast out as I planned. I do not care for your ways, never have and never shall. Do with me what you want," he demanded, his chin raised high in defiance to all within the Grand Hall.

Taken aback by his malevolent reply, Lama Norbu stepped down from his seat and edged closer to the insolent novice.

"Then it has been revealed here today, young Ketu. That it is you yourself who has chosen your own destiny in the lack of redemption you show to those who have cared for you." Looking back to the Panchen Lama, the old monk waited for his permission to continue.

Acknowledging young Nyima's wishes, Lama Norbu bowed once to Ketu and then held the boy in his sights.

"Ketu, my child. Your acts have been accounted for within Tashilhunpo's walls this very day. It is with the utmost regret that we seated here today must cast you out into the world beyond, with hope that you shall one day see the callousness of your actions."

CHAPTER FIFTEEN

Looking to her two young Geisha, Auntie reached to the table.

"I see you have both enjoyed my tea," she said, holding the empty tea urn up to them. "Would you care for more?"

"Yes, Auntie," Keiko nodded as she collect the assortment of ceramic cups.

The old woman glanced to Momoko's pensive state and rose to her feet.

"No, Keiko," she said. "I shall prepare another drink for us all. You and your sister remain seated, I will not be long."

Doing as instructed, Keiko watched her guardian make for the Okiya's small kitchen. She turned to Momoko with a faint smile.

"I am sorry, Momoko," she whispered.

Momoko hesitated for a moment. "I am sorry too, Keiko," she replied.

From the Okiya kitchen's small confines, Auntie studied the exchange between her young charges. She had been dumbfounded by the representative's description of their actions, although it had come of no surprise such an incident had occurred. The old woman had expected some confrontation between the two young women, yet not to the extremes recounted to her in the early hours that morning.

With a second tray of green tea prepared, Auntie paused and continued to watch her young Geisha. She smiled to her memories of how each had sat together in the same place since children.

Looking now to the beautiful young women they were always destined to become, she saddened that her dreams of an unbreakable friendship between them had never appeared. With a sigh, the old woman's view fell to the Okiya kitchen's window, her sorrow enhanced that she must now disappoint one of those she had raised.

Momoko watched the old woman gaze to the world outside. Hidden memories flooded to her as she recalled witnessing another from her past do likewise. Once more she pushed such painful thoughts away and turned to her younger sister.

"Can your Shamisen be mended, Keiko?"

"Yes, Momoko." Keiko lowered her head to her admission, aware Momoko's prized kimono was beyond repair.

Raising her chin, she smiled to the concealed remorse in her elder sister's voice.

"Will you let me buy you a new kimono, Momoko?"

"No, Keiko," Momoko shook her head. She too raised a smile. "To wear a white Kimono was a foolish idea. It was my mistake to think such a thing would not happen."

"Yes it was," Keiko smiled.

Her high spirits faltered in Momoko's scowl and the young woman looked down at the table. She raised her head to Momoko's unexpected laughter.

"Yes it was, Keiko," Momoko agreed. "Maybe I will find another in America."

"Or maybe I shall," Keiko giggled, enjoying the rare moment of bonding between them both.

"What is all this?" Auntie returned from the kitchen and joined her giggling Geisha. Containing her own smiles, she poured their tea and then looked across the table.

"Now both of you settle down," she said. "We have much to talk of."

Any kinship Momoko and Keiko had shared that morning faded. Auntie recognised this and hid her returning sorrow. Over the years, she had witnessed these moments so longed for, when both her dependants had laughed and played together. Yet as now, those times had been brief, more often than not hampered by Momoko's eager want for domination. Now proved no different and Auntie ignored her protégé's glare and looked to Keiko.

"My, sweet Keiko," she began. "I have been told your manner and demure traits gained you many admirers last night. As did your skills in the music that has become so important to you, am I right?"

"Yes, Auntie, I played as best I could."

"You played better than ever before I believe. From your heart I am told. Yes, Keiko, my guest this morning spoke highly of your talents in this field."

Keiko's modesty overcame her placid character, portrayed in the redden cheeks she tried to hide with a tilt of chin.

"Do not be shy of your abilities, child," the old woman said. "For, they have served you well in the eyes of those who count."

Seeing Momoko's anguish to her words, Auntie winked at her.

"And, Momoko. My, beautiful Momoko. It seems that your attributes more than impressed those who mattered also."

"Thank you, Auntie."

The old woman did not wait for the same modesty to appear as had Keiko's. Her wants for a glimpse of humility in the young Geisha had been discarded long ago along with the hopes of a blossoming friendship between her treasured girls.

"Momoko," she continued. "I have been praised this morning for raising a Geisha with the lightening wit and charm seldom accompanied by the gift of great beauty you also possess."

Momoko showed no reaction to her compliment. The old woman understood this, knowing her egotistical streak was as clearly defined as the stunning eyes and charismatic smile she had inherited from both her parents.

Auntie's view left Momoko and she smiled to Keiko once more.

"Keiko, your composure and popularity astonished my guest. He saw the love others in his company felt for you, he himself admitting to such an emotion. Yet," the old woman turned back to Momoko. "He enthused about the presence Momoko held also, telling me that never before had he encountered a young woman who commanded such silent respect as yourself." Leaning back she looked to each hopeful young face, her heart sinking once again to the predicted disappointment to come.

"Keiko, your sister's great beauty and charm impressed our guest so much throughout the night. He found her company to be as exhilarating as promised." For a second time and her eyes flicked to Momoko's proud expression. The old woman sighed as to what was to come and looked to Keiko with sadness.

"My, sweet child. Your musical talents were so admired, as was your soft nature." Auntie wiped a single tear from her cheek and then smiled to both her young Geisha.

"This is why, Keiko, you are the one who has been chosen to

leave for San Francisco."

Auntie watched the surprised reaction her words produced.

"Me, Auntie?" Keiko said, her young mind trying to comprehend the turn of events.

So sure that Momoko was the one destined for America, she had dismissed any notions of her being chosen over her beautiful elder sister.

"Yes, Keiko. It is you who must now prepare for a new life away from all you know. I hope you are able to accept this opportunity."

The old woman looked to Momoko.

"I am sorry, my child," she said. "Your talents were considered also, however, it was Keiko's kindness that led to our guest's final choice. Do you understand this?"

Momoko shrugged.

"Yes, Auntie," she mumbled, her eyes not leaving the old woman's. "Congratulations younger sister."

Seeing through Momoko's bitter disappointment, Auntie's admiration increased as true emotions were covered once more. Aware her other young Geisha saw this also, she turned to Keiko and smiled.

"Keiko, what is to come cannot be taken lightly. You must be certain in your actions. Are you truly ready for the unknown future ahead of you?"

Keiko glanced to Momoko and the old woman saw the guilt her soul carried.

"Well, Keiko? Are you to be the one?" She asked again.

Keiko gave no reply. Auntie knew the reasons behind the delay. The unwritten rules between her charges had remained from childhood and the old woman waited with Keiko for her sister's consent. Watching Momoko give a slight nod, she smiled to the broad grin greeting her.

"Yes, Auntie," Keiko enthused. "I am ready."

"Then that is settled, my child," Auntie replied and glanced to Momoko's fixed expression. She nodded once to her protégé and then looked back to Keiko.

"I have arranged for a few of you friends to visit the Okiya this afternoon, Keiko. So they may also celebrate your good news. Now, you must go and prepare for their arrival."

"Thank you, Auntie," Keiko jumped to her feet and bowed.

Momoko also began to leave the table.

"I would like you to stay, Momoko," Auntie said. "We also have much to discuss."

Momoko knew the words to come and watching Keiko run from the room settled back in her place.

"I understand your upset, Momoko," Auntie said. "But you must accept that it is Keiko who has been chosen and that your fate now lies along another path."

"As your Atotori, Auntie?"

"Yes, my child," the old woman nodded. "You were always the one to be my successor, of this we both knew. One day soon, all you see around you shall be yours. Is this not some consolation for your disappointment?"

Momoko looked over the Okiya walls and then back to her guardian, aware as she that her heart lay with the prize given to her undeserving younger sister.

"Of course, Auntie," Momoko smiled, once more hiding her true thoughts from those who loved her.

"Thank you, Auntie," Momoko stood and bowed. "May I go now?"

The old woman stared up at her chosen successor. This time it was she who placed a veil over her emotions.

"Yes, Momoko, of course you can," she replied.

"Thank you," Momoko bowed again and strolled back to her room, leaving Auntie alone with her doubts towards her prosperous Okiya's future.

Later that afternoon, Momoko reappeared from her bedroom to the sound of laughter. Walking into the Okiya dining room, she looked to the food and drink across its table and then to the surrounding Geisha present.

"Momoko," Keiko beckoned "Come and join us."

Momoko nodded to her and looked once more to the faces greeting her. She did not receive one smile or nod of recognition as she walked to her younger sister's side.

"You know everyone here?" Keiko whispered.

"Yes," Momoko replied. She looked to those who had also been vying for position alongside her the evening before. Aware that each had seen her outburst towards Keiko, the looks of distain she now encountered were of little surprise.

"Are you pleased for your sister, Momoko?" One of their guests asked.

Seeing past the formalities of polite acceptance Momoko remembered the Geisha who now spoke.

"Yes, very much so," she lied.

Recalling her time as a Shikomi, Momoko's sight flowed across the room. Realising those present had studied with her also in those days, she felt as far removed from their smiling faces now as she had then.

"Yes, it seems that Keiko's talents shone through," the Geisha continued. "The way in which her fingers found the right notes for her prize last night." She smirked to her friends and then back to Momoko. "I think I'm right in saying those notes were to be found above the table, Momoko."

Momoko suppressed her scowls as soft laughter filled the room. Aware her indiscretion had been noticed she gave her aggressor a polite nod and then backed away to the safety of the Okiya kitchen doorway.

Watching Keiko and her friends return to the laughter she had always known them to delight in, Momoko once again tried to understand the need for such joy. Since a child she had learnt to avoid these moments, finding her own company more favourable than being surrounded by those who she knew would one day betray her.

The solace Momoko found in her embedded methods faltered as she watched the happy faces around the dining table. For the first time she considered what would her life be like if it were she he was leaving for America. Who would be celebrating with her now? Momoko edged back into the kitchen and turned to the small window there. Looking out to winter skies, her memories returned to the two faces she had battled for so long to forget. With a final glance to the party beside her, Momoko walked to the kitchen door and left the Okiya's laughter behind her.

As the chill of late afternoon set in, Momoko was glad she had borrowed Auntie's prized winter jacket. Pulling its fur lined collars up around her neck, Momoko took pleasure in the soft touch playing across her nape as she walked the streets she had known since a child. She knew her guardian would not mind, for how could she allow her intended heir to be cold?

Continuing onwards, Momoko began to consider the position she now held. It was of little consolation to the prospect of leaving for the America she had always longed to see, yet her cunning mind saw the benefits of becoming Atotori and one day proprietor to such an affluent Okiya.

The young Geisha was aware she had been a significant factor to the success of her inheritance. Without her participation, Auntie's thriving business would have remained deep within the anonymity of Tokyo's other small Geisha houses. This, Momoko knew, gave her the undoubted right to become sole owner of the Okiya she had always treated as her own.

As Momoko continued along her districts small winding roads, she tucked her hands into Auntie's jacket pockets and smiled on finding what she sought. Auntie would not want her Atotori to go hungry she considered. Staring down to the collection of coins in her palm, she wondered what delicacy she would treat herself to in the small harbour front market place that lay ahead, the one place she would often visit in her hunt to find the peace of mind so scarce within busy Okiya life.

Nearing the waterfront's ramshackle stalls of steaming rice and noodles, Momoko's thoughts returned to her new role and what effect it would have on the Okiya's other two Geisha. Both Hanako and Tamiko had always been kind to Momoko over the years, proving more than the surrogate elder sisters they were destined to be. Yet with all their love, each had always treated Momoko with trepidation, somehow knowing that one day they would answer to her. This did not trouble Momoko. She already understood the ways in which to cajole and manipulate those under her control. Yes, Hanako and Tamiko would be of no problem to her Momoko grinned as she looked to the fare her treasured market place had to offer.

Choosing her reward, Momoko paid the vendor and turned to the harbour behind her. Walking to those pacific edges, she tried her best to ignore the ships that would soon take Keiko eastwards and into the arms of her rich American Danna.

Leaning against the small guard rail of her favourite spot, Momoko reached into her pocket and smiled down to the two small rice cakes. Still warm in their brown paper wrapping, Momoko unfolded a corner and then raised the treat to her lips.

Savouring the sweet soft crunch, Momoko gave a silent thank you to Auntie's generosity. The young Geisha paused on taking a second nibble, her memories triggered in the taste of her delight. Once more that day, her thoughts returned to her childhood and the kind old midwife who had first introduced the warm snack she now held. Memories of another came to her also and Momoko smiled to the recollections of the mother she had fought so hard to forget.

It seemed a lifetime ago since she had felt the safety of those arms. For a moment, Momoko allowed herself to recall such warm embraces, even though those cherished emotions brought with them a heartache she had spent years trying to subdue.

"They would have celebrated with me," Momoko whispered, remembering the glory her younger sister now basked in.

Glancing back to the ocean, Momoko pushed away her sorrow and smiled to the solace those calm waters always produced.

"Atotori," she said, and returned to her treat.

With another delicate bite, Momoko relished its sweet texture. She paused on feeling another's eyes upon her.

Further along the bay front, the man stared across to the young Geisha. As Momoko caught his gaze, he lowered his head to the old worn blanket laid out before him and then peered up to her once more.

Momoko knew of her onlooker. Having seen him here many times here before she had always paid little attention to his presence, wanting to keep from the pitiful story that surrounded such a soul.

Looking away, Momoko raised her treat back to her lips, wondering if her spectator had once indeed been as handsome as everyone said. Finishing the first of her rice cakes, the young Geisha's curiosity grew and she turned to him, determined to see for herself if he had at one time retained such beauty.

As Momoko neared the man, she looked to the deep scar running from temple to jaw line and considered if the tales of his injury were true. As with most characters along these stretches of Tokyo Bay, each one had a story and Momoko had often delighted in hearing these anecdotes within the safe walls of her Okiya. Now though, Momoko felt some apprehension as she edged closer to one of these fables.

Studying his scar once more, Momoko tried to catch a glimpse of the once handsome features she had been told of. She saddened on remembering the accounts of how he had obtained such a disfigurement, wondering if it were true that someone could survive such a fall.

Some said he had slipped from his bedroom window late one night making for the docklands he now frequented, in hope of escaping his poor upbringing for a life at sea. Others spoke of more romantic reasons for his accident. These Momoko had enjoyed hearing most and had often become lost in the idea of two lovers meeting in the dead of night to elope for new beginnings together.

Approaching the man's expectant gaze, Momoko realised how each of these explanations had become intertwined throughout the years in the whispers of others, leaving her young mind unsure of what to believe.

On reaching the man, Momoko smiled and looked to small collection of fish spread out on the blanket before him. She knew these were his catch of the day. Momoko saddened once more to the life that had once shown such promise, now reduced to selling his meagre wares much to the amusement of others passing by.

Momoko crouched down and smiled again.

"Hello," she said.

She knew no reply would come. Looking to the scar that had rendered him mute for over twenty years, Momoko reddened as the man reached a frail hand up to cover his affliction.

"I am sorry," Momoko gave a slight bow, her guilt pulling on emotions never experienced before. Understanding her words, the man gazed up to her once more. He frowned and tilted his head on meeting with Momoko's eyes.

"What? What is it?" She whispered.

Momoko was used to the attention her eyes often caused, learning to become comfortable through the years as both men and women alike stared endlessly to their unique rare beauty. The gaze she now received seemed so different to the fascination others always held. Momoko could not understand the unspoken recognition she felt flow to her. Staring back to the man's gaunt features, Momoko looked down to her remaining rice cake.

"Would you like this?" She offered the last of her treat to him.

The man glanced down and then nodded back to her, his hand outstretched ready to receive the delicacy he could no longer afford. Taking it gently from Momoko's delicate hand, he took a bite and gazed back at her.

"Tastes good?" Momoko smiled.

She knew this man had nothing to offer in return and could not explain the new emotions surging through her. Momoko wondered if this happiness never encountered within her before came from her simple act of giving with no want of anything in return. Watching the man devour the last of her cherished snack, Momoko's joy faded as he smiled up to her.

So many times before had she met with such a smile, but had never encountered it outside the reflection she had come to adore. In the years of staring at her own image, Momoko never imagined someone could share the same attractive quality presented to her now in the face of a stranger. The corners of her lips raised once more and she too frowned to the unknown similarity between them.

Reaching into her pocket, Momoko searched for what she knew would reclaim her mysterious joy. The young Geisha looked to the last of Auntie's coins. She smiled and pointed down to the row of small fish at the feet of the one who shared the same smile as she.

"How much are these?"

The man looked to his quarry, aware as well as she that no meal could ever come from such a paltry selection. Gazing back to Momoko, he replied with a shrug.

Counting her guardian's remaining money, Momoko thought of the two additional rice cakes that would see her through her journey back to the Okiya. Something within the young Geisha told her those delicacies would somehow not taste so sweet now. Smiling to the man, she placed each coin down beside a row of glazed eyes.

"Is this enough?" She asked.

Greeted once again by her own smile, the man reached forward and gathered his catch. Rising to her feet, Momoko watched, as with great care, he wrapped the fish in a sheet of discarded newspaper and then offered them up to her.

"Thank you," she took them from him.

Becoming lost in his familiar expression, she at last saw through features ravaged by time and to the handsome young man he had once been.

"I will come again," she said to him.

Momoko warmed to the expectant pleasure received in answer to her promise and with a short bow, began to walk back to the Okiya destined to be hers.

Leaving Tokyo Bay's water front behind, Momoko stopped at the entrance of the small winding streets that would lead her homewards. Looking back, she raised a hand in reply to her goodbye from across the harbour, her thoughts remaining confused as to the reasons behind her encounter. Lost once again to the warmth she had felt that day, Momoko turned from the man and continued onwards, unaware another set of eyes now watched her departure.

CHAPTER SIXTEEN

Ketu's expulsion came of no surprise to Tashilhunpo's inhabitants. Although each was aware of the boy's spiteful temperament, their observations only enhanced the love they shared for Tenzin, the young Lama who saw no wrong in those he encountered.

Giving all concerned an insight into the forgiveness and understanding their souls strived to reach, Tenzin's compassionate nature excelled in such harrowing times and only led to encourage his brothers to walk a similar path. No one had believed Tenzin was capable of harming his elders, and the whispers carried through Tashilhunpo Monastery's candle lit corridors and passageways told of who was truly to blame.

Ketu's swift departure came within hours of his admissions, a protocol called upon to ensure the boy's safe exit from his home of six years.

Lama Norbu was aware of the devotion containing Tashilhunpo's monks and feared any reprisals that may ensue.

As word spread of the young Lama's exoneration, within an hour of watching Ketu's small frame trudge from the monastery's walls, Tenzin was greeted with the subtle nods from all those he knew, confirming his absolution was now complete. Witnessing his acceptance, Nyima smiled to the Lamas huddled outside the Grand Hall's ornate entrance. His young features instilled a truth within wise aged hearts that also encouraged each soul to continue its glimpse into the reality sometimes lost in their coveted position.

Returning to his peers, Tenzin stood between Lama Norbu and the Panchen Lama's side and stared up to the gilded figures above them. Tenzin's famed endless smiles spread across wind chapped cheeks as he felt Nyima's hand fold into his.

"He is gone now," the young Panchen Lama said up to him.

Tenzin gave his reply in a short thoughtful nod before joining his fellow Lama's gaze towards the rich orange autumn sunset played out before them.

As the spring months came and Tenzin reached his fifteenth year, any memory of the boy who had caused such harm was soon lost in the first rays of warm sunlight cast across Tashilhunpo's courtyard and temples. Those welcomed beams brought with them their usual delights and Tenzin relished the optimism and returning smiles his birthday triggered in all around.

Continuing with his studies with a new found ease, the young monk was aware of the reasons for the peace that surrounded him. Free to work alongside those who held no malice towards his gentle soul, Tenzin's inner strength grew, revealed in the small steps he took under Lama Norbu's watchful gaze and developing a knowledge the was also noticed by the wise Lamas he would sit with each afternoon. Listening to his rising skills in the heated debates they often held, their wise hearts concealed their guilt as they dismissed the suspicions once held towards the child from Gyantse.

Aware of his peer's growing respect, Tenzin took no pleasure in his newly gained praise. He recognised the words he spoke were that of his own soul, a soul which had encountered these wise old men many times before in the guise of another's.

Throughout his training, the young monk came to realise his heart guided the ones who had shown him a path no dissimilar to the one he had always trod now.

As Tashilhunpo's Lamas accepted his expanding knowledge, he too began to discover the secrets locked within him, allowing his awareness to come forth so he may share with those he had always accompanied.

As the years passed, Tenzin developed the wise traits his predecessor had been acknowledged for and soon the young monk became the teacher he was destined to be.

From the back of Tashilhunpo's small classrooms, Lama Norbu would watch his apprentice open the young minds sat in awe before him. Introducing these young novices to the ways and beliefs of their new home, Tenzin's words rang true to the old monk and he would suppress his smiles, recalling how he himself had spoken of such things to Tenzin many years ago.

Tenzin knew Lama Norbu's thoughts and he too concealed his joy. Looking to his guardian across a classroom of newly shaven heads, Tenzin would bow to the old monk and then join with the laughter his students produced on recognising that their own teacher had once had one of his own.

As the winters came and went, a sorrow came to Tenzin on watching his peers advance through the years. Young Nyima, the Panchen Lama who he had witnessed grow into the revered head of state his fate led him to be, was no longer the small child with a wiseness beyond his years that Tenzin had first encountered. He too had grown and soon came to tower over his favoured contemporary. From his classroom's small window, Tenzin would watch Nyima and Lama Norbu walk together deep in conversation, the old monk's tired stoop enhancing his sadness.

Within the core of his teaching, Tenzin knew his sorrow held no ground. He understood how all those close to us at one time leaves, yet this did not alleviate his anxiety towards his elderly guardian's inevitable departure from this world. To lose the one who had seen him through the years would bring a heartache unimagined. Tenzin was aware their souls would meet again and tried to let these facts surface. His struggle to confront such matters would stay with him, even when attempting to let his unfounded ideas drift by, much the same way he instructed his young students to do likewise when gazing up with them to the clouds filling Tashilhunpo's blue Tibetan skies.

Tenzin's strength as a teacher to Tashilhunpo's new apprentices caught the attention of those far from the walls of the young monk's treasured home and soon his talents were asked for throughout Tibet's midland regions.

Hearing of this news, Lama Norbu devised a plan so all could share the wisdom his novice administered with such modesty. The old monk's plans were greeted with enthusiasm from Tenzin's curious mind.

Although he adored his home, the curiosity present within him since a boy resurfaced and he took to his new role with vigour, his only regret being that Lama Norbu's aged frail body restricted him from joining his travels.

Beginning with Shigatse's neighbouring towns of Lhatse, Shegar and Sakya, Tenzin's quest to enlighten young minds spread from the banks of the Yarlang Tsangpo river and to villages accessible only by horse. These journeys took Tenzin from Tashilhunpo's walls for several days at time and he would return to his brothers with great joy on each occasion, yet when walking through Tashilhunpo's doors once more, he considered the hidden sadness masking his soul.

He knew from where that sorrow came, choosing instead to ignore the confrontation he was aware would release him from his pain.

Mounting his ride to take him onwards to Tibet's smallest settlements, Tenzin would look down to his horse and recall his first venture from his birth place. So many years had passed since he had stood beside Nyangchu's rushing waters, and although he knew many of its residents had called for the services of the monk from Tashilhunpo, Tenzin avoided his return to Gyantse, his heart wary of the reception he may receive there.

For his first few years beneath the monastery's rooftops, Tenzin would dream he was back at his father's side working together in Gyantse's fields. Another would be present in those dreams also and Tenzin often longed for night time to come so he may hold his grandfather's hand once again.

Waking the next morning, he would sadden that his sleeping hours were over, yet as his time advanced within Tashilhunpo and he settled into the life he was destined to lead, his memories of being in his father and grandfather's company faded.

Tenzin tried to understand why these recollections resurfaced within him now. Was it because his travels triggered such memories? Looking out onto distant horizons, he wondered what had become of the one they called Gyaltso and he father. His thoughts soon became filled each day with the want to know what became of the one who gave him up for the monastic life he now led.

As the spring of 1899 began and Tenzin reached his twenty-third birthday, his want for knowledge towards those he had left behind waned. Accepting that the past remained where it belonged, he continued his travels across the Tibetan plains with no further thought as to what had gone before.

Finding comfort in the present moment, he continued to pass his awareness onto others in hope they too would follow a similar path.

Yet, his new found peace was soon disturbed as the summer months gave way for autumn when Tenzin met with a lonely figure from the past he had tried so hard to forget.

Approaching Tashilhunpo's walls after several days' absence, Tenzin smiled in knowing he would soon sit with Nyima and Lama Norbu once more. The young monk anticipated his return to them as much as the meetings he would hold with the village chiefs his work caused him to encounter. Never once did he tire of the wide eyed joy the young Panchen Lama revealed on listening to his tales of places unseen.

Lama Norbu too would show such enthusiasm, concealing his own thoughts as to the villages he already knew from his travels as a boy. This pleased Tenzin. He understood the lesson the old monk gave in his silence and adjured to his guardian's apparent modesty in not telling of his own journeys he himself now undertook.

Tenzin looked up to darkening skies and pulled his robes around him. After a long hot Tibetan summer he was thankful for the cool winds the new season brought and gazed ahead to the golden rooftops which always signalled his arrival home.

Nearing the monastery's entrance, he looked to the small market place beside his home's steep walls, recalling his time as a young novice when he had run between its stalls of fruit and vegetables. It seemed as though Tashilhunpo had always been the place in which his soul had dwelled and once again the young monk pushed away memories of the small house beside Nyangchu River's gushing waters.

"Tenzin, you are back," a voice called out.

Pulling him from painful recollections, Tenzin turned to the street vendor he had known since a child.

"Of that I am," Tenzin grinned.

The vendor nodded to him and without a word handed the young monk two shiny green apples from his stall.

"Thank you," Tenzin smiled and bowed to the man. The market trader returned his respects and watched his recipient walk from him. Recalling the same actions he had witnessed for almost two decades, he paused to enjoy the peace the young monk always gave his heart and then returned to his other customers.

Biting into the apple, Tenzin savoured its sweet taste and

continued towards his home. He stopped on seeing a lone raggedy figure sat beside Tashilhunpo's entrance.

Although it was not unusual to see the occasional beggar outside the monastery doors in hope of charity, Tenzin recognised something about the pitiful stature before him. Drawn to the beggar, he edged closer and glanced down to the second apple in his hand. He knew who deserved his treat more and stepped forward to pass on his gift. Standing before the man, Tenzin leant closer so he may see his features and smiled.

"Here," he said. "This is for you."

With arm outstretched, Tenzin waited for the beggar to reveal himself. The man at his feet kept his head bowed and pulled his tattered shawl over him to conceal his true identity.

"It does not matter," Tenzin reassured.

Many times before on his travels had he encountered those who shied away from another's gaze and he lowered the apple to the beggar's line of sight.

"Please," he insisted. "Take it."

Watching the beggar's slight hesitation, relief came to Tenzin and he smiled as he received a nod. His happiness faded as the man lowered the dirty torn cloth from his brow. Edging back from the figure of his past, Tenzin's body began to tremble.

"Ketu," he gasped to the haggard face grinning up at him.

Looking at the toothless smile, Tenzin's stomach sickened as his eyes fell to the lines etched across Ketu's parched cheeks. The young monk gasped once more as his old adversary combed back his mop of matted hair to reveal another myriad of aged grooves embedded in his grimy forehead.

"Is that really you, Ketu?" Tenzin whispered.

Keeping a distance from him, he peered closer to the one he had last seen as a boy some nine years ago. His heart sank on seeing his perception was true, confirmed by the continued grin directed at him. Awaiting a reply, it dawned on Tenzin that the mind which had shown such malice was lost from the beggar and wondered if his presence was registered by his former antagonist.

"Ketu," he moved closer. "It is me, Tenzin. Do you remember?"

Once more he waited for an answer from Tashilhunpo's past exile yet none came.

"How did you get here?" Tenzin spoke again even though his

heart knew no reply would come.

Looking to the filthy rags covering Ketu's small frame, he tried to imagine the life that had led to such an outcome and he crouched down before the beggar.

He stared into eyes that seemed far beyond rescue.

Recalling the remorse Ketu had always placed on him, a determination entered Tenzin not to succumb to the same emotional manipulation again. Resting back on his haunches, he glared back at Ketu. Memories of the hurt his soul had produced ebbed back and he battled the morals raging within him. Pushing his own wants away, Tenzin summoned a smile and tried to find the compassion he had always shown the boy.

"Ketu, it's me, Tenzin," he tried once more. The young monk sighed on receiving only the same inane grins he had encountered since their reunion.

Considering for a moment if he was mistaken, that this pathetic creature before him really was the boy whose malicious acts were fabled within Tashilhunpo's walls, Tenzin glimpsed something which confirmed his discovery.

"You want this?" He asked Ketu on recognising the same glare he had witnessed as a child. Holding the apple up to him, Tenzin sickened to the craving Ketu revealed to what belonged to him.

"You always did want what I had," Tenzin continued. "Tell me, why should you be no different now?"

The young monk felt little remorse to the confused frowns he now received. In his heart he knew his actions towards Ketu's mislaid wits was wrong, yet years of heartache surfaced within him, betraying the soul so dear to the young monk and all those who knew him. Trying not to continue with his unkind motives, Tenzin fought not to give the desired apple to his foe.

The mounting want in Ketu's eyes triggered more painful hidden memories within Tenzin. With some trepidation he stared down at the fruit and then placed it back into his shoulder bag.

"No, Ketu," Tenzin whispered. "Why should you deserve anything after what you did?"

Ketu watched the apple disappear from his view and then looked back at Tenzin. The beggar's frowns caused his lined features to contort in a way the young monk had never seen before. Startled by his reaction, Tenzin hesitated and reached back into his bag. He stopped in catching sight of Ketu's anticipation.

Pulling his hand back to him, Tenzin's determination to not let his childhood adversary sway his emotions again resurfaced and he stared back at the hunger in Ketu's eyes.

"No, Ketu," he whispered once more and rose to his feet.

Turning from the beggar, Tenzin paused to the grunt behind him.

"What is it?" He asked as Ketu's grins returned.

Following Ketu's gaze, the young monk's hand reached to his worn bead necklace. Glancing back to Ketu, Tenzin began to understand the reasons for the inaudible sounds coming from him.

"You recognise these beads?" Tenzin asked.

Ketu grunted again, this time accompanied by a frenzied nod. Crouching back before him, Tenzin thought of the apple in his bag, yet his attention drifted and he stared at Ketu.

"Then if you recognise my beads, then you must surely realise who I am."

Ketu raised his head and nodded, his grins replaced by a soft warm smile.

Holding each other's gaze, Tenzin considered his actions and reached for the fruit he had forbidden himself to give Ketu. He stopped once more as Ketu scrabbled through his ragged clothing and pulled out a small package wrapped in the same torn material he now wore. Holding the parcel up to Tenzin, he thrust it towards the young monk's hands.

"What is it?" Tenzin whispered.

Ketu motioned for the young monk to take it from him. A single tear fell from him as Tenzin shook his head and refused his gift to him.

"No, Ketu," Tenzin stood up.

Looking to the disappointment below him, the young monk recalled the trickery Ketu had shown.

"I want nothing from you," he said and ignored the beggar's pleas as he walked through Tashilhunpo's doors and away from the past which had caused him such anguish.

Watching Tenzin march across the courtyard, his unknown observer saddened on seeing the young monk reach into his bag and take a large bite from the fruit that had been meant for another.

With a sigh, he walked to the beggar whose hunger would have benefited more from the gift. Smiling to Tashilhunpo's former novice on his approach, Lama Norbu glanced back to Tenzin and hoped the young monk realised his delicacy no longer tasted quite as sweet.

CHAPTER SEVENTEEN

Unsure of why they had been summoned from their beds so early, Momoko and Keiko looked to one another.

"Momoko," Keiko whispered.

"Shhh," her sister hushed. Momoko watched Keiko lower her head and then look to their guardian. She understood the significance of the old woman's stance.

Auntie took her gaze from the Okiya kitchen window and caught her protégé's stare. She nodded to Momoko, aware it was time to tell both her young Geisha the news received that morning.

"Thank you for rising so soon," she joined them at the dining room table.

As Momoko and Keiko bowed in unison to her arrival, Auntie saw their respectful gesture could not mask the anxiety each held.

"Momoko, can you tell me where you went yesterday afternoon?"

Keiko glanced to the startled expression beside her. She too had noticed her sister's absence from the party. Putting her disappearance down to the upset of losing her passage to America, Keiko had tried to conceal her guilt from her friends. That remorse now resurfaced on realising how she had become lost in her celebrations that afternoon and had forgotten the lack of her fellow Geisha's presence.

"Well?"

Keiko lowered her head once more on seeing Auntie's eyebrows raise.

"I went to the harbour, Auntie," Momoko replied.

"And did you talk to anyone there?"

"Yes."

"Who, Momoko? Tell me who it was you spoke with."

Her encounter the day before had stayed with her since returning to the Okiya that night, much as it did now, her thoughts revisiting that familiar smile in her first moments of waking. Understanding something significant lay in their brief meeting, she struggled to bring her insight forward and stared back at the old woman.

"I spoke with a man, Auntie."

"What man?"

"The man who sold me two rice cakes."

"And no one else, Momoko?"

Momoko hesitated. "No, Auntie," she lied, remaining calm under the old woman's scrutiny. Something within the young Geisha wanted to keep her encounter secret. Holding her reserve, she recalled the happiness felt in sharing her treat. An emotion she longed to experience again.

"And how were those rice cakes?" Auntie raised her eyebrows once more.

"They were lovely thank you, Auntie," Momoko flushed.

Was this was why she had had been called from her bed so early? So she could be berated in front of her younger sister for the reward their guardian had unwittingly paid for?

"Yes, Momoko," Auntie gave her a wry smile. "My visitor this morning told me how much you seemed to enjoy my little treat." The old woman's smile faded. "But, this is not the reason I have called you both to me."

Keiko and Momoko turned to one another once more. Each shared the same confused expression.

"Hanako, Tamiko," Auntie called out.

She glanced back to her young Geisha as they watched their elder sisters enter the room and sidle up beside their former imouto-san.

"Thank you for joining us. Now I can explain my motives behind our small meeting this morning." She looked to each of her charges in turn and then returned to Momoko and Keiko's concerned features.

"It appears your movements were seen yesterday, Momoko," she began. "I too know of your fascination with Tokyo Bay's beauty, and my visitor this morning also witnessed the delight you hold in such a place."

Wondering who had watched her that afternoon, Momoko shifted in her seat, worried the old woman now knew of her secret encounter.

"Yes, Momoko," Auntie continued. "He told me of the purchase you made, and of his surprise in seeing the contemplation you carried looking across the waters there," she paused. "Eastwards towards his home."

"It was the representative?"

"Yes, Momoko. He was the one who knocked on this Okiya door as dawn hours broke, eager to tell me what he observed."

"Why? What else did he see me do?"

Searching for the cause behind her questioning, Auntie frowned at Momoko,

"He would tell me no more than what I have already told you of the matter."

Although aware of the old woman's suspicions, Momoko's worry eased. Seeing Auntie knew nothing of the actions that had brought such joy the previous afternoon, her thoughts returned to the smile encountered from her selfless gift. Momoko felt a possessive hold on those emotions never experienced before and glared back at her guardian, fearful they may be taken from her.

"Then why have you called us here?" She snapped.

Momoko's fellow Geisha paid no attention to her outburst. They had become accustomed to her capricious nature over the years. Also conscious of her protégé's impulsive behaviour, Auntie ignored Momoko's want for answers and prepared her reply.

"Besides your pensive manner yesterday," she continued. "It seems there was another incident my visitor witnessed. Yet once more, of this he would not explain."

Holding Momoko in her sights, Auntie leant forwards.

"Momoko, he told me only of the kindness unseen in his last meeting with yourself."

Tamiko knew the words to come and edged closer to Keiko.

"Whatever you did in your afternoon alone appears to have made quite an impression."

The old woman looked to Keiko.

"My, sweet child," she whispered. "Your kind nature has seen you through your journey to becoming the wonderful Geisha we all knew you would be. But it is for me to tell you that there has been a change of plans."

Watching Tamiko reach for Keiko's hand, Auntie's view returned to her other young Geisha.

"It is now you, Momoko, who has been chosen to leave for America. A decision I received only this morning from your new Danna's representative."

Keiko and Momoko exchanged glances once more.

"But, Auntie," Momoko was first to speak of their news. "I thought Keiko was the one the representative asked for."

"And so she was, Momoko," the old woman told them. "I am sorry Keiko for what I have told you this morning, but my visitor was adamant that Momoko is more suited to the needs of his superior."

Clenching her imouto-san's hand tight Keiko nodded to Auntie's words, her glistening eyes betraying the disappointment she now tried so hard to disguise.

"Do not be sad, Keiko," her older sister smiled. "We are happy that you will remain here with us. Take comfort in how much we would miss you if you were to leave."

Momoko sensed unconditional love flow between the two women. Looking to Auntie and Hanako, she wondered if her presence will now be missed as much as her younger sister's may have been. Turning to Keiko, Momoko leant forward and kissed her cheek.

"I am sorry, Keiko," she said.

Auntie concealed her surprise and saw her other Geisha did likewise.

"Momoko, before I would have questioned the choice that has been made today. Yet I see something within you has changed. I believe now that you shall represent your Okiya well in the years to come amongst others not of our world."

"Thank you, Auntie," Momoko bowed.

Still trying to understand her actions towards the man who had given nothing in return, she looked to the smile playing across Keiko's lips. Emotions seldom felt came to Momoko. She realised her gifts that afternoon had not been in vain, her sister's joy now prompting a slight rush of the same delight experienced besides the waters she would soon travel upon.

Watching the interaction between her young charges, Auntie caught a glimpse of the modesty she had longed to encounter within her treasured Geisha. Momoko's elder sisters saw this also and the old woman saddened that only now such a trait should appear, here in the final moments that would see the departure of the one always considered to be her true heir.

"Momoko, as with Keiko, I have raised you both in the foresight that one day I shall retire from the life that is now yours. I must admit my decisions to who would take my position have wavered throughout the years, yet it seems my selection has been made for me." Auntie glanced to each of the beautiful women present until returning to the one whose looks held the greatest command.

"Momoko, are you happy for your younger sister? Now she has achieved title of Atotori."

"Keiko?"

"Yes, Momoko," the old woman nodded. "She is to be the one who will follow the path that has proved me so well."

"But, Auntie, I thought I was your Atotori?"

"Momoko," the old woman laughed. "And I am sure you would have been a great one at that. But you are to set sail for a new life few of us could ever dream of. Did you really think you could have both?"

Keiko lowered her head. Aware of Momoko's glare she hoped her sister's temper would not rise. The reprisals she had witnessed in their lives together remained etched within her and hoped the prospects of a life shared under the wing of her unnamed Danna would calm that familiar rage. Yet Keiko's initial disappointment in not being the one to enter that new life faded. Realising the responsibility she now held in becoming her guardian's successor, her placid nature faded also and she raised her chin to Momoko. Her defiant expression faltered to Momoko's smile.

"Congratulations, onee-san," Momoko said climbing to her feet.

The Okiya's new Atotori gazed up in awe to the deep bow she now received. Smiling up to her charge with newfound confidence, Keiko too saw the change within the one whose shadow she had always tried to escape.

"Thank you, Momoko," she whispered, confused by the pleasure Momoko gained in seeing her apparent happiness.

Time soon came for Momoko to leave the life she had always known behind.

Sitting with those she had known since a child, the young Geisha looked to the gifts presented on the eve of her departure. Her view fell once more to those who would no longer be a part of her daily existence.

"Thank you, Hanako and Tamiko."

Momoko's hand rested soft on the pure white kimono received from them. Her finger tips brushed over the red kimono besides her older sister's gift and she smiled to her guardian, filling with the memories of the red kimono given in their formative days together.

"And, Auntie. This is beautiful also, thank you."

"It is my pleasure, Momoko. I am sure these shall see you well in your new home. Are you excited?"

"Yes, Auntie."

Concealing her fear in leaving the security of the Okiya, Momoko looked from the empty dishes and plates of their last meal together and then to Keiko.

"I am sure Keiko will become the formidable proprietor this Okiya shall now need without my presence."

"Thank you, Momoko."

Keiko knew her sister's words were true. Momoko had indeed raised the Okiya's standing within Tokyo's Hanamachi district. Without the calls for her charm and unique beauty, Keiko realised the fortitude she would need in up keeping her home's status. Looking to the one she was to soon succeed, she saw the old woman also understood no malice was held in Momoko's words. As with the Auntie, the young Atotori wondered what catalyst had brought about the change in her elder sister. The one she had longed to befriend.

"We shall miss you greatly, Momoko," Hanako reached for the large bottle of sake between them. "Now we must drink to your leaving, so that one day you shall return."

"Do not look so worried, Keiko," Auntie giggled. "Only a few sips this evening."

Keiko joined with the table's laughter as old memories of their last toast together flooded back to her.

"I am glad," she said, warming to the selfless bonds shared amongst those she loved.

"To, Momoko," Auntie raised her cup and waited for her charges to follow. "May your new life give you all you have ever desired."

"And more," Hanako, Tamiko and Keiko chorused.

Draining their sake, each Geisha frowned to the tears falling down Momoko's cheeks. They looked to their guardian for answers to their sister's unexpected display of emotion only to find Auntie's tears fell also. The old woman took her protégé's hand in hers.

"Why is it only now you show us what we have waited for so long, Momoko?" she whispered to her weeping Geisha.

Momoko knew of the unbridled emotions she now portrayed. She did not care. Only one week had passed since her encounter besides the waterfront she was soon to depart and her heart ached for that peace once more. Looking up to the blurry figures sat around her, she wanted so much to tell them of the joy she had experienced, to speak of her unknown pleasure in giving to another. She saw her small family longed to hear those words and Momoko smiled to each of her sisters before looking to the old woman who had raised her with such kindness. Momoko hesitated, years of training in concealing her true thoughts pushing forwards.

"This sake is strong, Auntie," she said, escaping her admissions in the drink they had shared. "Another?"

To the nods of each disappointed face beside her, Momoko poured all a second shot of clear liquor, veiling the frustration held in not sharing her feelings.

Auntie recognised Momoko's wants. She saddened that her protégé had come so close to releasing them. Watching her raise her cup, the old woman remembered the frightened child she had first accompanied through her Okiya doors. She realised that even then Momoko had hidden her true emotions from the eyes of others, a coping mechanism Auntie had witnessed evolve alongside such unparalleled beauty. Aware her want of disclosure had passed, Auntie submitted to the return of Momoko's emotional barriers and leant to her.

"Momoko," she smiled. "I have a surprise concerning your intended journey. It seems that if goes well, you shall arrive in San Francisco on the last day of March."

"On my birthday?"

"Yes, my child. An auspicious day for you to meet the one you have never seen before."

Momoko glanced to her sisters. Seeing they too wondered what her encounter would bring, she turned to her guardian.

"Auntie?"

"Yes, Momoko?"

"Will they have Hanami in America?"

The old woman saddened once again to her young Geisha's words, aware of the bond Momoko held with the pinks and whites that signalled her arrival into this world. Looking to the eyes that had enamoured so many, she worried for the new sights they were to see.

"That I do not know, Momoko," the old woman drew on her own skills of masked emotions.

"But I do know you are to see many wonderful things. I have I told you of the stop you shall make one month before reaching your new Danna?"

"No, Auntie," a smile returned to Momoko's lips. "Where?"

Auntie looked to her other Geisha. "Hawaii," she announced.

"Hawaii?"

"Yes, Momoko, but do not get too excited. Your ship will only dock there for a short time to take its new passengers onwards to your final destination, yet you will have the opportunity to see the places I have always longed to see for myself."

Seeing the delight in her features, the old woman was satisfied she dispelled some of Momoko's doubt towards her forthcoming journey.

"Momoko, it is late. Tomorrow we must rise early to leave for the harbour." Auntie's joy faded and she climbed to her feet. "It is now time to say goodbye to your sisters."

As the remainder of the room stood also, Momoko walked to her elder sisters and fell into their warm embrace.

"Be careful," Hanako whispered.

"Yes, Momoko, take care," Tamiko joined her sister's sentiments.

Nodding up to each of them, Momoko turned and watched Keiko run from the room. Frowning to her actions, she smiled as her younger sister soon returned, her hands held behind her back.

"Momoko," she said. "I have something for you."

Keiko brought her hands forward and smiled down to the gift. "Would you like her to come with you?"

Auntie watched Momoko smile to Keiko and take the treasured doll from her palms.

"Thank you, Keiko," she whispered, pulling its red dress to her. "I will look after her, I promise."

Fighting her want to weep once more that night, Momoko wrapped her arms around Keiko, both unaware of the silent tears surrounding them.

Auntie stepped back as her young charges broke apart.

"Come now, all of you," the old woman smiled to each of her Geisha. "I am sure we shall hold Momoko close to us once again."

Hanako and Tamiko wiped their eyes and bowed to their guardian.

"Good luck, Momoko," they said before walking from her.

"Yes, good luck," Keiko echoed. She hovered for a moment and then with a final bow, followed her sisters to leave Momoko and Auntie alone.

Glancing over the deserted table they had shared so often, Momoko turned to Auntie in silence. The old woman met with the frightened eyes encountered long ago.

"My beautiful, Momoko," she bowed to her cherished young Geisha. "Now you are ready."

Momoko leant across the ship's rail and peered down to the harbour below. Watching the old woman's cheeks glisten in early morning sun, she smiled a silent goodbye, longing to be held in those arms for one last time.

Knowing this would not happen, her thoughts were confirmed as engines rumbled to life beneath her. Looking to her guardian once more she understood their time together had come to an end.

"Goodbye, Auntie." she whispered as the ship edged away from its temporary home, her tears matching those of the one who had steered her towards the life she now departed for.

Pulling the collars of Auntie's treasured jacket around her neck, Momoko found some comfort in the old woman's final gift to her. Breathing in its familiar scent she considered her unknown future without her guidance. Thoughts of her sisters came to her also in those moments and she wondered how her life would now be without them.

Recalling the hidden emotions she had revealed during their last meal together, Momoko searched once more for the catalyst that had triggered such feelings within her.

Momoko felt some guilt that she had not upheld her promise to revisit the man who carried the same smile as she. The days between their meeting had advanced so quick in preparation for the journey she now embarked, giving her no time to return to the joy experienced that afternoon. The memory of her encounter had not left the young Geisha and she had anticipated seeing him again as she and Auntie had walked together to the harbour that morning for their final goodbye.

As the Tokyo dockside drifted away, Momoko looked one last time to Auntie's small figure. Raising her arm high, she waved and giggled to the exaggerated gesture received in return. Tears fell from the young Geisha realising how she would miss the humour and kindness she had come to accept from that wise old woman over the years.

With all she knew flowing from her, Momoko glanced across the bay. Her eyes widened to the small arm waving to her.

"Is that you?" she questioned, straining to make out the second figure's farewell to her. Momoko smiled on recognising his ragged blanket and its display of small fish. The same bliss encountered on their first meeting returned and she waved back to the man who had taught her so much in such little time.

"And goodbye to you too," she whispered out to him, a sadness entering her young soul that their time together had proved so brief as both he and Auntie faded from sight.

Auntie wiped her cheeks as Momoko disappeared from her view. Turning from the pacific waters her unique young Geisha now sailed, the old woman glanced to the one who had also seen to her departure that morning. She wondered of the exchange Momoko and the man had shared.

Looking to the bustling market place behind her she walked from his stare. Alone in her thoughts, she knew what she was to buy and headed for the stall she too would often frequent.

The old woman returned to the waterfront, her hands warmed by the brown paper package in her hands. Looking out once more for a glimpse of Momoko's ship she raised the package to her and breathed in the aroma of hot rice cakes, the treat that reminded her so much of the one who had now gone from her life.

"Momoko, be safe," Auntie whispered out to her and then walked to the man fishing for his meagre days catch further along the harbour.

On her approach, Auntie looked to the deep scar that had caused such heartache, her memories of those times producing their usual pain of regret and sorrow. The man smiled on seeing his visitor near and set down the makeshift fishing rod he would use each morning. He bowed to the old woman and smiled once more.

"Hello," Auntie returned his gesture. Her heart sank to the familiar smile before her.

"Any luck this morning?" She asked.

Beaming back to her, he pointed out to the ocean and to the small dot on its horizon.

"Yes, I know," Auntie handed him the two small rice cakes. "She has her mother's eyes," she whispered as he unwrapped the delicacy she had brought to him every week for the past twenty-three years.

In her first several weeks on board ship, Momoko often thought of her encounter on Tokyo's waterfront, as did she of Auntie and the sisters she now missed so much. Alone in her cabin at night, she would fall asleep clutching Keiko's doll tight to her chest, longing for the familiar smells and sounds of the Okiya. Waking each morning those memories would fade as she resigned to the unknown life ahead of her.

Lying in her bed Momoko thought of the Danna she had yet to meet, wondering how she would be treated by such a man. In her own experience, those with the wealth and status admired by so many, seldom carried the kindness her previous guardian held. Her returning doubts only added to the loneliness Momoko experienced in her daily life on those Pacific waters, her seclusion enhanced by the reaction of her fellow passengers to her presence.

Momoko was more than used to the unwanted attention of men. Since her days as an apprentice, she had known the power her looks commanded. The interest of others had always been confined to Tokyo's male dominated tea houses and banquets and the dynamics of those settings had now changed. Where once she would have laughed and talked freely with these men, her observers shied away from such pastimes, dissuaded by the jealous wives a their side.

Momoko could cope with the looks of distain she received each day. She did not care for the frumpy middle-aged women whose eyes held such venom. Using the skills imbedded within her, Momoko would pass the time smiling to their errant husbands, and then, when their yearning view became distracted by said wives, Momoko would use her infamous glare to discourage any reprisal from those envious of the beauty she held.

Aware her actions proved for a lonely life, eating unaccompanied every day became customary to her, as did the afternoons spent alone in her cabin studying the English books Auntie had given her so she may converse with her future patron.

It would not be until evening when Momoko glimpsed the foolishness in her games, when she would watch a golden sun melt into the horizon, alone with no one to share its beauty.

Those solitary days passed with relative ease as Momoko's strength came from traits learnt as a child, finding comfort in the belief that she needed no-one and no-one needed her. The ways that had served so well in the past waned in the memory of the smile identical to her own.

Looking to the mirror each night before bed, Momoko's recollections of the joy she had felt that day on Tokyo's harbour front would surface in the smiling reflection before her. Although those insights were brief, it proved enough for Momoko to gain some hope towards her uncertain future. A future she was aware may also provide her unspoken needs. For something deep within the young Geisha called for the companionship which had always eluded her.

Soon the moment Momoko anticipated arrived and she looked to the crystal clear waters surrounding the island before her. From her solitary position on the ship's prom, the young Geisha hoped at least one of the new passengers bound for America would pay her some attention.

"Hawaii," she whispered, smiling out to the lush green hillsides so similar to the ones she had once known as her ship nudged against its new moorings.

Auntie's words that their stop would be brief proved true. No sooner had the ship's new intake boarded its engines reached their monotonous pitch once more.

Watching those figures step up onto their new home the young Geisha's heart sank in seeing only the familiar round faces of her American counterparts. Turning from their arrival, she paused and looked back for a final time, optimistic in the search for her elusive companion. Momoko gasped. Peering closer to the cropped black hair amongst a sea of blonde, she smiled on seeing the same almond shaped eyes she was accustomed to. Her smile dropped as their owner caught her gaze. She recognised his frightened stare. Looking to the emotions she experienced also, any hope of an escort for the rest of her journey dissolved as she glanced down to the burgundy robes he wore. Momoko knew the young monk's calling far reached the needs of her own.

For her remaining voyage, Momoko watched the young monk from afar, feeling some guilt when his view returned her curious stare with a shyness that intrigued the young Geisha. Fascinated by his presence, Momoko considered why it was he travelled alone and had made his destination the same as hers.

Standing alone on deck each evening she would watch the sunset play out before her, longing for him to join her so they could talk and maybe laugh together. Those wishes never surfaced and with some sorrow Momoko accepted their meeting was not to be. Although this did not dispel her interest in the mysterious young monk and she would often consider what it was he did in the endless hours spent alone all day in his own small cabin.

On the morning of Momoko's twenty-fourth birthday she looked from her cabin's small window to the land that was to be her new home. Considering once more if San Francisco played host to the cherry blossom season celebrating her day, Momoko's thoughts returned to those from the past who had accompanied her beneath newly formed buds of pink and white.

"Happy birthday," she whispered turning to the room's small mirror and checked the elaborate hairstyle she had spent the previous day preparing. Looking to Auntie's red kimono she smiled, aware once more of the beauty she possessed.

"Your Danna will love you," Momoko's reflection smiled, yet the young Geisha could not escape the uncertainty in the eyes staring back at her.

"He will," she reassured and reached a hand out to steady herself as the ship came to a stop, signalling the arrival of her destination. With a final glance to her appearance, Momoko lifted her small bag from the bed and made her way towards her unknown fate.

From the ship's prom, Momoko ignored the attention her formal Geisha attire produced as she waited for those from the lower decks to depart. Watching the ones who had once despised her presence, Momoko raised her chin in defiance for the esteem her fellow passengers now held towards her, empowering the young Geisha with confidence for her approaching encounter.

"Now you see," she whispered down to the milling crowds below. Her pride faltered to the smile she received in return.

Momoko's fascination returned and she smiled back to the young monk, disappointed they had not shared a moment together no matter how brief. Pulling his burgundy robes over his shoulder the young monk nodded up in recognition of her wants.

Something within the young Geisha called her to run to the smiling figure, to be close to him in a way she could not understand. She hesitated. Remembering her patron and the duty such concerns held, she bowed to her unknown friend and watched with regret as he smiled to her once more before becoming lost in the busy harbour crowds.

Watching those crowds disperse, she took a deep breath and walked towards dry land. Edging forwards, she tried to catch a final glimpse of the young monk. Her disappointment returned and she sighed. Collecting her thoughts as to the reasons for her arrival to the new land spread out before her, Momoko submitted to the fact that their meeting was not to be.

On stepping closer towards her unknown destiny the young Geisha wondered what such an encounter may have produced.

CHAPTER EIGHTEEN

Within one hour of Tenzin's return there was a loud rap on his bedroom door.

"Lama Tenzin," the young apprentice stared up at him. "Lama Norbu wants to see you in the Grand Hall straight away."

Thanking his messenger, Tenzin prepared himself for his calling, finding it strange that his presence was required so soon.

He was aware of Nyima's enthusiasm to hear of his latest travels to the Tibetan midlands outer reaches, but those tales would usually be recounted over a hearty supper within Lama Norbu's quarters, never in the sacred chambers he had been asked to go to now. Changing into fresh robes, the young monk paused on leaving his room. Confused by his peer's wants, he glanced back to his room's small window and then climbed up onto his bed to see if the courtyard below provided any answers.

The courtyard below remained the same as he had always known and he allowed himself a moment to recall his first days in Tashilhunpo when he had peered down to his new home much the same way he did now. Those times seemed lost to him now, so much had changed as the years had passed and he considered what that young frightened child would have thought then if he knew of his destiny to come.

Looking to the classrooms he longed to return to, Tenzin thought of his students and the joys his own heart would gain in being before them once again. Turning from the scene, the young monk's thoughts fell back to Lama Norbu and with some trepidation he left his room to meet with his cherished guardian.

Walking through the candle lit corridor anxiety filled Tenzin as

Ketu's pitiful features came to him in his thoughts. The guilt he recalled harbouring since their last encounter flooded back to him and by the time he reached the passageway's end his heart filled with remorse for his actions that day.

Never before had he dismissed the compassion ingrained within him. For a slight moment he considered returning back to the monastery entrance so he may make amends for his lack of empathy. Torn between Ketu's needs and Lama Norbu's call for his attendance, Tenzin glanced back to Tashilhunpo's opening and then to the Grand Hall's gilded eaves. Would his guardian understand if he arrived late? Would the old monk appreciate the reasons why he had been kept waiting? Tenzin once more battled his emotions as to where his intentions lay.

"Ketu can wait," he whispered as he continued across the courtyard, his hopes that Ketu still sat beneath Tashilhunpo's walls pushing him forwards to meet with his guardian.

Walking into the Grand Hall, Tenzin saw not only the old monk, but also Nyima and the other Lamas sat waiting patiently for his arrival. Bowing to each in turn, he tried to understand the reasoning behind Lama Norbu and his peer's solemn features.

"Tenzin," the old monk said. "Thank you for joining us so soon, now maybe you can tell us your thoughts on compassion."

Startled by Lama Norbu's sudden request, Tenzin view ran across the aged Lamas before him. Not understanding their severe manner, he straightened and looked to Nyima.

"Yes, Lama Tenzin," the Panchen Lama smiled. "What are your views on the core of our beliefs?"

Glancing to Lama Norbu, the old monk's nod gave Tenzin the courage to speak, yet in his heart he knew the reasons behind his questioning within the Grand Hall that day. Turning back to Nyima, the young monk bowed once more and began to recount his philosophies behind what proved his life's work.

"Compassion is forgiveness," Tenzin smiled. Seeing his audience did not share his sentiments, Tenzin realised the seriousness surrounding him and suppressed his smiles as he continued. "Forgiveness with understanding, Panchen Lama. Without this our souls cannot progress onwards to that which we all reach."

"And what is it that we reach for, my child," Lama Norbu asked.

"We reach for that moment when we hold great reverence to all that lives and breathes. Without thinking we become one with all we know, giving us an understanding to the reasons behind the motives and actions of others."

"And then?"

"And then, Master, the suffering we hold within our hearts is released in the forgiveness we give to others as we learn to forgive ourselves and our own misdeeds."

Silence descended over the preceding, broken only by the hushed whispers between each Lama present. Tenzin watched his guardian listen to his fellow holy men's views before turning his attention back to him.

"Tenzin, the words you have spoken today match the thoughts and beliefs we all cherish within the life we have chosen to lead."

"Thank you, Lama Norbu."

Tenzin's stomach churned as the old monk raised a hand to silence his gratitude.

"Yet, Tenzin. Although you reveal what your heart has always known. Your fellow Lamas and I cannot understand why you have betrayed that which your soul seems to treasure."

Tenzin lowered his head, looking to his feet he knew of what his guardian now spoke. As his awareness grew as to the reasons for his summoning, Ketu's haggard features returned to haunt him for the second time that day.

"Yes, Tenzin," Lama Norbu nodded. "Your actions towards the one who at one time caused such suffering were witnessed. Tell me, young Lama, why did you not demonstrate what you have told us here today to that poor wretched soul?"

His redemption surfaced in the tears falling in a steady stream from the corners of his eyes. Wiping his cheeks, Tenzin fought to find his composure in the eyes of the audience who awaited their answer.

"I do not know," he replied, his words lost within in the stares before him.

"I tried so hard, but I could not forget the harm Ketu had caused to us all so long ago."

"That maybe so," the old monk nodded. His eyes softening to his young apprentice's admission, he glanced to the young Panchen Lama at his side and spoke once more.

"We too recall the suffering young Ketu's soul bestowed on us all.

But, Tenzin, what emotions do you see your peer's hold towards the child's spiteful acts?"

Once again Tenzin's view flowed across aged wise faces. His conscious eased as he watched each Lama smile back to him, giving the young monk an understanding towards his own actions. Seeing the release they held in forgiving the one who had caused such suffering to them, Tenzin's compassionate soul resurfaced and his heart returned to the characteristics he had known since taking his first footsteps on this earth.

"I understand," he said. "My actions towards Ketu were indeed wrong and have only caused my soul to feel the same suffering evident in his own."

"Yes, young Lama, now you value of what you speak. By understanding the root of Ketu's suffering, you in turn now see why his malicious acts harm all those around him. Is it no wonder his mind has become lost within the turmoil and torment in the years his own suffering had produced?"

"Yes," Tenzin whispered.

Looking back to the wooden floorboards beneath him, he began to see how his own suffering had only been brought about by not absolving the resentment held towards his former charge. Recalling Ketu's misplaced stares, the young monk began to feel the empathy lost within him, his compassion towards his adversary's wicked ways pushing forwards on sensing his heartfelt forgiveness flourish. Ketu had indeed become what his soul produced. As Tenzin considered a life holding such sorrow, his sympathy led to the full compassion his heart had searched for since Ketu's exile from Tashilhunpo's grounds.

"Yes, Tenzin," the young Panchen Lama recognised his friend's eternal comprehension. "It is now you see that your actions this day gave nothing to aid the recovery of what has been lost to young Ketu. Are you now aware how your forgiveness would have shown a kindness that may have guided his misplaced soul to find the tranquillity we ourselves experience?"

Warmed by the Panchen Lama's smile, Tenzin looked to those sat beside Nyima and fell into their familiar loving gaze. Realising the compassion they now gave to him for his own callous actions his thought returned to Ketu.

No longer did he see his childhood foe as the malevolent spirit he was accustomed to, now Ketu's tormented features were replaced by the lost soul the young monk knew him to be and his heart filled with empathy for him. Once again, Lama Norbu witnessed Tenzin's understanding. Encouraged by his fellow Lama's approval, the old monk stepped forwards.

"Tenzin," he said. "Today you have learnt a great lesson. One we are all sure you have always known." The old monk glanced back to his peer's smiles before returning to Tenzin. "However, young Lama, your actions towards Ketu cannot be disregarded. You yourself and the position you hold should have produced the forgiveness and compassion expected within you." Tenzin frowned as his guardian glanced back to Nyima. The Panchen Lama's smile faded as he nodded to the old monk and Tenzin's disquiet returned as the Lama Norbu sighed.

"Young Tenzin, your brother's and I must now deliberate the actions we must take towards your misdemeanour." The old monk pointed to the Grand Hall's doors. "Please, my child, you must leave us now so we may consider our options towards your unknown future. We shall call for you when ready."

It would be two hours before Tenzin was summoned back to meet with those he revered within the Grand Hall once more. The young monk had spent his time sitting alone beneath its entrances golden statues of those whose path he followed.

Considering if he should revisit the ragged beggar so he may show the new found compassion instilled within him, Tenzin had decided not to take such an action, his heart wanting to stay close to the chambers of those he feared he would soon be asked to leave.

Tenzin's remorse remained tantamount to the one broken from years of embittered torment. His optimism for Ketu's recovery left him as he stood before the Lama's grave faces once again. Determined not to lose his stare to the floorboards beneath him, the young monk raised his head and gazed over to his guardian. His body straightened so he may retain his dignity on hearing of his fate.

Lama Norbu recognised Tenzin's tenacious spirit. With memories of his old friend triggered by the young monk's posture, he raised a smile, ready to speak with the young apprentice who had brought such joy into his life.

"Thank you once more, Tenzin for joining us again," he began. "We have discussed a possible future for you so you may learn of that which you have forgotten. We have made many choices towards the teaching your soul requires. All seated here before you understand that you are aware of your transgression, as am I. Yet we have chosen for you to continue with the teaching of others you carry out so well."

Tenzin's shoulders fell and a lone tear escaped his worried eyes.

"Thank you," he whispered out to his peers.

"Do not thank us so soon, young Lama," the old monk looked to those sat beside him. "It is true that we could never bring an end to the lessons of hope and optimism you give to all those you encounter, but we are aware there lies a greater amount of people who are in need of your words."

"But I already travel for miles to reach those you talk of. I do not know where else I can go to please your decisions."

"Tenzin," Nyima said. "We are more than thankful for your contributions in the towns and villages far from Tashilhunpo's walls. The place we have chosen for you to continue your good work lies further from where even Lama Norbu here has ever ventured."

"Yes, young Lama," the old monk continued. "We have many brothers there already who would only be happy for you to join them."

"Where? Where is this place I am to go?" Tenzin asked, not knowing which of his emotions to follow.

The thought of leaving his home for another grieved the young monk, yet his want for adventure and travel melded with his sorrow. "Where?" He asked again.

"It is not the question of where your destination lies. Do you not understand that it is the journey which is more important?"

"Yes, Tenzin," the young Panchen Lama joined the old monk. "Your travels towards your objective may give you an insight into the compassion mislaid to the one who needed such sentiments."

Tenzin began to realise the reasons behind his intended trip. Watching the other Lama's Tenzin nodded.

"I understand," he said "Tell me Lama Norbu, where am I to go?"

The old monk's tears pushed forwards from the sorrow he now held.

"America, young Lama," he said. "The city of San Francisco."

In the two weeks respite before partaking on his journey to the continent he knew little of, Tenzin studied the books given to him of the unknown language he would soon need. Joined by Lama Norbu and Nyima, those days were filled with laughter as each helped the young monk achieve the words and sounds so alien to them all.

Tenzin showed great promise in his grasp of his new found dialect, although his eagerness to speak to others who knew such words in no way masked the sorrow he experienced in leaving his cherished friends and home.

The young monk understood the reasons behind his looming departure. Even in the darkest moments leading up to his leaving, the awareness Tenzin held towards his travels calmed any unease his soul touched upon. With his thoughts remaining with his encounter with Ketu, each day he had searched for the beggar outside Tashilhunpo's walls. To no avail did his hunt produce the forgiveness he yearned to portray bringing Tenzin a deeper understanding towards his trials ahead.

Ketu's absence meant his soul must continue the compassion once lost from him, leaving his own thoughts to do so without his wrongdoer's physical presence before him. This he knew would prove greater in the long run, something that would see him through his journey to come.

As the day came for Tenzin to take his first steps from Tashilhunpo, he bid farewell to Tibet's ninth Panchen Lama and his fellow Lamas, wondering when he would speak with them again. Looking down to gold coins given to him to aid his travels eastwards, Tenzin looked to the old monk walking at his side who had chosen to escort him to Tashilhunpo's doors.

"Those should serve you well, my child," Lama Norbu smiled.

"That they should," Tenzin replied.

Placing the coins carefully into the shoulder bag that had seen him through many journeys before, he considered how and where his new found currency would find a home within his intended passage to come.

Walking together in silence both neared the outside world and stopped beneath the monastery's large wooden doorframe.

"I can go no further, Tenzin," Lama Norbu said.

Looking out to the distant horizon he turned to his apprentice.

"It seems only yesterday you entered these gates for the first time, and now I see to your leaving."

"But, I shall return, will I not?"

"Oh yes, my child," the old monk laughed. "I know for certain we shall sit together once more."

Watching Tenzin ease to his words, he reached forwards and held the young monk he would miss dearly. Tenzin fell into his embrace, his spirit warmed by the love Lama Norbu instilled within him.

"Now you are ready to face the adventure ahead of you," the old monk smiled as they broke free.

"Thank you, Lama Norbu."

"No thanks are needed, young Lama. For my heart tells me there is a reason for the journey you are to take, maybe another's soul shall teach you that which you have yet to learn."

Sensing Tenzin's attempts to conceal his fears towards that unknown fate, Lama Norbu knew it was time to give his young apprentice his parting gift. Reaching into his robes he produced what had been intended for him.

"Here, Tenzin, we here at Tashilhunpo have decided that maybe this shall enhance a new understanding towards your past actions."

Tenzin stared down at the familiar package resting in his guardian's wrinkled hand. Recognising it as the gift he had refused from Ketu's own hands, he reached out and took the package, wondering what lay within its ragged cloth wrapping,

"Open that which you once refused, Tenzin," the old monk encouraged. "Only then may you see what your own salvation may have missed."

Tenzin began to carefully unwrap his gift. His heart sank to what he found within its tattered bindings.

"This was what Ketu tried to give me that day?" He asked, his eyes not leaving the roughly fashioned wooden flute.

"It seems that Ketu's bedraggled mind managed to remember his spiteful act towards you from many years ago."

"Ketu made this? For me?"

"Yes, Tenzin. By his toil in trying to replace that which he once took from you, can you see the compassion lost within his soul resurface in his actions?"

"Yes, Lama Norbu."

Tenzin's shame was brought forward by the heart felt gift lying in his hands.

The old monk recognised his young apprentice's remorse and

smiled, hopeful the flute's notes would provide Tenzin with the insights he required.

"Good luck, young Lama," he bowed to his charge.

Returning his respects, Tenzin saddened as his guardian turned from him and made his way back to sit within the Grand Hall he himself longed to be. Looking down to Ketu's gift, the young monk placed the flute with care into his bag and stared ahead. With a deep breath, he glanced back once to Tashilhunpo's golden rooftops before taking his first footsteps towards his unknown destiny.

Travelling with ease over Tibet's southern regions, Tenzin steered clear of his home town of Gyantse. The young monk's uncertainty to his welcome there still remained and he pushed away unwanted emotions once more as he continued his route through Sakya and Tingri's familiar streets. Within one week of leaving Tashilhunpo's walls, he reached Nepal's border.

Glad of his guardian's advice to walk with those of his own kind, Tenzin felt some relief as he mingled with the Tibetan traders who would see to his safe passage towards Kathmandu. Resting for one night in the Nepal's capital city, Tenzin's lost enthusiasm towards his journey returned. The gold coins in his bag proving their worth, with a new found vigour the young monk trekked southwards, his heart anticipating his arrival to India's vast lands he never before imagined he would step foot upon.

Crossing into that mystical country, Tenzin's presence was readily accepted. Finding no animosity from those who looked so different to him, his smiles returned, bringing hope to all those encountered as he walked the banks of the Hoogly river towards Digha, the harbour side town resting at the mouth of the Ganges which would see his departure from his own continent.

As Tenzin walked alone, his thoughts would return to the monastery that had proved the foundations of all he knew. Enjoying his travels towards that which he did not know lay ahead, the young monk could not help but think of the small community he had left behind where he had known every soul and every soul had known he.

Aware his journey was more than necessary, Tenzin's memories of laughing with Nyima and Lama Norbu would enter his dreams as he slept, causing some heartache on waking the next day and remembering his solitary quest. Yet so many things now surrounding the young monk gave cause for him to continue his passage.

It seemed strange for Tenzin to walk in warm sunlight. Tibet's harsh winter months were all he had ever known, and now as November approached, he at times wished for the snows that would alleviate the mounting heat he met with on his push southwards.

In the knowledge that his first intended route would have provided a similar climate from the one he now encountered, once again the young monk was thankful for Lama Norbu's directions. The wise Lama's concerns for Tenzin's safety were revealed on talking of the dangers should he decided to travel through China's plains.

Reaching the beginning of Hoogly's waters, he entered Digha's town walls. Delighted in the greetings he received from its kind community, his burgundy robes ignited the reverence its community held for their own many Gods and Deity's.

Spending two days waiting for the ship that would carrying him onwards towards his destination, Tenzin relished his time amid Digha's townsfolk, his heart recalling Tashilhunpo's corridors and passageways as he marvelled up to their sculptures and bright colourful relief's of Gods and Goddesses so different to his own.

With some sorrow the young monk left the ones who had shown such kindness to the stranger he knew he was, unaware how his smiles repaid his debt as he waved to them from the stern of the ship he now boarded.

Amazed by the vast waters spread out before him and knowing most of the people of his own landlocked country had never witnessed such a sight, Tenzin soon became accustomed to the searing heat he met with as he sailed south eastwards across the Bay of Bengal. By the first days of December he reached the Malaysian peninsular and his met with his introduction to the Pacific's immeasurable waters. Yet with all Tenzin's optimism and fortitude, there would be one unseen destination which brought a new unbridled fear to the young monk's heart.

On the eve of a new century, deep anxiety came to Tenzin as his ship steered into Shanghai's chaotic harbours. Ignoring the celebrations which marked the end of 1899's last day sounding through his quarters, the young monk hid within his cabin as Lama Norbu's stories of the Chinese government's want to take his Tibetan homelands for themselves hounded his thoughts. He had not considered his journey would take him into the heart of the nation that for centuries had already attempted to do such a thing.

Not daring to leave his sanctuary to discover how long they would remain within China's dangerous harbour, Tenzin remained hidden in his cabin, the worn wooden beads he had worn since child his only company. Flicking each bead across finger and thumb, Tenzin's mind reached out to the safety he recalled sitting between Lama Norbu and their treasured Panchen Lama.

The memories of their time together eased the young monk's soul and soon his recollections drifted to play within his dreams as he succumbed to much need sleep.

Waking the next morning to the ship's engines familiar rumble beneath his berth, Tenzin stared down to the necklace held tight within his hand, and rising from his bunk, he tentatively looked from his cabin's small window. On seeing the expanse of blue green water stretched out to the horizon before him the relief Tenzin encountered on escaping the clutches of his enemy enhanced his want to continue onwards and he anticipated his next stop before meeting with his unknown brothers in America.

As the new century reached the first day of its third month, the young monk stepped onto the island unheard of in his own country. Glad to be on dry land once more, he looked to the lush greenery covering the surrounding hills of the place they called Hawaii.

Watching the ship that had brought him in safety to the island on which he now stood sail from him, Tenzin took pleasure in his respite from life at sea, wondering how he would fill his time in the week ahead before his new ship arrived to take him onwards to America.

As he explored his new brief home, never before had he seen such foliage and he marvelled in the delight its alien fruits carried, wishing his peers could only taste the sweet pineapple and mango he discovered lining the serene beaches he now spent his time sitting upon.

Using his time wisely, Tenzin would fall into the medative states he had tried to master since a boy. With all the new sights surrounding him, his thoughts would flow into the space reserved for the clear blue skies he imagined above him.

Looking onto Hawaii's gentle lapping waves, Tenzin considered another way as to reach the peace of mind evading his soul. From past experience he knew the one thing which would aid that want for a calm mind. For the first time since Lama Norbu's warm farewell embrace, Tenzin took Ketu's flute from his bag.

Looking to its rough holes gauged into the hollowed wooden piece, Tenzin recalled the reasons for his journey halfway across the world into the unknown. Studying Ketu's craftsmanship closer, he saw the love and care put into the makeshift instrument. The young monk's shame returned in refusing his adversary's souls attempt at reconciliation.

Tenzin raised the flute to his lips not knowing what noise its crude form would make. He smiled on hearing its pitch.

Surprised by the quality in its tone, Tenzin realised that with only some minor adjustments, Ketu's gift to him would soon emit the same melodies his grandfather had played.

Thinking of the treasured flute his former charge had destroyed, Lama Norbu's wise features came to Tenzin, he realised the reasons behind the old monk's ideas. He understood how his own work on the instrument would maybe bring his and Ketu's soul together at last. Placing the flute back into his bag, Tenzin vowed to make the instrument rival his grandfather's sweet tones on his final passage towards San Francisco's forthcoming port, and once again considered the auspicious meaning behind arriving at his destination on the day marking his twenty-fourth year.

The morning soon arrived when Tenzin would make the last leg of his journey. Hoisting his robes across his shoulder, he looked to the new ship that would take him onwards towards his unknown fate.

Reaching its gang plank, the young monk glanced back to the island which had proved the re-emergence of his lost compassion. Looking to the endless green forests he had come to know and love, the young monk turned from what once had been his pleasure and stepped forward with his fellow passengers.

Fear gripped Tenzin as he looked to the sea of blonde hair surrounding him. It was then he realised the enormity his trip entailed and he stared up to his ships other travellers in hope of finding the same almond shaped eyes he was accustomed to. He paused on seeing that which he sought. Any relief he held faltered as he saw the same fear within the beautiful young woman who now caught his gaze. Watching her striking eyes fall to his burgundy robes, he averted his gaze from the sheer beauty and presence the young Geisha held and made his way to his small cabin he had secured with one of Tashilhunpo's favoured gold coins.

Tenzin stayed within his cabin for most of the remainder of his journey, his soul determined to perfect Ketu's gift so it may one day play the tunes that brought happy memories of the home so far from him now. Leaving only to eat from the ships dining rooms, he would not stay amongst those who stared endlessly to the strange robes so different to their own attire.

The young monk would smile, understanding how his presence seemed so mysterious to others unaccustomed to his fellow countrymen's ways. Feeling no animosity towards their unwanted stares, he too noticed the fascination the beautiful young Geisha held towards him whenever their gaze crossed. Wondering the reasons behind her own travels to a new land, Tenzin would watch his observer stand on their ships highest deck each evening, his heart feeling the sorrow her eyes portrayed as she stood alone before magnificent sunsets of orange and red.

As the morning of Tenzin's twenty-fourth birthday arrived, he looked from his cabin's small window. Seeing San Francisco's port loom in the distance, the anticipation towards the end of his journey filled Tenzin with fresh hope towards his future.

Lifting his bag across his shoulder, he walked from his cabin and made for the expectant crowds waiting to alight the ship and onto dry land once more.

Feeling the ship bump across its new moorings, Tenzin steadied himself and looked once again to the faces around him. Wondering how many of these strangers were now departing for a new life also, he followed their gaze up to the ships second tier.

Seeing the beautiful young woman who shared the same eyes as he, Tenzin smiled to the soul he regretted having not shared a moment with. As the young Geisha smiled back to him, the young monk's remorse increased on seeing the mysterious young woman housed those very same sentiments as he. Pulling his robes across his shoulder, he nodded to her once in recognition of her wants.

Enchanted by the bow he received in return from the young Geisha, the young monk smiled back to her for a final time before becoming lost within the crowds of San Francisco's busy harbour.

Stepping onto American soil for the first time, Tenzin looked back to where he had last seen the young woman. He saddened on seeing she was no longer there.

With some disappointed he continued onwards, his heart considering what fate their encounter may have produced.

CHAPTER NINETEEN

Momoko stepped onto dry land and looked once more for the mysterious young monk she had felt so drawn towards. Staring through the harbour front's thinning crowds, her optimism faded on seeing his memorable deep red robes were nowhere to be seen.

The young Geisha sighed and glanced back to her former floating home. The security she had found within its small cabin began to dwindle, replaced by an anxiety now welling in the pit of her stomach. Ignoring her want to return to the home she had always known, Momoko pushed away memories of the Okiya, her sisters and Auntie's kindness. Turning from the ship that would have seen safe passage back to Tokyo's familiar streets, Momoko raised her head high and continued onwards to meet with her unknown fate.

Walking from San Francisco's waterfront, Momoko became aware of the attention her presence gave. Passing by those who vied for her affections with bawdy calls and whistles, Momoko disregarded the welcomed interest she received. The young Geisha suppressed her smiles. She knew these men were of no use to her, not now the promise of life surrounded by her prospective Danna's riches lay ahead. With thoughts of a future filled with the delights and pleasures she had always longed for, Momoko left the Pacific's gentle lapping waters behind and looked to her new home's steep streets and cable cars.

Taking the small map from her bag, Momoko stared down to the directions her Danna's representative had given to her. Finding it strange she had not been met on disembarking from her long voyage, the young Geisha gave no further thought to her lack of greeting party and smiled. She understood how her new position still retained the secrecy her life's work contained, even here, thousands of miles away from the tea houses and banquets she knew so well.

Momoko delighted in the sense of adventure rushing through her thoughts. Not only was she heading towards the pampered life style she and her fellow Geisha's dreamed of, but now there was an added twist to the pleasures awaiting her. Looking down to the map's neat pencil lined streets, Momoko quickly gained her bearings and began to follow its directions, enjoying her quest with a curiosity she knew she had always held.

Walking onwards, Momoko sensed the stares beside her. Wondering if there were others like herself hidden somewhere within the city streets she now climbed the young Geisha's confidence grew. If this was the awed reception she received from each stranger she passed by, then what kind of welcome was she soon to receive from the one who called for her services? With these thoughts, Momoko strode onwards, her expression not faltering once in the anticipation of her intended encounter.

Reaching the street's summit, Momoko stood and looked to the city spread out below her. Once again considering if other Geishas had walked the same path as her, Momoko's gaze fell to the docklands to which she had arrived. Anxiety returned across her torso as she watched her ship rest at its temporary port. Knowing the vessel would soon leave back towards her homelands on the stroke of midnight, loneliness entered the young Geisha as she hampered for the world of women she was so accustomed to. Looking to the harbour's crystal blue waters, memories of moments shared within the Okiya confirmed she was now alone and she recalled her voyage to where she now stood.

Although her hours had been spent alone, those solitary days had caused reflection to surface within the young Geisha's heart.

Remembering the life now left behind, there was one from her past which would fill the majority of those memories. Recalling her last weeks before knowing of her intended journey to American shores, the image of the mute fisherman who had shared her rice cakes on Tokyo's harbour front came to her often. From her small cabin, the young Geisha longed for the joy experienced in her selfless act, considering the true identity of the one whose smile mirrored her own and found their way into her dreams each night.

Momoko looked back to the docklands and thought of another whose presence had touched her so. Although not a word had been shared between the two, the young monk's recognition towards her only hours before filled Momoko with regret that she had not followed her heart and raced after him.

Not understanding the attraction she held towards the robed stranger, Momoko shook her head and stared back down to the map held tight in her hands.

"Remember the reasons why you are here," she told herself.

Dismissing her foolish notions of maybe seeing the young monk again, Momoko's thoughts returned to the rich patron awaiting her arrival and once again began to follow the directions towards her proposed future.

Walking street after street, Momoko considered the riches that lay ahead of her. No matter how hard she tried to picture her future unknown benefactor, another's features would come to mind each time. The young monk's eyes pierced her thoughts. How could one slight glance have revealed so much to her? Recalling how those eyes so similar to her own had also shown the same fear on arriving to this strange land, the young Geisha considered what significance that recognition supposed in their silent exchange. Lost within her contemplation, Momoko paid little notice of the continued gazes her attendance caused to all around and looked to her map once more. Annoyed her daydreaming had cast her two streets past her destination she glanced to wide eyed stares and raised her head.

"I will show them," she muttered and with a swift graceful turn, she retraced her steps, not caring who now watched the refined gait she had spent a lifetime perfecting.

Momoko's pace slowed as she neared the town house circled in black ink on the representative's map. Wondering if her new home was aware of her birthday, the young Geisha came to a stop and glanced to her reflection in her Danna's neighbour's window. She smiled. Of course they knew she reassured herself.

Becoming lost in her own gaze, Momoko grinned as she thought of the celebrations that lay ahead, and of the praise she would receive for the unique beauty she held.

Breaking free from her reflection, the young Geisha stepped forwards. Her heart raced as she looked to the doorway before her.

Smiling once more to her reflection in its black paint work sheen, Momoko pulled the bell cord beside her to signal her much anticipated arrival.

Running through the words chosen for her introduction, Momoko was thankful for her solitary time on board ship. With no distractions to hinder her studies, the young Geisha had become immersed within the English books Auntie had presented. Waiting for the town house door to open and the greetings that lay within, Momoko looked forward to at last utilising that which she had learnt.

Returning to her reflection, Momoko frowned and pulled the cord once more. She wondered if her delayed welcome was due to the festivities marking her birthday appearance. Stepping back from the entrance she looked up to her new home's three tiers.

Taking note of the green vines covering a third of the house, she smirked to the treasures that lay beyond those walls, sure that such a fine façade held the wealth she had envisioned one day lavished upon her. Momoko's joy grew as the door creaked open before her and she stepped forwards ready to be greeted.

The young Geisha's optimistic smile faded to the scowl she received.

"Yes," the portly maid frowned.

Taken back by her welcoming committee's harsh tone, Momoko regained her composure. Lowering her chin and gazing up to the maid she readied her rehearsed lines.

"Well?" the maid snapped before Momoko could utter a word. "What is it girl? What do you want?"

Seeing her coy advances cut no thread with the woman, Momoko raised her head.

"I am here," she said.

"Well I can see that," the maid laughed. "And why is it that you are here?"

Her patience worn thin, the young Geisha glared back at the woman.

"I am expected," Momoko stepped closer. "Now, if you tell my sponsor that I have arrived, then you will see who it is I am. Here, take my bag."

The maid stared back at the young Geisha stood on her master's doorstep and positioned herself so no one could pass through the doorway she now fiercely protected. Looking to the bag held out in front of her, she laughed once again to the young Geisha's request.

"Take my bag," Momoko insisted. "That is what servants do. Isn't it?"

Placing her hands on her hips, the maid reddened and leant towards Momoko.

"How dare you, who do you think you are talking to me that way?" Straightening, her stout arms folded across her expanding midriff.

Momoko scowled back at the determined expression before her. Aware in no way its owner would allow access to the delights laying in wait behind her, the young Geisha's manipulative skills returned. Edging back from her aggressor, Momoko tilted her chin to the floor once again. Her eyes widened as she stared back up at the maid.

"Please, forgive me," Momoko summoned the soft tones she had relied on so many times before. "I am tired after my long journey. Please, can you tell the owner of the house that I have arrived?"

Keeping her pose, Momoko's optimism resurfaced in seeing a broad grin spread across the maid's ample cheeks.

"Now I understand," the woman said. "You have been called for, haven't you."

Momoko watched the maid's arms rest back to her side and nodded.

"Yes," she whispered. Retaining her bashful performance, the young Geisha motioned to step forward. She paused as the maid raised her hand.

"Stop right there. It seems another has made yet another futile trip to this doorstep." With a quick glance back over her shoulder, the maid lowered her hand and leant to Momoko.

"My master has these whims," she said. Glancing back into the house once more she returned to Momoko's confused stare. "You are not the only one to have been summoned in such a way."

Raising her chin, the young Geisha lost her timid stance. Was this a joke? A test of her resilience to be allowed to live in the grand house she now stood before? Not knowing her prospective Danna's true identity, she felt sure she could one day adjure to such humour. The corners of Momoko's lips raised and she smiled to the overweight servant.

"Have I passed my test?" She asked. "Can I now come and join my birthday celebrations?"

Momoko's joy vanished in seeing the maid sadden.

"It is your birthday today?" She said, losing her harsh tone.

"Yes. But you knew this already," Momoko brightened.

The maid shook her head slowly from side to side.

"I am sorry, my child. But it seems your journey here has been wasted."

Feeling her legs weaken, Momoko's stomach turned on realising the implications in the maid's words. How could this be? Was this true? Momoko's thoughts encircled her emotions as she battled her tears.

"What am I to do now?" She whispered.

Momoko looked to the maid. The woman's concerned eyes triggered the tears the young Geisha had fought so hard to contain.

"What am I to do now?" Momoko repeated as the maid's blurred features took on the appearance of the one she known long ago. Recalling the old woman who had shown such kindness to her in the past, Momoko dabbed at salty tears running down her cheeks.

"I am sorry," the maid said. Her eyebrows rose to the calls behind her. "You must go now, my child," she hushed and glanced back to the house "Quickly, now," she added, before turning from Momoko's sobs.

"Wait," the young Geisha called out. "Where will I go?"

The maid's concerned stare returned and she stepped from the doorway.

"You must go back from where you came. I am sure there is someone waiting for you there."

Holding each other's gaze, Momoko nodded to the kindness she had always tried to push away, her heart once again filling with memories of another as she nodded back to the maid.

"I understand," Momoko winced as the door slammed shut before her.

Panicked by her encounter, Momoko stumbled back into the street and looked up to the green vines etched across the face of her promised home. She could not believe the turn of events and reached for the bell cord.

Hesitating for a moment, the young Geisha recalled the familiar maid's advice and lowered her arm as distant memories surfaced within her. With a final glance to her tearful reflection she turned from the doorway that had promised so much.

Retracing her footsteps, Momoko soon stood on the steep street's brow once more. Looking down to the docklands below, her spirits lifted some on seeing her ship remained tight against the harbour's quayside and she began her long walk back to its safety. Keeping her goal in sight, Momoko realised that the floating vessel was all she knew in this continent once anticipated to be her new home.

Momoko stopped and looked to her surrounding streets.

"No," she whispered. "There is another," she continued onwards, her thoughts refreshed by the enigmatic smile her fellow passenger had given.

Thinking of the young monk who had ignited something deep within her soul, the young Geisha forgot the hardship met only moments before and wondered where and what he was doing now.

Those thoughts stayed with Momoko as she descended the cobble stoned street, becoming lost in the imagined words they may have shared on their long voyage together.

On standing at the bottom of the hill, Momoko glanced back to the path taken and then to her feet. Cringing down to the traditional wooden sandals so unused to the steep inclines they now encountered, the pain in her ankles was accompanied by pangs of hunger.

Only a few hours had passed since leaving the ship she hoped would carry her homewards that evening, and as the spring sun rose to its midday apex, the young Geisha looked for somewhere to satisfy her growing appetite. Recalling the small marketplace she would often visit on Tokyo's harbour front she wondered if San Francisco shared a similar setting of stalls and vendors also. Walking into the dockside area, Momoko smiled on finding such a place and strolled past more curious glares, intent on feeding her empty stomach.

Reaching the small collection of stalls, the young Geisha glanced back to her ship, longing for the security it once gave.

"Can I help you?" A voice called out. Momoko turned to the vendor and nodded.

"And what would you like?" He asked, his hand flowing over the fruit and vegetables between them.

Leaning forwards, Momoko pointed to a pile of green apples.

"Two please," she smiled, warmed by the pleasant manner the vendor showed. Reaching into her small bag, Momoko searched for her purse. She sickened on not finding it lying in its usual spot.

Searching once more, dread coursed through the young Geisha as she crouched down and rifled through her belongings.

"Is everything ok?" The vendor joined her side.

Momoko gazed up to him and then to the brown paper bag in his hands, anxious to know how she would now pay for the apples which lay within.

"It's gone," she mumbled. "My purse, I, I've lost it."

"Look again," the vendor encouraged, his soft voice instilling some hope within the young Geisha.

Doing as instructed, Momoko searched several times again.

"No," she stood and gazed to her feet. "It's not there." Feeling her tears return for a second time that day, Momoko looked the vendor's kind smile.

"Here," he said and placed the paper bag in her hands. "A present," he added and returned to his place behind his wares.

Forgetting her troubles, Momoko held the gift to her and bowed.

"Thank you," she said to his generosity. "Thank you so much."

"Think nothing of it," he nodded. Momoko followed his gaze to the shoreline. "Maybe you would like to eat your lunch over there," he pointed.

Momoko looked to the small jetty beyond the market place. True, its wooden slat floorboards looked inviting enough, as did the wooden bench at its end.

Staring from the quiet sanctuary and back to the ship preparing for its moonlit voyage back to all she knew, the vendor leant across his stall on seeing the young Geisha's trepidation.

"Your ship will not be leaving for half a day yet. Take some time to collect your thoughts," he motioned towards the peaceful jetty once more. "Maybe your answers lay upon its wooden bench," he added with a wink.

Lightened by the man's comical gesture, Momoko lifted her hand to mask her giggles. Her actions brought delight to the vendor and he nodded for her to take his advice.

The young Geisha bowed to him.

"Thank you," she said for a final time, placed her gift into her bag and made for the jetty and its alluring wooden bench.

Stepping onto the first of many worn wooden floorboards, Momoko calmed to the waters lapping beneath her. Remembering the same peace found on the banks of her homeland's harbour front, the young Geisha's pace quickened, determined to find sanctuary on the bench before her. She soon reached her objective.

Lowering herself down, Momoko gazed out to the serene ocean before her. Watching sunbeams play over its gentle waves, she glanced back to the small market place, past the kind hearted vendor and then to the ship she knew she could no longer afford. As her dilemma entered her young mind once more, the young Geisha reached into her bag and took one of the apples from there.

Biting into green polished skin, she smiled to its replenishing sweet taste and continued to do so until all that remained of her gift was stem and core. Throwing the remnants out into the ocean, the young Geisha watched the ripples caused spread out and disappear from view. It was only then that the enormity of her situation dawned upon her.

With no rich Danna to keep her in the life she had yearned for and with no money to her name, Momoko's anxiety returned, leaving her dejected and alone like never before. Searching deep inside for an answer to her predicament, Momoko looked out to sea and recalled the vendor's words to her.

"How will my answers come?" She questioned from the end of the jetty.

Although Momoko was grateful for his kindness, she battled to understand how her new location could aid the position she now found herself in.

"Auntie," she mumbled. "Where are you?"

She realised it was not her former guardian for which her soul craved.

"And where are you?" she raised a slight smile, her thoughts returning to the one whose burgundy robes had disappeared from her, much the same way her promised life had now done so also.

CHAPTER TWENTY

Beneath a bright morning sun, the young monk pushed forwards through the diminishing crowds and away from San Francisco's harbour front. Tenzin smiled to the new sights and sounds confronting all his senses. Never before had he seen such people and he wondered if all this young nation's citizens went about their business with such verve. Thinking of his own homelands, he recalled its quiet streets and peaceful manner, so different to the calls, shouts and laughter surrounding him now. The young monk's confidence wavered as he considered what Lama Norbu and young Nyima would have thought of such a place were they to walk with him now. Taking a few more steps, he paused, his want for companionship overriding the reasons for his journey.

Forgetting his fellow brothers he was due to meet in the city, Tenzin turned back to the ship that had brought him here. He looked once more for the beautiful young woman whose glance had touched him so. Rising up onto his toes, he stared through his ship's last remaining passengers and then to the small water side market place further in the distance. Searching in vain he at last hoisted his robes over his shoulder and turned back to the harbour exit, considering why he felt so drawn towards the one he had never talked with.

Walking onwards, Tenzin challenged his reasons for wanting to be beside the young Geisha. Aware of the life these women led, his heart knew the causes for his fascination did not rest in the earthly pleasures their company produced. The motive for his wants lay unseen from his soul, hidden within the depths of his being and he considered what Lama Norbu would have made of their brief exchange on arriving at these distant shores.

Nearing the harbour exit, Tenzin's thoughts stayed with the one who had raised him within Tashilhunpo's walls. Did the old monk too wonder where his young apprentice now stood? A smile returned to Tenzin's lips as he thought of years past when he and the old monk had walked together on his birthday. Those happy recollections left him as he realised he now shared that day alone. Did his fellow brothers know that his arrival marked the first day of his twenty-fourth year? Reaching into his bag, Tenzin remembered his long journey neared its end and produced the small map given to him in his home's Grand Hall. Studying its lined streets, he raised his head and looked up to the steep street before him. Glad his path pointed him another direction, Tenzin turned from the mountainous incline and walked northwards, anticipating the welcome from those of his own beliefs he was soon to receive.

Enjoying his adventure, Tenzin strolled through the busy streets. Amazed by the sights surrounding him, he too came to realise his own presence created as much interest as his own mind fashioned. Smiling to his observers, he lowered his head and continued his path, understanding the stares he now received held no malice towards his being amongst those so different to himself.

Tenzin longed for the moment when he could at last speak with these new people. Thinking of the many hours studying in his cabin, Lama Norbu filled his thoughts once again and he smiled to the laughter shared on attempting the strange words he would now use in his new home. Looking up to cloudless skies, a shard of homesickness came to the young monk and he quickened his pace, intent on reaching those who knew a similar vast deep blue backdrop.

Looking to his map, he turned from the busy street and onto a quiet tree lined avenue. Walking beneath newly opened buds, the young monk recalled the mountain peaks overlooking Tashilhunpo. They too would soon signal an advancing spring as their winter shroud of snow and ice melted, giving way for the lush greenery welcomed by all, adding to the joy that would now fill his distant monastery in seeing another harsh cold season pass. He saddened on not being able to share such joy and considered when he would once again witness the changing landscape he had known since a boy.

Leaving the flowering avenue, Tenzin marched onwards. Passing through more residential streets he noticed a change in the homes he now walked beside. As he followed the map's intricate pencilled lines, the affluent appearance he had encountered in the heart of the city became replaced by dilapidated buildings and broken fences. Pulling his robes closer to him, Tenzin felt the menacing ambiance accompanying the neighbourhoods he now walked and continued with some trepidation to the home his brothers kept.

Tenzin saw no-one as he walked through the foreboding streets, yet his heart lightened on at last finding the house which marked the close of his momentous journey.

The young monk looked up to the chipped paintwork walls that contained those he had travelled so far to meet with. Taking a moment to reflect his journey to these doors, Tenzin's thoughts carried him through Nepal, India and then the white sandy beaches of Hawaii he had cherished. His memories bringing him forth to his final destination, he pictured the beautiful young Geisha who had shared his smiles. Becoming lost in her memory, he wondered the reasons for her arrival and was in no doubt they differed greatly to his own. Was she now sitting within her own American home? Surrounded by those who knew and cared for her? Certain the young Geisha's beauty and composure could only surmount to such a setting, Tenzin cast aside his day dreams and stepped forward.

Checking he now stood outside the correct address he matched the corresponding house numbers and then placed the map back into his bag. Straightening his robes he knocked three times on the chipped varnished door.

Would his brothers expect him to speak the language of their new homelands? With ease he recited his intended introduction in his mind, taking a moment to congratulate himself on learning his prose. Running through his greetings for a second time, the young monk knocked again. Not understanding the reasons for the delay he edged back and stared up at the house's decaying walls.

His expectant eyes flowed across its wooden exterior and came to rest at the glass shards which had once been windows. Yellowed newspaper covered those openings. With still no answer, he raised his hand to knock again. He stopped as the door creaked slightly open.

"Whada ya want?" A small grimy face growled between its gap.

Startled by his reception, Tenzin regained his smiles.

"I am here," he bowed.

The door crept open and the young monk stared at the

dishevelled old man stood before him. Looking to his unkempt beard and grey wispy hair, Tenzin continued to smile.

"I can see you're here," the man replied and scratched his head. "Whada ya want?"

After travelling so many miles, Tenzin could not understand his abrupt welcome. Peering over the man's shoulder, the young monk tried to see into the house promised as his new home. The man followed Tenzin's stares.

"There's nothin' in there for you," he snapped and pulled the door back to him.

"Wait," the young monk called out. "My brothers, where are they?"

"How do I know?"

"But you must know."

"Look kid, I don't know who or what you're talking about. Now leave me be."

Worried the only person who could aid his search now rebuked his calls, the young monk's voice trembled as he spoke again.

"But, they are waiting for me."

The man loosened his grip on the door and leant to his unexpected visitor. His features lost their grizzled appearance as he ran his eyes across the young monk's robes and a smile formed beneath his whiskers.

"Your brothers you say?"

"Yes," Tenzin nodded. Stepping forward, he stopped as the man growled once more.

"You won't find them here."

"Then you know of them?"

"Yes," the man saddened. "Good to me they was, before…"

Watching the man's words trail from him, concern entered the young monk.

"Before what? What has happened to them?"

The man looked past Tenzin and out to the streets the young monk had walked.

"Before they left," he lowered his head. "Miss them I do," he added with a sniff.

His worst fears confirmed by the pitiful nods before him, Tenzin wondered what he would do now in this strange foreign land. Summoning his strength he spoke once more.

"Where did they go?" He asked. "Tell me so I may find them."

The man raised his chin. "Gone home they have," he whispered. "Far from here, long way off."

"Home to Tibet?"

Tenzin's optimism returned to the slight recognition his homelands name gave.

"Ahh, that's the place they talked of. Seemed they'd had enough of us kind. Said we was too hard to show a better path to."

The man paused and scratched his dirty scalp once more. "Wha'dever that means?" He looked to the clouds drifting above him. The old man shrugged and his view returned to the young monk.

Not believing his fellow monks had given up with such ease he questioned if this land and its people really were beyond seeing the noble path he and his kind trod?

"How? How could they leave? Did they know of my arrival?"

"Yes, that they did if I remember right. Wait," the man brightened and gave a toothless grin. "They talked of a visitor from their own home. Must have been you."

Tenzin glanced down to the grubby finger pointing at him and then back up to its owner.

"They talked of me?"

"Yes, many times. I remember what they said now. They told me sumthin' real important."

"What? What did they tell you?" Tenzin tried to calm his impatience and looked up to the clouds in hope of finding solace there. Watching their white wisps drift by, his eager wants vanished from him and he looked back to the man.

"I am sorry," Tenzin smiled. "Please, can you tell me what they said?"

The man returned the smile, eased by the good manners shown to him.

"They said they'd leave word for you. Yes that's it. They said one of them would wait somewhere along your journey so they could tell you to go no further."

"Where? I would have met them already. Tell me, where were they to wait with my message."

The old man's face contorted as he concentrated once more.

"Shanghai," he finally cackled. "That's it, that's the place one of them brothers of yours was waiting."

As the man congratulated himself on recalling such news, Tenzin paled. How could this be? China was too dangerous a place for his own peoples, that Tenzin knew. Having not forgotten the fear experienced hidden in his cabin whilst moored overnight in Shanghai's dreaded port, the young monk tried to comprehend why such a place had been chosen.

"But that's in China," Tenzin said.

"Yeah, so?"

"Well my people are at risk there, are you sure they said Shanghai?"

"Yes," the man nodded. "Don't you know those ports belong to them Brits and Frenchys?

Even I knows that," he laughed.

The man's joy subsided as he watched sorrow etch across his young guest's features. Sensing empathy within his stares, Tenzin shook his head. Realising his terrifying night spent alone beneath his covers had been in vain, he wondered what Lama Norbu would say of his foolishness.

"No, I did not know that," the young monk whispered to his feet and then looked up to with tear filled eyes. "Tell me," he asked. "What will I do now?"

An uncharacteristic warm smile spread across the old man's features.

"Young man," he said. "I'm sure there's someone in your own homelands who expect your return. Go back to them, so they may once more see the one they have missed so much."

Listening to his advice, Tenzin could not help remembering the same tones his guardian had used in difficult times such as these.

"I understand," Tenzin nodded as the door to his supposed new home closed before him.

Knowing no other solution to his dilemma, Tenzin walked from the dilapidated house, ashamed he had missed his fellow brother awaiting his arrival on China's eastern shoreline. His foolhardy attempts at joining those he was meant to meet contained the young monk on retracing his footsteps back to San Francisco's harbour front and soon he walked once more beneath newly formed cherry blossoms. Stopping on the avenue he had only taken moments before he recalled the trust and anticipation that had surrounded him then. Reaching up he picked a single flower from above. Gazing at its emerging pink and white petals, Tenzin breathed in its sweet aroma and then placed it into his bag, hoping its purity would in somehow aid his journey back to where he belonged.

As the buildings around him regained their affluent appearance, Tenzin thought of what consequences would come from his intended actions. The gold coins Nyima and his peers had entrusted to him would safely see to his return home, yet Tenzin wondered what would be said should he spend Tashilhunpo's small fortune. For a brief moment he considered staying in the city and attempting to teach those who were willing to learn. Those thoughts passed by Tenzin on realising how hard that vocation would prove. He knew no-one in this city and no-one it seemed was aware of him. Tenzin came to a stop once more.

"No," he whispered. "There is someone."

With thoughts of the beautiful young Geisha encircling him again, Tenzin shook his head. He shrugged and continued onwards, wondering what luxury she now basked within.

Reaching the entrance to the harbour he had only left a few hours before, the young monk smiled on seeing his ship still stood at its temporary home. Feeling the coins through his bag's coarse material, Tenzin considered if he should return back to the country of his birth.

Walking to the ship he stopped next to the huge ropes holding her in place. His view fell to its worn, scratched grey panelled sides. Eyeing the wear and tear the vessel had yielded to over the years, Tenzin tried to picture the ship in its infancy, sure its finery had enthralled all those who had boarded her then. Staring across its aged hull, he remembered his encounter with the grimy old man who now lived within his fellow brother's home. Had he too captivated a willing audience in his younger years? Not knowing how to discover such a thing, Tenzin smiled on recalling his parting words.

"Yes, I am sure somebody awaits my return," Tenzin's whispers reassured and he felt for the gold coins again. Holding them through his weathered shoulder bag, Tenzin knew then that it would matter little to Lama Norbu if he soon returned.

Turning to the small market placed further along the harbour he recalled the same stalls and vendors vying for business outside

Tashilhunpo's gates, wondering if these stalls shared the same fruits and vegetables his homelands would now be sowing in the event of early spring.

The clearing skies above accompanied his walk towards the market place. So many times had he seen such a view, yet the blues he witnessed now seemed not to hold the stark beauty he often sat beneath. Watching the few clouds remaining as the midday sun reached its highest point, the young monk questioned if now, miles from his beloved home, he could make them disappear in his overflowing mind. Closing his eyes, Tenzin inhaled and then let his breath go in the manner he had been taught many years ago. Repeating the pattern several times, his cluttered thoughts faded and a new found peace entered his soul.

Lost within the tranquillity of the moment, Tenzin did not notice the stares of others who watched his actions. Continuing his peaceful stance, the sun's rays invigorated his senses. On opening his eyes once more, the young monk smiled to the results he had longed to teach others of this continent.

Tenzin blushed as he turned back to the market place. Looking to those familiar stares he had encountered on first stepping onto dry land once more, his head lowered on walking between his spectators, his understanding to their interest returning as the crowds parted for him.

Glancing back to the ship, he longed to be held in its security again and considered how he would spend the next twelve hours before setting sail back to his home. Tenzin's view fell back to the market place and to the small stall and its familiar fruits.

On reaching his chosen stall, Tenzin smiled to the young vendor and pointed to the fresh green apples piled high before him.

"An excellent choice," the young man placed two apples into one of his many brown paper bags hanging up beside him.

Reaching into his bag for its collection of coins the young monk stopped as the vendor raised his hand.

"That is not necessary," he said. "Please, this is my gift to you."

Taking the apples from the youthful vendor's out stretched arm, Tenzin smiled again Placing his hands together beneath his chin the young monk gave his kind benefactor a deep bow.

"Thank you," he said. "Your kindness shall not go unnoticed."

As the vendor nodded in reply Tenzin saw the wise soul which lay behind his eyes. A fleeting recognition came to the young monk as he and the youthful stall holder held each other's gaze. Their acknowledgement was soon broken as Tenzin's ship sounded its horn across its bows. Looking back to the vessel which would soon see the start to his voyage back to Tashilhunpo, Tenzin turned back to the vendor's calls.

"You have a long wait," the young man winked. "Maybe there is somewhere you can enjoy your time before returning to the one who has missed your presence."

Tenzin's memories filled with his time spent besides Nyangchu's flowing waters, and to the familiar kind expression he had encountered there many years ago. Looking to the one who had lifted his spirits after the shock of finding his brothers no longer stayed upon these shores, Tenzin followed the young vendor's smile to the small jetty at the far end of the market place.

"Maybe there you shall find the reasons for your journey here," the young man whispered to him.

"Thank you," the young monk said, and walking from the soul he felt sure he had once known so well, made for the small wooden jetty in the distance.

Biting into his apple, Tenzin placed the other into his bag, not knowing when he would eat again. Its sweet taste brought with it recollections of the reasons for his journey and his guilt returned as Ketu's dishevelled hungry expression came to him. Had his voyage here taught him the lessons he needed learn? Taking another bite, Tenzin thought of those he had encountered on his long journey to where he now stood. Recalling the kindness given with no want of return, he saw the compassion in all those features. The Nepali tradesmen and the inhabitants of Digha, on the banks of the Ganges, all these had shown great kindness to the solitary stranger who happened upon them. Looking down to his lunch, Tenzin realised how that same generosity had been shown to him only moments before and he stared back to the young vendor.

With the ship looming behind him, the stall holder waved to Tenzin and encouraged him onwards. Tenzin raised his arm, waved back and continued towards the wooden jetty. He hesitated on seeing someone sat alone on the wooden bench at its end.

Watching the young Geisha throw her apple core into the water,

Tenzin stepped forward, his joy building in at last meeting with the one whose presence had remained with him since sharing their brief smile together.

Stepping softly across the jetty's worn floorboards until reaching the wooden bench, the young Geisha turned to his arrival and looked up to the young monk at her side.

"Hello," Tenzin smiled. "May I sit with you a while?"

CHAPTER TWENTY-ONE

Looking up to the warm smile encountered once before, Momoko nodded and shuffled along the jetty's small wooden bench to make room for the young monk. Her heart racing as she bowed her head to the one she had longed to know.

"Thank you," Tenzin lowered himself down beside her.

Noting the young Geisha's coy pose, he stared ahead and took the final bite from his apple. Raining her chin Momoko watched her new companion throw core and stem into the still waters before them, much the way she had done so only moments earlier, taking in the apparent joy the young monk took in gazing at the fine ripples spreading out and beneath their tranquil setting.

"Good shot," Momoko she said.

Looking to his apple's remnants, Tenzin watched the remains of Momoko's own lunch bob softly next to his.

"Yes," his replied. "I suppose it was."

Lowering her head as Tenzin looked to her, the young monk's smile wavered to the young Geisha's bashful pose and he frowned as she gazed up to him with a slight tilt of her chin. Momoko reddened. Seeing the ploy she had always used to gain the affections of others was lost on the young monk, she raised her head, wondering what other skills she would utilise in order to enchant him. Sensing the pause between them, the young Geisha drew on her teachings.

To let silence penetrate a moment between a Geisha and her companion was a cardinal sin, and although she was aware the young monk in no way fell into that category, the lessons instilled in Momoko within her Okiya's walls came forward.

Looking back to Tenzin, she hesitated. Watching the young

monk's view return to their floating apple cores, Momoko considered the comfort she now found in the silence between her and the robed stranger beside her. Falling into the new found safety she now felt at his side, her want for conversation faded and she too gazed over to the ripple's ever decreasing circles.

"They fit," the young monk said as the encircling fruit joined together with ease.

"That they do," Momoko whispered and turned to Tenzin's profile. Her heart raced once again as he turned to her and nodded.

"Even nature finds a way home" he said, "and makes a mark on all that surrounds it."

Both watched the harbour's small waves nudge their lunch closer together.

"And every meeting causes similar ripples to touch all those it encounters."

· The young Geisha giggled as surprise spread across Tenzin's features to her words.

"You know of my beliefs?" He asked with cheeks sharing the same flush he had witnessed in their first meeting.

"No, not really," Momoko shrugged looking out to the distant horizon. "It's something I've always known," she added.

Each fell back into the reassuring stillness held between them.

The young monk's gaze mirrored Momoko's as he turned from her and looked to the ocean spread out before them. Aware of the shared peace each assumed in one another's presence, Tenzin recalled their first brief smiles only weeks earlier. Regret entered the young monk. Realising his solitary journey may have held the same comfort his soul now experienced he reached for the wooden beads which had accompanied his lonely travels. Momoko watched on as he began to flick each worn bead over finger and thumb.

"What are they?" the young Geisha asked, finding it strange how she felt so drawn to the aged necklace. Momoko had always dreamed of silver, gold and jewels, the trappings of which she thought would come in arriving on these distant shores. Yet here she was, her dreams of such riches shattered and she frowned to the attraction the young monk's worn necklace held towards her.

"These beads are many things," Tenzin smiled. "Each one holds a prayer for me and those of the world I do not know."

"Those you don't know?"

"Yes," he held the necklace up to Momoko. "You see, my people believe that we have not five, but six senses. Sight, sound, touch, smell and taste are accompanied by another." Lowering the necklace, he continued to replace each bead with the next over finger and thumb. "We believe that that extra sense is the foundation for all reverence held towards those who walk this earth."

"And what is this additional sense?"

"Consciousness," Tenzin replied. "For without consciousness, how can we hold compassion for others?"

"So every time you turn one of the beads, a prayer goes out to others? Even if you have never met them?"

"Yes. But I like to think they show me other things also. To me, each bead represents a moment in my life. As I replace one moment with another, that past remains yet is separate from the next bead between my fingers. Moving on from that one, all I have ever done, thought, or said, stays with me, connected by the string that holds these moments together in succession."

Looking to the young Geisha, Tenzin saw she understood his words.

"Everything you have ever done?" Momoko's eyes widened. "Both good and bad?"

She frowned as the young monk's smile vanished and he lowered his head. Sensing his remorse, Momoko leant to him.

"I can't imagine you doing anything bad," she said.

Giving no reply on recalling the reasons behind his journey away from all he cherished, he placed his beads back around his neck and turned to the beautiful young Geisha's concern with a smile.

"Every soul holds some regrets," he looked to the apple cores drifting from them out towards his own homelands. Joining his view, Momoko settled back once more and wondered what secrets the young monk held.

Sitting together in a familiar comforting silence, Momoko thought of the young monk's beads and how she too held some regrets towards past actions. Her fleeting repentance soon vanished. Remembering how her own kindness had brought her to these shores she now sat, the young Geisha pushed away the disappointment shrouding her dismissal from the luxurious life promised by another. Momoko glanced to the young monk at her side and began to giggle. Turning to her laughter, Tenzin's spirits lifted in seeing the joy displayed in such beautiful eyes.

"What is it?" Tenzin asked. "Tell me," he said as the young Geisha shook her head and stared back at him.

"We have shared this bench and have talked some for more than an hour, but."

"But what?" Tenzin asked as Momoko's giggles resurfaced.

"But, I don't even know your name."

Tenzin began to laugh also. The safety and belonging he knew each of their souls held appeared to have always been with them, as if they had never been apart. Yet sitting next to the one whose company brought such calm, he too realised the young Geisha's true identity remained hidden from him. Rising to his feet, Tenzin adjusted his robes and gave a bow.

"Tenzin," he said. "My name is Tenzin."

Regaining her composure, Momoko stood also and repaid his courtesy with a similar bow

"And I am Momoko," she smiled. "How do you do?"

With a slight pause between them, both Momoko and Tenzin burst into laughter, each remembering the strange greetings studied in the English books they had poured over.

"I am fine, thank you," Tenzin grinned. "And you?"

Momoko giggled and lowered her chin. "I am fine also," she replied sitting down on the wooden bench once more. "Won't you join me?" She continued their charade.

"It would be my pleasure," the young monk replied, enjoying the laughter shared from the foreign etiquette which had confused him so.

With introductions complete and sitting beside each other once again, their laughter subsided and Momoko turned to Tenzin.

"So, Tenzin," a smile played across Momoko's lips on saying his name for the first time. "Tell me, what are you doing here?"

During his and Momoko's laughter, he had forgotten the events leading up to their meeting. Taking a moment, Tenzin remembered his distress in finding those he was to meet with had left before his timed arrival.

"I came to stay with my brothers," he replied softly.

"You have brothers here? Then where are they now? How is it you are now alone, sitting here with me?"

Watching her new friend's sorrow, the young Geisha fell quiet in hope her silence would encourage Tenzin to continue. The young monk acknowledged her stillness with a respectful nod and gentle smile.

"They left before I arrived," he said. "Back to my homelands, disillusioned by those we now sit amongst."

Wanting to reach out and comfort the young monk, she paid heed to her desires. Aware such conduct proved improper towards a man of Tenzin's beliefs, the young Geisha also held her silence towards her own unexpected dismissal, confused by her want to put someone else's needs before her own.

"Your journey must have been long to arrive here, Tenzin," she said. "Please, tell me of the lands you passed through before finding yourself here, with me."

As his troubles faded he looked to the beautiful young woman. The security he found within those deep brown eyes gazing back at him gave the young monk the courage to speak of his voyage, and of the eventual disappointment which had greeted him only hours before.

Leaving Momoko's expectant stares, Tenzin looked out onto the ocean as he began to recount his journey. Glancing from the far horizon, Tenzin would smile to his new friend as she listened intently to his tales of foreign lands.

Telling of the kindness encountered throughout his trip, Tenzin saddened once more as he explained how his brothers had waited for him in Shanghai's bustling port to tell they no longer remained in the city he now sat. Bowing his head, he admitted the foolishness he felt in not venturing out from his cabin to receive such news. Momoko saw his shame and again battled her want to reach out and hold the young monk beside her.

"Then where did your travels take you?" She persuaded him to continue.

On seeing Tenzin lighten as he spoke of the idyllic beaches he had encountered on Hawaii's coast line. Momoko's lightened also on seeing the young monk's smiles return, her heart intrigued as he spoke of the time he had spent in quiet contemplation there.

"And then you saw me," she whispered.

Momoko's smiles turned to giggles as Tenzin blushed.

"And you saw me also, Momoko, if I remember."

Matching Tenzin's flushed cheeks, Momoko frowned as concealed emotions surfaced within her.

"Then why did you not approach me?" She asked. "At least then we could have shared those sunsets you watched me enjoy alone."

Wanting to speak of his longing to join her on their ship's highest tier so they may have basked together in daytimes closing hours Tenzin held his tongue. Knowing it was not his place to speak of such matters he gave a slight shrug and gazed out to the midday sun once again. Recognising his trepidation, the young Geisha sat back, feeling some guilt in her eager want for answers.

"Maybe we will share a similar sunset this evening."

Tenzin turned to Momoko and smiled as the young Geisha nodded to his offer of consolation.

"And then, Tenzin? What happened when you left this harbour. Was that when you found your brothers had gone?"

Telling Momoko how he had followed the small map given to him at the beginning of his journey, he described the rundown dilapidated streets walked before finding his brothers' former address. Tenzin laughed as the young Geisha cringed on hearing of the old man who had spoken of his brothers' departure. His high spirits weakened as he spoke of his decision to follow those who he had come to stay with back to where he belonged.

Taking in Tenzin's story, there was one factor Momoko could not understand.

"Are you not angry with your brothers?" She asked. "To have left you here alone, with nowhere to stay?"

"No, Momoko. How could I be angry with them? They have only followed the path shown to them."

"Yes, but they have now left you in a terrible position. Do you not feel any upset towards them?"

"How can I? They planned to tell me on China's coast line did they not?

"Yes, but you didn't get their message."

"That is true. But I am aware of their attempts to warn me against continuing."

"And that makes everything fine?"

"Yes," the young monk smiled. "Yes, in a way it does."

Seeing Momoko did not understand his approval in his brothers' actions, he leant to her.

"Momoko, I have forgiven them for not staying to greet me. I understand their reasons for leaving and this has led me to release any hurt or anger I may have held against them."

Considering Tenzin's words, she wondered if her own wrath towards the one who had offered a life surrounded in wealth and fame would end also if she were to understand and forgive her Danna's position.

"Forgiveness with understanding," she whispered under her breath.

Unbeknown to her, the young monk caught her words. As Momoko leant forwards on the edge of the bench, he studied her exquisite profile beside him. The sheer beauty portrayed in her high cheekbones and the jet black hair which framed such striking eyes, were overridden by Tenzin's brief glimpse to the knowledge he understood her soul contained. Continuing to watch Momoko gaze out onto the ocean, Tenzin considered the reasons behind their encounter here on the shores so far from both their own homelands.

Aware of Tenzin's gaze, Momoko settled back beside him. Looking to his black cropped hair, her eyes fell to his and she smiled to the comfort found within them.

"Your forgiveness amazes me, Tenzin," she told him. "Your brothers should be truly thankful."

The young Geisha's frowns returned to Tenzin's faint laughter.

"It is not they who should thank me. More so, it is I them."

"But why? After what they did."

"They have helped me find the compassion I once thought lost within me," Tenzin continued. "Without their actions, I would have forgotten the reasons for my travels."

Calmed by Tenzin's words her gaze returned to the sunlit waters ahead.

"And your forgiveness towards those who have caused such suffering has released you from your anger," she said.

For a second time, Tenzin was taken aback by Momoko's insights into the life he had been raised. Nodding in reply to her words, the young monk again wondered the reasons for their meeting. Reaching for his necklace, he held its worn wooden beads between his fingers and then looked back to the beautiful young woman smiling beside him.

"Yes, Momoko, that is true," he dismissed his ideas towards the identity of Momoko's true soul on falling once more into the wholeness experienced in her presence.

"Now it is for you to tell me," he said. "How you came to find yourself sat alone on this bench we now share."

As Momoko had done so also, Tenzin listened in silence as she told of her solitary journey to America. He too felt the urge to comfort the young Geisha on hearing of the treatment her fellow passengers directed to her. Understanding the reasons for the jealousy caused by Momoko's unique beauty, he hoped she too saw the forgiveness that would in turn release her anger towards them, somehow knowing that liberation lay within her.

"And then you appeared," Momoko smiled.

Recalling the brief welcome he had encountered on Hawaiian shores he nodded to her.

The regrets of not talking to the young Geisha sooner returned and as she had to him, he encouraged Momoko to continue.

"I looked for you, Tenzin," she lowered her chin from his gaze. "When I stepped from our ship."

"And I you," his cheek's redness deepening. "And then what did you do?"

"I too followed the directions to my new home," Momoko replied after some hesitation, her recollections bringing forth a sorrow forgotten in Tenzin's presence.

"A new home?" Tenzin pressed. "I thought you were stepping into a known life. One filled with the luxuries I could not even begin to imagine."

The young Geisha winced to Tenzin's words.

"So did I, Tenzin," she replied. "So did I."

Tenzin fought his want to reach out and comfort Momoko's sadness. He instead settled back and persuaded her to carry on with her tale.

Sensing the young monk's empathy Momoko smiled to him, secure in his company.

"I was called from my home for the life you speak of, Tenzin. One which contained those riches you say you cannot imagine."

"Then why are you not enjoying them now?"

"My Danna. My patron," she corrected on seeing Tenzin's frown. "He called for me on impulse and when I arrived to his door, it seems his desires for me no longer remained."

"He asked you to join him and then when you did he told you to leave?"

"In a way, yes, Tenzin," Momoko leant to him. "But I never saw his face."

"You mean someone else told you?"

As she recounted the portly maid's words to her only hours prior to their meeting, Tenzin wondered if the compassion he had talked of had begun to surface within the beautiful young woman at his side. Momoko read his thoughts.

"Yes, Tenzin," she said. "He was a weak man, his own selfish desires overruled the consideration towards another's feelings. I understand the reasons behind my dismissal."

The shame he now felt from his assumptions were revealed in his fading smile as he looked to Momoko.

"Tenzin," she giggled. "Feel no guilt towards that which you supposed. I know your thoughts were in my best interests and for that I am grateful."

"Then you have found your compassion to the one who hurt you so?"

"As I have said, I understand the causes of my dismissal," the young Geisha's smiles continued. "But, that does not mean my forgiveness has arrived to his callous actions." His embarrassment leaving him, Tenzin looked to the young Geisha's sudden sorrow.

"What is it?" He asked, concerned for his new friend's sadness.

Momoko looked from the ocean and to the ship that had carried her here.

"My plan was to return homewards, so I may be amongst the one who care for me."

"Me also," Tenzin nodded.

Confused by Momoko's sadness he smiled to her once more. "Our wait will not be long," he reassured. "And my company cannot be that bad."

Watching the young Geisha raise a smile to his words, her joy waned and she glanced back to their ship and then to him.

"No, Tenzin. Your company is all I've ever dreamt of. I am sad that we shall spend such little time together."

"We shall still talk on the ship, will we not?"

Momoko shook her head.

"I cannot join you on our journey home," she told him. "Not only have I lost my promised life upon these shores, but also my purse holding the money needed for my fare homewards should such a thing of happened."

Staring back to Momoko's admission, Tenzin's compassion towards the young Geisha and her sad tale pushed forwards. With a brief glance back to the ship he would board at midnight, his view fell to his bag beside him.

Lama Norbu's parting smiles came to him as he thought of the small fortune contained within, and his guardian's reaction should he return without Tashilhunpo's golden funds.

CHAPTER TWENTY-TWO

Welcoming the cool breeze blowing in from the ocean before them, Tenzin turned to Momoko. Seeing she too shared the same delight, he smiled and then glanced back down to his bag. Considering once again his want to help the young Geisha's passage homewards, Tenzin wondered if his aid would prove the reason behind their meeting on San Francisco's tranquil harbour front. His thoughts were soon interrupted by Momoko's giggles.

"And where have you gone?" The young Geisha laughed beside him.

Tenzin's smiles returned on sensing Momoko's sadness lift.

"Just thinking," he replied, hesitating in telling his intended plans of funding her travels. Although Momoko had lost her money and now had no conceivable way of getting home, Tenzin admired her optimism yet held his silence towards his proposed gift.

"And what were you thinking of, young monk?" Momoko's eyes narrowed.

"Nothing that concerns you, young Geisha," Tenzin laughed, his eyes too sharing the playful seriousness between them both.

"Fine," Momoko huffed. Looking away from Tenzin she soon returned to him.

"You are to leave tonight, back to your home?"

"Yes," Tenzin once again battled his want to tell of his intentions.

"Then may I sit with you as you wait?"

"Of course," he said.

His smile vanished as he leant to her.

"But only on one condition."

Lowering her head to the young monk's sudden change in mood, she then peered back up at him, her eyes half closed.

"And what condition is that?" She whispered.

"That you tell me of the lands from which you come," Tenzin replied. "Tell me of your life, Momoko," his whispers matched hers.

Embracing the young monk's soft tones Momoko nodded to him.

"It would be my pleasure," she replied, even though aware of the pain such memories still carried within her soul. "But I have one condition also, Tenzin," she raised her head. "You must tell me of your past too."

Agreeing with the young Geisha, Tenzin's own anxiety came forth on thinking of the past he had pushed away from him for so long.

"Of that I shall," the young monk joined Momoko's contemplation out onto the ocean, becoming as lost as she in shards of flickering sunlight played across its gentle waves.

Tenzin waited for Momoko to begin her tale of the life led before their meeting. As the young monk's own hidden memories crept forwards he looked to Momoko and his anxiety eased. Comforted once more by being in the young Geisha's presence he at last anticipated talking of what had passed.

With Tenzin's eyes upon her, Momoko turned to him and smiled.

"I was born in Kyoto," she said. "In the opening days of spring."

Closing her eyes as another cool breeze drifted over her she stared back out onto the ocean, its fresh respite from the midday sun encouraging her to continue

"The first day of Hanami," she said. "Does your home have Hanami also, Tenzin?"

"No," he said. "Tell me of this, Hanami."

As she spoke of the cherry blossoms she would walk beneath each birthday, Momoko's eyes sparkled and Tenzin wondered if the young Geisha would talk of those who had accompanied her. Seeing the pain such recollections contained, he too understood the concealed hurt of those lost to him also.

"I can see those trees of pinks and whites which marked my birthday now, and hear the small stream I would paddle in beside them."

As the young Geisha's words trailed from her, she returned to Tenzin.

"Now, young monk, it is your turn," she gave a faint giggle.

"Gyantse," Tenzin said. He grinned to Momoko's frown. "The

place I was born," he explained. "I too was born beside water, Momoko, and would paddle there also when young."

The young Geisha's surprise gave Tenzin the confidence to continue and he soon became lost in his memories of Nyangchu's flowing waters. Telling of the melting mountain snows that fed the river each spring, he did not speak of the birthday which coincided with such an event, his thoughts returning for a moment to Momoko's supposed identity.

Wanting to speak of the ones he had walked between on those banks, Tenzin's heart saddened as he edged around memories buried deep within.

Recognising the young monk's pain, Momoko tried to lighten Tenzin's soul.

"It sounds wonderful," she said.

Understanding Tenzin's trepidation to talk of those who had raised him, her own emotions hid a similar fear. Remembering the features that had accompanied her formative years, sorrow came to Momoko and her view fell back to the ocean.

"Yes, Tenzin, I too remember those from my past. More so today, than any other."

"And why today?" Tenzin asked, although he supposed the answer he would receive.

"Because." Momoko paused. Turning to the young monk, she looked to the eyes which gave her such peace and summoned a slight smile.

"Because, Tenzin. Today is my birthday."

Staring back at Momoko, Tenzin dismissed the notions swimming through him and once again did not speak of the birthday they shared. Confused by his silence, his thoughts drifted as he too recalled the kind features he had known throughout his childhood. Remembering the birthday walks they would take beneath thawing mountain peaks, the young monk calmed his fears towards recalling such times.

Smiling to Momoko, he leant down beside him and reached into his bag. The young Geisha's surprise returned as she looked to what Tenzin held out to her.

"Happy birthday, Momoko," Tenzin said as the young Geisha leant forward and took the flower from him.

"Hanami," Momoko gazed from the delicate pink and white petals of her childhood and then to Tenzin. "How did you know?"

Seeing the joy his gift provided, Tenzin remembered how he had been drawn to the cherry blossoms on his walk to meet with his brothers. Tenzin's regret of their absence returned and looking to the young Geisha's pleasure he pushed away his disappointment for a second time that afternoon.

"Is this the same as the birthday flowers you have told me of, Momoko?" he asked.

"Yes," Momoko replied, her eyes moist with gratitude. "Thank you."

Raising the flower up to her, she breathed in its subtle aroma. A single tear fell from her as she looked to Tenzin once more.

"What is it?" he asked, concerned for the sorrow the blossom's fragrance produced.

"It is so beautiful, the flower," Momoko dabbed her cheek, reassuring Tenzin's worry towards his gift to her. "It is the memories its smell invokes that causes my sadness, Tenzin."

Inhaling the flower's scent once more, another tear rolled down Momoko's cheek. "Hiroko," she recalled the old midwife who she had once adored. "Cherry blossom always reminds me of her, Tenzin."

Knowing the young Geisha needed no further prompt in unearthing her young memories, Tenzin simply nodded and waited to hear Momoko's recollections of the one she called Hiroko.

"She was so kind to me," Momoko began. "It seems so long ago now, but I still feel her presence."

She lifted the flower to her once more.

"Tenzin, isn't it funny, the smallest things we remember?"

Listening as Momoko talked of the old midwife who had shown such compassion towards her, Tenzin's own thoughts filled with another's smile and similar gentle ways. His eyes glistened as he explored buried memories, his heart no longer avoiding his grandfather's kind features.

"I too knew such a person once," he said as Momoko's words faded. "My grandfather held such traits you speak of."

"And he left you also?"

"Yes, Momoko," Tenzin nodded, heavy with the forgotten pain experienced in his loss. He smiled on catching the young Geisha's stare.

"An older generation gives us much more than we perceive, Momoko. They clearly see the trials of the young, an understanding which gives us something more sacred than we can imagine in such infancy."

Momoko smiled. "Freedom," she whispered.

"Yes," he returned her smile. "They allow the younger generation to explore life's trials and tests they too once faced, providing a liberty unrivalled by the generation between them."

Warming to the understanding his new friend showed in his words, the young monk considered how Momoko knew the ways of his forefathers. His ideas towards their meeting returned, only to once again be interrupted by Momoko's soft voice.

"Tenzin," she leant to him. "Who was the generation between you and the grandfather you talk of?"

As Tenzin looked away from her, Momoko watched the young monk reach for the comfort his beaded necklace gave. Studying him flick each wooden bead over finger and thumb, she wondered if she should continue, her soul recognising the hurt such recollections held.

"I am sorry, Tenzin," she said to him. "It seems I too share the same torment."

Aware of Momoko's gaze, Tenzin's view remained on the soothing waters before them.

"Sometimes our memories hold the keys that will unlock the freedom you have talked of, Tenzin," Momoko told him.

"This I am aware of also," he said. "Tell me, Momoko. How do you know such things?"

"I just do," Momoko giggled. "These are things I have always known, but the knowledge I hold has never surfaced until…"

"Until we met," Tenzin thoughts towards the identity of the beautiful young woman's soul beside him grew by the moment.

"Yes, Tenzin. Until we met."

As gentle waves edge towards them only disappear beneath the old wooden jetty where they now sat, Tenzin turned to the young Geisha.

"It was so long ago I left his side, Momoko. Yet I can still recall our last meal together and the laughter we shared that night. For so many years I have tried to forget those times, but they have stayed with me, hidden within the deepest corners of my heart."

Tenzin spoke of his formative years and how after his grandfather passing he had left his father alone besides Nyangchu's eternal waters. The young Geisha hid her surprise to the way the young monk's life experiences paralleled hers. For years, Momoko too had tried to forget her childhood and had dismissed her Kyoto home as just a distant dream. The one who had held her close before watching her leave for the destined life within Tokyo's Hanamachi district had always remained with her, brought back each time the young Geisha's reflection gazed back at her with the striking eyes both shared.

Recalling her mother's beauty, Momoko reached out for the young monk. Betraying her understanding towards his devout position, she cared little for the formalities such consequences gave and wrapped her fingers around Tenzin's forearm.

"I too hold a similar memory, Tenzin," Momoko whispered, her smile enhanced on seeing the comfort her touch gave. "My own childish wants also caused me to dismiss all I had ever known and leave those behind who had little else."

Warmed once more by the young Geisha's understanding, he glanced down to her tender grip and smiled. Looking back into Momoko's deep brown eyes, he searched within them for an answer to his anguish and regret. In some way he knew they held the knowledge in which to ease his remorse.

Holding the young monk's gaze, Momoko gave his arm a gentle squeeze before her hand fell back into her lap.

"We search for the same thing, you and I," she too sensed the growing bond between them.

"Of that we do, Momoko."

Confused by his want to feel her touch again, he remembered the comfort such warm contact had given in the years they now talked of. Recalling how his hand had once wrapped around his father's, he smiled on finding his answers in Gyaltso's gentle guidance.

"We are our parents," he said. "Yet we are also not."

"How can that be, Tenzin?"

"Momoko, we come from them, but we are not them. Although we share a connection with those who brought us into this world, our souls are still separate. The choices we make are for us to choose and ours alone."

The young Geisha lost puzzled stare as she too began to see the basis in Tenzin's words.

"Then the decisions to leave those who once guided us, share no connotations with the wants of others?"

"Yes, Momoko. It is true that it is our path to follow, made by these choices, decisions made with no association to the wanted direction of others. It is for us to choose to step forward towards our preferred destiny."

Their understanding expanded as they placed their words with the situation each had faced at such a young age. As forbidden memories eased within the insights summoned by another's existence, Momoko and Tenzin retuned to the timeless stares each had held, their anxiety to the past slowly released by their discovery.

Settling back against the wooden bench, Momoko reached out to Tenzin again. With her hand rested soft on the young monk's arm once more, they both gave the other a soft smile and looked out to the late afternoon sun, each aware its diminishing arc indicated the little time they would have together.

Comforted by the young Geisha's touch, Tenzin thought of the words they had shared. Momoko's admission that the knowledge she held was triggered by being in his presence matched the young monk's, and he reflected on the new found awareness he too now experienced, brought forth by their auspicious encounter.

Knowing the young monk's thoughts beside her, Momoko fell into the peace she had sought for as long as she could remember. Recalling her younger days, she began to see how the knowledge surfacing within her now had always been there, laying dormant in her heart until ignited by Tenzin's gentle attendance.

In silence, they continued to look ahead. Their souls entwined within the lessons each gained from one another, considering the significance behind their meeting and of what more they might learn from the other.

At last breaking their silence, Momoko turned from the pre-dusk haze forming before them.

"You talked before of leaving your birthplace, Tenzin," she said. "Tell me, where did you go?"

Holding his view on the horizon, the young monk remembered his two day trek at Lama Norbu's side.

"They came for me, Momoko," he looked to her, considering what she would make of his tale.

"Who? Who came for you, Tenzin?"

Momoko wondered if the young monk's experiences would once again match her own.

"Lama Norbu. He became my new guardian. And friend," Tenzin added, his smiles growing in recalling the old monk's console. Telling Momoko of his travels to the monastery that was to become his home, Tenzin saddened as he spoke of Tashilhunpo, a familiar ache retuning to him for the security offered beneath them its golden rooftops.

"And you, Momoko," he avoided such sorrow. "Where did your decision to leave your true home behind take you?"

Speaking of her Okiya's enclosed walls, Momoko delighted in the young monk's awe as she told of the intrigue and mystery held within them, witnessed only by those with the sufficient funds to do so. Recounting Auntie's kindness and guidance, she too saw the similar traits Lama Norbu had shown to Tenzin and considered once more if the young monk's life would continue to parallel the one she now remembered.

"And you lived there with your sisters?" Tenzin asked.

"Yes," Momoko lowered her head on recalling the ones who had accompanied her chosen upbringing, the features of one in particular standing out above the rest.

In seeing the young Geisha's remorse Tenzin leant to her.

"I too had many brothers," he smiled. "And for me also there is one who comes to me now."

With a slight smile Momoko raised her head looked to Tenzin, holding no surprise his memories matched her own. The young monk was aware of the building synchronicity each shared too and his want to know more of Momoko's life raced through him.

"Why were you chosen to leave your mother's side?" He asked.

Also aware her words were already known Momoko continued.

"Tokyo holds much call for those with my unique appearance."

Out into the advancing sunset ahead, the young Geisha spoke of her mother's debt to the one she too had called Auntie, of the beauty first witnessed by the old woman when walking beneath Kyoto's treasured cherry blossoms and of her first footsteps into the Okiya.

"And you, young monk," she raised an eyebrow. "Were there reasons for why you were chosen also?"

"Yes," Tenzin looked out to their dimming sun. "I too was chosen, Momoko."

Recounting his younger days, Tenzin told of his encounter with Lama Norbu on Gyantse river banks and of his guardian's returning visit. Momoko's eyes widened as he talked of the beliefs that his soul was that of Lama Jampo. On watching her awareness grow as he spoke of the tests given so he may lead the life he was destined to, Tenzin saddened on telling of the melody which confirmed his place amongst Tashilhunpo's Lamas. The features of another returned to his memories. Looking down to his bag, Tenzin thought of the roughly fashioned flute lying within and the reasons for his journey across many lands.

"Lama Jampo," Momoko whispered beside him. "Lama Jampo," her eyes sparkled as she said his name once more.

"Yes, Momoko," Tenzin nodded. "I am him, and he is me."

The young monk's sorrow vanished as he joined Momoko's giggles.

"You are him, and he is you," she laughed, knowing Tenzin also recalled the strange nuances their newly mastered language produced.

As their laughter fell back into the comfort each held sat beside one another, Momoko and Tenzin settled back and watched the falling sun touch the horizon.

"It seems at last we get to share our sunset," Momoko said.

Turning to Tenzin, she revelled in his smiles and then looked to the beaded necklace in his hand.

"May I see, Tenzin?"

Following the young Geisha's eyes, Tenzin nodded and carefully handed her his string of wooden beads.

"Thank you," she whispered to him.

Taking them from the young monk, Momoko's fingers rubbed gentle across each worn bead and began to flick them one by one over her thumb. Watching her do so, Tenzin warmed to the comfort the young Geisha's presence gave and looked out to the clouds passing before him. Becoming lost in their golden tinged edges, he recalled his treasured Tibetan skies, and the memories of the birthdays he had shared beneath them with those from his past.

CHAPTER TWENTY-THREE

Pulling his robes to him, Tenzin glanced to Momoko as she also adjusted her jacket in the prevailing cool winds. Sensing his gaze, Momoko looked out across the ocean to the pink and red hues building before them.

"See," she said. "I knew we would watch the sun fall together."

"You did?"

"Tenzin, now we are free to enjoy such a sight in each other's company."

Pointing to their sunset she settled back with an added smile as Tenzin did likewise beside her, both at ease in the unexpected comfort found on San Francisco's harbour front.

As if the sight was theirs alone, the young Geisha and monk watched a golden sun melt into its calm horizon. With Tenzin's beads still held tight in her hand, Momoko loosened her grasp on the precious necklace, lost in thoughts of how fast their afternoon together had passed. With all her years spent in the company of men, never before had she felt such ease beside another. Recalling Hanako and Auntie's formative training in the art of conversation, Momoko remembered the tricks she had utilised to accompany her unique beauty.

Taking the old woman's advice, she had told her clients that she too had shared the experiences they spoke of, even if such words deemed untrue. This, Momoko knew, would entice her clients to shower her with gifts both material and emotional, leading them to think the young Geisha before them held an uncanny union to their own feelings having experienced the same moments also.

Feeling the young monk's warmth beside her, Momoko

considered the similar paths she and Tenzin's life had taken and how there was now no need for the false experiences she had been taught to speak of. The young Geisha's eyes left the dimming sun and she looked down to the single cherry blossom rested in her lap. This simple gift of petals of pink and white gave Momoko more than she ever imagined possible. Returning to the fading sunset, her heart was fulfilled that she at last shared the closing daytime hours at Tenzin's side.

Momoko recalled her solitary days aboard ship and how she had longed for the young monk to join her so they may watch the view playing out before them.

Her wishes granted, the young Geisha wondered once more how Tenzin had spent his time alone in his cabin. Turning to him, her curiosity grew in his smiles and she once again broke the peaceful silence between them.

"Tenzin, you remember our travels here?"

"Yes, and how I too longed to join you so we may enjoy this sight together." He lowered his head as Momoko flushed beside him. "I am sorry to embarrass you, Momoko."

"You do not embarrass me, young monk. I knew you wanted to join me," Momoko giggled." She paused. "May I ask you a question?"

"Yes."

"Tell me, what did you do alone in your cabin for most of your journey?"

Tenzin looked to the worn wooden beads in Momoko's hands, wondering if the young Geisha already knew her answer.

"I was emptying my thoughts," he replied.

"How?" she said. "I have never heard of such a thing."

"Would you like me to show you?"

Tenzin hopes that the young Geisha would accept his proposal were justified as she nodded to him.

"You see the ocean before us?" He began. "Look to the waves as they rise and fall. Now close your eyes and picture that which you have just seen."

Watching Momoko do as instructed, Tenzin placed his hands into his lap and cupped one hand into the other, forming a circle as the tips of his thumbs touched together.

"Can you see those waves, Momoko?"

Smiling as she nodded, he too closed his eyes as he spoke once more.

"Now, think of nothing else but those waves, and then."

Feeling the young Geisha's intent want to continue, he warmed to her presence. "And then, Momoko, picture the same ocean, yet still, with no waves upon its surface."

Falling into his own focus, Tenzin pictured the still waters he spoke of and smiled on hearing Momoko's breathing slow to match his own.

Opening his eyes, Tenzin looked to the young Geisha beside him. Her great beauty was overshadowed by the tranquil appearance she now held and the young monk considered his companion's true identity once more as her breathing slowed yet again.

She opened her eyes and stared back at him.

"I did it, I did it," she said. "But..."

"But only for a brief moment?"

"Yes," Momoko saddened. "How did you know?"

"Oh, I know," Tenzin laughed. "It takes such practice and dedication to remain in the emptiness we try so hard to reach. Yet even a brief glimpse of that peace gives us an insight to what treasures such moments contain."

"So I did well on my first try?"

"More than well, Momoko."

"Thank you, Tenzin," the young Geisha whispered. Her hushed tones echoed the return of reddening cheeks. Looking out to the ocean waves her mind had released for those fleeting moments, she turned back to Tenzin..

"What is the purpose in finding this peace, Tenzin?" she asked. "I mean, I understand the benefits of resting my mind in such a way. But there must be other benefits held within calming my thoughts."

"Look out to the ocean once more, Momoko," Tenzin replied. "Tell me, how does it make you feel?"

Casting her view on the vast seas before them, the young Geisha's frown deepened.

"It makes me feel small," she answered.

"Me also, Momoko," Tenzin agreed. "You too see its immense size. We sitting here on this wooden bench seem so insignificant in comparison."

Momoko nodded, her frowns easing as she listened to the young monk's words.

"If we stop for a moment and forget its vast size, we allow ourselves to concentrate on only one bit. Where we are now, Momoko. Although we know these waters are far bigger than we can see from here, to think of such enormity will only confound us. By just thinking of the little we can see, this brings the ocean into perspective."

Seeing Momoko's frowns remained, he leant to her.

"Think of these waters as being moments in time, Momoko," he continued. "We have both travelled upon this ocean to arrive here, yet we can no longer see the passage we once took. This is the same as our past. It is gone from us now, out of our view. Now, think of the seas we have neither seen nor travelled yet. These waters are our future and are also hidden from us."

Tenzin warmed once again as Momoko smiled in understanding his words.

"Then what of the ocean spread out before us now, Tenzin?"

"The waters we see now, Momoko, are neither the past nor the future. They are the present moment."

Momoko's eyebrows rose as she saw what Tenzin spoke of.

"So by living in the present moment, we no longer think of the things that have passed. Or of our unknown future."

Excited by her new discovery Tenzin's spirit lightened also to Momoko's perception. His thoughts returning to the causes behind such quick understanding, the young monk dismissed his ideas and looked back across the ocean to their sunset's dying embers.

"There are no problems in the present," he said. "We can cope with anything that happens in these present moments."

Joining with Tenzin's unread thoughts, Momoko felt his sorrow also that the skies which had held such vivid colour now gave way for night.

"I understand now, Tenzin," she said. "Thank you for showing me such ways."

On hearing Momoko's words, Tenzin shook his head to her praise.

"Momoko," he smiled. "A great teacher learns as much from his students, as they do from him. It is I who must thank you."

Understanding Tenzin's gratitude she wondered what Auntie would have thought, should she have listened to the words spoken between the young monk and herself. Considering the guardian Tenzin had recalled with a similar fondness, she wondered what he would also have made of their conversations.

"Did Lama Norbu teach these ways?"

"Yes, Momoko. But there were many others also."

"And, Lama Jampo? Did he know of such things too?"

Concealing his surprise to Momoko's question, Tenzin saw she subconsciously flicked each worn bead in slow succession. Looking back into her striking eyes, he nodded to her.

"Yes, Momoko, I am more than sure he did."

Tenzin's heart pounding with each flipped wooden bead beside him.

Sensing his surprise she too looked to the necklace.

"Here, Tenzin," she held the beads out to him. "I have held these for far too long now."

"No, they are for you, Momoko."

Looking to the beads, Momoko mirrored the young monk's denial. "No, Tenzin," she said. "They are yours. You cannot give me such a cherished gift."

"And why not? They suit you better than I. Have you never been given a gift before?"

Momoko flushed to the young monk's questioning. Seeing Tenzin's insistence towards her acceptance, she lowered her hand and held the necklace to her chest.

"Thank you," she said.

Feeling the warm wooden beads against her, Momoko recalled another who had given such a treasured gift. Looking to her bag, she thought of Keiko's red doll contained within and the generosity her younger sister's soul had portrayed. The young Geisha's cheeks coloured once more as old memories entered her. Younger recollections she had pushed away resurfaced and Momoko looked to Tenzin, her shame evident in her eyes.

"There was one who also gave me something they held dear to them," she said. "Yet I am undeserving of their kindness."

"In what way, Momoko?" The young monk frowned, his forgotten memories also brought forward by his own questions. "How could that be?"

Momoko looked to the emerging full moon high above the vast ocean before them. Remembering how only she and Auntie knew of the event which had marred Keiko's arrival to the Okiya, the young Geisha considered that if Keiko had been aware of her spiteful actions, would she still have given the doll to her only months ago. Momoko raised a weak smile. Yes, she thought, I suppose she still would have.

"Your memories still stay with you, Momoko," Tenzin said, his observations causing him also to glance to his bag. Remorse accompanied his gaze towards Ketu's red flute buried deep beneath his belongings.

"Yes, Tenzin," Momoko nodded. "They do."

Turning to him, she told of her hurtful act in taking Keiko's much loved possession for herself. With years of hidden regret, the young Geisha shed a tear as she spoke of Auntie's kindness in keeping the incident between them and how she had not once spoken of the matter again.

Momoko feared the reprisals from the young monk beside her in her admissions.

"We were all young once," Tenzin said. "And although that does not excuse our malicious acts to others, it is a test to ourselves if we feel remorse for those actions in our later years."

Seeing Momoko gained some peace from his words, he looked from the young Geisha, and recalled the hurt Ketu had inflicted on him and to the remaining pain his heart experienced on finding his grandfather's red flute laying in shards across his bunk. Glancing back to his bag, Tenzin felt a familiar regret return and he too lowered his chin in shame for the actions that had instigated his long journey to these American shores.

"You also hold such regrets, young monk," Momoko whispered beside him, her understanding enhanced as her hand found its home on Tenzin's arm once again.

Feeling the young Geisha's soft touch, Tenzin battled to tell of the reasons for his arrival in San Francisco. Yet as he eased into the security Momoko's tender contact provided, those words would not come. Looking out to the ocean, Tenzin tried to regain the peace found across its waters. Attempting to clear its rising waves in his mind, his concentration faltered as Ketu's lost eyes returned to him.

"It is ok, Tenzin," Momoko smiled as the young monk looked back to her. "There are many things within us to talk of. Those moments in time will come forth, if and when they are ready to do so."

"Thank you," Tenzin replied, his soul strengthened by Momoko's kindness.

"It is my pleasure," she replied as together they watched moon beams dance across gentle waves ahead of them.

Losing themselves within such a view, Momoko wondered of the new found understanding she felt at Tenzin's side. Once again, her thoughts explored the past she had tried so hard to forget. Momoko's eyes widened as she stumbled into the reasons behind her behaviour towards those who had held her best interests at heart.

"Tenzin," her sight remained ahead. "When someone tries to break your dreams, we sometimes try to break everyone else's."

Momoko raised her chin to the ocean.

"But when we try to destroy another's dreams, we only end up destroying our own," she said.

"Then what is the answer, Momoko? How do we keep from doing such a thing?"

"That's easy, Tenzin," the young Geisha giggled. "All you have to do is dream a better dream."

Forgetting his repentance, Tenzin fell into the same laughter beside him, his soul surrounded by Momoko's good humour. Never before had he encountered such a one as the young Geisha, his gratitude increasing his forgiveness towards his brothers' hasty departure.

"Thank you, Momoko"

His appreciation mirrored Momoko's own sentiments, conveyed by the dark brown eyes now penetrating his. Avoiding her stares, Tenzin felt his cheeks burn and he reached down for his bag.

"Are you hungry, young Geisha?"

Momoko nodded and she too leant to her belongings.

"Here," they said simultaneously, and laughed again as each looked to the apple in the other's outstretched hand. Taking the offering from one another, they smiled and then took a bite from the fruit, holding their gaze as they did so, neither surprised by the gifts received from one another.

Taking his final bite, Tenzin smiled as he watched Momoko continue her delicate nibbles.

"Does it not taste sweeter?" He asked.

"My apple? Yes, I suppose it does. Why is that?"

"Why do you think, young Geisha?"

Momoko finished her apple and followed Tenzin's stares behind them.

"He's gone," she said.

"The trader gave you his gifts also, Momoko?"

As both looked back to the empty market place where the young stall holder had given them his apples, each realised they had once more succumbed to a similar fate.

"Yes," Tenzin whispered.

The ship looming in the distance caught his attention and he watched its crew readying her bows for the journey he would take at midnight. Turning from the vessel, he considered his decision to aid Momoko's passage back to her own home lands, wondering if her soul would benefit from such charity. Still undecided on his actions, he looked to Momoko and sensed her thoughts towards his sudden aloofness.

"What is it, Tenzin?" She asked, concerned for her companion's distraction.

"Nothing," he simply replied.

Looking to the apple core in his palm, he raised a smile to calm Momoko's anxiety.

"So why did the apple seem sweeter? Are you going to tell me?"

To Momoko's playful demands, Tenzin leant back against their wooden bench.

"When a gift is given to us in joy, it enhances all that is present within the item, be it food, drink or object. The said gift holds that love from its bestower so we may too enjoy the pleasure it once gave them. That, Momoko, is what gave our apples their characteristic sweetness."

"A double sweetness, young monk."

"Yes, your right, a double sweetness. We also contributed to the love which surrounded the trader's gift, by offering them on towards each other."

Settling back beside him, Momoko felt Tenzin's warmth again and fought her want to move closer to him. Remembering his holy position, she forced her wants from her. Raising her hand, she smirked to Tenzin.

"Come on," Momoko pulled her arm back. "Who can throw the furthest?"

Taking her lead, each threw the apple cores as far into the ocean as they could. Both looked to the other as they listened to the plopping sounds before them.

"I think I won," Momoko whispered, folding her arms in defiance.

"Yes," Tenzin answered. "Maybe," he added, aware of Momoko's need for the comfort of his presence, Tenzin's thoughts remained with the vows he had taken beneath Tashilhunpo's sacred rooftops. Fighting his longing to hold the hand which had lain on his arm twice, he dismissed his growing reasons towards their meeting.

"Tenzin?" Momoko pulled him from his thoughts. "What if you receive a gift that is not given with the kindness you speak of?"

"Then the opposite happens. Those delicious apples would have proved a bitter tinge to them had they been given in spite."

"And so we must always give only with the good intentions we want to pass onto those we care for?"

Momoko watched the young monk nod in reply. Seeing the delight he held in her growing awareness, Momoko fell silent as she recalled her encounter on Tokyo's waterfront days before her departure. Memories of the old fisherman returned. Remembering how his smile had mirrored her own, she wondered of his true identity, and of the scar which tarnished the once handsome looks she was sure he had held in his younger days. Wanting to tell Tenzin of him, Momoko instead kept her silence. Losing her purse, she was aware that now without such means her return to Japan lay in doubt. The sorrow she felt that she may never see the homeless fisherman again was lightened by her memories of the joy encountered on giving him her remaining rice cake.

"To give is also a pleasure," she whispered into the night sky.

"Yes, Momoko," Tenzin caught her words beneath the silver moon lighting their features. "The joys of giving meet with those of receiving, coming full circle until..."

"Until that which we provide comes back to us in the most unexpected ways," Momoko finished Tenzin's words.

The young Geisha raised her hand to her mouth and giggled to Tenzin's returned surprise.

"Do not seem so astonished, young monk," she said. "I too am aware of what you speak."

"Yes, Momoko, I know," his heart ached to speak of his ideas, but still he held his silence.

Fearful of the reaction the young Geisha would give should he speak of what he believed now, he instead nestled back in his robes, longing for Momoko to sidle up to him so he too could feel her warmth.

Momoko's experience told her of Tenzin's wishes. Hesitating, she surrendered to her wants and shuffled across the seat towards him. Stopping a hairs breadth from him, she knew the young monk's gratitude.

"It is cold," she warranted her actions.

"Of that it is, young Geisha," he acknowledged the deepening bonds each held between them.

"Tenzin," Momoko whispered as they sat in comfort together. "You speak of your homelands with such fondness. Tell me, why did you leave the place you love so much?"

Have spent so long hiding his longings for the crystal blue skies he had forsaken in his moment of forgotten compassion, Tenzin decided to speak of what tormented him so.

"There is a reason behind my journey here. Of this I shall tell you."

The young monk turned to the beautiful young woman sat so close to his side.

"Yet, Momoko, are there not causes for your leaving your treasured Okiya also?"

CHAPTER TWENTY-FOUR

Momoko looked from Tenzin and out to the full moon before them. Breaking free of silver tinged clouds, the moon's glow pushed forwards to cast a line of highlighted waves towards her. The young Geisha's view settled on its silvery trail.

"Look, Tenzin," she smiled. "They have found each other again."

Tenzin followed Momoko's view out to the ocean's flickering ripples. He too smiled on seeing their apple cores encircled one another. Watching Momoko's delight his heart pounded as their small dinner brought yet more answers to him.

"It seems they were destined to meet, Momoko."

"Yes, it does, young monk," Momoko replied, her head bowing to conceal the thoughts towards her and Tenzin's encounter as she too considered the significance of all that had been shared between them as day turned into night.

Memories of her homelands rushed back to the young Geisha. The events which had led to her arrival came to her also and Momoko wondered if she should tell of the actions that gave rise to her leaving the Okiya's relative safety.

"We both know of the reasons why we travelled to these shores, Tenzin," she said, "you to meet with your brothers and I with my patron. But yes, you are right there were certain events that led to my being here, as I am sure there were for you."

Watching the young monk lower his head, Momoko sensed his shame and reached for him once more.

"I will tell you of the causes behind my arrival here, Tenzin." Momoko paused, her eyes narrowing. "If only you promise that you shall share the moments towards your departure as well."

Looking to Momoko's delicate fingers rested on his arm, Tenzin raised his head and nodded to her.

"I promise."

Understanding his admissions would prove the release he craved, the young monk relaxed in Momoko's gentle touch, his heart warmed by the forbidden contact between them.

The young Geisha's fingers trailed from Tenzin's arm. Aware of their prohibited touch, she smiled and held Tenzin's necklace in both hands. Running her finger tips across its beads, Momoko looked out to the ocean and the apple cores continual dance around each other. The fruits trepidation caused by each rising wave mirrored her own feeling towards the young monk beside her and she smiled to the brief moments when the remains of their meal touched together.

Falling into the silence between them, Momoko smiled down to her gift. Knowing the necklace had been given with the love she and Tenzin had talked of, another's smile came to her, evoking the pleasure she had received on Tokyo's harbour front.

Remembering those moments, the young Geisha looked to her bag, aware Keiko's red doll lay somewhere within.

Keiko's kindness surrounded Momoko as she began to share the shame Tenzin experienced also. Recalling her younger days when she had left Hiroko's treasured gift in Kyoto, Momoko told Tenzin of how she had taken Keiko's cherished doll for her own. In silence, she remembered her guilt towards her treatment of her younger sister's forgiving soul, and of the generosity shown only months ago in parting with her treasured possession.

"There was another whose actions prompted your arrival in San Francisco?" Tenzin asked on seeing Momoko's disquiet.

"Yes, Tenzin. In a way there was."

"Then tell me," Tenzin encouraged. "Speak of them so we may share our regrets towards those of our past."

As Momoko turned to him, the young monk recalled Ketu's appearance within Tashilhunpo's walls. Pushing his past from him, anxiety resurfaced on remembering his vow to speak of such events.

Seeing Tenzin shared a similar hurt, Momoko's hand returned to his arm. A smile accompanied her finger's tender squeeze.

"I have talked of my younger sister before," Momoko began. "Keiko," she whispered glancing down to her bag once again.

Looking back to Tenzin she told of Keiko's arrival to the Okiya and of their schooling together. Realising no judgement came from the young monk, Momoko continued with her tale and of her disrespectful treatment towards her young charge whose unconditional smile would always greet such harsh words.

Remembering how Keiko had ignored the resentment placed upon her, Momoko saddened as her actions became more apparent to her on releasing past mistakes.

In the liberation the young Geisha gained from unfolding her history Tenzin wondered if he too would receive the same peace of mind from his own admissions. As Ketu's features returned to him, he recalled the misplaced soul which had glared back at him through vacant eyes. The memories of such a stare haunted Tenzin, his sorrow mounting in his easy dismissal of another's cry for help, trusting his own lapse of compassion would find the reprieve he yearned.

"The forgiveness Keiko held towards you was always there, Momoko. Can you not see this?"

"In a way," Momoko sighed. "But how can that excuse my behaviour?"

"This is it, Momoko. Keiko waited for you to feel the regrets you do now. She saw through all the resentment you took to her presence within the Okiya. She understood."

"Then all the time I was so horrible to her, Keiko knew the true feelings my soul held?"

The young Geisha raised a soft smile as the respite she sought flourished inside her.

"Then, Keiko understood the reasons behind my bitterness towards her? She knew all along?" Momoko paused. "She waited for me to reach my own understanding."

"Yes, Momoko," Tenzin's own hopes lay in that Ketu's distressed mind also shared the same understanding towards his own soul. He frowned as Momoko's joy left her.

"What is it, Momoko?" he asked, concerned for the young Geisha's sorrow.

Momoko shrugged. "If only I had known then," she mumbled out to calm waters.

Seeing their apples were no longer before them, Momoko looked back to Tenzin.

"Then I would not have acted the way I did that night."

"When, Momoko? What night?"

Leaning back, Momoko recounted the night she and Keiko had vied for the representative's affections. Tenzin smiled on occasion as he listened, optimistic his silence would persuade the young Geisha to reveal her story to him. Trying to imagine the finery and abundance the banquet offered, his eyes widened as Momoko described how red wine had seeped into her expensive kimono from Keiko's hand. Tenzin glanced down to his own burgundy robes. Was this another indication towards him and Momoko's true bond? His want to tell of his theories amplified. Shuddering as Momoko told of the damage inflicted to Keiko's beloved Shamisen, he recalled the hurt his heart experienced many years ago to Ketu's similar spiteful act. Yet it was not the young Geisha's actions which gave such shock. More so it was the continuing similarities between their past.

Momoko saw Tenzin's reaction and lowered her head.

"And then what happened, Momoko?" Tenzin whispered, the need to clarify his thoughts developing with every word spoken.

"Keiko was chosen to come here. Here to San Francisco to start the new life promised to me also."

"Then how is it you and not she who sits here beside me, Momoko?"

Tenzin's frown deepened as the young Geisha shook her head.

"Tenzin, there was another event."

Momoko's heart filled with memories of her brief encounter on Tokyo's dockside. Recalling the joy her selfless actions had produced, she raised a smile, her shame replaced by the warmth felt that day.

"And what was that event?"

Summoning the courage to speak of her meeting with the one who shared so much with her, she hesitated.

"All in good time, young monk," she whispered.

Glancing back to the moon's silver glow, she met with Tenzin's gaze and nodded to him.

"Now," she tentatively placed her hand on his. "Have you not got something to tell me?"

Feeling the young Geisha's fingers curl around his, Tenzin acted like wise.

Comforted by the warmth his soul emitted, he fell into her tactile touch, aware their joining ran deeper than the mere meeting of two strangers.

"Yes, Momoko, I too have reasons behind my arrival here. Reasons of which I hold no pride towards," he said out across the dark waters before them.

Encouraged by Momoko's delicate hand in his, Tenzin told of Ketu's arrival to Tashilhunpo. Explaining how he had welcomed his new brother with affection and understanding, he saddened on speaking of how his young charge refused the care his soul presented. Momoko concealed her frowns on hearing of such moments, she herself beginning to consider the causes their deepening bond portrayed. Listening to Ketu's conduct towards Tenzin, Momoko searched for an explanation to why she and the young monk's lives echoed each other's in such a way. Discovering Ketu's behaviour towards Tenzin matched hers to Keiko, she paled, her mind dismissing the ideas of her and the young monk's true identity, and the reasons for their meeting here on American shores.

Momoko looked down to her bag as Tenzin spoke of finding his grandfather's flute lying in shards across his bed. Keiko's red doll pulled on her emotions and Momoko shamed once again in realising how she and Ketu shared such similar traits.

As Tenzin spoke of how his duties had been taken from him and given to Ketu, Momoko recalled the moments she too had been cast aside to allow Keiko to wait for her older sisters until the early morning hours. Yet as she listened to how Tenzin had helped Ketu in his chores, Momoko saw how in some way she too could have aided Keiko with hers. Seeing Keiko's position through fresh eyes, the young Geisha once more understood Keiko's unfaltering compassion towards her, her insights bringing with them the further release her heart craved for.

The young Geisha gave Tenzin's hand a calming squeeze as he told of Ketu's acts of harming his treasured Lamas. Witnessing the pain such memories produced, she raised a smile as Tenzin shook his hurt from him and told of the relief felt on Ketu's banishment from Tashilhunpo's walls.

"And you never saw him again, Tenzin?"

"Oh yes, Momoko," the young monk replied, his heart heavy once more. "We were to meet again."

Drawing his hand from hers, Tenzin reached down for his bag and pulled it to him.

"What is it you are looking for," Momoko asked.

"The reason behind why I am here."

He smiled to the young Geisha's surprise in seeing Ketu's flute.

"You mended it?"

"No, Momoko," Tenzin saddened. "My grandfather's gift was far from repair. This," he held the flute out to her. "Is Ketu's handiwork."

Raising the instrument to his lips he began to play the notes he had known since a boy. Losing herself in its melodic tune, Momoko's ideas towards their encounter grew. Looking out to silver tinged clouds the young Geisha wondered how such notions deemed possible.

As Tenzin's recital came to an end he smiled to Momoko.

"That was beautiful," she whispered to him.

Her hand reaching for his once more.

"What troubles you so, young monk?"

Gazing down to the string of wooden beads, Tenzin saddened as he recalled how another had recognised the necklace Momoko now held to her.

"You already know of Ketu's misdeeds towards myself and my peers, Momoko," he said. "But it would be my own insensitivity towards such a misguided soul which caused me to leave my home."

"Then you must speak of these things, Tenzin," Momoko encouraged, aware of the release the young monk craved. "If only for yourself than any other."

Knowing he understood, Momoko was certain he too sensed the new found freedom she experienced from her admissions.

"Speak to me of what has gone before, Tenzin," she whispered. "For as did you to me, I shall hold no judgement towards your wrongs."

As Tenzin's fingers folded soft around hers he began to recount the moment he faced his childhood adversary once more.

Recalling his shock in seeing Ketu's bedraggled appearance, Tenzin told of the emotions such recognition triggered.

"My heart pounded in witnessing the advanced years his features portrayed, Momoko," his hand squeezed gentle in hers. "So many seasons had passed since our last encounter, yet it seemed Ketu had witnessed many more."

"And what were your feelings towards him, Tenzin. Did you pity such a character?"

"At first, Momoko," Tenzin admitted. He paused and looked to the arcing moon above them. "But then…"

"But what, Tenzin," the young Geisha pressed. "Tell me."

"But then I remembered all that had gone before, the deceit and hurt he had exposed to those who had only ever shown kindness towards him."

As Tenzin spoke of the fleeting compassion he had held towards Ketu, he fell silent once more on telling of the anger which had surfaced within him that day.

"It is understandable that such emotions came to you, Tenzin," Momoko heartened. "We all fall prey to these feelings from time to time."

"Yes, Momoko, but until that point, I had never experienced the rage which contained me. My life had been spent within the compassion my soul endeared, yet as Ketu sat before me I could find no empathy towards his soul."

Tenzin turned from Momoko and gazed out onto the ocean, his heart trying to find peace within its moonlit strip.

Momoko looked to the young monk's profile. Feeling his sadness, she watched the night sky reflected in his tear filled eyes and placed her other hand on his.

"But I see you have found that compassion now."

Tenzin turned to meet her gaze.

"Yes, Momoko," he gave a faint smile. "It is only now I understand the circumstances Ketu faced in arriving alone to Tashilhunpo. It could not have been easy to be with one such as I, whose destiny proved my belonging within those walls. It is only now I see how Ketu projected his fears and resentments onto me, bringing me the understanding and forgiveness lost in our reunion."

"Then now you are free, Tenzin. Can you not see this? You have released your anger towards Ketu and his crimes. Do you not feel the liberation I too now experience?"

Acknowledging the freedom of which Momoko talked, some guilt remained.

"There is more, Tenzin?" Momoko's wisdom resurfaced in the young monk's company.

"Yes, Momoko. There is," Tenzin's view retuned to moonlit waters.

"Then once more you must tell me," Momoko smiled.

Describing how he had offered Ketu his remaining apple, a single tear fell from the young monk as he spoke of how he had taken the fruit from Ketu's hungry eyes and placed it back into his bag. The redemption encircling the young monk touched Momoko in a way never experienced before and she once more considered the ideas towards their soul's true identities. Casting aside her theories, she cupped her hands around Tenzin's and leant to him.

"But you gave me your final apple, Tenzin," she smiled. "Does that not show the compassion and empathy you once thought lost within you was there all along?"

"Yes," Tenzin frowned. "I suppose it does."

Tenzin's regrets ebbed from him, and although some doubts towards his actions remained, he felt sure his past transgressions towards Ketu had in some way been absolved.

The corners of his lips rose as he too joined Momoko's smiles.

"Thank you," he whispered to her. "How is it you make me see that which I thought lost?"

"And do you not think you do the same for me, young monk?" Momoko giggled, happy he understood the lessons they spoke of.

The young Geisha glanced to Tenzin's flute.

"Then how is it you now hold Ketu's gift?"

Listening to Tenzin recall his refusal of Ketu's crude present and how Lama Norbu had witnessed his callous actions, Momoko nodded. She too accompanied Tenzin's smile on hearing how Ketu's promised fruit came with such a bitter tang.

Understanding now the reasons behind why the young monk had left his beloved homelands, her thoughts returned to Lama Jampo. Wondering if Tenzin's predecessor would have made the same errors, Momoko's heart beat faster in recalling his name. Dismissing such feelings, she gladdened once more in seeing Tenzin's smile return.

"And now you have found your answers, Tenzin," she said.

"Yes, and it seems much more besides, young Geisha," Tenzin's soul lightened by freeing the admissions harboured within him for so long.

Momoko blushed to the young monk's words, she too acknowledging her thoughts. Tenderly unravelling her hands from his, Momoko reached down into her bag. She grinned on finding Keiko's red doll and held it up to Tenzin.

"You returned to your mother's home?"

"No, Tenzin," Momoko saddened. With thoughts of her Kyoto's famed rows of cherry trees, she raised a smile on recalling Hiroko's birthday gift. "Keiko gave me her doll," she explained, "to keep me company on my travels."

"A kind soul this Keiko holds, Momoko," Tenzin smiled. "Tell me, young Geisha, what kindness did you portray to receive such a gift?"

Unsure of Tenzin's question, Momoko frowned.

"In what way do you mean, Tenzin?"

"Well, for you to be given such a prized possession, your actions towards another must have triggered Keiko's generosity. Was there not someone who received such kindness from your own soul before you accepted your gift?"

The single rice cake she had given that afternoon on Tokyo's harbour front came forth in her memories. Considering if her selfless act towards the fisher man had some way in turn prompted Keiko to part with her cherished doll, the young Geisha looked before her, hoping an answer lay across its highlighted gentle waves.

"So if I had given something I treasured to another, than that act would somehow be repaid back to me, Tenzin?"

Turning to the young monk, Momoko saw her words rang true.

"Yes, Momoko. Each of our actions holds great consequences.

"Even the bad ones?" Momoko shuffled in her seat. "I mean, when we hurt others, we shall one day experience such a pain also?"

Great anxiety shrouded the young Geisha as Tenzin nodded to her.

"Yes, Momoko, this is true also. But these actions and consequences are not separate, they are a whole, without each other they would cease to exist. If you are involved in a certain action, then you shall be part of the consequence each and every time. Even the slightest ill will towards another's soul will come back to us in some form or other. These are the rules on which our lives run, Momoko. Everything we do, say or feel holds with it its own costs, be them good or bad."

"Have you too experienced a consequence from your own misdeeds, Tenzin?" Momoko avoided her own sins.

"Yes, Momoko," Tenzin replied aware of her evasion. "As have you also against those we have talked of this night."

"You mean, Keiko and Ketu?"

"It seems our actions towards them may have led to the situation we now find ourselves in."

Understanding Tenzin's words, her cheeks lost their flush and she stared at Tenzin.

"So if my behaviour had held more respect to Keiko, I may not have been turned away from my proposed benefactor's door?"

"That just may be," Tenzin agreed. He paused and leant to the young Geisha. "And also, if my own conduct towards Ketu's lost soul had been filled with compassion, then maybe I would now be sitting amongst by brothers."

"And just maybe, young monk," Momoko grinned. "We would never have met and not be sitting here together also."

"That is also true," Tenzin joined Momoko's good humour.

Recalling another who he had been told once shared the same jollity beside him, Momoko he saw the concern held in such striking eyes.

"Often when we have completed a circle of the consequences we ourselves have set before us, then our past actions come to us and mirror that which we have just concluded."

"So if our bad acts have caught up with us, and we have received that penalty, then the good that is waiting for us from previous selfless deeds appears?"

Tenzin nodded again. This time it was he who reached for the young Geisha's delicate hand. Smiling as she accepted his grasp, he leant to her once more.

"We cannot determine from what good acts our rewards come, Momoko. Maybe our encounter was brought about on my behalf by the help I gave Ketu in his duties for so many years. No one can tell."

"Well, young monk," Momoko giggled. "I am glad you did help him."

In the delight within Momoko's eyes, Tenzin once again recalled the humour he had been told his predecessor had held. Wanting to tell the young Geisha his ideas on their meeting and of the identity he was sure she held, the young monk hesitated once again.

"Was there not such a good act you carried out which may have led to our meeting?"

"Yes, Tenzin," Momoko whispered. "There was," she added, picturing the Tokyo fisherman's smile on receiving her last rice cake from her hand.

Momoko no longer found it strange that she and Tenzin held a similar history and her ideas towards the young monk's own identity surfaced again as it had throughout their time spent together. Aware he too contained the same needs to speak of such matters, she smiled.

"What?"

"I think we have both come to understand who our souls are, Tenzin."

"Yes, young Geisha, I know. But before we speak of our ideas, you must tell me what prompted your arrival to these shores."

Momoko nodded and then looked out onto the waters she and the young monk beside her had each travelled. Knowing it was time to talk of her encounter of the one who had shared her smile, Momoko gazed upwards.

Watching dark clouds diminish and the moon's full light burst forwards, the beautiful young Geisha smiled up to the sky's emerging stars and then back to Tenzin.

CHAPTER TWENTY-FIVE

Cool breezes whipped past Momoko and Tenzin. In its slight chill, Momoko sidled up to the young monk and stopped just from him once more. Looking back to the night sky, she felt his view match hers.

"It seems strange, Tenzin," Momoko said, her eyes fixed on the mounting pin points of light above them.

"What seems strange?"

"That our lives have always shared the same stars we now sit beneath, yet in all that time we were never aware that the other existed."

"But in a way we both knew we did, Momoko. Am I not right?"

"Yes," the young Geisha nodded. "I too feel our connection, Tenzin, as I am sure you do too. We each know our meeting was meant to be. Of this I have my own ideas towards, but, young monk, I wonder if my theories are shared by you also."

"I think we already know of our answers, Momoko," Tenzin's own thoughts towards their souls uniqueness eased by Momoko's apparent understanding.

He wondered if he should now approach the matters which had chased his beliefs since their first words together. Aware his assumptions needed the final part of Momoko's history to be told he looked back to the night sky's flickering band of stars.

"Momoko," he said. "What brought you here so we may meet?"

The young Geisha knew what Tenzin asked of her now. In the months since her encounter with the lowly fisherman on Tokyo's peaceful harbour front, not a day had gone by when his smile had not appeared to her. Seeing his innocent expression now, Momoko felt her joy return, prompting her to speak of the humble actions she thought lost from her own character.

"My own homelands share a similar dockside as the one we sit at now, Tenzin," she began. "As I suppose the world does all over. But the harbour I talk of now, young monk, has always given me a peace so seldom found within my heart."

Tenzin smiled as Momoko described her waterside sanctuary, remembering how he too had shared such tranquil settings amongst Tashilhunpo's hidden annexes and chambers. Witnessing the young Geisha's delight in recalling her private haven, he glanced back to the empty market place behind them. Memories of his own home's stalls and traders mixed with Momoko's as she talked of the two rice cakes she had bought with Auntie's money.

"They tasted good?"

"Yes, Tenzin," Momoko nodded.

Once again her view fell to the ocean's gentle waves before them. "Although," she whispered. "I was only to eat one of my treats that day."

Holding his words in hope his silence would encourage Momoko to continue, she understood the young monk's stillness. Giving him a coy smile in return to the unspoken respect for one another, she told of her walk to the Tokyo bay waters so far from where they now sat, and of the homeless man whose smile had drawn her to him.

"And you knew the man you approached?"

"Not as such, Tenzin," Momoko shook her head. "I had seen him fishing on the harbour front many times before and had always paid little attention to him, but that afternoon, it was so strange. I felt drawn towards his smile."

As Tenzin heard of the man's ragged clothes and glazed stare he recalled Ketu's haggard appearance. His soul reached for the compassion hidden from him that day. Hoping Momoko would tell of her actions towards the humble fisherman, the young monk's thoughts remained with the similarities the young Geisha and he held. Thinking if her admissions would counteract his own past wrongs, Tenzin knew such words would prove his ideas towards their soul's distinctive connection.

Telling of the deep scar running down the fisher man's cheek, Momoko recalled how his affliction faded from view, overpowered by the smiles they had shared together.

"It was then, Tenzin," she continued, "that I gave him my remaining rice cake."

"And how was your treat received, young Geisha?"

"With delight," Momoko flushed. "But, it seemed it was I who received much more in return."

Looking from Tenzin, Momoko remembered the rich warmth her actions had produced, and how she had longed to feel that emotion once more. Momoko swung her head back to him, her eyes wide.

"Our actions were the same, Tenzin," she said remembering Ketu's sad tale. "Well the situation at least."

"Yes, Momoko, I know. Were as you gave with your heart, I instead gave nothing to the one who needed my help most."

Tenzin lowered his head as Ketu's image returned to him, yet his spirits lifted as he thought of his former charge. Knowing for certain the implications of his and Momoko's meeting together, the young monk wondered how his news would be greeted by the beautiful young woman beside him.

"Where I helped, Tenzin," Momoko smiled. "You did not. But do not be disheartened, for we both know my previous actions have always opposed yours. Is this not part of the reason why we have met this day?"

"We may never know the reasons for our encounter, Momoko. But tell me, have you considered that the bonds we hold together may outreach that which we both believe to be true?"

As Momoko nodded to him, Tenzin realised his explanations would soon be accepted. He raised his head and returned to the young Geisha.

"Tell me more of the man who shared your smile, Momoko."

Feeling Momoko's hand rest on his arm, her tender touch matched the sentiments his heart received on hearing she had bought the fisher man's paltry catch.

"And how did you feel in making such a selfless act, Momoko?"

Momoko's chin fell to Tenzin's question.

"Wonderful," she replied, tears running freely down her cheeks.

Casting aside his want to comfort the young Geisha, Tenzin glanced down to the delicate fingers entwined within his. Aware their touch was forbidden in the eyes of his peers, the young monk experienced no guilt in their tender hold. Knowing for certain the significance of the bond shared between them both, any fears towards Momoko's reaction to such matters faded from him and he smiled back to her tears.

"Momoko, what you felt that day, in those moments you talk of now. Do you know why your heart filled with such joy?"

"Because I gave to another, with no want of anything in return?"

"Yes, Momoko. But tell me, how did you feel as you walked from that man? Was your step lighter? Did your troubles vanish and all seem right in the world?"

"Yes. How do you know this?"

"And you have searched for this feeling again and again?" The young monk continued.

"I felt whole that day, Tenzin, as though everything around me was new and fresh to my eyes. My problems left me and it mattered little what others said or thought of me. I knew all was well in my world." Momoko stared before her on recalling such emotions. "Yes, Tenzin, I have searched for the same peace since that day."

"And have you found that which you seek?"

"I have glimpsed it," Momoko turned back to the young monk. "In the moments we have shared together."

On hearing Momoko's admissions, Tenzin nodded to her reply.

"I too have felt such things, Momoko," he whispered. "Do you know what triggered these emotions within you?"

Momoko settled back against their wooden bench. Her hand still held in Tenzin's gentle clasp, she remembered the fisherman's innocent smiles in gratitude to her kindness. The young Geisha's thoughts returned to the moment she had given her remaining apple to Tenzin, and of the laughter shared with the young monk beside her.

"It seemed my true soul surfaced within those moments, Tenzin, giving me the strength to continue onwards." Momoko paused, her hand squeezing soft on the young monk's. "Giving me the knowledge that everything will work out for the best," she told him.

"Your true self, your true soul, came forward in your selfless actions. In those quiet moments, you understood the reasons locked away in your heart. That the peace you have sought throughout your life was there all along, just waiting for you to release its harmony so you may experience your higher self."

"By giving to others? By putting another first and pushing aside my own wants and desires?"

"This knowledge was within you from the moment you took your first breaths, Momoko," Tenzin nodded. "It is in us all. Everybody can experience the feelings we speak of now. Yet often on our search for that peace, we look to others and the riches that bring us material pleasures in hope that they hold our answers."

"When, young monk, what we seek most lays within us already."

Tenzin's joy matched Momoko's in her understanding. Each gazed out to the full moon before them in silence, shrouded in the wellbeing their hearts had always longed for.

Watching new stars emerge above them, Momoko glanced back to the ship which would soon take Tenzin from her. Meeting with the young monk's gaze once more, she saw he recognised her sorrow.

"Our time together is coming to end, Tenzin."

"Yes, Momoko, but do you see how we have never been apart?"

Momoko gave no reply. Her view returning to the gentle waves lapping across the moon's highlighted glow, she came to understand the thoughts that had entered her since the day light hours made way for darkness. Lowering her chin, the young Geisha looked up to Tenzin.

"I too am beginning to understand our identities, Tenzin," she smiled. "Please, tell me more of Lama Jampo?"

Tenzin's closed his eyes to Momoko's question. At once relieved she too had considered their connection, he still wondered what the young Geisha's response would be. Taking it upon him to speak of the ideas he was sure Momoko thought also, Tenzin began to tell what little he knew of his predecessor's character. Explaining the nuances of monastic life, he stopped and stared deep into Momoko's eyes.

"What is it, Tenzin?" Momoko asked him, not understanding his silence. Tenzin smiled once more to her and he too glanced back to his awaiting ship.

"We have shared our history here this day and night. Yet it as if we have shared so much more also. Our lives have run parallel with one another's. It seems our actions have opposed the others, yet complimented them also."

"I know," Momoko replied, her voice soft. "I feel it too. We're like two halves, Tenzin."

"Yes, like two halves."

"And why do you believe this so, young monk?"

Tenzin hesitated in his reply as he searched for the words to explain his ideas.

"Could it be that we share a similar destiny?" Momoko grinned.

Looking back to the young Geisha, Tenzin joined her humour.

"You have known all along, Momoko?"

"I suspected," Momoko giggled. "At first I dismissed my ideas, but as you mentioned Lama Jampo's name such thoughts came to me and have stayed ever since. But how can this be?"

Preparing his answer, he knew somewhere deep inside his heart Momoko already had an inclination towards his answer to come.

"It is believed that when a soul returns, sometimes on rare occasions it chooses to split into two, so it may experience dual lives within one life time."

"And Lama Jampo's soul chose us to continue his work?"

"From what I have learnt of Lama Jampo, it seems his good humour has carried with him in his decisions to return back to this world."

"So, we are both Lama Jampo?" Momoko's understanding combined with Tenzin's and their hands wrapped tight around the others,

"Of that I am sure, Momoko," he nodded. "As I have said, our lives have mirrored the others from our first day on this world, and…"

"Our first day?" Momoko's eyes widened. Her surprise gave way to a smile as she rose to her feet. Looking down to Tenzin the young Geisha gave a deep bow.

"Then happy birthday, young monk," she giggled and then returned to his side.

Momoko's laughter confirmed Tenzin's ideas and he too began to marvel at what had come to pass. Sensing Tenzin's wonder, Momoko also submitted to their related fates.

"But, Tenzin, can this really be true? How can we be certain of such things?"

"That I cannot say Momoko, but what we have told one another, does this not prove our ideas?"

"Yes, young monk," Momoko whispered. "There seems to be no other way."

As both fell silent, each moved closer together until at last the young Geisha's elegant clothing touched with the young monk's robes. A smile came to them both as they felt their energies combine, and together as one, they looked from the small wooden jetty where they had discovered their soul's true identity.

Wrapped within that warmth, Momoko and Tenzin's minds recalled the histories each had shared with the other. As the young Geisha imagined the snowcapped peaks that had towered over Tenzin's formative years, the young monk pictured row upon row of cherry trees, his heart filling with the scent such pink and white petals produced. Continuing with his exploration of a past no different to his own, Tenzin felt the love and protection Momoko's mother had shown. Experiencing the sorrow containing Momoko on leaving for a new life at Auntie's side, the young Geisha beside him felt Tenzin's similar pain in leaving his father for Tashilhunpo's golden rooftops.

Looking back to one another, the Geisha and the monk nodded. Each understood the emotions they now experienced together as one. Falling back into their recollections of each other's past, Momoko and Tenzin leant into one another, the warmth of the other's body enhancing memories shared.

As Auntie's kind features came to Tenzin, he frowned to Keiko's arrival, his heart saddened by Momoko's treatment towards such a kind soul. Momoko sensed the young monk's upset, yet she continued her recollections of Lama Norbu and Nyima, the young Panchen Lama, finding the joy experienced once before in the welcome given to Ketu. That joy faltered as she felt Tenzin's hurt and disappointment towards Ketu's actions so similar to her own.

Their hands still clasped tight together, Momoko's pain continued as Tenzin's memories pushed forwards through the years and she pictured Ketu's aged form at her feet. Feeling the lapse in compassion towards his adversary, a single tear fell from the young Geisha, her memories recalling her behaviour towards her younger sister, Keiko.

Feeling Momoko's grip across his fingers, Tenzin knew of what the young Geisha saw, yet his remorse towards such actions faded as he too stood before another's homeless disposition. The young monk smiled out across the moonlit ocean as he experienced Momoko's empathy towards the humble fisherman, his own salvation coming in feeling the compassion once lost from him.

Tenzin's heart filled with the joy Momoko had told of and came to understand how the young Geisha had arrived on the American shores they now sat upon. Sure that Momoko had experienced the same as he, Tenzin turned to the same soft smile he had just left besides Tokyo's harbour side and nodded to her.

"So your selfless actions were witnessed by another, young Geisha," he whispered to her.

"Yes, Tenzin," Momoko answered. "It seems our acts truly have paralleled the others."

Falling silent once again, neither spoke of how the other's memories had played out before them. A deeper understanding encircling them both, their souls eased, as did their hand's grip around the others.

"Tenzin," Momoko said. "What does this all mean? What has brought us to meet this day?"

"That I am not sure, Momoko."

"But there must be a reason, Tenzin. The things we have discovered between us both must hold some significance."

"We both know the answer, Momoko. Are we not the same? Does our soul not share the same knowledge? Look deep within, young Geisha, there you will find what you seek."

Momoko smiled down to the wooden beads still resting her lap. Realising how she had worn them a life time before, she gazed out to the ocean and closed her eyes, determined to still its gentle waves in her minds eyes.

Watching the young Geisha follow the path their predecessor's soul had mastered once before, Tenzin settled back and waited for their answers to come. As the tension around Momoko's eyes ebbed away he too joined the tranquillity encompassing the young Geisha beside him.

Picturing the full moon cast its beams across still waters, Tenzin knew he had reached that which his peers had instilled within him. Opening his eyes he glanced to Momoko, his heart delighting that she too attained a similar image. Sensing the young monk's stare, Momoko pulled herself from the peace once lost within her.

"Once again, young monk, you saw the same as I?"

She saw is nod and turned to him.

"We have never been alone. Even in our darkest moments, our souls have been together and have paid little attention to the distance between our homelands. Do you not see why we have met, Tenzin? Why we have arrived to sit here together?"

"So we may continue."

"Yes, Tenzin. So we may continue along our paths aware that the other exists, so those feelings of loneliness and uncertainty that have haunted us from time to time carry no meaning anymore."

"As we know the other is somewhere out there in the world," Tenzin said. "Holding their own against any adversity with the aid of the other soul's unique strength, no matter how far away from each other we may be."

Momoko withdrew her hand from Tenzin's.

"What is wrong, Momoko?" the young monk asked. "Are my words not true?"

"Your words are more than true, Tenzin. More than you and I can imagine. Do not doubt that I take as much comfort as you from such a discovery."

"Then why does you sorrow return, young Geisha. Tell me, so you may banish your sadness."

Holding Keiko's doll to her chest, Momoko looked onto moonlit seas, its silver light reflected in her tears. Pulling Tenzin's wooden necklace to her also, she sighed and wiped her eyes.

"Never before could I have imagined our meeting and what we would share together. It is not your company and our discoveries that hurt me so. It is the unknown future that lies ahead of me I grieve for now."

Understanding the young Geisha's sorrow, Tenzin looked to his ship and then averted his eyes from the line of passengers already boarding the vessel.

"We do not know what the future holds for us both, Momoko, only that the other is out there somewhere. Our meeting has taught us this. We are both destined to leave these shores and return to our homelands, of that I am certain."

"That may be so for you, Tenzin. But I have no means to return to Tokyo's docklands. How will I ever see those who we have talked of again?"

Tenzin shook his head and reached into his bag.

"Momoko, you are me, and I am you. Is it not that our paths have taken the same route throughout our lives?"

"Yes, Tenzin, but…"

"But what, young Geisha?" Tenzin held his hand out to her.

"But."

Momoko's lips parted and she gasped to the gold coins within the young monk's palm.

"How could I leave my other self alone now?" Tenzin grinned.

Both jumped to their ship's bellowing horn sounding out across San Francisco's busying harbour. Laughing to one another's startled expression, their view returned to Tashilhunpo's golden fortune.

CHAPTER TWENTY-SIX

Momoko and Tenzin stood side by side on their ship's highest deck. They looked to each other as the small wooden jetty upon which they had discovered so much faded from them.

"Thank you," Momoko whispered to the young monk.

Tenzin shook his head to her gratitude.

"No, Momoko, it is I who must once more thank you."

Leaning onto the deck's metal rail looking to the diminishing American shoreline, Tenzin smiled to the young Geisha's frowns.

"But, Tenzin, without you I may never have been able to return to my home. Why is it your generosity overrules my thanks?"

As the young Geisha too looked across moonlit waters, Tenzin turned to her delicate profile.

"Momoko, the moments we have shared together have brought such understanding to me. Picturing your kindness towards the soul whose needs were greater than yours has given me an insight to my own lapse in compassion."

"Towards the one you call Ketu?"

"Yes, Momoko."

The young Geisha sensed Tenzin's sorrow and moved closer to him until their clothing touched once more.

"Have you not shown a similar kindness in funding my passage homewards, young monk?" She said to him. "Are not your actions now those you thought lost from you?"

Brightening to the smile accompanying the young Geisha's words, Tenzin fell into deep brown eyes that held such unique beauty. Recalling the moments he had turned from the one who had needed his help, he began to understand how his compassion had never left his soul, but had rested within him only waiting to be revealed once more.

"Can you see how you have carried with you the forgiveness you searched for all along, Tenzin?" On seeing his recognition, Momoko glanced down to his bag. Reaching down, he took the wooden flute from there and then stood tall besides her.

"Yes, Tenzin, your absolution was at your side all the time," she said. "Why else would Ketu hand his gift to Lama Norbu, knowing it would soon fall into your possession?"

Looking to Ketu's gift, Tenzin's heart at last found the freedom longed for throughout his travels. Feeling the love containing the instrument, he placed his fingertips across the flute's crudely shaped holes and raised it to his lips. Watching Momoko close her eyes as he began to play, the young monk wondered if the young Geisha also noticed its soft tones seemed sweeter than ever before.

Each morning the Geisha and the monk would leave their separate cabins and sit beside one another before the ocean's vast horizon. Their bonds growing by the day, those hours were spent discovering more of the other's past, their knowledge bringing them a deeper understanding to parallel histories shared.

Filled with laughter and little sorrow, Momoko and Tenzin delighted in their time together and never mentioning the steady approach of the Hawaiian port which would bring an end to their encounter.

Although aware such a destination loomed, with each passing day they dismissed their thoughts, concentrating only on their moments held together.

Momoko and Tenzin would fall silent as the daylight hours faded and a glowing orange sun descended into the waters before them. At last enjoying the sunsets they had longed to share together, their hands would find a place within the other's as they smiled out to pink and red edged clouds passing by them. In their silence, each knew to have shared such a sight before may not have brought about the knowledge they held now. Taking comfort in their time spent as one, they forgot the lonely hours on their previous voyage. Realising the timing of their meeting on San Francisco's quiet wooden jetty took place as it should have, both smiled to the calm such memories contained.

Speaking of all that had gone before gave them both the console their souls had sought throughout their young lives apart. Remembering those memories with clarity once unknown, they would often pause in their recollections, once again bringing themselves back into the present moment so they could enjoy the precious times held in one another's company, with no thoughts of the time spent without the other, or the unwritten future which lay ahead.

Learning more from each other as the days passed, Tenzin saddened one morning on seeing land for the first time in weeks. Recognising the lush greenery covering the group of tiny islands, his heart sank that a view which had once given such delight now carried with it the foreboding of his and Momoko's farewell. Tenzin saw the young Geisha held a similar sorrow as he joined his side on their ship's top deck in those early hours.

"It seems we have arrived, young Geisha."

Momoko saw her sadness shared in his eyes.

"That it does, young monk," she replied, holding back tears she knew were to come.

Resting against the metal railings they had shared throughout their journey together, Momoko looked to Tenzin. She smiled once again as their hands found a home within the others. Grasping her fingers around Tenzin's, the young Geisha gazed up to him and then back to the advancing islands.

"You know our meeting need not end here, Tenzin," she whispered to him.

"Yes, Momoko, of that I am aware," he replied, his heart heavy with the implications his new ideas carried towards their future.

Momoko's eyes opened wide. "Then you too have considered a life together?"

"Yes, Momoko," Tenzin's eyes matched the young Geisha's watery film. "But do you think this is the reason for our meeting? So we can share the remaining years we have missed together?"

She kept her view on Tenzin.

"We know the true reason behind our meeting, one that will stay with us both until the end of our days."

Momoko reached for Tenzin's other hand and glanced back to their nearing port.

"I suppose Lama Jampo would not have chosen such a way, would he?"

"No," Tenzin concealed his own sadness to their inevitable parting. "Momoko, what we have shared together is unique, unknown to most who walk this earth. We must take comfort in this knowledge, so we may find the strength to continue on alone along our paths."

"But imagine, Tenzin," Momoko smiled. "Imagine the life we would share as one."

"Then what lessons would we learn? No matter how much our bonds were to deepen."

Momoko's understanding surfaced in Tenzin's words. Looking to him she began to giggle.

"It was just a thought, young monk," she grinned.

"And a good one at that," Tenzin laughed with her.

Pushing away the pain of not knowing what their unknown life together may have held, he gazed back to the young Geisha. Considering the years they could have shared at each other's side, he at last found solace in those unseen moments as he recalled Tashilhunpo and felt the monastery's golden rooftops pull upon him. Somewhere within Momoko's gaze, he too saw her own homelands held a similar draw.

"Yes, Tenzin," Momoko whispered. "It seems we are both destined to return back to where we truly belong."

Tenzin's silence acknowledged the young Geisha's foresight. Each knowing the other's thoughts towards such dreams, they turned to the island which would set the scene for their postponed farewell. Aware their goodbyes advanced with every passing minute, Momoko and Tenzin squeezed soft on the other's hand, determined to enjoy their last moments together.

Lost within their finger's tender grasp, the Geisha and the monk's souls encircled one another's once more, instilling within them the courage needed to continue onwards alone as their ship bounced gentle across its new moorings.

Momoko and Tenzin edged closer as the ship's gantry touched down onto Hawaii's dockside. Together they watched a handful of passengers step onto the island, knowing as Tenzin, they would now remain for several days until boarding their connecting ship bound for China and beyond. For a brief moment, the young Geisha considered stepping with Tenzin to join him in his wait. The young monk sensed his companion's wants. "Momoko," he smiled softly to her. "Our time together has now reached its end."

"I know, young monk," Momoko's tears escaped as she lowered her head.

Feeling such sadness enter him, Tenzin cast aside his thoughts towards the forbidden touches they had already shared. Raising his hand, he lifted the young Geisha's chin with a gentle finger.

"We are the same, you and I, Momoko," he smiled. "We are one and whole."

"I am you and you are me," Momoko replied, her smiles bathed in new found tears. "I understand," she continued. "We shall always be together no matter what distance lies between us."

"As have we always, Momoko," Tenzin nodded.

"Yes, Tenzin," the young Geisha whispered. "As have we always."

Lost within the other's gaze, their eyes portrayed the sentiments each had experienced in their brief moments as unified souls. Raising a smile, Momoko accepted it was time for them to part ways. As the ship's engines whirred to life beneath them once more after its brief stop another tear fell from the young Geisha.

"I am sorry, Tenzin," she wiped her eyes. "Goodbyes are never easy."

"Goodbyes are not important, Momoko. It is the time spent with those we love which matter most. Remember these moments we have shared, young Geisha, for they will stay with me also."

Grinning to Momoko's nods, he pointed to Lama Jampo's beaded necklace resting around her slender neck.

"These wooden beads mark our bond as the one soul we truly are, Momoko. They signify all that has happened and will happen in our unwritten future. They are yours now, returned at last to their other rightful owner."

"Tenzin," Momoko said, her hands clutching their necklace. "I have not given you anything in return."

"You have given me enough, Momoko," he smiled. "More than enough."

Tossing his bag over his shoulder, Tenzin glanced back to the awaiting waterfront and then returned to Momoko's gaze.

"Goodbye, young Geisha," he whispered to her.

"Goodbye, young monk," Momoko replied through tear filled

eyes as he walked from her.

Following his path as she had done so once before, Momoko gave a warm smile in understanding as Tenzin turned and waved to her from the harbour side.

"Yes, young monk," she whispered out to him. "You have given me more than enough also."

Holding Tenzin in her gaze, she smiled on seeing he acknowledged her parting whispers.

As the young monk's burgundy robes faded from her view, the lush green island upon which he now stood soon faded also and the young Geisha turned from her past, ready at last to face her unknown future.

Momoko kept to herself in the weeks that followed. No longer troubled by her fellow passenger's attitude towards her presence she delighted in her time alone.

Each morning the young Geisha would sit on the ship's highest deck where she and Tenzin had explored one another's past. No sorrow came to Momoko in those moments. The strength gained from the knowledge she now shared with the young monk dispelled such emotions, her heart at last reaching the peace sought throughout her life.

Returning to her cabin, she would smile on recapturing the stilling ocean waves Tenzin had taught her to see in her mind's eye, bringing an extra awareness to events passed. Each evening she would leave the sanctity of those moments and return to the ships top deck. Gazing out to a pink and red horizon, Momoko would relish the pacific sunsets she had once enjoyed at the young monk's side, her joy enhanced in knowing that somewhere, out in the same world she had once felt so alone, Tenzin also shared a similar view.

Soon, Momoko's solitary journey neared its end and as Tokyo's bay approached, the young Geisha looked to the harbour front she had thought she would never see again.

Anxiety rose in her on seeing such a familiar setting. Considering what reaction would greet her on returning to the Okiya, Auntie's aged features came to her. As did the presumed shock she was sure her sister's would produce on seeing her premature return.

These worries stayed with Momoko as her ship settled once more against her homeland's shores. Stepping from the security of her temporary home, the young Geisha looked to the streets that would lead to her unknown welcome.

Momoko sighed. Knowing of no other option than to return to the life she had known since a child, she raised her head and prepared for what to come. She paused on remembering her previous moments besides Tokyo's harbour front. Smiling as she caught sight of the fisherman who had triggered forgotten joys within her, the young Geisha froze on seeing another now paid the same attention she had once given to him.

Looking closer, Momoko backed away so her presence remained unseen. Hidden behind one of the docksides many signs, she watched as the old woman leant down and across the man's meagre row of fish and hand him a brown paper bag. Momoko's heart pounded as he bit into the warm rice cake and then gave Auntie the same smile Momoko also shared.

Confused to why her childhood guardian now stood before the man she too had given such gifts, Momoko stayed her ground, unsure of the feelings now encircling her. Within minutes of seeing the old women she was soon to confront and explain the reasons for her untimely return, the young Geisha calmed as Auntie bowed farewell to the man and made for the streets Momoko would soon take.

Sure that the old woman remained unaware of her arrival, Momoko stepped towards the man, her uncertainty as to his true identity fading from her with every footfall.

As the man beamed up to Momoko on her approach, the young Geisha looked to the deep scar running down from his temple and across weathered cheek. Wondering once more of the tales behind such a wound, she pushed away her suspicions as she came to a stop before him.

"I told you I would return," she smiled. "Not many fish today?" she pointed to the tiny catch between them. The fisherman grinned back up to her. Momoko's heart beat increased once again on recognising the expression both shared.

Glancing behind her to check Auntie had left the harbour side, Momoko crouched down and pointed again to the man's wares. Reaching into her jacket pocket she found the last of Tenzin's gold coins he had given her and held it up to the man.

"I think this will cover your catch for the day," she whispered.

The joy she recalled experiencing once before faltered in seeing the man's deep frown.

"What is it?" Momoko saddened. "Does my gift offend you in some way?"

The man shook his head.

"Then what is wrong?" Momoko continued. She paled as he gazed at her and opened his lips.

"What is it you are trying to tell me?" she asked him. Leaning forwards, the young Geisha tried to decipher his words. She trembled on hearing her mother's name come from him.

"Miyako," the man mumbled once more, his view held on Momoko's striking eyes. In an instant Momoko understood the connection made so many months ago.

"Yes," she whispered to him. "We have the same eyes, do we not? And you and I share the same smile."

The fisherman nodded to the young Geisha's tears.

"Now I know," Momoko smiled and handed her father her golden coin.

Looking to her gift resting soft in his palm, he turned his head and raised his chin towards the roads that led from Tokyo's bustling city streets. Returning to the young Geisha, he smiled once more in seeing she understood his directions.

"Thank you, father," Momoko said wiping at her wet cheeks.

"Miyako," he mumbled to her once more before his view fell back down to his catch.

Momoko watched transfixed as he carefully wrapped her fish and then handed them to her.

"Thank you," she said once more on rising to her feet. "Until we meet again," she added with a deep bow. The man returned her familiar smile and then lifted his chin towards Kyoto once more.

"Miyako," he whispered to her and grinned as the young Geisha glanced to the streets leading to her Okiya. Looking to him, Momoko nodded and with a final bow, she turned her back on all she could remember and towards her birthplace's silent call.

Finding a ride to Kyoto, Momoko smiled to the young driver and his wife, wondering on the luck she had found only minutes from leaving Tokyo's harbour. Watching the two talk between themselves, the young Geisha's thoughts returned to her time with Tenzin.

Considering his explanation for the kindness shown to her now, she knew his words and smiled to the pleasant consequences of her previous actions towards the man she now deemed her father.

As they continued onwards to their destination, Momoko looked ahead. Raising a smile as the young woman rested her head on her husband's shoulder, Momoko's view ran down her cascading silk black hair. The young Geisha reached for her own coiffured locks. Taking out the delicate silver pins holding her elaborate hair style in place, she reached for her bag and the wooden paddled brush laying within. The young woman woke to Momoko's yelps. Leaning to her, she and the young Geisha shared their giggles as each fought to comb out matted tresses so used to such ornamental designs.

Within an hour their battle was complete and Momoko nodded a silent thank you to her aid before the young woman returned to her husband's side. Running her fingers through soft strands, Momoko smiled to the release that came from her actions.

Experiencing the freedom lost to her since a child, her act of defiance towards a Geisha's public display brought with it the realisation that she no longer paid heed to such rules, her understanding growing as Tokyo receded from her.

For a brief moment her thoughts filled with Auntie and with those she had once shared the Okiya. Aware that not one knew of her return, Momoko settled back in her seat and closed the eyes that had been the envy of many.

Waking to a gentle nudge from the young woman hours later, Momoko looked out onto Kyoto's southern suburbs. In her first moments of consciousness, her confused frowns faded on remembering the journey that had brought her back to the place she had been born.

"Kyoto," she whispered out into the early evening rush, finding peace in the sights before her. Thanking the generosity given, Momoko watched the young couple drive from her and then looked to the surrounding streets. She smiled on recognising the familiar lanes and avenues she had played upon when young and made for the destination that had fuelled those moments.

Walking those memorable streets came with ease to Momoko and soon she found her goal. Pausing before the old wooden porch that had once housed such laughter, Momoko reached forwards and rapped on its red painted door. Momoko sighed as she knocked again, her tears forming as she leant against her younger home's entrance, her soul filled with doubt towards her arrival.

Walking homewards, Miyako smiled to all those who paid the respect once given to her predecessor. Many years had passed since the people of southern Kyoto had gained their new midwife, yet those times had brought with them gratitude towards the one who had taken Hiroko's place. Thinking often of the old midwife, Miyako had continued with her work knowing her guardian and friend had always remained at her side.

Miyako quickened her pace anticipating the rest her body craved. Continuing to reply to the welcoming nods she received, she recalled her vow to take on an apprentice in her work. Smiling as she remembered how Hiroko had taken her under her wing, Miyako's thoughts returned to the other soul who had once shared their home.

With each passing spring, Momoko's absence had laboured on Miyako's heart. Recalling the walks they would take together on the eve of Hanami, she would push away her recollections, aware such times lay in an unforgotten past.

Never marrying, Miyako had shunned her many admirers. The fear of losing another so close to her enhanced the quiet dismissals she had presented for the previous two decades spent alone. Miyako knew her work redeemed any want of companionship, the souls she delivered into the world presenting her with the love lost from her.

As Miyako turned the corner onto the street she had known most of her adult life, she came to a stop on seeing a young woman stood outside her door. She sighed, recalling how many other young Geisha had found their way to her home in hope of having her former profession's forbidden children.

Although Miyako seldom received such callers, on each occasion she had taken the frightened women into her home, remembering the kindness given her by Hiroko's gentle soul.

Great joy had come to Miyako in her actions, and as her callers left her home with the loved child in their arms, southern Kyoto's midwife had delighted in seeing the pleasure her skills had attributed to. Readying herself to face another's fears, Miyako stepped forward and smiled to the expectant face watching her approach. She paused once more as her unexpected visitor raised her head.

Miyako's gaze fell to the young woman's torso. She frowned to the flat stomach before her. Looking up to the tears forming in the same striking eyes Miyako herself had once been famed for, her body trembled as old memories resurfaced.

"Momoko?" she whispered.

"Yes, Mamma, it is I."

Miyako looked down to her daughter's midriff once again. She raised her head to Momoko's giggles.

"No, Mamma. You are not to be grandmother yet," Momoko smiled. "That is not the reason for my return."

Miyako joined Momoko's joy, she too releasing her tears as mother and daughter embraced on the spot they had last held one another close so many years ago.

In the weeks that followed, mother and daughter came to understand the missing years between them. As Momoko told of Auntie and her time spent within the Okiya, Miyako would smile on recalling a similar rite of passage. Miyako's own heart filled with forgotten memories, yet the pain and loss of her treasured child faded. Aware Momoko had seen at last seen through the painted façade of false, moneyed love, her joy was boosted in recognising the modesty and humbleness that accompanied her daughter's words.

Momoko too listened to her mother's tales of life within the community she had forsaken at an early age. However, the shame to her premature leaving remained brief. Momoko was more than aware that without the journey her youthful soul had taken at that young age would not have caused her to encounter the young monk who had opened her eyes to the world around her. Wanting to tell her mother of Tenzin, Momoko hesitated in her story.

'Not yet,' she would whisper on retiring to her childhood bedroom, her heart longing to hold his memory in her silence.

On one such night when the young monk's words denied the sleep she desired, Momoko looked to the wooden beads beside her. Smiling to the necklace and then to the two red dressed dolls sat upright next to her cherished gift, she rose from her bed and walked out to her small home's kitchen. Preparing the green tea she hoped would ease her restlessness. Momoko looked from the window there. She smiled on realising how she now took Hiroko's stance.

"Momoko, it is late," Miyako called to her from the fireplace.

Turning to her mother, Momoko saw she too recognised Hiroko's favoured position.

"What plays on your mind, my child?" Miyako continued. "Come, sit with me and tell of what has gone before."

Momoko nodded. She knew it was now time to share her encounter with the one who had guided her back to where she truly belonged.

Waiting for the hot water that would accompany their talk of the young monk, Momoko looked back to the moonlit cherry trees far in the distance.

"Tenzin," she whispered out to them, her soul lightened by the memories she knew she would carry with her always.

CHAPTER TWENTY-SEVEN

Tenzin opened his eyes to the golden sunset before him. In the days passed since his and Momoko's farewell, the young monk had found solace each evening sitting before such a sight. Glancing down to Hawaii's white sands beneath him, his view returned to the vibrant display he knew the young Geisha enjoyed somewhere also.

"Momoko," he whispered her name out to the far horizon.

Although alone once more, Tenzin's soul understood the reasons behind their parting, yet the sorrow he had expected to accompany those moments were lost from him. Warmed by the times he and the young Geisha had shared, Tenzin closed his eyes once again, his mind returning to still the gentle waves rising and falling in the distance.

The young monk rose to his feet within an hour of finding the tranquillity he sought. Slinging his bag over his shoulder, Tenzin bowed to his temporary beach home and then walked to the harbour and the awaiting ship which would take him back to his beloved Tibetan mountains, so different to the lush green hillsides he walked beside now.

On reaching his ship, Tenzin paused at the foot of its long ramp. Looking back to the island that had brought such calm he recalled his last words to Momoko. Recognising the lessons each had learnt in their time together his spirits lifted and he stepped up onto the gantry, aware the knowledge they had shared as one would carry with them both until their end of days.

These thoughts stayed with Tenzin on his voyage back towards his own continent, once again bringing with them great understanding to the reasons for their encounter. Sitting alone on the ship's highest deck each evening, Tenzin's memories flooded with the words spoken between them and the timeless bonds that connected one another. Finding comfort in such moments, the young monk would smile out to clouds of vivid pink and red, his awareness to his and Momoko's unique union increasing as dusk give way for dark blue skies littered with stars.

Returning to his cabin each night, the young monk would think of the wooden beads he had worn since a child. Picturing Momoko holding Lama Jampo's sacred necklace gave Tenzin the console he longed for in his solitary journey, the young Geisha's image providing the strength each had promised to uphold. Reassured by Momoko's presence no matter of the distance between them, the young monk's heart eased and he would soon drift to sleep, his dreams anticipating his return to Tashilhunpo's white washed walls and ornate gilded rooftops.

Spending his time within the security of his small cabin, Tenzin longed for when he would at last walk through Tashilhunpo's gates once more and be with Lama Norbu, Nyima and his fellow Lamas again. Wondering what they would make of his premature return, the young monk considered his peer's reaction to the tales he held.

At times, Tenzin doubted he should tell of his encounter with the young Geisha who had taught him so much, his worries surfacing in the forbidden touch each had shared.

Thinking of the warmth Momoko's tender hand had given, he was sure Lama Norbu would understand and Tenzin would smile on realising such physical ties did not matter, he and the young Geisha were the same soul, were they not?

Remembering his home's tall wooden gates, Tenzin's thoughts returned to another. Ketu's lost eyes came to him and he wondered what fate his former charge now faced. Aware that Lama Norbu's compassion outweighed that of his childhood adversary, the young monk confronted his reservations to the one who had caused such heartache. Within these thoughts, he gradually found the forgiveness with understanding he and Momoko had discovered together towards the troubled soul.

Tenzin's ideas towards what lay within his unknown future left him as his ship drew closer to China's eastern coastline. Recalling the anxiety experienced on his last arrival to Shanghai's bustling port, the young monk raised a smile to the events that had passed. Remembering how his brothers had waited with their news on his outward bound journey, the young monk recognised how his decision to stay hidden that night had led to his and Momoko's eventual meeting. Wondering if his brother's still remained on Chinese soil, Tenzin decided on retiring to his bunk once more, his soul delighting in the recollections of his unnecessary fear, and the destiny prevailed from such apprehension. As the dawn light spilled into Tenzin's small cabin so did the whir and hum of the ship's engines beneath him. Such familiar sounds filled the young monk with optimism. He knew his voyage was coming to a close and he would soon once again walk across India's parched roads and northwards towards his own homelands.

Within weeks of leaving Shanghai, Tenzin watched the Pacific waters he had gained such knowledge sat before pass from him. As his ship rounded Malaysia's tropical peninsular, he marvelled to the deepening sunsets, their colour enhanced by the memories shared with another.

Momoko's laughter and kind words surrounded Tenzin as he continued to watch a dimming sun meet with the horizon each evening. He wondered if she too recalled such moments shared. Knowing that were true, the young monk held the young Geisha's soul to him, confirming his understanding towards the brief time spent together on San Francisco's peaceful harbour front.

Looking one day out across the Bay of Bengal, his heart longed for his return to the small portal town where he would begin his long walk home, considering if his presence would be remembered on entering Digha's town walls once again.

On walking from his ship as that day came, his questionings ran true on being greeted by the same smiles he recalled sharing months earlier. Welcomed once more by Digha's small community, the young monk felt some sorrow that he was unable to speak of the sights he had seen. Yet the lack of words spoken between him and his hosts mattered little, as for two days, Tenzin relished in the unspoken kindness shown to a stranger far from his own home.

As his brief stay came to an end, Tenzin experienced a familiar sadness in leaving. As he waved farewell to the crowd gathered on his departure, the young monk looked to those smiling faces. He bowed to those who had shown the compassion he had at last discovered once more and then turned from them to take his first step towards Tibet's cooler climates.

It would be several weeks until Tenzin reached Nepal's strict borders. Finding refuge in the company of those of his own homelands once more, Tenzin relished being able to talk in his own tongue again. Although telling the traders little of his trip, the young monk enjoyed the easy banter shared on their long trek from Kathmandu and northwards through the district of Sindhupalchowk and to the lands he had missed dearly.

Reaching his longed for border front, Tenzin stepped soft onto Tibetan soil. Breathing in the scents surrounding him, Tenzin looked to fields full with mustard seed and wheat, his smiles bathed in summer's rich sunlight. Childhood feelings returned to the young monk and he recalled the hot humid days when he would work beside the one he had once called father. Continuing onwards, Tenzin pushed such recollections from him and again strayed from Gyantse roads, aware Shigatse's famed monastery called to him now as it had done since a boy.

Following the roads through the Tibetan small towns of Tingri and Sakya, Tenzin quickened his march, his heart pulling him towards the monastery in which he had spent his formative years. Within a week of leaving the Nepal's steep mountain ranges, the young monk at last came to stand on Shigatse's city outskirts.

Looking onto his home, Tenzin recalled the first time he had seen the same view he now witnessed. He frowned on sensing the same trepidation he had felt then. Putting his emotions down to the long journey undertaken to return to his home, Tenzin stepped forwards, ignoring his want to return to be at another's side.

Feeling Momoko's strength enter him again, Tenzin lowered his head as he walked through Shigatse's busy streets and lanes, raising his eyes only to stare up to the golden rooftops that had filled his dreams throughout his voyage from American shores.

Walking into Tashilhunpo's surrounding market place, Tenzin smiled to the same stall holders he recalled. He grinned to the trader who stood before the shiny green apples that had triggered his new found knowledge and then gazed up to his cherished monastery. Walking forwards to meet those with which he had grown, Tenzin stopped. The young monk stepped back into the shadows as he watched three familiar figures look from Tashilhunpo's high walls. Tenzin's heart pounded to the thoughts now encircling his arrival.

Tenzin stared up at those gazing out onto Shigatse's busy streets. He smiled on recognising the old monk, his heart beat slowing in being in his guardian's presence once again. Looking to the young men stood either side of Lama Norbu, Tenzin warmed on seeing their Panchen Lama, Nyima. He then realised who accompanied his peers and he lowered his head.

"Ketu," Tenzin whispered into his chest.

Gazing back up to his former charge, Tenzin frowned to the emotions rushing through him. At first, the shock of seeing Ketu dressed once more in the deep red robes he had so shamed brought anger to Tenzin. Not seeing how a malicious soul was permitted to wear Tashilhunpo's sacred attire again after committing such wrongs, Tenzin's heart embraced the compassion regained from his time away. As fresh understanding shrouded the young monk he tried to calm his racing mind.

Gazing back up to Ketu, Tenzin began to accept all that had gone before, his new found empathy releasing the final shards of dislike held towards his childhood foe.

Tenzin studied the joy in Ketu's features and he too soon joined his smiles, recalling the lost stares and bedraggled appearance he had witnessed only months earlier. Warmed by seeing Ketu now enjoyed a different path from the one his soul had taken in his shaping years, Tenzin heart eased and any repulsion remaining towards the boy disappeared.

Stepping back from their view once again, the two young monks spoke up to Lama Norbu and then one another. Watching Lama Norbu bow to them each in turn, Tenzin felt some remorse that they were now leaving his guardian's side. Aware he needed a little more time to observe those of his past, Tenzin hesitated in moving forwards and announcing his return. The young monk's trepidation stayed with him as both Nyima and Ketu left Lama Norbu and Tenzin smiled up to the old monk now stood alone gazing out from Tashilhunpo's ornate tiers.

Pulled to calling out to him, Tenzin tried to shake the feeling that another longed for his company also. Tenzin remembered the comfort the young Geisha had instilled deep within him. Her memory bringing his wants to the surface, he knew of no other way to confront his needs and with a deep breath he motioned forwards. He paused as Lama Norbu nodded down to him. Realising the old monk had been aware of his presence all along, Tenzin stepped out from the shadows and bowed to his guardian.

As Lama Norbu repaid Tenzin's greeting, the young monk's footfalls stopped once more in the understanding stares above him. A wise smile spread across the old monk's lips and he nodded again, aware of the desires Tenzin harboured within his soul.

"You knew before me, old monk," Tenzin whispered out to him, his calls for another's company confirmed by his guardian's perception.

Lama Norbu grinned down to his young apprentice, concealing his sadness that their reunion was to be postponed for a little while longer.

Tenzin matched Lama Norbu's smiles. Feeling some sorrow that the laughter they had shared since his first arrival to Tashilhunpo was to be delayed, the young monk's sadness soon faded. He understood the future lessons he was to learn.

Knowing he and his guardian would laugh together once more, Tenzin nodded up to him in farewell, his heart lifted by the prospects of the path he would now follow. Watching the old monk return their goodbyes, the young monk turned from his cherished home and made for the one who called his soul back to him.

As Tenzin walked from the monastery he dared not glance back once, aware that if he did so his decision to continue onwards would be overturned and he would soon return to the safety of what he had always known. Feeling Lama Norbu's gaze upon him, the young Geisha's smiles came to Tenzin, once more giving him the courage to continue towards his destination.

Breaking free of Shigatse's town walls, Tenzin's soul carried him towards his birthplace and the unknown welcome he was soon to receive. Sleeping little on his two day trek southwards, the young monk's view filled with the sights he recalled as a boy. Recognising the tall snow-capped mountain peaks towering on either side of him, memories of his grandfather accompanied his gait and he thought of the San Franciscan street vendor who had shown such kindness to both him and Momoko. Savouring those moments along his journey homewards, Tenzin wondered of the life the young Geisha now lived so far from where he now walked. He warmed to her memory.

Somehow he knew her life path had taken a similar route to the one he now stepped and on nearing the edges of Gyantse, wondered if he was to be given the good reception he was sure Momoko had received.

Tenzin's anxiety left him as the sounds of rushing water filled the air. Pushing forwards, the young monk strode towards the river. His smiles grew on seeing the churning rapids fuelled by the surrounding mountains melted coverings of snow and ice.

As Tenzin stood on the banks of his young home's life blood, comfort came to him in realising that in all his years away nothing had changed, his beliefs brought to life by observing nature still ruled the seasons of those who lived within Tibet's peaceful midlands.

Following the waters of his childhood, Tenzin paused on recognising the small house he had shared with his grandfather and the one he felt so drawn to be with once more. Quickening his pace, he made for his home and on reaching its old wooden door rapped gently across its weathered boards. Knocking several times again, Tenzin turned and walked to the fields far in the distance.

The young monk's smiles as he continued out towards crops of barley and maize, remembering his childhood summer days when he had worked at his father's side.

Returning to the river banks on which had taken his first tentative steps, Tenzin looked ahead to the fields that provided the needs of Gyantse's small community. Tenzin paused. Shielding his eyes from the sun, he gazed across the raging waters and to the small plot of land he had played and laughed as a child. Looking from the lone figure there, the young monk glanced up to the vivid blue skies each now shared. He smiled on seeing not a cloud remained above them.

"Now you are ready, Tenzin," he whispered and strode forwards to meet with his past.

Walking through fields of golden strands, his palms ran across tips of barley and wheat. Aware these crops would see his village through the harsh winter ahead, Tenzin's thoughts returned to Momoko's striking eyes and he wondered again of the greeting he was sure she had encountered on returning to such familiar childhood settings.

"And did you undergo the same anxiety, young Geisha?" Tenzin smiled. "Yes, I am sure you did," he added, once more aware of the feelings their dual soul experienced.

Nearing the man crouched down before him, Tenzin stopped and watched aged hands perform the work they had always known. Remembering how he too had carried out such labour he glanced down to his own. The young monk smiled, realising how even then his destiny had lain elsewhere, portrayed by the smooth skin his fingers now carried.

Looking back to the one they called Gyaltso, Tenzin smiled on seeing he noticed his presence.

"Can I help you?" his father asked, a worn hand raising to his brow from the sun's glare.

Tenzin gave no reply as Gyaltso edged towards him.

"Are you looking for someone?" He continued and came to stop before the young monk.

"It seems I have found them," Tenzin smiled.

Gyaltso frowned. Peering closer to his visitor, his eyes widened on recognising the smile that still entered his dreams from time to time. So many years had passed since he had fallen into the warmth such an expression held and he lowered his hand to his side.

"Tenzin?" he whispered. "Can that really be you?"

"Yes, father," the young monk replied. "I am here now," he felt his tears combine with his father's on their embrace.

That evening, Tenzin smiled to his grandfather's empty chair as he and Gyaltso ate together in the home they had all once shared. Listening to his son's tales of a life he could never imagine, Gyaltso's joy of Tenzin's return faded on hearing the love he held for Tashilhunpo's grounds. Tenzin recognised his father's sorrow and smiled to him once again.

"Father, it feels my life in Tashilhunpo has served its purpose. Maybe one day I shall return to the comfort found there, that I do not know."

"Then where are you to go now, Tenzin?" Gyaltso concealed his wishes.

Glancing back to the bunk where he had taken his first breaths, Tenzin returned to his father's hopeful gaze.

"Those crops are too much for one, old man," the young monk grinned, his smiles enhanced by the delight Gyaltso held before him.

As the weeks passed them by, Tenzin and Gyaltso brought in the crops that would see them through the approaching winter. Retiring early from the fields each evening beneath a darkening sky, father and son would hold their silence, comforted to be in one another's company once more.

Watching Gyaltso prepare their evening meal, Tenzin's thoughts would often return to his former life in Tashilhunpo and he would look down to the clothes he now wore, so different to the heavy burgundy robes he had known. Although no words were said of the revered attire remaining besides Tenzin's bed, both he and Gyaltso knew that clothing mattered little as he continued his path within the beliefs he was destined to carry.

As winter drew in and their work was completed for another season, Tenzin and Gyaltso would sit before a raging fire recalling the years they had missed together. Listening to his father's tales of life within their small village, Tenzin would recognise the love his father still held for the mother he had never met. Tenzin understood how his presence rescinded such sorrow, his smile mirroring the one lost so young.

Although the bonds between them grew with each passing day, Tenzin said nothing of the young Geisha whose words had prompted his return. Wanting to keep her memory to himself, the young monk slowly began to realise the release he had encountered from their meeting may in some way be improved by the telling of their time together. Sure that his father saw his son carried such a story, Tenzin's respect for him grew in his silence to those matters.

Each night Tenzin drew closer to revealing the words spoken between them, yet still he retained his want to speak of the one with striking eyes of dark brown and the smile which had set his soul on the path he now followed. Recalling the moments they had shared brought with them memories of others and Tenzin would often glance back to his revered robes folded neat beneath his bed. He knew his return to Tashilhunpo held the same inevitability as the spring time which would soon be upon them, yet he calmed his thoughts aware also that he was where he should be at this present moment in time. Gyaltso also realised his son's return. He too pushed away his ideas, knowing as Tenzin that the moments they now shared together once more were to be savoured.

One night as the winter's chill faded and the first signs of spring approached, Tenzin's recollections of Lama Norbu and his fellow

Lamas filled the young monk's heart. Resting his head onto his pillow, he gazed across his home's single room. Watching his father shrouded in the sleep Tenzin craved, he smiled to the fire place's rich amber light highlighting Gyaltso's blanket.

Glancing to where his grandfather had once slept, Tenzin left his bunk and reached for the robes he had learnt so much within. Wrapping them around him, Tenzin eased to the forgotten comfort they gave and crept outside. Closing the door behind him, he gazed up to winter's final full moon. Sitting down within its silver light, his thoughts returned to the young Geisha and the unique bonds held between them both.

Momoko glanced back to her sleeping mother. Turning away, she crept from Miyako's bedroom door careful as not to wake her. Walking to the kitchen, Momoko looked out from its small window and across to the cherry trees that would soon make their mark on Kyoto's landscape once more. Momoko smiled out to the approaching blossoms. Considering why sleep had not come to her that night, Momoko became lost in the moon's silver highlights playing over fragile branches. Gazing up to dawn's slow advance, Momoko's thoughts filled with Tenzin on seeing the last full moon before spring shine above and she reached for her jacket and then the kitchen's door handle.

Sitting down in her home's small garden where she and her mother would often watch the morning sun rise, Momoko recalled the silence they would hold between one another in such moments, tired but happy the delivery of another soul into southern Kyoto's community had gone well. Momoko smiled up to the fading stars above and she remembered sharing the same view with the young monk who had given her the strength to return to her birthplace. She longed to tell her dual soul the joy she had found in working besides her mother and of her delight in becoming a midwife's apprentice. Momoko grinned to her notions.

"Yes, young monk," she whispered. "I am aware you already know."

Looking back to her small home, Momoko thought of the old woman who had watched over her formative years. She wondered what Hiroko would have thought of the profession she now undertook.

"And I am sure you know also, Hiroko," Momoko nodded.

The life Momoko had chosen long ago seemed so far from her now. At times she would miss the banquets and affection Tokyo's wealthy men had showered upon her, yet she understood those days were gone from her now. On each occasion when that charmed past came to her, she would thank Tenzin for the given courage to leave such a lifestyle behind. Momoko often longed for Tenzin's company once more. Those wants would soon withdraw. Sensing his presence with her always, Momoko knew Tenzin felt those emotions also, as was she somehow aware of the similar path to hers Tenzin had taken on his return to his own homelands.

As the Geisha and the monk returned their view to the full moon they knew both now shared thousands of miles apart, each smiled in the warmth of knowing the other was out there in the world. The loneliness that at times had filled their hearts remained hidden from them, lost in the love and compassion that had encircled them from their first words together.

Comforted by their new found understanding of the special destinies each now followed, Momoko and Tenzin glanced back to where their parent slept and decided to stay a little while longer in the place where they truly belonged.

The End.

ALSO BY THE AUTHOR

FICTION

SUBWAY OF LIGHT

A novel by Julian Bound

Because Sometimes a Second Chance is All We Need

Following an accident Josh finds himself sat alone at the back of an empty New York subway car on a deserted station with no memory of how he arrived there.

A man approaches and tells Josh he has been taken out of his life to take a journey on the train. Acting as a guide he explains they will make several stops and that each station visited may seem familiar to him.

Arriving at their first stop they witness a young couple meet for the first time. Their ensuing subway stations follow the young couple's life as they experience courtship, marriage, tragedy and happiness. Watching their lives unfold Josh's memory begins to return until it is he himself who must decide the fate of his own final destination.

A story of awakening, 'Subway of Light' is a healing book of love found, lost, and regained through the act of belief and trust, not only within others but also in ourselves.

A heart-warming tale of kindness, understanding and forgiveness.

Life's Heart Eternal

A novel by Julian Bound

One Man's Journey Through The Centuries

'My name is Franc Barbour. I was born on the 20th July 1845 in the town of Saumur, deep in the heart of the Loire Valley, France. The truth of the matter is I simply never died.'

These are the opening words a young nurse reads in an old leather bound journal given to her by a stranger. She soon uncovers the story of one man's journey through the centuries.

From 1845 to present day, and to a backdrop of the world's conflicts and wars, Franc loses then encounters those closest to him again as they are reincarnated time and time again in different bodies.

Be it brothers, friends, soulmates or enemies, those met with once more hold lessons as to how our actions in each lifetime often hold consequences in the next.

In Franc's travels and adventures across the world an encounter with those reincarnated from his past is never far away…

'For who has never wondered what it would be like to live forever?'

THE SOUL WITHIN

A novel by Julian Bound

In releasing our thoughts towards a lifetime imagined,
only then may we have the life our soul awaits.

Falling ill in his home town of Puri on India's eastern shoreline a young boy is visited by a mysterious woman. Taking him on a journey around a tranquil lake, together they observe those living along its banks.

Acting as a guide the woman explains the life lessons they encounter through gentle teachings. As the boy begins to realise the significance of their walk his emerging awareness to matters of the soul leads him to discover the true reason behind their meeting.

A heart-warming tale of awareness, The Soul Within provides readers with an insight into awakening, guided by subtle teachings grounded in love, kindness and compassion.

OF FUTURES PAST

A novel by Julian Bound

Past lives and reincarnation, one soul's journey

Following her death, a young New York art restorer finds herself on a deserted beach. An older man approaches and introduces himself as George.

Explaining she is now between lives, George guides her to a cliff top library. Inside she finds a book containing all the past lives she has ever lived. She begins to read of her past lifetimes lived throughout the centuries.

Be it an artist's model of 16th century Renaissance Italy, a geisha of ancient Japan, or a Tibetan Buddhist monk living in the foothills of the Himalayas, each lifetime holds answers towards the progression of her soul, as seen in those met with through the years, be them friend or foe, or ultimately her soul mate she encounters in her many lifetimes.

Between uncovering the events of her previous lives, George explains the reasons for the situations that unfolded within her past. His explanations provide awareness to characteristics unique to her soul, and of the trials she at times has been faced with.

Of Futures Past is a story of discovery, giving an insight into how our actions in one lifetime can effect moments in those to follow.

A Gardener's Tale

A novel by Julian Bound

'It's funny the people you meet in a lifetime.
Looking back it wasn't so much how many crossed my path,
more so it was what they had to say.'

With these opening lines a sheltered man recounts his life spent working as a gardener in his hometown's park. Recalling those encountered he tells how they shared their problems with him, resulting in him offering them his own unique perspective on life and so touching the hearts of all he meets.

Unbeknown to them all, his wise insights for their woes arrive from the numerous jigsaw puzzles he and his mother complete together each the evening. Yet as tragedy strikes, it is he who must search for the missing piece within his own life puzzle.

Because Everybody Searches For Their Missing Piece

BY WAY OF THE SEA

A novel by Julian Bound

One monk's journey of discovery

Struggling with his beliefs, Tenzin, a Tibetan Buddhist monk, begins a journey to see the sea he has always imagined. Travelling on foot through Tibet, Nepal and India to reach his goal, those he encounters along the way start to restore a faith lost to him.

Since a young novice Tenzin has longed to stand before seas never witnessed in a landlocked Tibet. Travelling through his homelands he walks beside holy lakes and over high attitude mountain passes until stepping into Nepal, where within the gardens of Buddha's birthplace his fading beliefs begin to be rekindled.

Crossing into India he journeys south once more until meeting with a path he is destined to take.

Encountering many on his travels each hold a valuable lesson for Tenzin as together they explore the concepts of attachment, impermanence, kindness and compassion and karma and reincarnation. With each insight gained he continues onwards, his pursuit to see the sea accompanied by a want to understand the faith in which he has been raised.

FOUR HEARTS

A novel by Julian Bound

*'You walk into a room filled with all the people you've ever met,
who do you seek out first?'*

Diagnosed with an incurable illness, one man begins a journey across the world to meet with those from his past.

Travelling to India and Nepal's ancient cities and to Thailand's tropical islands, those he encounters hold a message for him. Exploring the concepts of love, friendship and heartache it is he who must ultimately face a destiny shaped by life choices made.

Four Locations, Four Souls, One Journey. - *'Four Hearts'* a tale of wanderlust and self-discovery.

All Roads

A novel by Julian Bound

A journey of awakening in the foothills of the Himalayas

When Josh's intended two month holiday in Thailand heads in an unexpected direction the doors of a new world are opened to him.

Pulled away from his comfort zone and led across South East Asia by a turn of surprising encounters and events, he finds himself in locations never thought of before.

From Thailand and Cambodia's golden temples to the banks of China's Li River, and from the high altitudes of Tibet's ancient monasteries to Nepal's sacred lakes, Josh gains insights into Asia's Buddhist concepts and principals while walking a path he is destined to take.

NON-FICTION

IN THE FIELD

A Memoir by Julian Bound

Tales of capturing world events, conflicts and culture on camera whilst living on the road as a documentary photographer.

From the boy soldiers of a Burmese liberation army to photographing the moment Nepal's 2015 earthquake struck, *In The Field* tells of Java's active volcanoes, Cairo's Arab Spring, Bangkok's coup d'état, and a venture into covert photography for a government in exile.

Alongside tales of conflict and natural disasters another journey is recounted, one of documenting Buddhism throughout Asia and South East Asia, including Bhutan's fortress monasteries, Tibet's remote temples, chanting Tantric monks of the Himalayas, and meeting His Holiness the 14th Dalai Lama at his 80th birthday celebrations.

Stories Featured Include

The Karen National Liberation Army
Nepal's Maoist Civil War
Rebellion on the streets of Bangkok
Tibetan refugees
A journey through Tibet
Mumbai's Dharavi slums
Cambodia's Killing Fields
The Nepal earthquakes of 2015
His Holiness the 14th Dalai Lama

ABOUT THE AUTHOR

Born in England, Julian is a documentary photographer, film maker and author. With photographic work featured on the BBC news, his photographs have been published in National Geographic, New Scientist and the international press. His work focuses on the social documentary of world culture, religion and traditions, with time spent studying meditation with the Buddhist monks of Tibet and Northern Thailand and spiritual teachers of India's Himalaya region.

His photography work includes documenting the child soldiers of Myanmar's Karen National Liberation Army, the Arab Spring of 2011, Cairo, Egypt, and Thailand's political uprisings of 2009 and 2014 in Bangkok.

With portraiture of His Holiness the 14th Dalai Lama, Julian has extensively photographed the Tibetan refugees of Nepal and India. His other projects include the road working gypsies of Rajasthan, India, the Dharavi slums of Mumbai, the riverside squatter slums of Yogyakarta and the sulphur miners at work in the active volcanoes of Eastern Java, Indonesia.

Present for the Nepal earthquakes of 2015 he documented the disaster whilst working as an emergency deployment photographer for various NGO and international embassies in conjunction with the United Nations and the World Wildlife Foundation.

With published photography books Julian is the author of nine novels.

Printed in Great Britain
by Amazon

30052201R00179